LAND OF RIVERA

LAND OF RIVERA

TRUTH AND EVOLUTION

By

KmCarey

Hardcover ISBN: 979-8-9909087-1-0

TABLE OF CONTENTS

Zuku

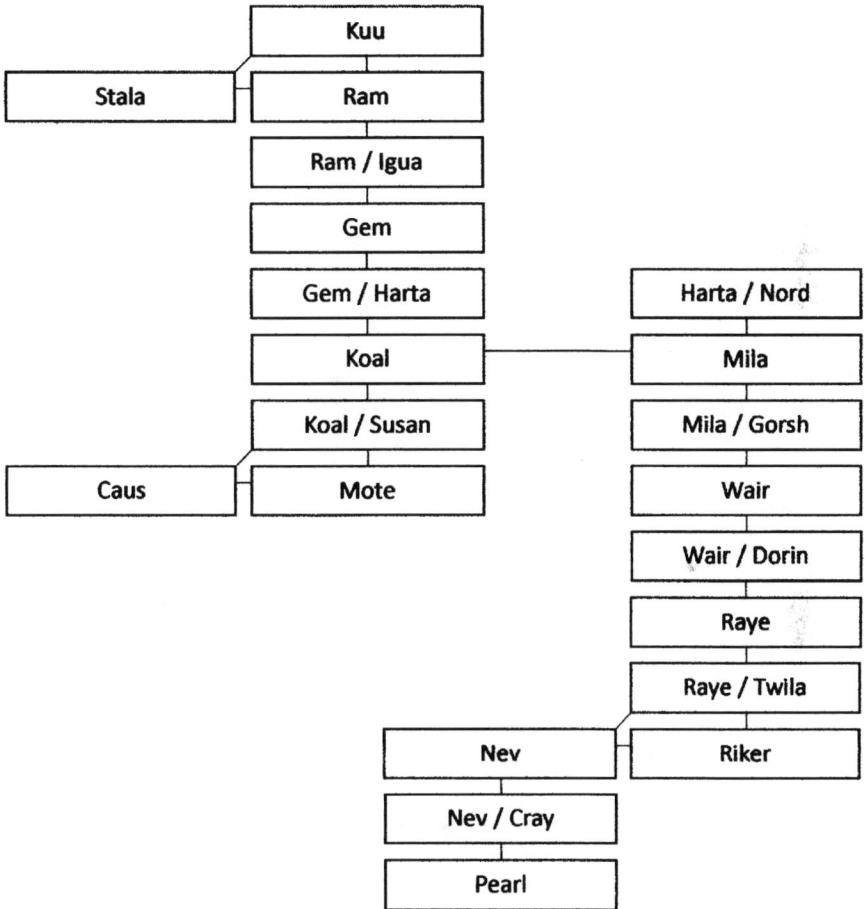

Tuz

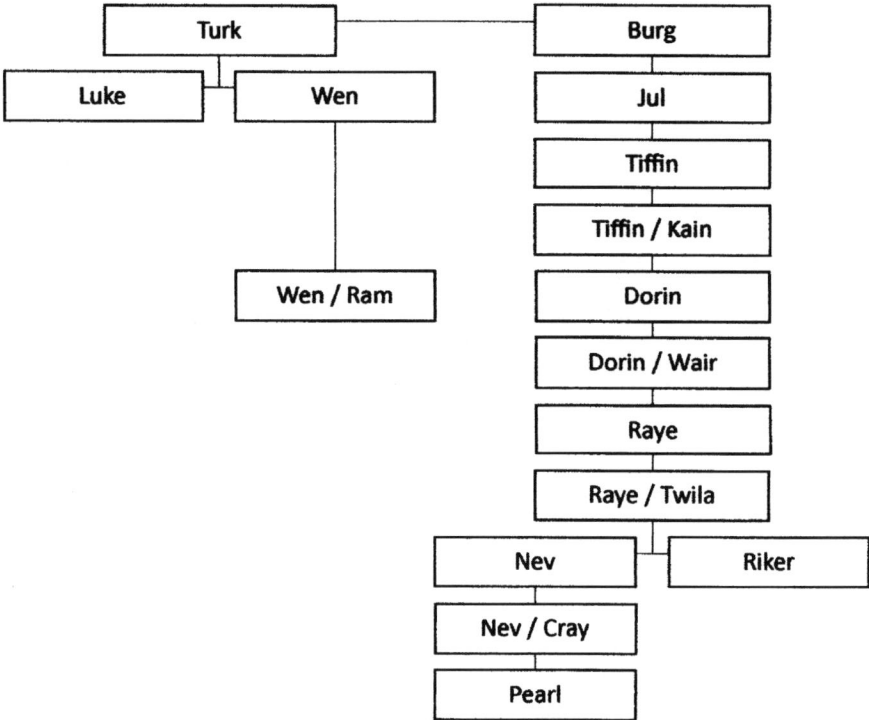

Symlander

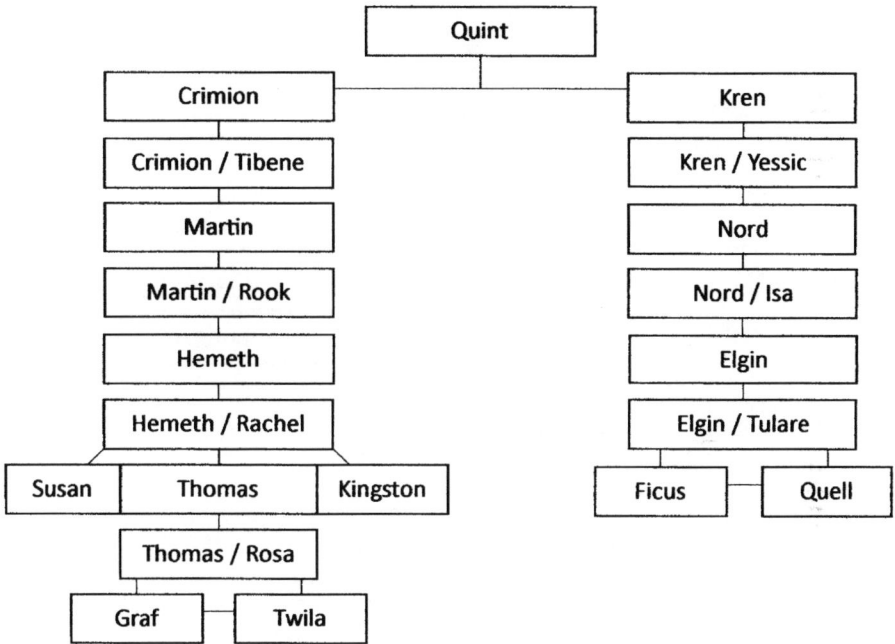

Cantor

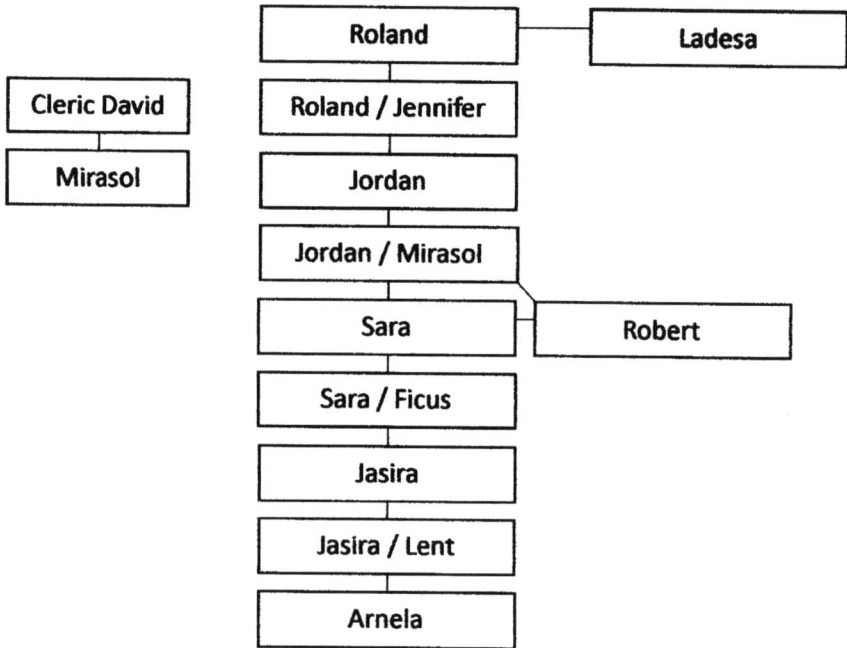

Rivera

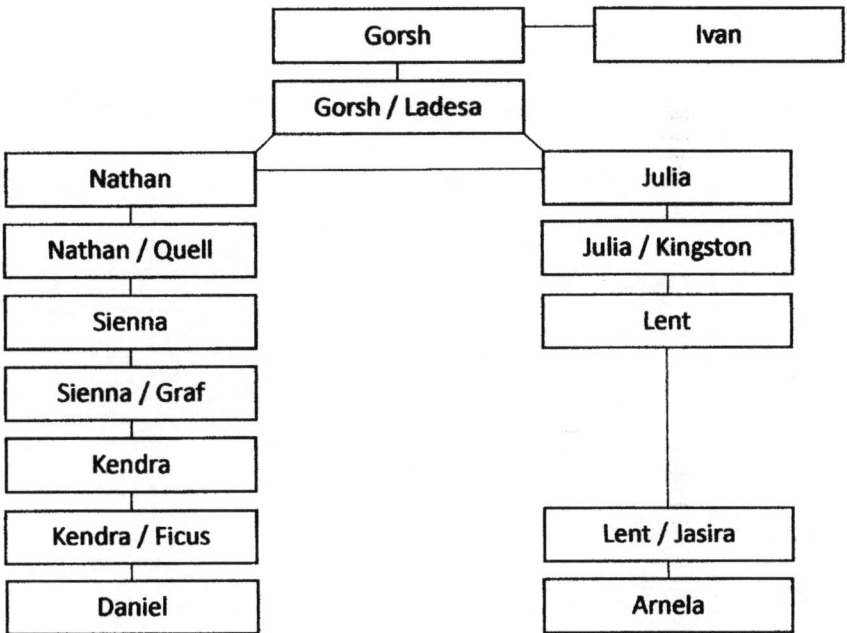

PART I

CHAPTER 1

SUCRENE VALLEY

It was daybreak and Arnela pressed on. She had walked through the night with the full moon's encouragement. Prior to that, she had traveled a fair distance by vessel. Although she was enriched with outstanding endurance, the lack of sleep was challenging her pace.

The sun's rays peeked into the forest, along that gentle stream. Up ahead sat a large rock, perfectly shaped to sit on. Arnela climbed up and did so. She slid the backpack off her shoulders and opened it on her lap. Inside were a flask of fresh water and plaka—the heavy bread would add weight to her fatigue.

Looking up at the swaying canopy, she yawned and rubbed her eyes. Rest would find her, but only for a short while. She must hurry back to Sucrene, where her mother anxiously waited.

The young wizard lay back against the rock and drifted away in thought. *I was sixteen when I left that valley. A wonderful place for sure, yet all I ever knew. Five years have passed—and everything has changed. I have perspective.*

* * *

Arnela's journey began in Montro, a private island controlled by the royals of Sym. The Academy for Special Studies was located there.

She adapted well to academy life, advancing to the abilities program after two years of required courses. Ficus was never more encouraged to evolve a student. "You are a wizard with extreme potential," he assured her.

Mostly because of David, Arnela was not so sure. He was a classmate she had become curiously fond of, a direct descendent of the Mystic Wizard Kren, with abilities (she believed) far more polished than her own. Tragically, he became gravely ill before their graduation.

* * *

Time passed peacefully, as did the water in that gentle stream, until a dorken frog let out a huge CROAK and jolted her awake.

"Oh dear. Oh dear. Mother, I'm on my way!"

Sitting up tall, Arnela stretched for the sky. Then she tucked her white tousled hair into the hood and dropped to the ground. As she kept to the well-worn trail an assortment of creatures appeared. Monarch butterflies fluttered among the eucalyptus. A family of brown-freckled turtles paddled in a shallow pool. And then there was this bothersome crow who shadowed her every step.

It was a rather unseemly bird, with shifty dark eyes and oily black feathers. When she paused, it paused. When she moved, it moved. *Very odd*, she said to herself. Stopping in her tracks, she looked up at the pesky crow, who not surprisingly stared back down at her.

"Time to get to the bottom of this," she grumbled.

Arnela's crystal-blue eyes narrowed as she glared up into the tree. Her chest warmed, and her left arm began to rise. Holding the pointed finger steady, she ensnared the unsuspecting nuisance.

"Crow!" she called out. "What reason do you have for following me?"

The flightless bird hopped down from limb-to-limb, landing on the one that was closest to her. "You are a most talented wizard."

"Just answer the question."

"I am Hendrick, your scout and traveling companion."

"I am Arnela, and this is absurd! Who is behind all this?"

"Your mother," he disclosed. "It was she who gave me a name."

Kendra's involvement was unexpected, and resulted in a moment of silence, during which time the sound of others could be heard in the distance.

"My wings?" he cautiously asked.

"Your wings," she begrudgingly gave in.

Hendrick flew up toward the disturbance, while Arnela sought cover among the ferns. She crouched low and cinched the hood around her face. The crow swooped back down and onto her shoulder, his scowling expression ever so close. She crossed her eyes to look at it.

"What is this," she whispered with annoyance, "perched upon me now?"

Ignoring her, he revealed his findings. "Three Tuz with a Zuku guide. Interesting . . . so far outside their territory."

"This isn't the route I intended to take, but rail service has been disrupted. Something about a commotion in Truth." A perplexed expression came over her. "I feel it is me they are searching for."

"That's it, then. You must be splattered."

"Splattered?"

"Something your mother prepared as a precaution, to take away your scent. I was told it is harmless."

A deep crease formed between her thick white eyebrows. "You will never in your soon-to-be short-lived lifetime do such a dreadful thing."

"We have no other choice," the crow insisted. "Unless we do this, the Zuku will smell you out. And if discovered—"

"Enough already. For Mother's sake, get . . . on . . . with . . . it."

Hendrick tilted his head straight back and gaped his beak. The potion was released and misted down on her. Much to Arnela's surprise, the splatter was light and fragrant. *I smell as lavender.* She chuckled to herself.

The travelers approached and were in full view. They were armed with weapons and extremely observant. Even so, they passed without incident.

"Ready to continue?" asked the crow.

"Let's do it," said Arnela, with an easy smile and confident nod.

He continued to perch on her shoulder, and she was fine with that.

"Arnela."

"Yes, Hendrick."

"Thank you for giving me a voice."

"Me? I thought it was my mother."

"Never!" The crow shook his glistening head. "She only made it so I could understand her demands—uh, instructions."

"Well then, now your opinions can also be expressed."

Hendrick happily bobbed his beak.

He asked, "Your talents, tell me more?"

The wizard rolled up her eyes for a moment. "I've always had conversations with creatures as yourself. I kept that from mother for the longest time. My guarded secret." She quietly reflected.

"Arnela?"

"Oh . . . what else? Until my training is complete, so much remains unclear. Then again, there *is* the obvious."

"Your finger."

Her eyes opened wide. "Yes! But before that—an energy." She pressed against the center of her chest. "It begins here. And even though it's an unconscious impulse, what happens next has never not been my intention." She emphatically shook her head. "It's impossible to explain."

"No! Please continue," Hendrick implored. "I find wizardry . . . fascinating."

"Oh my," she blurted out. "Let me try to show you."

"This is getting good."

She took a deep breath. "First, I feel a warmth—"

"The energy."

"Next, I channel it like this." She curved her finger and steadied it at the crow.

His claws squeezed tighter on her shoulder.

"No need to worry, Hendrick. For this example, my finger is harmless."

"But if you wouldn't mind not pointing it at me? I'm still *tingling* from our introduction."

"Alright then . . . we'll skip that part."

The relieved crow sighed and relaxed his grip.

She circled her chest with another deep breath. "Most often it stays here. But sometimes"—she placed a fingertip on the side of her head—"it moves up here. And on the rarest of occasions, I feel it EVERYWHERE."

She threw her arms up and burst into laughter, while Hendrick flapped his wings and held on.

"More! More!" begged the elated crow.

"Growing up, Mother would sometimes say, 'Arnela, aren't you the wizard.' And this was before she confirmed it."

"Your mother—"

"Is magical," Arnela concluded.

"*Yes . . . magical*," the crow kept to himself.

"My confusion is this, Hendrick. I have known my mother primarily as a teacher. And from the beginning, she has guided me well. I listened carefully and did my best to please her. I wasn't always perfect, but she had patience for that. Yet, there was a divide between us. Maybe now—after Montro, after five years of being away—could I be on that level she has waited for me to reach? A place where she will open up and let me in? I want to *know* her."

By chance, the crow had witnessed Arnela's most personal thoughts.

"I hope this comes true for you. And I'm sure it will." He confidently bobbed his beak.

"Hendrick."

"Yes?"

"I hadn't expected to share all of this, no less with a lively crow."

"At first I was nervous."

"How so?"

"I imagined being turned to stone."

"Never turned anything to stone," she said under her breath.

"What was that?"

"Not so far from home, Hendrick. We're not so far from home."

The crow looked off into the near distance. "You see that ridgeline up ahead?

Arnela smiled warmly. "It glimmers."

"On the other side is our valley. You'll be at your doorstep with daylight to spare."

"Perfect!" she rejoiced and scratched his oily head.

* * *

The thinning forest exposed chiseled granite, framing a rich-blue sky. They went to an outcrop and took in the view.

"Look!" Arnela marveled. "Lake Sucrene and Mount Golder, and—" Suddenly, she was lost in the memories of that day. *Why would I ever go back there?*

Hendrick broke through the silence when he jumped to the ledge and spread his wings. "A glorious place to fly!" He swooped down then caught the updraft. "Caw! Caw!"

Arnela's mood was also lifted. "If only I could fly." And in that instant, her body warmed and became as light as a feather. *I can.*

Exhilarated and knowing no fear, the wide-eyed wizard stepped off the ledge. Surrounded by the thermals, she floated without effort. Her radiant white hair blazed upward.

"Hendrick!"

"Arnela, what is this! What have you done?" The crow was astonished. Here they were facing each other, high above the valley floor.

"I watched you take flight and felt your joy. It moved me beyond compare. It stimulated that *something* . . . that delayed—whatever." She shook her head and laughed. "When I told myself to step off, I was already there. The feeling has never been stronger."

"It must have been very strong. Look where we are."

"Yes, Hendrick . . . look where we are!"

"CAW. CAW."

Arnela thought it wise to return to the outcrop. *Better not to be seen like this, suspended in the air. Someone watching could become unnerved. When does the wizard crossover to the witch?*

Hendrick flew up ahead, finding a pine tree to perch on. When Arnela caught up, he had yet to notice her, preoccupied as he was with grooming himself.

He stared down at the speechless wizard. "From time to time, I do tidy up!"

After he finished and was back on her shoulder, they continued on their way. And before long, they had reached the valley floor.

"Well now." Arnela cheerfully acknowledged the familiar landmark.

It was a prominent greeting from the time of royals, an impressive redwood arch with *SUCRENE* carved into its center, spanning the convergence of two main trails. A warkin, sculpted from volcanic rock, sat anchored on each side.

WARKINS

Warkins were related to the wolf but with far more intelligence and ferocity. Their muscular bodies and long bushy tails were covered in a dense and surprisingly soft gray-patterned fur. An exceptional few were born with silver highlights. Their large heads with upright ears had pronounced canines and intimidating amber eyes. The female, despite being slightly smaller, was no less imposing.

Originating from the Mystic Mountains, they were first encountered by the Zuku. Domesticated by the tribe and receptive to training, they were valued for their hunting prowess and loyalty.

As the years went on, warkins retreated deep into the forests and were not often seen. Inside the castle's Zone, a pack was said to roam.

CASTLE GOLDER

The castle was built by Cantor royals and constructed on Mount Golder, a long-dormant volcano. Its observation deck, windows, and passageways blended seamlessly with the natural contours. Surrounding the castle was a large restricted area called the Zone. Outside its perimeter by the western gate stood the cottage where Arnela was raised.

Arnela

Arnela was an only child. Her father died in a mining accident before she could remember. Her mother made a living as a healer and frequently traveled. While she was away, it was Aunt Murn who looked after her.

When Arnela turned eleven, things abruptly changed. Her mother seldom left the cottage, and rarely overnight. The time had come for the young wizard's first evolvement.

The structured process was most often serious. There were, however, lighter moments, times when Kendra, lacking her own creativity, seemingly fed off her daughter's abundant supply. During those surprising situations, Arnela caught a glimpse of her mother's true self. But it never went further than that.

By age fourteen, the evolvement was complete. Kendra returned to the business of healing, while Arnela fixated on the Zone. She was flatly warned, when her mother found out, to put away such thoughts.

* * *

Kendra's services had been requested in Kurth, a small mining village, one day's travel from Sucrene. Arnela's insatiable curiosity finally got the best of her. An opportunity emerged and the decision was made. Before leaving for Montro, she would explore the forbidden.

CHAPTER 2
THE ZONE

The Zone was created to deter trespassing and preserve the castle's privacy. Entrenched around its perimeter was a gnarly hedge bearing poisonous thorns. Roaming the trails within the buffer were the warkins. Even so, an occasional unfortunate did find their way inside, never to be heard from again.

Although the royals had long since departed, the castle was never abandoned. There was evidence of a custodian. During times of darkness, flickering lights and marching shadows played upon its walls. Large covered wagons with hooded drivers came and went through the western gate. The castle remained an accepted mystery, not openly discussed.

* * *

Arnela's bountiful hair was tied in a tail, and she was dressed in layers. In spite of being late solar, the valley's high elevation made for cool early mornings. She packed roasted oats with honey, and a waterskin. Her plan was simple and well-considered: avoid the warkins and explore the castle grounds. That would suffice for one adventure.

The enthused young wizard raised her hood and charged out the door. She headed south away from the western gate, soon enough reaching the woodlands and her favorite trail. It was uncommonly still that morning. A silent apprehension occupied the air. She paused and looked around. Her eyes locked with those of a squirrel standing on a fallen tree, larger than the average of its kind.

That squirrel can gather. She chuckled to herself.

Suddenly, a familiar feeling simmered deep within her chest, an energy encouraging her arm to rise and her finger to take aim. "What is your name?"

The robust squirrel responded, in a higher-than-expected pitch. "I haven't got a name!"

"Then I will give you one!" she shot back with a glare. "Or better yet . . . name yourself."

"CLEO," the squirrel blurted out, with a smug twitch of its nose. "And you are the wizard, Arnela."

She stepped ever closer. "That I am, Cleo. Now tell me . . . why so quiet today?"

"There's been talk of your intention."

"And might you be the one to help me over there?"

"No way." The squirrel emphatically shook its head. "That is pure nonsense."

"There's something about the Zone that calls to me."

"I suggest you stop listening. There is nothing of importance in there . . . only trouble."

"You *have* been inside," she determined with a knowing stare.

"Purely because of necessity."

"What necessity do you speak of?"

Cleo jumped to the ground and explained. "It was an ordinary day, and unsurprisingly . . . I was hungry. The prevailing breeze brought with it the most enticing smell of ripening fruit. My appetite took control of my better judgment and I followed the aroma. It led me over there." The squirrel looked in the Zone's direction. "Once inside, I discovered an abundance of wonderful food. And this contributed to my generous size."

Arnela burst out laughing, with Cleo joining in.

Their joyful engagement returned the woodlands to life.

"Take me inside," Arnela pleaded. "I will obey your every direction. You know the Zone better than anyone . . . except the warkins."

"Never again mention those hideous beasts!" Cleo spat out. "Disgusting they are, and seemingly always hungry. Thankfully, they are not interested in the foodstuffs that I prefer. But still"—the squirrel frowned and rubbed its belly—"they wouldn't think twice to devour this."

Arnela thought, *I see cause for that concern.*

"Not sure what they would make of you. The strange young wizard that you are."

"Strange?" She scowled, both hands firmly on her hips.

By the way, how are your tree-climbing skills?"

"I can climb 'most anything."

"Hmm," the squirrel twitched its nose and scampered down the trail.

"And Cleo! I will do my best not to mention those *things*."

"Good!"

An idea suddenly came to her. "Wait a moment!"

The squirrel stopped and turned around.

Arnela caught up and reached inside her daypack. "Here . . . try this."

"Wizard food?" Cleo said with an open hand. "I don't know if I should."

"And?"

"Mmm—tasty."

"I'm glad you like it, roasted oats with honey."

"Arnela, I need a promise. We go in, but only as far as I take you."

"I promise."

They left the trail and managed their way through a thicket.

"There it is," said Cleo.

"Impressive." Arnela surveyed the ancient oak, straddling the poisonous hedge.

"The limbs are low enough on both sides. But be careful and look to where I go. We must avoid the thorns."

"And those *things*, they cannot climb?"

"They respect the buffer."

"Buffer?"

"It travels alongside the hedge. Apparently, they've been instructed not to pursue in there."

"Why would you believe this?" she asked.

"Because I've seen it."

Arnela marveled at the oversized squirrel's agility, the way it sprung up onto the oak and escalated across. She took off her pullover and tied it around her waist. Standing on the tips of her toes, she reached a limb to swing up on.

Cleo was waiting at the center of the tree.

"Arnela."

"Yes?"

"A bit more of those sweet and crunchy oats?"

She chuckled. "Of course."

One last bite and the mood was tempered. "Stay close to me, Arnela, with all your senses alert. No regrets for leading you over there."

"No regrets, my friend."

"Then . . . let's go."

Using branches to steady herself, she followed Cleo to the other side.

They sat together on the lowest limb.

"Soft voices now," whispered the squirrel.

Arnela observed the Zone's surroundings. The buffer was clearly defined, a wide strip of dirt and small rocks, with sparse vegetation. The dry grass that lined it would rise up to her chest. A web of trails was inside that.

"Warkins," she thought out loud.

"What did you say?"

"Nothing really," she softly replied. "Testing the volume of my voice. It's good, right?"

Cleo stayed silent and sprang to the ground.

Arnela swung down and stuck her landing. "Perfect," she commended herself.

"Quiet."

Although the sight of the castle inspired her, she also felt a measure of guilt.

Forgive me, Mother, she said to herself. *Everything will be fine.*

"Through here." Cleo tunneled through the grass.

Arnela parted the yellow blades and went inside. After three paces, she was on the trail.

The spirited squirrel waved her on. The undulating path descended to a final corner, where a flourishing oasis was revealed. It was a spring-fed orchard of bountiful fruits and nuts. Cleo had indeed made an incredible discovery!

"Try this one."

She took the apricot and brought it to her nose. "What a wonderful smell."

"And this one." The squirrel presented a deep-purple plum. "Amazing, aren't they?"

Arnela nodded with a mouthful of fruit.

"Wait, there's more."

"Cleo! Please, a moment to swallow."

The deflated squirrel hung its head and sighed.

"Cheer up. The fruit is the best ever . . . peak perfection." She finished another bite of plum.

Their heads jerked in the same direction, startled by the frenzied sounds.

"It's *them*," said Cleo.

They both shot forward and rushed to where they had come from.

Arnela jumped up as high as she could. "They're closing in!"

"And they're hungry . . . always hungry!" screeched the squirrel. "Faster, Arnela. Faster!"

Faster . . . faster, she encouraged herself. Her breathing was labored, her legs becoming numb.

Cleo shouted, "I've reached the buffer!"

"The oak?"

"Almost there!"

Arnela broke through. "Made it."

"Up here!" Cleo yelled from the tree.

Arnela bent over and gulped some air. She raised up, wobbled forward, and then stopped. She sensed a presence and turned around. There they were, perfectly still and staring at her. She counted twelve, all but one with their large heads poked through the grass. The leader's front paws were just inside the buffer.

Arnela's chest swelled with heat, energizing her pointed finger. "What is your name, warkin?"

The beast's upper lip curled, exposing enlarged canines, worn and discolored yet impressive nevertheless.

"My name is LUTZ," he bellowed. "What brings you to the Zone, Wizard? Only to gather food with an overstuffed rodent?"

She kept her eyes on the leader while slowly stepping backward toward the oak.

"Warkins," she said in a pleasant tone. "It's time for us to go. Return to what you were doing."

"Not so fast," Lutz snarled.

The other warkins did not flinch, their attentive ears straight up.

Arnela probed the eyes of the pack. Even though their leader was a menace, she *felt* they were not. One of them in particular piqued her interest. She was directly behind Lutz. Unlike the others, her forehead shimmered with silver.

Arnela privately asked the exceptional warkin, *You will succeed your father?* Ever so slightly, she lowered and then raised her glimmering head.

The leader's patience was waning, his snarl growing thick and wet.

Arnela reached up and grabbed the sturdy limb. "Goodbye, Lutz."

"I'm not through with you, Wizard!"

"You are NOT allowed in the buffer, and you know it!"

He closed the gap between them. "Does your mother know about this?"

"What about my mother?"

Not waiting for an answer, she swung up onto the tree and climbed away.

Lutz crouched down and then powerfully leaped to a limb. Cautiously, he started across the oak.

The warkin was vulnerable until safely on the other side. Once there, he would kill her.

From high above at the center of the tree, Cleo crashed down on the beast. Its clawed fingers latched to his eye sockets. Stunned and writhing in pain, Lutz violently shook his head.

Arnela heard the ruckus and turned to see the fight. "I'm coming, Cleo!"

"No—Arnela!" the squirrel screeched. "Save yourself!"

"Lutz! Go BACK," she demanded.

Cleo's strong fingers dug deeper. Squishing the right eyeball, while the left one popped free.

"Get off me!" roared the beast.

The courageous squirrel clamped its teeth on the warkin's ear and ground them together.

Lutz yelped from the piercing pain, in desperation ramming his head against the oak's main stem, hitting with such force his hind legs slipped out from underneath him. Down they tumbled, breaking branches and bouncing off limbs, all the way to an abrupt silence. Their bodies were lacerated by the poisonous thorns, their last breath quickly taken.

Inside the Zone, the warkins HOWLED.

CHAPTER 3
CANTOR ROYAL FAMILY

With the exception of Truth, the royals of Rivera laid claim to all the regions in the land. The southwest peninsula was of strategic importance and had yet to be developed. The queen's brother, Roland, was offered the coastal basin and plateau. The Principality of Marina would be autonomous, with conditions that favored the kingdom.

Ten years after its establishment, Marina was struck by a catastrophic tidal wave. Fishing boats were tossed as toys and smashed into driftwood. Fertile farmland was flooded and poisoned by brackish water. All low-lying structures were destroyed. Virtually all life on the bottom land perished without warning. Prince Roland and Princess Jennifer were swept away from the harbor, leaving their son, Jordan, the surviving heir.

* * *

In a tangerine sky above the now-calm sea, a falcon circled and screeched. The young royals stood on the balcony, overlooking the misery, holding each other as if for the last time. As the water receded and the cries diminished, they wondered what would bring the new day's dawn.

Prince Jordan and Princess Mirasol had only briefly returned. They had been away celebrating their union.

The Aftermath and Sucrene

Pillars of smoke rose from the mass cremations—humans and animals alike. The smell of death was everywhere. Fearfulness pervaded the thoughts of most survivors. The open sea could no longer be trusted.

Encouragingly, food stocks, fresh water, and shelter were available on the plateau. The castle opened its doors for medical care and took in orphaned children. Jordan and Mirasol's compassion consoled those who were desperate for hope.

Led by the royal couple, a committee was formed to relocate the principality. Their resources were plentiful, as the treasury suffered no losses. Lancaster was the favored choice. Located nearby, it boasted a surplus of opportunities.

The kingdom also valued this area, its future already drafted. Many Riveras clamored to settle there. The Cantors were offered an alternative: the Sucrene Valley.

Located in the northeastern highlands, the valley at the time was inhabited by hardened trappers and miners. The growing season was short, but the land fertile. There was an abundance of fresh water, including the expansive Lake Sucrene. Isolated as it was, the kingdom had yet to make a meaningful commitment. Although, they did anticipate its eventual development. Through chance circumstance, the opportunity had arrived.

The committee was not thrilled with the offer, but would go there and see for themselves.

It was early renewal, a favorable season for an introduction. Jordan and Mirasol admired the natural beauty, yet were not blind to the hardships they would face.

Rights to the valley were secured. The kingdom's share was thirty percent of the mining revenue.

* * *

The first two years were extremely difficult, and Marina was sorely missed. The mild climate they were accustomed to was replaced by four assertive seasons. Dark was formidable, with bitter cold and snowfall. Even so, the royals maintained a positive front. They believed with sincere effort, a bright future would prevail.

Privately, they did share their misgivings. But through it all, remained devoted to each other.

Jordan said one moonlit night while staring at Mount Golder, "We will build a castle there, and live in this enchanted place."

"And raise a family."

"Yes, my princess."

"And the warkins you favor," she playfully reminded him, "we will have those as well."

He smiled broadly. "How could we not."

They embraced and shared a lasting kiss.

During the dark season that second year, joyful news arrived. The royals welcomed their first child, Sara.

Soon after her birth, a pair of warkins were acquired and bred. Symbolic of Sucrene's sporting lifestyle, the royal warkins led parades and performed at festivals.

After two years with mixed results, seasoned miners were brought in to better manage the assets. Equipment was upgraded and the latest techniques applied. By year three, productivity had vastly improved.

During year five, a significant discovery was made: gold. The new-found wealth sparked Sucrene's remarkable transformation. Castle Golder became a reality. The village's infrastructure was modernized. The livery stable was moved to the outskirts, and its services expanded. Lake Sucrene was tapped to serve the entire valley. Additional tracts of farmland were cultivated, and pastures teemed with livestock. True to the royals' belief, life became better for all those who lived there.

Instead of loathing the bleakest time of the year, Mirasol decided to celebrate it. She created the Dark Season Festival. During the inaugural event, an important announcement was made. Prince Robert would arrive at the beginning of renewal.

* * *

To commemorate Sucrene's twentieth anniversary, a grand celebration was planned. Dignitaries from the kingdom and neighboring lands were invited to join the festivities. The once-undeveloped valley would be proudly put on display.

Sara and Robert were ecstatic. Sucrene had earned a favorable reputation, but special guests seldom traveled there.

CHAPTER 4
ZUKUS AND *TRUTH*

For a span of time in the distant past, the land now called Rivera was inhabitant by the Zuku.

All Zukus were similar in appearance, with strong facial features and large hazel eyes, and finely textured dark red hair tied to make a tail. Their bodies were short and muscular.

Most were born common, and lacked significant emotions. They were easygoing and not often disturbed. Their lack of understanding was rebalanced with resourcefulness and determination. They recognized there was more to life than living only to survive.

Each generation, uniquely gifted Zukus were born. A select few that could *feel* the thoughts, or *truth*, of others while also concealing their own. When of age, they provided the tribe's leadership and guidance.

Mating occurred but once each year, considered an act of purpose, one's responsibility to replenish the tribe. Commons by nature were not amorous and did not seek attachments. Without the need to partner, they led an independent and celibate life. The gifted, however, were capable of desire. Culturally obligated to restrain those feelings, at times they wrestled with their true self.

During the growing and harvest seasons, the tribe occupied the Western Encampment. The environment was peaceful and ideal for birthing. Within the encampment was Mothers' Village, an integral component of Zuku life. The younglings were insulated and nurtured there.

A new Zuku was carried in a sling and absorbed their mother's scent, which stayed with them a lifetime. At age six, the youngling left the village as a learner, transferred to a guide, and were given a name. For the next ten years, they came to know the ways of the tribe. At seventeen, they were acknowledged as mature and fully independent, eventually becoming an elder at the age of twenty-seven.

The tribe planted a variety of crops. Plaka beans and corn were staples, and the basis of their traditional bread. Flax was grown for oil and fabric, jute for rope and flooring.

A large protected cove contained a bounty of seafood. Canoes and nets were relied upon for their harvest. Closer to shore, an experienced hunter would wade in with a spear. A portion of the catch was smoked and preserved for the migration. Oysters attached to the barrier rocks yielded a prized pearl on occasion, the celebrated treasure put on display at Zuku House.

Not so far to the north was the Coastal Jungle. Most of the tribe's fruits, nuts and medicines were sourced from there.

Wild horses, long since domesticated, were essential to their way of life, harnessed for farming and travel, ridden for hunting and leisure.

After the crops were in the ground, hunting-team tryouts were held. The competition was open to those fifteen years of age. Females accepted to the team no longer qualify as mothers. A premium was placed on those with the skills to hunt. To be leader of the tribe, one first had to be a champion hunter.

Twice each year while on migration, they confronted the Lackland elk, a tradition since the earliest of times. The large impressive animals provided a multitude of their needs.

FESTIVALS

Festival of Family: A joyful event before the fields were planted. It coincided with Zuku births and the younglings' first steps.

Harvest Festival: The most exuberant gathering of them all, a time for abundant food, storytelling, games . . . and mating. A rare occasion when shillig—a specialty beverage, distilled from fermented plaka beans, sweet and smooth with a nutty finish—was toasted.

Festival of Blessings: A reflective and somewhat-spiritual occasion, held before the eastern migration. Although the Zuku were not a faith-based tribe, they did recognize the many blessings of life. Symbolically, a display of fire burned throughout the night, an offering, to the Great Deep Sky.

IGUA

An extremely gifted and humble Zuku, Igua understood the tribe's well-being always came first.

Zuku Governing Council:
Igua · · · · · · · *Leader of the Tribe*
Rono · · · · · · · *Leader of Mothers' Village and Younglings*
Carrib · · · · · *Leader of Learners and Guides*
Stala · · · · · · · *Leader of Wellness and Matures*
Ram · · · · · · · *Leader of Hunters*
Kierka · · · · · *Leader of Farmers*
Raj · · · · · · · · *Leader of Builders*

* * *

Soon the tribe would migrate east. Final preparations were being attended to, and everyone had a task. Traveling supplies were packed and inventoried. Wagons were serviced and health checks performed on the animals. After the majority of the work was done, they paused for the Festival of Blessings.

Igua began her day as any other, with a walk around the encampment, by habit starting at the Mothers' Village, a place she enjoyed the most.

"Blessings, Rono," she said with a smile.

"Blessings, Igua." The leader smiled in return, and they shared a warm hug.

"The village is prepared for travel?"

"Yes of course . . . and still you ask."

Igua lightly chuckled.

"Follow me," said Rono, her voice subdued.

They walked a short distance, exchanging greetings along the way.

Rono spoke softly, at the entrance to the tent. "This youngling is different."

"How so?"

"You will see." She took a deep breath. "Harta! I am here with Igua."

A few moments passed before the young mother arrived.

"You came to see the youngling?"

"Yes," said Rono.

"She is resting."

They went to a section in the back of the tent, where the youngling was asleep on a cot.

"She is five years old, and soon a learner," Harta said with hesitation. "There have always been differences, but now . . . even more so."

The leaders took notice of the child's striking appearance.

"Her hair is *wild*," Rono remarked. "And these roots," she pointed out.

"White," whispered Igua.

Rono pulled down the blanket.

"She looks to be ten," Igua blurted out.

"And her feet are slender," Rono added.

"What of her eyes, Harta?" asked Igua. "The color of her eyes?"

"Blue, Tribe Leader. They have turned from gray to the clearest blue." She meekly lowered her head.

"She is Zuku?" said Igua.

Harta responded with her head kept down, "She is my offspring."

The youngling stirred as the voices grew louder.

Rono stared at the restless child and firmly reminded them, "I was there when she was born. I delivered her."

The youngling's eyes opened wide. "Mother, what is it?"

"The tribe leader is here to extend her blessings."

Igua smiled and offered her hand. "Yes, for you and your mother."

The youngling reached out and *felt* something more.

"Igua," Rono said softly. "Time is passing."

The youngling spoke up. "Blessings, Tribe Leader." Her crystal-blue eyes were moist. Her warm hand was caring . . . and strong.

"Blessings," Igua replied, with thoughts that were flustered. The child was gifted.

The leaders left the tent and engaged in conversation.

"It is true you were there for the birth," said Igua. "But you were not there for the mating. Has Harta shared words of the father?"

"She does not remember the father. Most of that night is a blur. I asked her to try—"

"She must remember," Igua insisted. "What will be our explanation?"

"Harta remembers only this," said Rono with steadfast eyes. "On that night, much shillig was toasted. She ran into the darkness that led to the cove, waking up at sunrise, alone on the beach, her clothing torn and misplaced."

"The youngling has the look of those who were shipwrecked."

"Yes, I believe this as well."

"She can no longer stay hidden."

"No," Rono agreed.

"I need time to think about this. Blessings."

"Blessings."

They parted with a brief hug.

Walking out of the village, Igua asked herself. *What is the answer?*

No matter her experiences, no matter her gift, the revelation of a Zuku with mixed blood was inconceivable.

"Blessings, Igua!" a common shouted from a distance.

The preoccupied leader did not respond. Her thoughts drifted. *I must have guidance.*

"Blessings," Ram offered, while stepping in front of her path. "Are you there?"

"I am . . . blessings."

"You are not," he gruffly disagreed.

"Ram!" She glared into his probing eyes.

He smiled. "There you are."

"I am calling a meeting."

"When?"

"Tomorrow morning. I know it's sudden, but what must be discussed cannot be delayed."

"Tell me?"

"Tomorrow—"

He reached out and placed his hand on her shoulder. "Is it your health?"

"This isn't about me."

"I can listen?"

Igua could depend on Ram, always. He was wise, and his opinions were valued.

"I must prepare for tonight." She took a moment—then shook her head. "No . . . sit with me."

They walked up the gentle hill and sat on a familiar bench.

"Twenty years." Her eyes began to wander. "We've been on the council for all this time." She turned to him and softly smiled. "We have worked well together."

"That we have," he replied, unsure where the conversation was leading.

"And before this, we were close—without boundaries."

"I've never known a closeness as I have with you," said Ram.

"I am troubled."

"And I am listening."

"There is a youngling, birthed by Harta."

"The Zuku who lost her parents."

"Yes, Gem's friend. Her offspring is soon to be a learner." Igua gazed out, far beyond the encampment. "She is not full Zuku."

He studied her profile. "How can you say that?"

She took a deep breath and turned to him. "On this new day, I saw for myself. The youngling has the length of a Zuku twice her age. Her eyes are blue. Where does this come from?"

"We both know the answer." He nodded.

"It happened the night of the Harvest Festival. She ran off and slept at the cove. Whoever was there—with her—remains unknown."

Ram felt an uneasiness. "That night is familiar."

Igua looked down at the encampment and sighed. "We are a tribe of almost seven hundred, one of us an obscure youngling." Her words were suddenly not her own. "Does she belong?"

He held her hand, and their fingers interlocked. "She belongs."

*   *   *

The tribe had gathered in the central courtyard, most seated on the rows of sturdy oak benches. The night was pleasantly warm, the surroundings illuminated by lanterns and starlight. Igua stepped onto the platform and walked to its front center. From there, she was visible to all. What happened next was expected from her, ever since she was a youngling. She smiled, a radiant and engaging smile.

"Blessings, Zukus!" she proclaimed with outstretched arms.

"BLESSINGS," the tribe responded as one.

There was an extended pause and the courtyard fell silent. Those gifted *felt* Igua's private conflict, no matter her smile.

How do I begin? She struggled with her thoughts.

Igua.

She distanced herself from Ram's inner voice and took a slow, deep breath.

"Zukus! As the seasons change, so, too, will our tribe. Change is a natural progression. We will adapt and find balance."

The tribe was transfixed by the unusual message.

"Remember your blessings and hold them close. Keep them with you always. Tonight, we light a special fire, an offering to the Great Deep Sky, an expression of our gratitude, for the many blessings of life. Blessings!"

"BLESSINGS."

As Igua stepped down, Ram reached out his hand. Brushing it away, she left him in the shadows. Dismayed by her rejection, he stepped back further into darkness and revisited the past.

Ram and Igua

The Harvest Festival was comprised of two areas: general and mating. Most of the tribe gathered in the general area. Those preselected to mate were equally numbered by gender.

Mating was a matter of duty, a process, with expectations well defined. For Ram, it was never that clear. He envisioned his mate, a champion, forced to retire due to injury. In her presence, he felt immense joy.

The new matures arrived with their guides.

"Enjoy the festival," she said with a hug.

Ram softly nodded and went inside. He acquainted himself among the surroundings, with food and drink stations over there, and tents behind that.

Where is she? Up ahead next to a fire pit was a group of six, evenly paired. He observed their lively conversation. *Most likely the shillig,* he suspected.

The beverage was altered to provide encouragement, its herbal recipe known only to the leaders. Toasting was mandatory.

He recognized Max, Lona, and Krig, and then he excitedly blurted out, "Igua!"

"Ram!" shouted Lona.

"Hello, everyone," he started over. "Have you been here long?"

"Long enough to toast!" said Max with gusto.

Igua spoke up through the laughter. "Excuse me for a moment."

I'm too late, thought Ram, disappointed he had not arrived sooner.

Igua returned, with a toasting cup in each hand. "I've actually waited until now. Ram, would you like to share my first toast?"

Her intention was evident to the others, and they took their conversation elsewhere.

"Might we toast to a night of togetherness?" he suggested.

She smiled and lifted her cup to his. "Let us toast to that."

His face nestled against her bare shoulder. Their closeness was unlike anything he had experienced. *How much of the pleasure was brought on by the shillig?* he silently wondered. *Tomorrow, will this all be forgotten?*

"Ram."

"You were listening?"

"For me," she answered his thoughts, "the desire was greater than the shillig. After all, we only toasted once before—"

"This is true." He chuckled

"But let there be no misunderstanding"—she combed through his hair with her fingers—"I desired to mate without the shillig. And I wanted more than to create a new."

"Something more?"

"Like this." She lifted his chin and offered her lips.

They shared a tender kiss, then clutched each other tight in laughter and rolled from side to side.

* * *

After their one night of mutual bliss, they returned to the ways of the tribe. Igua immersed herself in the Mothers' Village. She *felt* Ram's presence in the youngling and was comforted, though at times an emptiness prevailed without him truly there.

During those moments, the youngling would ask, "Mother, why are you with sadness?"

Unlike the others, Igua and her offspring carried a wealth of emotions. She kept strong and guarded. Her son's inherited feelings, over time, would grow unrestrained.

Ram's access to the village was limited, as it had always been that way. He was a proud Zuku, and considerate of tradition.

* * *

The youngling would leave the village soon, and Igua sent word to Ram. They met outside the perimeter. He attempted to *feel* her thoughts.

"Are you searching for something?" she asked before continuing to walk ahead.

"You know me—when it comes to you, I am impulsive with little control."

Suddenly she stopped and faced him. "Once we are alone, I will share myself."

They looked at each other with deep care.

"Igua, I have missed you."

"Inside . . . let's go inside."

They slipped off their sandals and stepped into the visitors' tent. A jute mat covered the floor.

She reached out and invited his hands. "I have also missed you."

Their wanting lips touched and pressed warmly together.

"Let's talk." She smiled and then, unexpectedly, returned her lips to his. "There!" She exhaled.

They sat on the floor.

"The youngling is well?" he asked.

"Our youngling is very well, but in need of a guide. I asked you here to consider this."

"Igua, I—"

"Would you be willing and able? Ten years of your time."

Even though he was deeply involved with the hunting team, the idea had crossed his mind. Her offer flooded his emotions with gratefulness.

She *felt* his joy and acceptance. "It brings me great comfort, knowing our son will be with you."

THE COUNCIL

Tribal business was conducted at Zuku House, the encampment's most prominent structure, an expansive two-level log building that sat on the only hill.

The seven leaders settled around the large square-shaped oak table. Igua, alone on one side, stood up and opened the meeting.

"Good day, council members, and blessings for your thoughtfulness."

"Blessings, Tribe Leader!"

"A profound development has been brought to my attention, and I am challenged by its nature. There is a youngling—soon-to-be learner. She is of mixed blood, and not full Zuku."

"What is she, then?" asked Carrib.

"Zuku!" Ram impulsively shouted and then concluded in a less aggressive tone, "a member of our tribe."

Rono spoke up. "Tribe Leader . . . Let me explain to the council."

"Go on."

"At first the differences were peculiar, but well concealed in the sling. Once the new became a youngling, Harta made every effort to disguise the obvious. Coloring her hair, shaping her footwear. Until recently . . . her eyes were undecided."

"And now?" Carrib muttered.

"Blue—and they sparkle."

"Blue . . ." the members echoed. "Blue eyes."

Kierka asked, "Why did you not advise us sooner?"

"I fought my feelings to do so!"

"Rono," Igua reached out in a caring voice.

"The youngling was to be protected. First by Harta, then even more so by me." Rono's eyes were moist and distant. "I cared for her as if she were mine."

"And the father?" asked Stala.

Igua spoke up, "What happened that night remains a mystery."

"Not to her mate!" Raj blurted out. "Whatever he is."

"I would like to evaluate the child," said Stala.

Ram stood up. "This is not the youngling's making. She is to be respected, as any one of us."

"She cannot be a mother!" Raj insisted.

"I agree," said Stala, nodding in his direction.

"The half-Zuku," Raj continued, "will be respected until her final breath. However, when she passes . . . so, too, will the blood of her kind."

"Let our leader speak," said Ram, who then sat down with the others.

Igua stood and waited for quiet. "Your concerns are clear. Yet if this is about the purity of our blood—our culture—differences have always existed among us, differences not plainly seen." She looked with sincerity at each face there. "The learner will have my full attention, as I will be her guide. My time as leader is over, and I nominate Ram to take my place."

Stala spoke up, "Ram, do you accept?"

He rose to his feet. "I am honored to accept the nomination."

"Members of the council," said Igua, "show your hands in support."
All hands were raised.

"What now with the hunters?" asked Stala. "Who will lead them?
Ram, do you have a nomination?"

"Although he is two years from being an elder, Gem is worthy."

Igua forcefully raised her hand. "Those in favor?"

CHAPTER 5

ZUKUS AND TUZ

Ram greeted Gem with a smile and a firm handshake. "I have something of interest for you."

The two Zukus stared eye to eye.

"The tribe has selected a new leader?" Gem wryly suggested.

Ram crossed his arms and groaned. "Once again, you have obtained privileged information. Leave it to your mother." He quietly added, "Leader of the hunters."

"What? Yes—Mother . . . but leader? Not me!"

"Imagine that."

"There was no mention . . ." The stunned Zuku continued to ramble. "How is this possible? She conceals so well."

"Unbelievable!" Ram laughed. "I have finally surprised you. We made an exception, and everyone approved. However, you are still not an elder."

Gem had followed Ram's path, first as champion and now leader.

"You know of your mother's plan?"

"To guide the half-Zuku."

"Listen to me," said Ram. "Do not refer to the learner as anything less than a Zuku. She is a full member of our tribe."

Gem nodded. "She is Zuku."

Kierka appeared in the distance, running up the path that led to the cove. By the time she reached them, her breath was labored, the words forced from her mouth. "There's been a wreck at the point. It happened during the night. Again, the rocks without mercy. Bodies . . . some have washed into the cove."

Ram focused his attention on Gem. "Get help. Bring two wagons and include the warkins. We'll need water, blankets, carriers . . . anything else you can think of—and hurry."

"I'll meet you there!"

This was not the first time a vessel had smashed against those rocks, foreigners forsaken by a violent sea. Outside the cove's protective barrier, unpredictable winds, swift currents, and dense fog lay in wait.

Ram and Kierka hurried down the wide pathway, to a beach of light brown sand.

"Oh my," Ram said with squinted eyes. "There's not much—"

Remnants of the vessel were scattered everywhere.

"The tide is rising," said Kierka.

Between them and the point, bodies encrusted with seafoam had been discarded on the shore.

"We'll take care of those we can, and leave the others for the warkins."

The first foreigner lay face down, and noticeably longer than a Zuku. His hair was dark and shoulder length. He had a marking on his wrist. His clothing was in two pieces, the fabric not unlike the tribe's one-piece tunic. However, the fit was tailored and the stitching more refined. Once he was rolled over, empty eye sockets revealed only that.

The next body was a female, lying on her back, the length and color of her hair similar to the male's, her facial features softer.

Kierka knelt down and carefully pulled up an eyelid, exposing a dark-brown iris. "These foreigners are much different."

Ram crouched down beside her. "Yes, and I remember them well. Tangled white hair, and eyes the clearest blue. Their bodies left unmarked."

The leaders got to their feet and proceeded toward the point.

They came across a larger piece of the vessel. Slowly, Ram walked around it, the woodwork was less elaborate than before.

By the time the wagons arrived, eight lifeless foreigners had been moved to higher ground.

"Go!" Gem commanded.

The pair of warkins raced up the shoreline. If not for their task, they would have jumped straight into the cove.

The tribe maintained a small pack of warkins. They were well cared for but not spoiled. The loyal beasts were trained to be of service. They obeyed commands, *private* and spoken. They had an affinity for the water.

Ram looked past the fast-approaching warkins, to where Gem and the others loaded the bodies. He stood in disbelief, immersed in stark images and a flurry of thoughts.

As the leaders reached the point, they discovered another body. The foreigner's upper torso had wedged between two rocks, her exposed legs a pendulum controlled by the tide. Ram motioned the warkins closer, and they did so with nostrils flared.

The scent they trapped would lead them to the others.

WRECK OF THE *ROYAL SYMLANDER*

Fifteen years earlier, on the point's unforgiving rocks, a magnificent vessel had met its fate.

Gem had not been allowed to witness the recovery but could smell the aftermath of bodies being burned. He sensed the leaders' uneasiness and asked his mother to explain. She told him Kuu would do so later.

Kuu had been the Zuku leader for many years. His knowledge of their history deep and faithful.

The tribe leader stood on the platform, a setting sun at his back. Hundreds of large hazel eyes fixed upon him.

"Zukus!" his familiar voice rang out. "Outside our cove, a vessel was lost upon the rocks. Those from another tribe, lifeless and without explanation. It is true! A similar event happened long ago, put to sleep by the leaders of that time . . . to be forgotten. Today, we choose to remember! For as the daylight turns to dark and then returns again, so, too, is this for certain . . . we are not alone. There are others, who live in distant lands. And one day, they will return."

Voices and movement spread among those who were gathered.

Kuu raised his hands. "Zukus! We will share all that we know and learn what we can."

The tribe was instructed to meet at Zuku House, where objects salvaged from the wreckage were put on display.

In the main room were Kuu and Stala. They provided the initial guidance and maintained an orderly flow. Behind them, two foreigners, a male and a female, lay crudely embalmed and fully exposed.

Igua stood by in the next room. On three tables was a collection of unfamiliar items, including fine dishware, colorful fabrics, and intricate jewelry.

In the final room was Ram. He discussed the vessel's composition, providing examples of its advanced materials and design.

Ram asked Gem, "The thoughts you have *felt* around you?"

"Somewhat troubled," the wide-eyed Zuku conceded. "While I am equally inspired."

Four days went by and Gem was at the cove. He sat alone, carving into the wet sand with a stick of driftwood.

What more is out there? he pondered. *Other lands . . . where are they? Other tribes . . . who are they?*

High-pitched screeches interrupted the calm, sounds that were new to him. Looking up into the bright midday sky, he discovered the bird in flight. A falcon, soaring away with something glimmering in its talons.

THE TUZ

Again, without survivors, Ram was left to wonder. *What was their purpose?*

Venturing deeper into the rocks, the warkins retrieved more bodies and dragged them to the beach. Almost twenty had been recovered and loaded on the wagons. When the beasts returned this time, they became excited with nostrils flared.

Kierka said, "The scent is fresh."

"Go tell Gem, and return with the carriers."

She hurried to the beach.

Ram scrambled after the warkins, who jumped from rock to rock. They disappeared around the point and began to growl.

"Wait!" he commanded.

The growls subsided but were no less intense.

"Back!"

Retreating from the shallow cave, they exposed the two huddled bodies.

He stood there in the silence and listened. *They breathe.*

"We are here," a winded Kierka announced.

Ram said, "Gem, take the foreigners to Stala. They are weak, yet still alive."

The warkins were inclined to remain with the scent, but Ram ordered them to stay.

Kierka *felt* the leader's tension. "Let's take our time," she suggested.

Once over the rocks, she stood in front of his path. "Stop and share a moment with me." Her words though firm—were caring.

As leader of farmers, Kierka was nurturing and patient. She steadied Ram's strained emotions. Only a select group of Zukus understood the difficulties they could present.

She placed her hand on his shoulder and firmly gave it a squeeze. "I am here."

He took a deep breath. "Blessings for you."

"And you." She smiled.

The warkins flared their nostrils and raised their snouts.

"GO," Ram shouted.

The anxious beasts bounded into the cove.

Kierka pointed at a floating object. "Over there!"

The leaders walked down the sandy bottom until the tepid water reached their chests. The warkins gave one last nudge and then paddled back to shore.

Ram slowly turned the makeshift raft so the foreigner's head was next to his. With inquisitive fingers, he moved aside her matted hair, astonished by the face revealed.

Kierka *felt* Ram's beating heart. It was strong.

He privately asked, *Are you there?*

Her swollen eyelids twitched. "Yes," she whispered.

Ram took the foreigner over his shoulder and carried her up the beach. Once on the pathway, he shared the burden with Kierka—four turns each. Curious Zukus met them along the way and followed them to the clinic.

Gem was there when they arrived. "Another!" he blurted out.

"Yes," Ram said, "only by chance."

"Lay her here," directed Stala.

In one capacity or another, Stala had been a Zuku leader for many years. She was extremely enlightened, with much wisdom and strength. Traits passed down by Kuu. During her training, they developed an unbreakable bond. Although it had never been discussed, she *felt* the tribe leader was more than just a guide.

Stala took a cloth infused with herbal oils and tamped the survivor's forehead.

"How is she?" Ram asked with fascination.

"Stable."

"And the others?"

"The same . . . and resting."

Ram looked over at Gem. "Find your mother, and let her know where I am." He turned back to the survivor and gazed in curiosity.

Stala could feel his stare. "We have foreigners in our midst," she said softly, "and they breathe."

Igua soon arrived and silently stood at the doorway. Ram sat on a stool, holding the survivor's hand. His *truth* was open, and uniquely familiar.

He sensed her presence. "These foreigners, they are different than before."

"I see that," said Igua. "And what does she say to you, Ram?"

"That she is determined to live."

Stala spoke up, "They all are."

"The council will meet?" Igua thoughtfully asked, as she was no longer the tribe's leader.

"Yes," he replied. "If you could arrange this? Your support and familiar voice—"

"I will advise the leaders, and greet you at daybreak." She left without another word.

"Ram."

"Yes, Stala?"

"This will be a long night. I will leave for some moments and bring back food. Stay with the foreigner until I return."

"I will be here."

Ram never considered leaving. The foreigner's presence provided a calm within him, a peacefulness, as slow and steady as the beat of her heart.

He pressed his ear gently against her chest.

She stirred, and he immediately straightened up. Her eyes remained closed, but there was movement behind the lids. He felt her fingers—exploring his. He saw the markings on her forearm. *What is the meaning of those stars?*

Her eyes slightly opened.

"Where am I?" she whispered.

"A place where you are safe."

"My vessel?"

"It is no more," he said with care. "You and two others were saved. The rest have departed."

"Stay with me?"

"Yes." He tenderly squeezed her hand and offered a comforting smile. "Sleep for now, and restore your strength."

* * *

Ram was awakened by the tap on his shoulder. "It's time for council," Stala reminded him.

The leader nodded and got to his feet. "Let me splash some water on my face, and I will see you there."

He looked over at the foreigner. She was sound asleep and glowed.

It was early, and half the tribe had yet to rise. The meeting was urgent. They would migrate in three days' time. Ram was the last to arrive at Zuku House. He took his place at the table standing next to Igua.

"Good day, council members." He greeted everyone with an open *truth.*

"Good day, Tribe Leader!" The members responded with vigor, despite the time of day.

"Please be seated." He sat down and instinctively placed his hand on Igua's. "The situation upon us calls for action. Igua will help provide our guidance."

She eased her hand away. "Stala and I will stay here and evaluate the foreigners. Gem, Harta, and the learner will also remain. Once this is over with, we will join you at the hunting camp."

Obvious to everyone, Igua had taken control.

Kierka asked, "What do we share with the tribe?"

"The changes in leadership."

"And what of the foreigners?" Carrib muttered.

"The visitors will be mentioned in passing. More than this would detract from the journey."

"All in agreement?" asked Ram.

Raj stood up. "One moment! We present them as *visitors*? Even for us, their temperament is uncertain."

"I will keep watch over them," Gem assured the leaders.

Ram asked again with determined eyes. "Are we in agreement?"

All hands were raised.

As was her way, Igua shared a warm smile and sincere appreciation. "Blessings for your care of the tribe. Together, we have much to discover."

"Blessings!" they responded and left the room.

She glanced over at Ram, conflicted by what lingered inside her.

* * *

Daylight arrived at a quiet encampment, as the tribe was well on their way. Soon, the stay-overs would also leave. Until that time, Harta looked after her offspring and helped prepare for their travel.

Later that day, Stala escorted the visitors to Zuku House, where Igua and Gem were waiting.

On their walk up the hill, she emphasized the importance of openness. "Gaining a familiarity with your culture is to better know you, and attain a meaningful understanding."

Excluding Jon, she was satisfied with their response.

"I have brought the survivors," Stala announced, leading them into the room.

"Blessings for their health," said Igua.

Stala nodded. "Their strength is returning, and our communication is clear. They are of the tribe named Tuz. Their land, far across the open sea. Explorers, searching for a better place to live."

Igua smiled warmly at the Zuku leader. "Your gift of wellness has provided these Tuz a new beginning."

Stala stood behind the visitors and formally introduced each one. "This is Wen, second-in-command of the vessel . . . Jon, the cook . . . and Kelp, a valued deckhand."

Gem searched each *truth*. Stala had expressed her concern with Jon, and he primarily focused on him. Compared to the others, his thoughts were dark and misplaced.

Stala wished everyone well and left the building.

Igua motioned the visitors to be seated. "Welcome to our land."

As with Stala, Igua communicated with the Tuz both openly and *privately*. Through her gift, they were able to assimilate each other's language. Wen appreciated Igua's straightforward approach. Her message translated with clarity and candor.

They met again the following day, and four more times after that. Their extended visits were productive. Igua and Wen dominated the conversations, discovering through the process their surprising commonality.

Wen's mind was inventive and sharp. However, unlike the gifted Zuku, she could not access the thoughts of others. Igua, was thankful for this.

Gem sensed his mother's distress. It bothered him to *feel* the hurt. Igua had an awareness of her son's frustration and was ashamed because of it.

* * *

Wen was intrigued by the tribe she woke up to. Males and females so closely resembled each other. Commons were less complex than the average Tuz. The gifted were akin to wizards. The tribe's non-repressive state of order was astounding, how each Zuku unselfishly understood and accepted their required task. She was convinced they had achieved the unthinkable: harmony.

Gem attracted her attention, with his silent presence and unclear relationship with Igua. But it was the memory of another that held her interest—most of all.

They sat on a bench overlooking the encampment.

"Igua."

"Yes, Wen."

"During my recovery, I was not altogether present. There was a Zuku I vaguely remember."

Igua was caught off guard. She wanted to hear her name, and be called away. But they were alone without distraction.

"I believe you speak of Ram, the leader of our tribe. It was Ram and Kierka who found you in the cove. They carried you to Stala. That first night, he stayed by your side."

"Not a dream, then," she whispered.

Wen's *truth* was open and pure, Ram's appeal relatable. And Igua foresaw herself losing his favor.

* * *

Harta and the learner prepared the wagon as Jon stood nearby, watching. He was drawn to the Zuku mother and sought her out, whenever an opportunity arose. Although Harta noticed his interest, she had no idea what he was thinking.

Gem *felt* Jon's disturbing *truth*. The pent-up desire, envy, and rage— emotions the gifted Zuku suppressed.

Later that evening, those in the encampment had settled in for the night. The next day, they would begin their journey east. Harta tucked in the learner and softly kissed her cheek. Next to Kelp sat an empty cot. They were not close, and he never asked what took him away after dark.

By now, Jon could walk there blindfolded, to the place he stared from a distance, adrift in fantasy, imagining the positions in which she slept. Blame it on the open sea, or his close encounter with death. Jon the cook had gone perversely mad.

For him this night was different. She was awake and would be waiting.

"Where are you going, Jon?" said the voice, deep and assertive.

"I am going to visit Harta," he confidently replied. "She asked me to join her."

"Did she?"

"Yes. And you, Gem, what brings us together at this time of night?"

When they were learners, Harta and Gem had become close friends. He was the gifted one, inheriting a wide swath of abilities and emotions. She was common, and nothing more than that. Once a mature, his feelings for her changed, in a way only his guide could explain. She, however, remained unmoved.

Gem stepped closer. "I am here to stop you from doing something wrong."

"Something wrong?"

"I know your intention, Jon the cook. Harta has been hurt before, and it will *never* happen again."

"How can you claim I will hurt her?" he said with a veiled smirk.

"Come!"

"What is this?"

Two warkins appeared from the shadows.

Wait, he silently ordered.

Gem's connection with the beasts was as if he shared their blood.

"We can talk this out," suggested John.

"I'm not much for conversation. Lead us to the cove."

"We can . . . talk there."

"Now!"

Gem turned Jon around and shoved him forward. The warkins growled, their aggressive instincts aroused.

45

Disturbed by the fracas, Harta had been watching from the doorway. Halfway down the path, Jon spoke up. "I need to relieve myself."

"Over there." The Zuku pointed to an area of bushes.

While Jon was away, Gem picked up a rock. He held it to his side and gripped it tightly. The warkins were keenly alert. *No!* he admonished himself and dropped it. *They should not be here for this.*

He silently commanded them to the cove.

Jon returned to find Gem looking up and the warkins nowhere in sight. Instantly, he felt a reprieve.

"Tell me, Jon, how often do you search the stars?"

As the Tuz raised his head, Gem, jumped knees first onto his back. The forceful blow took his breath away and rendered him defenseless. With his thick forearms wrenched around his neck, the Zuku squeezed with purpose. They fell to the ground without a struggle, the last of Jon's air vanquished.

Gem slung the limp body over his shoulder and continued to the cove. At the waterline, he lowered it down, to where the warkins patiently waited.

Take him to the outer waters.

Exhausted, Gem lay down on the cool damp sand. Afraid his *truth* was beyond repair, he stared up into the starlight and begged for an answer. Grimacing, he rocked his head from side to side and moaned.

Explaining Jon's disappearance to Harta would be without complication, but to his mother would offer no such relief.

She was awakened by a familiar presence. "Gem?"

"Yes, Mother."

She knew by him calling her in this way, the late-night visit was concerning.

"Son." Igua got up and gathered him in her arms. His body trembled, his *truth* concealed.

She stepped away and lit the lantern, and then looked at him with care. "Tell me."

"I have taken the life of Jon the cook. He was sick, and I took him with these hands." He raised them up and moved the fingers, confirming they were under his control.

"The body?"

"Delivered to the outer waters."

"I know you had just cause."

"He intended to mate with Harta." His voice grew angry. "I could not restrain myself. I have disgraced our tribe!"

"Open yourself to me?"

Gem did as he was asked, and the pain began to ease.

* * *

Early the next morning, Igua met with Stala and discussed the night before. After this, she made another visit.

"Good day, Igua," said Wen, with a bright voice and broad smile. "Is it time?"

"Almost," she solemnly replied. "Gem continues to rest, and that is why I am here."

"You are troubled?"

"I am."

"What is it?"

"Late last night, Jon was on his way to see Harta. He believed she desired to mate."

"That is senseless."

"Yes . . . and impossible. Harta is without those feelings."

"What happened?"

Sadness washed over Igua's large hazel eyes. "Gem was waiting for him and—"

"Ended his life."

"My son was protecting Harta."

"Gem is your son?"

"He is, and I assure you, before last night, he caused harm to no one. I have never seen him so distressed . . . the guilt."

"We can take a walk?"

"Yes."

"What now—for Gem?" asked Wen.

"After this, I am not for certain. The finality of one's life living on in another."

"Violence happens in our land."

"Here . . . never."

"Strong emotions are present in all Tuz," Wen explained. "Most of us do well keeping them in balance. Yet there are those as my brother, who are incapable. Jon, I suspect, also struggled in this way. During our voyage, he was mostly quiet and kept to himself. There were times, however, he became ill tempered and thick with others. Even so"—her eyes opened wide—"the food was well prepared."

Igua shook her head in disbelief that she could say such a thing. "We could have used a good cook on this journey."

"Yes." Wen softly chuckled. "Kelp is a fine Tuz, and will help to lighten the mood."

"But can he cook?"

After a moment of silence, they gratefully welcomed the laughter.

"Wen"—Igua had been wanting to ask—"those markings on your arm . . . the *stars*. What is their meaning?"

"In our culture, the Great Deep Sky is also of significance. We align ourselves with the stars that reside there, and honor them in specific ways. Here in the land of Zuku, they are only markings and nothing more."

"And beautiful."

Wen abruptly changed the subject. "The learner, she does not have a proper name?"

"By tradition, not until after the hunt."

"There is Symlander in her blood."

"Symlander?"

"Reckless hair the color of white cotton. Crystal-blue eyes that sparkle. I have been to Sym, and am familiar with their kind."

"Yes, her blood is mixed," Igua confirmed. "What else about the Symlander."

"They are uniquely gifted, as you can relate. Treasured as partners, among those favored in neighboring lands."

Igua shook her head. "This is all so new to me. *You* are new to me." As she said those words, her thoughts returned to Ram.

Wen blinked and smiled. "Everything is new."

"Meet you at the stables, then?"

"Yes. I will gather my things."

* * *

"Mother."

She looked down into Gem's tired eyes. "We are burning daylight."

"Ready the horses. I won't be long."

Igua arrived at the stables smiling softly. "Blessings."

"Blessings!" they all replied—except for one.

Wen glanced over at the silent Tuz. "Kelp is aware of last night's tragedy. Jon was a good cook but a poor swimmer."

Igua and Stala looked on, befuddled.

"To be clear," Wen continued in a sober tone, "Jon was not well and decided to leave us."

Kelp spoke up, "There were times, I did more than clean the kitchen. I can try to provide our meals?"

"Let us share those duties," suggested Stala with a nod.

Gem approached the group. "Forgive my delay. A difficult night, and—"

"It was!" Wen interrupted. "We understand the situation and have accepted it."

He glanced over at his mother with a furrowed brow.

Harta chimed in, "I believe it's time."

The learner stayed silent while searching the *truth* of those around her. She did well with Harta and Kelp, though lacked experience with Igua and Gem, faring better with Wen, who, for reasons yet unclear, perceived her as a *Symlander.*

The young Zuku could not foresee the life ahead of her, influenced by the blood of wizards.

* * *

Igua and Wen led the way on horseback. Gem followed, driving the four-team covered wagon. Harta and the learner sat up front with him. Kelp and Stala were in the back with the supplies.

Once they rolled along the grasslands, the repetitive landscape seemed endless.

"There's that rabbit again," Gem announced, to anyone who listened. "Look! That bird has returned . . . and those pesky flies."

The learner found it all amusing, regardless that those things could not have reappeared, no matter Gem's insistence. She stared up at him with every sighting and grinned.

Harta was preoccupied in thought. She wanted private time with Gem.

As the scenery faded into the dwindling light, the learner's eyes grew heavy. She snuggled against her mother's side and slept.

Harta studied Gem's unwavering profile. "What do you make of me?" she asked.

"I—"

"Simple? Without feelings? Disappointing? All of this . . . am I right?"

"No!" he turned to her and insisted. "I was young and self-serving. It was wrong of me. Gifted . . . can be a curse."

"How so?"

"I refused to accept what you could not feel, and blamed you without cause. I left you in a rage of frustration. I abandoned you . . . and—"

"That was long ago."

Staring off into the dim horizon, he searched for anything, to lead him away from the regret.

Closing his eyes in despair he whispered, "Not so long ago."

"That night, I do not remember well. But I do know it should have been different."

Gem winced to recall the festival, the night they were to mate, the shillig he forced upon her.

"Jon the cook was obsessed with you. He was sick and I took his life. I told him you would never be hurt again."

"I saw you and the warkins."

"You trusted me."

"Yes," replied Harta looking down at the sleeping child.

Gem said, "She resembles the foreigners. Kuu displayed for the tribe."

"The learner is special. Watch over her with me?"

"Over there!" Igua shouted back to the wagon, pointing to a group of trees.

* * *

Later that night, they all sat around the fire.

"Kelp!" Wen called out.

"Yes?"

"I believe you know a tale from our land. Perhaps these Zukus would like to hear it?"

"I would!" the learner blurted out.

"If it's better than those pods you over-boiled tonight," Stala added with a chuckle.

"I need to practice with those *things*."

"Go-ahead, Kelp!" Gem urged him on. "Tell us a story from the Land of Tuz." He looked over at Harta and the learner with an easy smile. His *truth* was calm, and his mind at rest.

"Where is he going?" the learner asked.

"To prepare," Wen replied with a blink.

Unbeknownst to everyone but her, the young Tuz was quite the entertainer.

Kelp walked away and into the darkness. Then, with dramatic flair, he slowly emerged and circled the glowing embers. "This story is from long ago . . ." The adventurous tale was full of suspense, and unexpected humor. Best of all, it had a satisfying ending. "And so it was, from that day forward," Kelp finished and stepped back into the darkness.

Wen began to clap her hands, and the others joined in. Especially the learner, whose hands became sore because of it. The smiling young Tuz reappeared and acknowledged the warm ovation with a bow.

HUNTING CAMP

Igua and Gem rode up ahead, on the journey's final day.

Igua said, "It seems these days of travel have been good for you."

"Yes, Mother, surprisingly so."

"This brings me comfort. I know you can *feel*."

"I can."

"And you and Harta—"

"I want to share my life with her, and also the learner."

"With your guidance, the learner will be a champion."

Gem was humbled by the thought.

For a brief moment, Igua's breath was taken away. Galloping toward them was Ram. He was energized, but not for her.

"Stay here!" She held Gem and the wagon back, then encouraged her horse to meet him.

Ram took notice and pulled back on the reins.

"Your travel went well?" he asked, sensing her urgency.

"Yes. Although we are missing one of the Tuz."

"Who would that be?"

"Jon the cook."

Her *truth* was open, and the situation was clear.

"He was a threat to the tribe." Ram agreed. "How is Gem?"

"Better. The journey served him well."

"What is it, Igua?" He felt there was something else.

"Your thoughts of Wen are familiar."

Ram stared up into the clouds.

"I also find her engaging."

He lowered his eyes. "Igua—"

"The tribe is my priority. You are its leader, and I will support you in every way." She looked over at the group and signaled them on. "I will be at the camp."

"See you there!" he shouted as she galloped off.

Wen guided her horse next to Ram, as Gem and the wagon proceeded up the rise.

She softly smiled. "You were with me that first night."

"Yes."

"My memory was faint. Igua confirmed your care."

He gazed into her rich-brown eyes. "A blessing, to discover you with life. And now here we are—"

"Rediscovered."

Ram *felt* Wen's *truth*, and it was pure.

* * *

A late-afternoon breeze swept over the hillside and rustled the leaves on the oaks. The tribe converged from many directions. They had been called by the leaders to gather.

Harta and the learner stepped up on one end of the platform, as the Tuz stepped up on the other. Ram and Igua stepped up at the center, turned, and faced the tribe.

Ram extended his open arms. "Blessings, Zukus!"

"BLESSINGS."

He nodded to Igua and then stepped back and to the side.

The Zukus waited with curious murmurs.

With a radiant smile she proclaimed above the stir, "Blessings!"

"BLESSINGS," the tribe erupted.

"So wonderful to be with you!"

Limited as they were, the commons, on occasion, were able to absorb emotions from the gifted. Igua could inspire them in this way.

"Zukus!" she powerfully continued. "Today we bear witness to change. Today . . . begins our understanding. Listen and watch closely as our leader explains."

Ram stepped forward and, with his finger, circled the tribe in the air. "Where you sit is the land we know. However, there are also distant lands."

He pointed to Harta and the learner. "Over there is the Land of Sym. Ten days' travel across the open sea. The learner's blood is not only from Harta but also from this place. Even though her appearance is different, she is Zuku and a member of our tribe. Over there"—he pointed to the other side— "is the Land of Tuz. Fourteen days' travel across the open sea. Wen and Kelp are from this place. Their vessel was lost outside our cove."

"Zukus come forward!" Igua shouted with encouragement. "Greet and welcome the learner and the Tuz!"

* * *

Dawn arrived at the hunting camp, and the learner slowly opened her eyes. "Stala?"

"Good day, fair Zuku." During their travel, she began to call her by this name.

"Where is mother?"

Harta felt undeniable bliss, lying there on the soft grass, staring into the early-morning sky, listening to the rhythmic sound of Gem's breathing.

They had been together under a new moon. It was her desire. She took his hand and brought him there, to be as one . . . without guidance or obligation.

She watched as he awakened. "Where are your thoughts on this new day?"

Gem rolled over and gazed down into her warm hazel eyes, "I believe you know . . . but if not, sure."

"Tell me," she said softly, as their fingers interlocked.

"I propose we become mates for life. I want this for us—you, me, and the learner." He offered a tender kiss.

"I want this also." She felt the vibration of her words through their lightly pressed lips.

As he pushed himself up a teardrop fell. She reached behind his neck and brought him back down.

Stala took a moment and considered the gifted learner. "What would you think if I said your mother is with Gem?"

"I would think what I *felt*."

"Fair Zuku?"

"Feelings provide the answer."

"And?"

She smiled brightly. "Joy."

Stala shook her head and burst into laughter. "Now, let's go find them!"

Gem and Harta approached the camp, walking hand in hand, a display of Zuku affection without precedent.

"Good day, Stala, fair Zuku," Gem said in a cheerful voice.

"Good day to you both," said Stala.

"Beautiful morning, isn't it?" he remarked, his thumb gently massaging Harta's hand.

The learner nodded with a smile.

He looked down at her with hopeful eyes. "Spend a little time with me today? The elk will be here soon, and the hunters must prepare."

The learner closed her eyes and held her breath.

"Yes!" Gem blurted out in astonishment "She said yes!"

Everyone, including Harta, could not keep from laughing.

*   *   *

"Now, not too close," Gem cautioned the learner. "Let the warkins get used to your Symlander blood."

"Not sure I'm happy with Symlander blood," she scoffed, keeping an eye on the pack.

Gem chuckled and pointed out the pup. "Look over there . . . a learner, just like you."

"There is a shimmer to his coat?"

"A silver warkin, unique and special . . . as you are."

She exaggeratingly snarled her nose.

"As he matures, the coat turns more brilliant."

"How special is he?"

"I've known only one before."

"When?"

"I was eight, or maybe nine. She was the leader of the pack with many years. We spoke *privately*. It was my first time."

"What did you say?"

"She was sick, and close to the end. I asked, 'Are you afraid to leave this place?'"

"And what was her answer?"

"She looked at me with calm and said, 'Why?'"

"There was no waver?"

"Warkins are fearless."

She slowly approached the silver beast. *Hello, pup . . . hello, pup.* She greeted him warmly with her inner voice. *They call me fair Zuku. I am a learner, just like you.*

The gangly warkin was receptive, his thick bushy tail wagging with excitement. Gem stood back and watched in amazement.

"I will call you Symlander," she decided. "Sym for short."

"Warkins have never been named," he said with an eyebrow raised.

She blurted out, "And for this very reason, now . . . I am *not* the only Symlander!"

See you later, Sym.

The pup came forward with his head tilted down. She reached out and scratched the back of his shimmering neck.

"Follow me," said Gem.

They went to where the hunters had gathered, sharpening their spears and knives.

He took her aside and explained. "Each group has four hunters, two warkins, and is led by a champion. They train every season for this moment."

"I'm trying to imagine this Lackland elk."

"They are magnificent, but also dangerous. Many capable Zuku have been injured or worse."

"You will join the hunt?"

Gem understood her uneasiness. "No need to worry, fair Zuku. I know my way around this Lackland elk."

They walked to the edge of a drop-off and peered into the canyon below.

"Down there . . . it will happen," said the learner with reverence.

"The element of surprise is vital. If we startle the herd too soon, our advantage is wasted. They are capable of great speed and will break through our groupings. I know"—he nodded—"because I have been left in the dust."

"Tell me more."

Gem was inspired by her interest.

"Each hunter enters the canyon on horseback. They carry two spears each round. The number of rounds depends on the pace. The warkins will dictate this. They are trained to separate and stifle the herd, but not to injure. They are rewarded after the harvest. The life of each elk is taken with respect. Much of our well-being is dependent on them."

"When will they be here?"

"Tomorrow or the next day. Our most sensitive scouts are positioned up the trail. Once their scent is recognized, they will pass down the alert."

She focused intently, as far as her eyes could take her.

He quietly asked, "Would you like to go back and visit with Sym?"

"Not now . . . I want to be with Mother."

RAM'S MESSAGE

The leaders gathered around Ram in the community tent. He searched their *truth*, and all were concealed.

"Good day, council members."

"Good day, Tribe Leader."

"We express our gratitude to the Lackland elk, and the many blessings they provide us."

"Blessings," Igua responded.

"Blessings," echoed the others.

"Understandably, the Tuz and fair Zuku have preoccupied our thoughts. However, there is much more that resonates within us."

Ram pressed his fingertips against his chest. "I ask the council to open their *truth*." He looked at each leader with conviction, saving Igua and then Gem for last. "By tradition, this knowledge has been kept from you. Gem . . . you are my son."

"Father!"

Each leader experienced a sudden release of emotions.

Blessings, Igua said to herself.

Ram eased into a gentle smile. "My son desires Harta to be his mate for life. Together, guide the fair Zuku. Ideas such as these did not exist before today's sunrise . . . or did they? Has anyone here desired a lifelong mate? Wanted to participate in the growth of their offspring? Yearned for their *truth* set free? Let us commit to tribal reforms, and support our evolution. We do this for self-preservation."

"I, too, endorse tribal reforms," said Igua. If Zukus resolve to become lifelong mates, it is by their choice. The commitment they have for each other, celebrated by all."

Ram could *feel* Igua's hurt, enough so he was unable to continue, and yielded to Stala.

* * *

Wen and Ram took a walk outside the camp.

"I have been told that Gem is your son."

"He is."

Then reluctantly she asked, "If at the time this were possible, would Igua be your lifelong mate?"

"If my proposal had been accepted."

CHAPTER 6
LAND OF SYM

Syms were a people from the Northern Frontier, a spiritual culture, honoring the natural wonders and one great Maker.

An unusual happening occurred among some of the children: they evolved *differently*. Not in the physical sense, as their appearance remained the same—tall and sturdy, white tousled hair, thick eyebrows, eyes of crystal-blue. It was their way of thinking.

Uniquely enriched blood fed their youthful minds an abundance of insight. Opinions once kept behind closed doors were openly expressed, age-old traditions were questioned. A new order had taken root, and the hierarchy felt threatened.

Before the movement grew any stronger, a solution was proposed. The progressives would relocate to a land of their own. Incentives of gold, breeding stock, and falcons were included.

A mysterious nomad passed through the village as the offer was being considered. She delivered a map (assured to be reliable) to the group's leaders, Crimion and his younger brother, Kren. It showed a land of promise, on the coast and free of jurisdiction.

The brothers asked their father to join them, but instead he chose to stay. Quint had raised the boys by himself, and cared for them deeply. Nevertheless, as with the others of his generation, he could not envision another life. He gave each son a family heirloom, the night before they left: a dagger.

They called themselves Symlanders, and laid claim to the favorable land. Those who stayed on in the Northern Frontier held firm to their beliefs, grew old, and faded away.

* * *

Located along the Crescent Coast were three distinct lands: Sym, Cantor, and Tuz.

Sym was the northernmost land, boasting a mild climate, fertile soil, and plentiful natural resources. The idyllic island of Montro and mineral-rich salt flats were also within its boundaries.

Even though the environment was unfamiliar, the confident young Symlanders were quick to adapt. Settling next to a large natural harbor, they developed the skills to build vessels. Once Sym was firmly established, the brothers sailed south along the coast. They came upon the Land of Cantor. Rich and prosperous, two monarchies—Cantor and Rivera—occupied the land.

The royal families shared common ancestry, yet the Cantors were elite. Their kingdom controlled the land's most valued assets. Both cultures were moderately religious and worshiped one God. The arts were prominent and generously supported. A noticeable difference between the two was gender equality. Rivera was a male-dominated society, and most females were treated unfairly.

The seafarers from Sym were well received, the worthiness of their vessel respected. Their presence was refreshing, and their exotic features captivating.

Following the favorable introduction, they frequented each other's land. Trade and knowledge flowed freely. In a few years' time, Sym's advanced development rivaled their neighbor's.

During those visits, the newly partnered Crimion and Tibene succumbed to the allure of royalty. They came to believe obsessively, their destiny was to rule. True to this understanding, the majority of Symlanders agreed. By the will of the people, Lord Crimion, Lady Tibene, and Sir Martin became Sym's first royal family.

The monarchy was not approved of by everyone, and a settlement was reached with Kren. He was granted the Dark Forest Territory, a sizable tract of land, one day's travel from Sym.

Mineral rights to the salt flats were equally divided between the brothers. Kren's growing fleet of sail barges provided transport, supplying not only Sym but also the Lands of Cantor and Tuz, returning with profitable imports.

Sym

"Good to see you, Kren!"

"You as well, dear brother, or should I call you *lord*?"

"Hmm," Crimion contemplated. "I have grown fond of . . . my lord."

They laughed and aggressively hugged.

"That look of yours." Kren raised an eyebrow. "Have you been spying on me again?"

Crimion chuckled. "Of course my ears are open. And you have partnered, from what I have heard. Finally, someone who accepts your . . . unusual habits. She has her balance?"

"Her name is Yessic, and yes, quite steady."

"And well cared for, I might add. The business of minerals has made you rich. Looking back, the forest should have come with a note."

"The minerals can be magical," Kren remarked with fascination.

"And lucrative."

"Not only for me, dear brother," he responded with a nod.

"We both have prospered. Though tell me, why do you hoard so much of it?"

"True, we keep a stack of bricks for safekeeping. And the more interesting crystals for research."

Crimion reached out and grabbed his brother's shoulder. "Let me show you something."

They stepped out on an expansive balcony, overlooking the harbor.

"Down there in the yard, isn't she breathtaking? The *Royal Symlander*!"

"That she is," said Kren. "I must confess, I've watched her progress. When is the dedication? If you like"—the corners of his mouth dimpled—"I can bring some lucky salt for the grand occasion?"

"No additional salt required. She'll be floating in plenty." Crimion took pause, absorbed in his contentment. "After the trials, we'll sail to Montro. A family holiday, full of sweet pineapple and vibrant sunsets."

"I haven't set foot on that rock in years."

"We've made improvements, with more to come. You should stay with us."

There was a telling silence as the brothers stared into each other's eyes.

"I know those feelings well," said Crimion.

Kren arched his thick white eyebrow. "Born on the frontier, they were. Impressive, aren't they . . . those *feelings*?"

Crimion peered deeper into his brother's absorbing eyes. "Yes, they are." He released his stare and turned to the open sea. "I've made my choice," he asserted. "Yet all of this would never be enough for you . . . would it?"

"This is not where I live, in body or thought." Kren looked up into the cloudless sky. "My journey has only taken flight."

DARK FOREST

Yessic asked, "What is on your mind, Kren?"

"I have something to show you."

At the laboratory, he stood in the center of the room. Next to him was an object draped in a white sheet.

"What are you hiding under there?" she asked.

He pulled the fabric from the altar.

"Impressive. And the round stone, where did you discover *that*?"

He raised his eyes. "It came from up there."

"The roof?" she playfully suggested.

"A gift from our Maker," he responded with praise.

THE GIFT

Kren awakened with a gasp, late into the night, guided by an inner voice. *Go to the shallows and look to the western sky.*

Once at the shoreline, he did as he was told. There it was! He watched in awe as it streaked toward him, a powerful energy with a white-hot tail, in an instant striking the volcanic crust. Across the dark waters, it glowed.

He rushed back to the royal residence. "Crimion!"

"What is it, brother?"

"We have to go there now!"

"Now? Where?" Have you gone mad?"

"You must be able to *feel* it?" His voice grew even more intense. "I know you can! Close your eyes and let it in."

He took hold of his brother's hands, and a rush of heat flooded between them.

Crimion's eyes sparked open. "YES . . . I feel it!"

They dropped the oars and rowed tirelessly across the shallows, guided by the mysterious beacon.

"Not so far from here," Kren said, pulling the skiff ashore.

"But first, we can rest over there?"

The brothers lay down on that patch of sand, without another word.

Crimion's eyes opened with the rising sun. He stood up and browsed the desolate surroundings, with vast amounts of sand and rocks, patches of haggard cottonwood trees, and opportunistic sage. He gazed across the turquoise shallows and admired Sym in the distance.

"What happened?" Kren moaned and slowly sat up. "My arms are worthless." He rubbed his eyes and gingerly stretched his back.

"It's all your doing, brother." Crimion smiled as he walked over, and helped him to his feet. "Follow me."

They found the scorched round stone and pried it loose. Kren picked it up, managing the dense weight between both hands. It was smaller than expected, yet no less fascinating. Thin, blood-red veins mapped its dark gray surface. Its texture (except for one blemish) was smooth all around. He brought it tight to his chest and laid his face against it.

Crimion stood by in silence, watching his brother weep.

Kren looked up and spoke with reverence. "I believe this is a *gift*, bestowed by our Maker." He raised the stone high above his head. "A gift . . . for all Symlanders!"

"Brother, this is *yours*. Its arrival . . . announced only to you. Let us not attract the attention of others."

"What are you saying?" He slowly lowered the stone past his downcast eyes.

"There would be far too many questions than answers. Probe for its meaning . . . its value. Who better than you, to unlock its purpose? One day, you will provide the answers. And for this, my dear brother . . . always remembered."

There was much to be done the next few years, and the gift was secured safely away.

The Voice

Kren went back across the shallows and explored farther inland. There, a vast salt deposit was discovered. Assisted by his brother, he began a mining operation. The voice returned during early surveys, leading him to pockets of unique minerals. He made a guidebook and detailed their locations, keeping samples for future studies.

With the monarchy thriving, Kren left Sym for the Dark Forest. He built a lodge on a private hilltop, in harmony with the natural terrain. From the top-floor windows, he could view the village, and the sunrise beyond the evergreens. Above the lodge, he added a laboratory and a falcon habitat.

The lab was Kren's sanctuary. After its completion, he barely ventured out. His work became a priority—an obsession. Oftentimes, he was influenced by the voice. It came to him without notice or regard for the moment.

He was instructed to create an altar, its pedestal carved from ancient oak, and on top of that a basin, ground from volcanic rock. The gift to be placed at its center, surrounded by spring water.

Through it all, Kren remained committed to the voice, though often he wondered, *why am I the chosen one? What else waits for me?*

Vivid dreams came to him, on five successive nights, each one revealing a recipe:

> 1: *Black/Evolve*
> 2: *Clear/Vision*
> 3: *Blue/Truth*
> 4: *Pink/Connect*
> 5: *Yellow/Fury*

Exhausted from the experience, Kren did not revisit the lab for a full cycle of the seasons. During that time, he reacquainted himself with the village and socialized with those who lived there.

It was Yessic who captured his attention. She muted the voice and freed his thoughts. While others dwelled on his achievements, their conversations did not. Her openness and attractive ways moved him like no other. As their visits became more frequent, a relationship blossomed.

Kren and Yessic were partnered, and soon after, the voice returned.

* * *

He stopped in front of Yessic on his way up to the lab and said, "It's time."

"For what?"

"To continue my experiments."

"Then . . . I will never see you again?"

"Only if, from now on, you could deliver my meals to the door?"

"Kren!"

"Of course you will see me," he teased. "We'll even have conversation . . . I suppose. And if you were wondering—" He leaned forward and initiated a long, passionate kiss.

"This is encouraging," she whispered.

"We'll have some of *that*," he whispered back. "If you would be so inclined?"

"I would be actually." She took a firm hold of his hand and led him away.

* * *

Yessic entered the lab, her face flushed and her steps uncertain.

"Still not feeling well?" Kren asked.

She pressed her hand against her moist forehead. "A little warm, and food refuses to settle. How is your work?"

"Progressively frustrating."

"Another deceptive potion?"

"It's truth, and yet again . . . something is missing." He thought for a moment and then motioned her to the altar. "Dip your fingers and close your eyes. Focus on the discomfort. Let us find this *something*."

As the blue water sparkled, a sense of calm came over her. She opened her eyes and announced, "I carry a child."

"I had a feeling."

She raised an eyebrow. "Now, what do you have there?"

He handed her a small walnut box. It was polished, with iron hinges and a simple latch. "Open it."

"But our child, Kren." She sighed. "I have to be cautious around your experiments."

"Odds of him becoming a toad are slim."

"A boy? And by chance you have a name?"

"Nord has crossed my mind."

"Nord?"

"I am confident to welcome a son . . . *Nord*, hopefully by agreement."

He watched with amusement as Yessic lifted the lid.

"Testing my knowledge of chemistry?" She scowled. "You know I have little passion for science. Unless it's the science of cooking . . . in the kitchen."

"Well then"—he chuckled—"you'll be doing exactly that."

"Black crystals . . . really?

Kren took his little finger and wet it with his tongue. Then he pressed it lightly against the fine granules and brought it to her mouth. "Taste it." He smiled as she evaluated the flavor. "And are you surprised?"

"Bitter, yet interesting."

"It smooths out during the brewing. I've been drinking the tea since the last new moon. I feel rejuvenated! Drink three full cups per day."

"So much black tea."

"We've lost time."

"And what results are you expecting from this strange brew? What about our son . . . Nord?"

"I expect nothing more than a strong and healthy boy . . . *with superior capabilities and limitless potential.*"

VISION

Kren reviewed the list of potions, cross-referencing the colors with the minerals collected. He filled the altar's basin, with water sourced from a natural spring.

Vision, he confirmed to himself.

Taking a pinch of the coarse clear crystals, he scattered them around the gift, and waited.

Nothing.

He told himself, *Another pinch and more concentration* (trusting that would make the difference).

This time, the water's surface transformed. It solidified—into an illusion of glass. As he peered through the window, an image appeared.

A light-blue sky . . . sand and rocks . . . the shallows? "The flats!"

He reached out with his fingertips and traced the smooth round stone— until they stopped. Underneath the waterline, he felt the indentation.

A missing fragment. Could it be?

Kren went to Yessic and made himself clear. The experiment was missing an important element. He would go to the flats and look for it there.

She had no reason to question his motive, yet the urgency stirred her interest.

Kren planned to spend the night in Sym and ask his brother to join him. But when he arrived, the royals were preoccupied—their latest remodel, and something had gone awry. Early the next morning, he continued on his own.

He pondered the challenge of remembering his steps as he rowed across the shallows. That concern was unwarranted. Once on land, the voice led him to the exact location. At the edge of impact was the missing fragment, embedded in the volcanic crust. His heartbeat quickened and he dropped to the ground, lining up his sight with the round iron wafer. The view matched that of the altar's window!

* * *

The long ride home along the Red Road provided ample time for thought.

"Follow me," said Kren.

Yessic paused as they reached the door. "Are you sure?"

"I am," he replied as they stepped inside the lab. "I want you here—with me."

"What use would I be?"

"Support." He nodded. "My work has become too much at times. You will help maintain my balance. I have made discoveries, unusual in their nature. A voice that speaks to me."

"And what have you heard from this *voice*?"

He went to where the writings were kept and returned with the list of potions. "These recipes were revealed to me in the most elaborate dreams."

"Colors?"

"They relate to minerals. In time, you will know everything." Kren extended both of his hands. "Join me on this journey?"

She grasped them without hesitation. "Of course I will!" Her eyebrows narrowed. "However, there will be no late nights, and mornings before sunlight." She laughed and gave his hands a tug. "That is . . . unless you're onto something."

He stared deep into her sparkling eyes. His words were slow and deliberate. "I am onto something. Let me show you—now."

"What do you have there, a piece of jewelry? A *new moon*, is it?"

The gift's fragment was secured in a bronze setting, and attached to a leather bewit.

"A medallion with vision," he said in a steady voice. "Attached to the falcon's ankle. We will view the forest as she does."

"If this is true, I have no other choice."

"Oh?"

"To believe what they are saying in the village."

"Yessic?"

"That you are a wizard."

"People will talk," he said with a sly smile. "Meanwhile, the falcon waits."

He went over to the dark-oak chest, and returned with a container of minerals. "I will provide the first pinch, and you the second."

Carefully, they scattered the clear crystals around the gift.

What happens next? she wondered as he walked away.

In the corner on the floor sat a wicker basket, below where the falcon was perched. Kren lifted the lid and brought out a smoked sardine. As she ate, he attached the bewit and slipped on the handler's glove. After her last swallow, she stepped onto his leathered hand. Once outside, he raised it up and watched her fly away.

He went back inside and stood next to Yessic, who was staring down in disbelief.

She softly asked, "This magic . . . where will it take us?"

* * *

Sardines, attach the medallion, take flight—over and over. The bird's path persisted without influence, no matter the incentives.

Kren's experiment had stalled, and his nights were restless.

"I'm beyond tired," Yessic grumbled. "Will you be tossing around until the sun comes up?"

"Most likely," he curtly replied. "While you go off and search for mushrooms, I will be here, struggling with deceptive potions and obstinate birds."

Though tired as she was, Yessic could not stifle her amusement. The wizard's predicament was unfortunate yet far from a crisis.

"You must find a way to reach them at a higher level," she determined.

"And this is not my intention? The sardines . . . never enough."

"Maybe a pinch of pink with the sardines?"

His eyes opened wide.

"I wasn't serious," she assured him.

"No! It is *you*, the true wizard in this bed."

Just before sunrise, Kren hustled away from the lodge. He first went to the habitat and then to the lab.

Perched on the basin with her head cocked to one side, the falcon watched his every movement.

He scattered the fine blush crystals around the gift. "Will this be the answer?"

Tapping the water with his fingertip, he enticed the bird to drink. She lowered her beak and did so.

"Am I a respectable wizard?"

He received his answer in her unflinching golden eyes.

Follow my finger, he privately commanded, and she did exactly that. *Up and down, side to side*—without a single sardine.

Perch—she flew to the corner.

He siphoned the basin and refreshed it with vision. He returned to her and attached the medallion. She stepped onto his glove and they went outside.

The wizard raised his hand. "*FLY.*"

Thrusting her powerful wings, she climbed up through the brisk morning air, screeching triumphantly above the treetops.

He hurried back to the altar's window. "Yessic! Yessic! We have reached the falcon!"

The Mystic falcon.

TEN YEARS LATER

Celebrating their union of fifteen years, Lord Crimion and Lady Tibene embarked on a special voyage. Guided by a crew of twelve, the *Royal Symlander* was set on a northwest course. After the third day, they would sail along an uncharted coastline.

While his parents were away, Sir Martin stayed with Uncle Kren. The young royal was fond of the Dark Forest and relished the freedom there. He also enjoyed spending time with his cousin, Nord.

* * *

Three days had passed since the *Royal Symlander*'s anticipated return.

Kren spoke with Yessic in private. His eyes were distant, his mood solemn. "The vessel has yet to reach Montro. I am sending a falcon. It could be only the wind . . ."

The raptor took flight and climbed high into the thinning air. She would retrace the vessel's course at maximum speed. Kren looked through the altar's window, a whale's spout and a school of dolphins, yet a vessel nowhere to be found. Meanwhile, the sun crept closer to the horizon.

Perch. The falcon flew to shore, where she would eat and rest, and then continue at first light.

Early the next morning, Yessic joined Kren at the altar.

"It's not good." He sighed. "She has flown a great distance. We have to prepare for the worst."

Yessic rested her arm around his neck. "I feel this too," she said softly.

The raptor swooped lower, bringing the sea clearly into view—wind-driven whitecaps, swirling currents, jagged rocks, and wreckage.

They gasped! Remnants of the vessel at the edge of a cove. No sign of life. Their bodies tensed up—then slumped.

Retrieve, the wizard commanded.

The flacon glided down to the rocks with her open talons.

They had seen enough.

* * *

Early the next day, they prepared to leave the forest.

Sir Martin asked his uncle, "My parents have returned?"

"Not yet . . . but we will wait for them in Sym."

They walked a short distance to the stables.

"Sit next to me," said Kren.

The young royal did as he was asked, while Yessic and Nord sat in the back. The horses were encouraged, and off the wagon rolled. They traveled without incident or conversation.

By the time they reached the royal residence, the boys had fallen asleep. They were carried inside and plopped down on Martin's bed.

Kren took Yessic's hand and led her to the balcony.

"We are waiting for the falcon?" she asked in a somber voice.

"Yes," he said, with eyes that were misting over.

She wrapped her words with care. "No one can be prepared for something like this. The unexpected loss, and emptiness that follows."

"My brother and Tibene have departed." Kren took a moment in contemplation. "Their absence will be challenging."

"We will look after Sir Martin. He is not of age to rule but is the rightful heir. I understand your distaste for royalty, however, we have an obligation."

Yessic's voice was one of reason and steadied Kren's nerve.

"Sym must remain strong and have order. I will represent my brother and lead us through this."

"And I will support you in every way."

"Tomorrow, I will gather the civic leaders and move forward. There will be a tribute and time for remembrance, invitations sent out to the neighboring lands. After the formalities, take the boys to the forest and stay there for two seasons. The peaceful surroundings will help Martin heal."

"And me as well," said Yessic.

They looked at each other in silence . . . affirming their grief.

Kren *felt* the falcon's presence before the distant screech was heard. Not long after, she spread her wings and descended. A shiny object was released from her talons, and it clanged on the balcony floor.

He picked it up. "Rigging, from the *Royal Symlander.*"

* * *

Early the next morning, the boys cautiously entered the guest room and crept closer to the bed.

"Nord! Martin!" the startled wizard blurted out.

"My parents?"

Kren sat up in his nightshirt and motioned Martin closer.

Yessic was awake by now, and Nord made his way to her.

"My parents, Uncle Kren?"

"I am saddened to say, they are no longer with us."

"What has happened?"

Kren picked up the brass object from the nightstand and handed it to Martin. "This is from the *Royal Symlander.* Your parents have been called to the stars."

He stared at the rigging in disbelief and squeezed it tight.

Kren glanced over at Yessic and Nord, and then returned his attention to the young royal. "Martin, we are here for you."

"We are family," added Yessic.

"What will happen . . . to me?"

Kren smiled warmly. "You will become lord in two years' time. Although not your father, I will prepare you with no less care."

He got out of the bed, and gathered Martin in his arms.

Kren's display of affection was awkward for Nord to witness.

LORD MARTIN

The Central District was festooned in blooming color. Bright and joyful music filled the air. The main avenue was lined with ecstatic Symlanders. Today was the culmination of healing, the promise of renewal. Today was Sir Martin's coronation.

The newly dedicated *Royal Symlander CT* slowly paraded through the harbor. Standing on its bow were Sir Martin, Kren, Yessic, and Nord. A crowd of onlookers waved and cheered as the vessel reached the dock.

The soon-to-be lord disembarked and climbed onto his horse. Side by side, he rode with Kren, as the others followed in carriages.

Martin waved from side to side as they processioned up the avenue.

Even though well prepared, the enormity of the occasion was far greater than he had imagined.

"Thank you, Uncle!" he shouted above the revelry.

Kren acknowledged his nephew's gratitude, with a subtle nod and smile.

On the residence's main balcony, Sir Martin was declared lord. After the proclamation, he stepped up to the railing and raised his hands. Down below and standing in front, a woman held a red rose.

She cocked her arm and shouted, "For you, my lord!"

"Wait! Wait!" Martin implored, pumping his open hands.

Disappointed, she brought the rose to her side and bowed her head. When she looked up, he was gone.

Moments later, he was walking toward her. "Is this for me?"

"Yes, Lord Martin. I chose this rose especially for you."

"How kind."

They shared a meaningful smile.

As he reached forward to accept the rose, their hands met at the stem.

"Rook is my name."

Passage of Time

The following years passed as a whirlwind.

Kren returned to the Dark Forest, while Lord Martin and Lady Rook continued with their royal duties.

Although not partial to wizardry, Nord did develop a fondness for the falcons, even more so after they were connected. On occasion, he would spend the night in their habitat. Once he matured, his interest waned and he turned restless. The Dark Forest was closing in on him. It was decided by his parents, he would be better off in Sym.

Sponsored by his father's mineral operation, Nord became a mariner's apprentice. He would stay at the royal residence when not out to sea. During this time, his friendship with Lord Martin thrived. When absent of commitment, the cousins often went sailing. Their conversations on the water ranged from serious to quirky.

* * *

Nord gazed out on the distant horizon. "Have you ever thought to sail . . . there?"

"There?" said Martin.

"Where your parents—"

"I have, but it soon passes. My mind is busy enough. The responsibilities of family and Sym."

"We could do this together and complete their voyage."

"Let me think on this." Martin reached over and gripped Nord's shoulder and then squeezed it with brotherly affection. "I will speak with Rook while you are away."

THE QUEST

Nord had only just returned when there was a knock on the door.

"Are you in there?" Martin called out.

"Come in, cousin!"

"I have an answer to our quest."

"Quest . . . I like the sound of that," said Nord with an optimistic smile.

"Are you able to take leave when the moon turns full?"

"I will give my notice!"

"Then go to the forest and advise your parents."

"And Rook, she is good with this?"

"She is."

Martin was not completely transparent. She was supportive, and also—anxious.

* * *

In the Dark Forest, halfway through the evening meal, Nord divulged the plan.

Yessic spoke up, "Extended sail?"

"A quest," Nord confirmed with satisfaction. "We will revisit his parents' voyage."

"I am not in favor," she said firmly.

"Everything has been carefully considered," he assured her. "Our crew is well seasoned, including a Cantor, with knowledge of those waters."

"I have one requirement."

"Yes, Father?"

"You must wear a special medallion. To keep you safe and provide us comfort."

"I will do as you ask."

"It is not to be removed until you return."

"I understand."

They got up from the table and shared a group embrace.

* * *

Kren and Yessic stood arm in arm, looking through the altar's window. They watched with keen interest as the royal vessel left the harbor. The cousins were in good spirits, and a favorable wind filled their sails.

"They are fine young Symlanders," Yessic remarked.

"That they are."

She playfully pinched the side of his waist. "Maybe one day we'll take a turn on that fancy vessel."

"Why . . . when we have lovely sail barges at our disposal."

"Kren!"

He chuckled. "You have my word, as soon as they return. For now, let us follow their quest."

* * *

Later that same day, Martin called out from the bow, "There it is, cousin!"

"Montro," Nord said quietly to himself.

The lord smiled at the captain. "Take us around before we dock."

For Martin, the island was a cheerful family reminder, a place of wonder, introduced to him as a child. Not surprisingly, their first night would be spent there.

They sat out on the balcony, as the sun began to set.

"If only for the pineapple"—Martin raved after taking a bite—"this place is without compare."

Nord smiled from ear to ear. "How sweet they are."

"In every season, cousin!"

Their laughter was rich and sustained.

* * *

The following afternoon, Kren and Yessic observed the elegant vessel gliding through an undisturbed bay. The wind appeared light—yet favorable. The cousins were waking from a nap.

"That was an interesting dream," Nord disclosed with a yawn.

"You too." Martin added while rubbing his eyes.

Nord stood up and took note of the serene waters. "Must be something about this bay."

"Shall we name it the *Bay of Dreams*?"

"Would a proclamation be required?" said Nord while scratching his chin. "And if so . . . being that you are Lord—"

"Proclaimed!" shouted Martin, thrusting his fist in the air.

They both bent over in laughter.

Kren said, "I don't know what happened there. But they surely woke up in one festive mood."

The vessel's course led to a peninsula, with a deep-water harbor.

Martin said, "What do you say we lower the dinghy and shake off the sea legs?"

"That's a great idea, my lord. You will name this finger of land as well?"

He smiled and shook his head. "Enough with the proclamations, cousin."

After a brief wander, they returned to the vessel and settled in for the night.

* * *

Early the next morning, the captain ordered, "Up anchor!"

On the western horizon was the mysterious open sea.

Martin raised his voice above the wind-whipped sails. "This is all so new and exciting! Look at those cliffs reaching up to the sky. What might be up there, staring down on us?"

Nord surveyed the aggressive conditions. "The waters are restless!"

"They've become small and vulnerable," said Yessic in a wavering voice.

"The vessel is sound," Kren assured her. "There is no urgency among the crew. Trust that the sea will lie down."

"We are managing through all of this!" shouted Martin. "I am grateful to be here, honoring my parents. I feel their presence!" A sudden thought compelled his eyes to mist. "Not so far now—" His words became lost in the moment.

* * *

Two days passed. A crew member knocked on the door.

"Yes?" said Martin.

"The point has been sighted, my lord!"

Kren silently peered through the window.

"Not too close," whispered Yessic.

As the sails were gathered and anchor dropped, the waters respectfully calmed. The cousins slowly approached the bow. Tears Martin had restrained for the longest time flowed free and without scrutiny. They were his parents, and his most personal loss.

They climbed into the dinghy and dropped the oars, a memorial wreath between them. The wreath was fashioned from Dark Forest fir, and rose buds from the royal garden, a garden Lady Tibene often tended. They quietly rowed ever closer. Martin lowered the wreath to the sea. The cousins solemnly watched as it slowly drifted away.

Overwhelmed by sorrow, Yessic and Kren wrapped themselves in each other's arms.

The captain said, "My lord, the winds are gaining strength. I recommend we take shelter for the night." He pointed to a narrow inlet. "We can access the cove from there."

"Agreed," Martin said with a firm handshake. "I am thankful for you and your crew. Let us enjoy a full meal and well-deserved rest."

Navigating the open sea presented challenges, and a peaceful night was welcome.

Yessic's eyes were happy—yet weary. "They are settling in for the night."

"Let us do the same," said Kren.

They shared a sweet kiss.

THE COVE

Nord's eyes flashed open, and for no apparent reason. In the depth of night, he dressed and walked out of the cabin. Up on deck, he stood under a full moon's light, with sounds of the gentle waters lapping against the hull. He gazed off to the distant shoreline—beyond that was a warm glow.

Fires? he asked himself.

Yessic was startled from her sleep. Kren stayed motionless, and she carefully left him that way. Compelled to do so, she went to the laboratory.

Nord eased himself into the dinghy and began to row. His chest was tight, his breathing labored.

Where is he going? thought the anxious mother. *Why . . . at this time of night?*

He raised the oars, and looked over his shoulder. The vessel a faint silhouette.

"Go back!" she appealed through the altar's window. "There's nothing for you to see."

He pulled off his shoes and straddled over the side. The soft bottom was gradually sloped, and the dinghy beached with little effort. It was good to be on land again. The cool sand felt soothing between his toes. He took a deep breath.

Yessic followed Nord's every step. *"What is that?"* She narrowed her focus on the huddled shape. *Someone alone and sleeping.* "What are you doing?" she whispered—then pleaded, "Leave her be!"

Yessic trembled, and her feet began to shuffle. This was not her son. This was an aberration, a wild beast. She grasped the basin with both hands. "NO," she screamed madly and pushed with all her might.

"Yessic!" Kren shouted from down below.

She ran aimlessly into the forest.

"Yessic! Answer me. Yessic!"

Kren barged into the lab, only to find the dismembered altar lying on the floor. "What has happened here?"

He rushed to the falcons. *Call out when you find her.* They immediately took flight.

Kren waited along the tree line, troubled and confused. *Over there."* He scrambled inside and followed the screeches. "Yessic!" Every time her name was shouted, the falcons answered back. She was close.

He fell to his knees. "Yessic."

She was curled up tight with hands unyielding, clamped beneath her rigid jaw. Carefully, he picked her up and carried her back to the lodge.

"I am here. I am here," he repeated, every step of the way.

Yessic's eyes were fixed and glossy, her skin patterned with blood. Kren took a damp cloth and cleaned the wounds, and then dressed them with ointment and gauze. He laid her down on a bed of fresh linen and kissed her forehead.

"Rest your fears, my dearest. I am with you."

The next day arrived—and for Kren, without sleep. Yessic's condition was desperate. During the night, he had brewed a special tea, confident it would provide a cure. But instead, she choked on it as if it were poison. Over and over—he tried to connect, but she remained lost.

"Yessic," he said softly. "We are waiting for Nord. Our son will soon be here."

He left her side and returned to the lab.

What was the reason for this? He raised up the pedestal. *Why would she?* He set the basin on top. *Why?* He picked up the gift and brought it to his face. "Why?" he demanded to know.

Listen to me, said the voice.

* * *

Eight days later, Nord walked through the door. The lodge was cold and stale. He went to the study.

Kren got up from his chair. "You've returned to us."

"Yes, Father, and good to be home." He could sense something was wrong. "Mother is here?"

"She is . . . but not well."

"What is it?"

"I wish I knew." He sighed. "Perhaps . . . with you here."

"I must see her!"

At first glance, Yessic was unrecognizable, her gaunt face extremely pale and eyes grossly fixed open.

"Mother, I've returned from the sea. The quest is over . . . Mother?"

"Stories of the quest can wait," Kren said calmly. "Have something to eat and a good night's rest. Tomorrow, I require your attention."

Nord bent down and cradled the tightly gripped hands. "Good night, Mother."

She did not flinch.

* * *

81

At sunrise, the wizard said, "Come with me."

"So early?" Nord asked.

"Yes."

Nord rarely entered the lab. Standing at the doorway, he reacquainted himself.

Kren took out the top drawer from the dark-oak chest, and brought it to a small table near the altar. Looking over at his son, he motioned him there.

"These minerals"—the wizard pointed out— "form the core of my experiments. Alone or in combination, their properties are impressive. If you had shown more interest—"

"I could learn from you now.

"Is it not too late?"

Kren unclasped the leather cord from around Nord's neck, and held it between them. "We followed your quest through this medallion. *New moon* is what your mother called it. You were our falcon."

Nord's face lost color, and the palms of his hands dampened. "What did you see?

Kren stared deep into his son's uncertain eyes. "We watched you eat pineapple in the midst of a sunset."

"Martin has invited us Montro."

"There was a tranquil bay, a deep-water harbor . . . majestic shoreline cliffs."

"Yes, those were all sights to behold."

"We wept with you, as the wreath floated away." He looked over at the altar with downcast eyes.

"Father?"

"That was the end of it," he said while shaking his head. "Later that night, the altar was damaged. The same night your mother ran away."

"I can assure you, the journey home was uneventful . . . and here I am."

"Yes, here you are . . . and I have an idea."

"What is it?"

"With the proper combination of minerals and influence, I believe we can salvage the missing record. Discover what happened that fateful night."

"Wizardry makes no sense to me," Nord said with built-up angst. "You witnessed the summary of our quest. The missing record was nothing more than endless sea and slumber."

"I do have experience with this *wizardry* you speak of. Let us give it a try."

"As you wish . . . Father."

Kren let the medallion slide off the cord and into the basin. "Place your hands in the water and relax. There is nothing to fear."

Perspiration beaded on Nord's forehead and then trailed down his guilt-ridden face.

"You are not feeling well?"

"Not at all," he replied in a shaky voice.

"Hopefully this will not take long. But there are questions that linger."

"We can take Mother to Sym, find treatment for her there. She will improve, I know it!"

Kren methodically browsed over the minerals. *Two pinches of the clear, to activate the window.* "Pay attention, Nord." He scattered the crystals above the water. "You see there, the surface is transforming." *Better than I imagined.*

"I see the changes."

The wizard then took a pinch of blue. "This special mineral will provide us the truth." He opened his fingers around the gift.

"Father, I—"

"Be quiet and watch."

They looked down and saw the smooth waters of the cove, Nord's arms rhythmically rowing toward the shore, his moonlit shadow striding up the sand, a shadowy figure lying in his path . . .

Kren furiously turned away and went back to the chest. He pulled out the bottom drawer and took out a sealed box. Nord attempted to raise his hands.

"STOP."

"Father!" The sharp directive froze his movement.

"Do not disturb the window."

Kren returned to the altar and opened the lid. Inside, the yellow fury glittered. He released a few grains above Nord's hands. After a brief moment, his fingers adhered to the stone.

"Father . . . my fingers are locked."

"Keep your eyes on the window, as your mother did that night." The wizard's thoughts were merciless. *Soon, you will know her suffering.*

"Father!" Nord cried out in growing desperation. "Where are you going? Please . . . do not leave me like this."

"I won't be long."

"I can't . . . explain," he continued to stammer, "what came over me . . . that night."

Kren walked down the path and into the lodge. He went to the vanity, for cotton and a hairpin, and after that the kitchen, for a large silver spoon. He lit the lamp at Yessic's bedside and held the pin over its open flame. When it glowed, he pricked her fingertip, collecting two drops of blood in the spoon. Finally, he placed cotton in her ears and returned to the lab.

"It's over, father. I am rowing back—"

"It's not over," he said to his face. "While you rowed across smooth waters, your mother ran recklessly through the forest. Crazed as an animal, fleeing a lightning-strike fire. I fear she will never be the same. As you . . . will never be the same."

"Why do you say this?"

The wizard stayed silent and finalized the potion. He added a pinch of fury to the spoon and lowered it into the basin. The water churned, and Nord's fingernails began to melt. Bright red bubbles rose to the surface, popping and splattering.

Kren put cotton in his ears and walked away. Halfway down the pathway, Nord's wailing grew faint. By the time he lay next to Yessic, they were gone.

* * *

The next morning, Nord woke up with bandaged fingers, swollen and throbbing. An expressionless wizard stood over him. "Father," he whispered.

"Go to the flats with our smallest barge. Fill the compartment half-way with the finest volcanic sand. I will meet you at the harbor in five days' time."

"Yes, Father."

Not another word was spoken.

Three days passed.

A falcon arrived in Sym with Nord's final instructions. They were simple and few.

* * *

Kren carried Yessic to the end of the dock and the specially prepared barge. She was dressed in her favorite pattern. A fresh corsage adorned the delicate fabric. Nord watched in silence as his mother's stiff body was carefully lowered through the hatch and onto a bed of shimmering sand. The cover was pulled shut.

On the stern of the barge, Nord stood alone. His eyes flooded with tears. He stowed the rope and set a partial sail. Once outside the harbor, it was raised on a due-west course. His task complete, he climbed aboard the dinghy and severed the towline.

Kren lit the damp cloth. A fragrant smoke slowly filled the compartment. Before drifting away, he placed his hand on Yessic's. Her fingers relaxed one last time, and he interlocked his—between them.

* * *

An overcast sky shrouded the crowded cathedral. Nord sat in the front row and quietly listened. Enlightened by recollections of his parents' admirers, he chose not to speak, leaving the eulogies to those without shame.

After the service, he took his place at the end of the reception line. Despite being shielded by custom-fitted gloves, his deformities kept him unsure. Instead of shaking hands, he extended a caring nod, or shared a light embrace.

Lady Jennifer said, "Nord, I am truly sorry for your loss.

"How kind of you to be here."

Jennifer was a friend of Rook's and frequented the residence. It was there she and Nord developed a friendship. They shared a passion for sailing. She traveled with him to the Dark Forest, a guest at the family lodge. The Mystic falcons were the highlight of her stay.

Prince Roland, fourth in line to the Cantor throne, made his way to Nord. "I am here to express our deepest sympathy."

"How thoughtful of you to deliver this message. My parents held your land in the highest regard."

Jennifer stood beside a column and viewed the conversation. The royal from Cantor roused her interest. After he stepped away, she happened upon his path. "My name is Jennifer," she boldly announced, her crystal-blue eyes bright and honest. The prince was instantly charmed.

"My name is Roland. Kren and I did business together."

"And I am a friend of Nord's."

They continued with their visit, indifferent to the time.

The prince pursued an idea. "I am traveling to the Dark Forest. Items belonging to his father, Nord wishes me to have. It is far too early, isn't it, asking you to join me?"

"Not so early," she said with an easy smile.

"I will advise Nord."

"Let me."

DARK FOREST

The Dark Forest settlers were independent minded and abstract thinkers. They followed Kren with enthusiasm and were deeded plots of land. Their village was communal from inception. Fresh spring wells, gardens, laundry rooms, and pastures were shared by all.

The villagers dropped by the lodge and offered their condolences. They brought with them kind words, food, and flowers. One neighbor provided a hog. As they came and went, Nord was left to wonder, had they heard his screams?

* * *

Jennifer and Roland were expected the following day, and Nord prepared for their arrival. First, he straightened up the lodge and then the laboratory.

Although a painful reminder, Nord had preserved the altar. He did so to honor his father. He also studied his writings, becoming familiar with the minerals and recipes.

With what daylight remained, he brought out his favorite falcon. They were strongly connected and shared a special bond. He attached the bewit to her ankle.

Fly high and free.

As the altar's window opened, he felt a measure of relief, watching the majestic bird soar into the vast blue sky.

The next day, Nord woke up refreshed. It had been a good while to feel this way. He was eager to receive his visitors—and curious. How would their relationship evolve? The prospect of a union intrigued him. Could it even be possible, a royal of Cantor and a lady Symlander? He looked forward to finding out.

Before they reached the village, he would surprise them with some magic.

The carriage continued down the Red Road.

Roland said, "You mentioned being familiar with these parts."

"Yes, I traveled through here with Nord. The sea is my favorite place, but I also appreciate the countryside."

"How did you occupy your time there . . . in the forest?"

"Oh my, with the falcons of course." Jennifer's face reflected those fond memories. "And also exploring on horseback."

"Actually"—the royal was embarrassed to say—"I'm rather uncomfortable on top of those beasts."

"Fear not, Prince Roland, I know just the old mare for you."

"Brilliant!" He joined her in laughter. "Your eyes . . . so *brilliant*."

The carriage entered the Dark Forest Territory.

"Look there!" Jennifer pointed up into the cloudless sky.

"A Northern Frontier falcon," recognized the prince.

"A *Mystic falcon*," she corrected him. "Nord communicates with them."

"Whoa!" Roland commanded the horses.

"What are we doing?"

On impulse, he reached over and squeezed her hand. "We are watching the Mystic falcon."

The performance was exceptional, and Nord was filled with pride. When the falcon returned, an extra ration of sardines was waiting. After she ate, he slipped off his glove and rubbed the back of her muscular neck, his gnarled fingers tenderly pushing through the soft feathers.

Seek a mate, and return with your unborn. We will raise and train them together. The wizard detached the bewit, and the falcon flew away.

* * *

Jennifer ran up the path and hugged her good friend. "Nord . . . that was amazing!"

"We've been practicing," he responded with delight.

"The prince stopped the carriage"—her eyes opened wide—"so we *all* could watch."

"All?"

"The horses included!"

* * *

The next morning, after a hearty meal, Nord walked his guests down to the stables.

"It has been mentioned," he said to the prince, "a spirited horse is your preference?"

"The more spirited, the better," he confirmed with a nod. Then he turned to Jennifer with an eyebrow raised. "Unfortunately, my back has been troubling me of late."

"Let the horses rest today," she suggested. "Instead, we will hike to Blue Ridge Meadow."

"A fine choice," said Nord. "I'll join you as far as the trailhead."

* * *

Later that afternoon, Jennifer and Roland returned to the lodge. They found Nord in the kitchen, preparing strawberries.

"How was the outing?" he asked. A broad smile across his face.

"Memorable," Roland sheepishly replied.

Jennifer let out a hearty laugh. "The prince was up that old pine before I could finish yelling, mother—"

"BEAR. And I know one when I see one!"

Jennifer's lips curled into a smile. "We did have a nice visit . . . up there in that tree."

"That we did."

Nord said, "Sit down and relax. Enjoy the fresh strawberries and cream. Afterwards, we will go up to the lab. I have an idea."

What has he planned? she wondered.

* * *

Nord stood beside the doorway. "Go on in."

Roland dramatically searched the room. "So this is it . . . the wizard's laboratory."

"In all its glory," Nord confirmed with a wink.

"Tell me, where was the creature kept?" he asked.

The wizard took his gloved fingers and rubbed his chin. "The creature?" With rolled-up eyes, he thought some more. "Oh yes . . . the *Dark Forest creature*."

Unbeknownst to Roland, a falcon perched silently behind him. Without warning, the raptor let out an unnerving screech. The unsuspecting prince nearly jumped out of his skin. His subsequent scream nearly matched the falcon's.

Jennifer burst out laughing. "I told you he had a way with those birds!"

"NORD," Roland blared, once his breath returned.

After the commotion was over the wizard spoke up. "What happens here is between us."

"Of course," they both agreed.

"Very well, let us proceed." He gazed about the room. "My father spent a great deal of time here, often directed by an inner voice. He understood this presence divine. I was told this by my mother."

"Have you also heard this voice?" asked the prince.

"No, and I don't expect to. Wizardry isn't my calling. However, there is an experiment, or—"

"Potion?" Jennifer suggested.

"Connect . . . first developed by my father, to become one with the falcons."

"Interesting," remarked the prince.

"Tell us more," said Jennifer.

Nord approached them both. "There are layers to this *potion*, each one dependent upon the subjects. Their natural chemistry, attraction and comfort. If these elements are not present, the potion remains dormant. To be clear"—his Symlander eyes sparkled—"there has to be *something* already there."

The uncertain prince first looked at Jennifer, and then over at Nord.

"What is it, Roland?"

"*You* are the wizard."

"But not a mind reader."

Jennifer spoke up, "Are you considering us?"

"I am willing," the prince jumped in. "What would be the harm?"

"Yes," she agreed. "What would be the harm?"

"Wait for me at the altar," said Nord.

He went to the drawer of minerals and placed two pinches of pink in his open glove.

Roland whispered, "Even now I feel that *something*."

"Me too," she whispered back.

Nord approached the altar. "Stand across from each other and join hands. Rest them in the water and close your eyes." He sprinkled the shimmering minerals around the gift. "Free your thoughts . . ."

A moment of silence passed before he spoke again.

"Answer this simple question, my friends. Is your desire and care for each other . . . strong enough to last forever?"

"Yes," they mutually agreed.

* * *

The union of Roland and Jennifer was the social event of the year. Never had a Symlander exchanged vows outside their culture.

Nord, sought out for more of the same, became convinced this was his calling. He commissioned a special robe, headdress, and gloves. The laboratory was expanded and given a proper name: Center for Connections—or the center, for short.

Those privileged of both genders sought an appointment with the wizard, aspiring to leave the forest with a Symlander. In-depth interviews prior to the ceremony were crucial to a perfect match.

The majority of connections were successful, and Nord generously rewarded. Because of this, he sold his interest in the mineral operation.

As demand increased, Nord sought out an assistant. Impressed with her demeanor, he offered the position to Isa, an original settler whose partner was lost to illness. From the beginning, she was invaluable, accompanying him on travel, managing the interviews, and organizing their daily routine. They were inseparable.

Six Years Passed

Isa was asked to return later that evening. They would meet at the center and go through some notes. Nord was there waiting, dressed in ceremonial attire.

"The paperwork?" she asked.

"Everything is in order."

"Then why am I here? And why are you dressed so formal?"

"I've been thinking about us for some time."

"And?"

"Do you believe in second chances?"

"I'm not sure."

He stepped up to her with care in his eyes. "I desire a closeness with you."

Isa had not anticipated or pursued a relationship with Nord. Suddenly, she was compelled to inventory her feelings. "I was not expecting this," she responded with candor. "And without the slightest of warnings."

"Connect with me, Isa."

"We can try?"

He pulled out the drawer of minerals. "I'll take the first pinch."

"And I'll take the second."

One Year Later

Nord asked, "How are you feeling?"

Isa smiled broadly. "*We* are very well. The tea provides us strength and confidence."

"My mother felt the same, from what I was told." He said with mixed emotions.

"With a touch of the yellow for energy."

He stared at her in disbelief. "How long have you been drinking this blend?"

"Just a few days, and the difference is remarkable."

Nord's troubled expression gained intensity. "Isa!"

"I add but one or two grains."

"This mineral is caustic, and not to be tampered with."

"I want our child to be fearless."

He ripped off his glove and exposed the mutilated fingers. "This is what *fury* is good for, pain and humiliation!"

"Nord." Isa reached out and brought his hand to her chest. "I only want what is best for our son."

They held each other in silence, until their pounding hearts settled.

He left the room with the box of fury, and Isa soon followed, quietly, watching through the doorway, cradling her midsection—she felt a *kick*.

CHAPTER 7
LAND OF TUZ

EASTERN ENCAMPMENT

Tribal Reforms
- Emotions: openly expressed.
- Lifelong mates: recognized and celebrated.
- Fathers: equally acknowledged and involved.
- Guides: parental first option.

All hands were raised.

"The reforms have been accepted!" Ram confirmed. "This meeting is complete."

* * *

The new learners had come of age, their names to be revealed.

The fair Zuku stood front and center, wearing the broadest smile. On the platform behind her were Gem and Harta; behind them were Ram and Igua.

Harta stepped forward. "Blessings!" Her voice carried through the air, stronger than ever.

"BLESSINGS," the tribe enthusiastically replied.

"I am the mother of Mila!"

"Blessings, MILA."

When she heard her name, unlike the others, she waved her hands up high.

Even though you are not of my blood . . . would you know me as your father?

The learner turned around and pulled Gem down, then whispered in his ear. "Yes—my father."

Harta observed the special moment and then continued to speak. "I will guide Mila, with Gem!"

He stepped forward. "I am Harta's mate, the offspring of Igua and Ram!"

Wen, standing among the tribe, never felt so alone.

WESTERN ENCAMPMENT

As was their tradition, the Zukus journeyed west in time for planting.

Not long after they resettled, Ram was approached by Wen. He was uncomfortable peering into her *truth*, yet did so anyway.

She asked, "Could you help with building a vessel?"

"Not for fishing, I suppose."

"Fishing is optional," she said with a forced smile. "more so for travel."

"To the Land of Tuz."

"Yes . . . and a small crew—ten, maybe twelve."

"We will assist you in every way."

She gazed off and then returned to him. "I was prepared to stay here and grow old . . . but only with you. I know you can *feel* this—"

"I can."

"And now you've heard me say it."

"Wen"—his eyes looked deep into hers—"know this for certain with the sound of my voice, you will always be a blessing in my life."

The instant Ram first saw her, an absent warmth returned. After the tribal reforms, a reunion with Igua was inevitable, a future with Wen sacrificed.

"The life you have made here is beyond belief," she remarked with admiration." I will share with my father a vision of this place. The Land

96

of Zuku is open and plentiful. We would never encroach on your tribe. But where I come from, resources are scarce and most have very little."

Ram reached out his hands, and Wen did the same. They came together in a natural fit.

Igua was at Zuku House, overlooking the conversation. Although she could not hear what was said, she understood the purpose.

Soon after, Ram arrived at her dwelling. They both were vulnerable, and their *truth* concealed.

"We were sharing final words."

"I imagined this," said Igua.

"Wen has decided to go back to her homeland." Ram's *truth* was exposed by the hurt in his voice. "She asked me for our help."

He believed it best not to mention her possible return.

"And us?" she asked.

"Is there room for another in your dwelling?"

THREE YEARS LATER

The vessel's construction was slow and demanding, its design unflattering yet soundly built. They would sail off before the tribe's migration. As for the crew, only a few spots remained to be filled.

"Mother."

"Yes, Mila?"

"I would like for us to join the crew."

"That's impossible," she said without hesitation.

"Remember our first wagon ride with Gem? How this travel brought us closer together?"

"And all the wagon rides ever since. But sailing across the open sea"—she shook her head—"is much different than rolling across the grasslands."

"Ask Father?"

"I will mention it."

* * *

Later that day, Mila kept quiet and listened from the other room.

"Welcome back—my mate," said Harta.

Gem had grown accustomed to her greeting and delighted in the familiarity. On this day, however, the tone was not familiar.

"Good to be back." He welcomed her hug. "You have something to tell me?"

"Our learner has an idea."

"An idea, does she?"

"She would like for us to travel."

"Where?"

"The Land of Tuz."

"Hmm . . ." He took a moment to consider the adventure. "And you are against this idea of hers?"

"So much time away." She sighed. "Your responsibilities."

"Mila's idea is not unreasonable." He reached out and took hold of her hands. "Season after season is the same in this land. The tribe can manage without me. I'm sure my parents will agree."

"Then go and speak with them."

"And are you willing to go?"

"Yes."

* * *

"Gem," said Ram, somewhat surprised by his visit.

"Hello, Father." He looked over his shoulder. "Mother is here?"

"I am!" she called out. No sooner had he asked.

They greeted each other with a warm hug.

Open yourself, she privately requested.

He did so, then stepped back and faced his father.

"Go on," said Ram. "What is it?"

"The voyage . . . Mila wants us to join the crew."

"The crew," he murmured.

"I haven't spoken with her myself, but Harta says she's determined."

Igua looked at Gem with a clear understanding. "Let me discuss this with your father."

"I'll leave you alone for that."

The door closed and she turned to Ram. "Tomorrow, I will speak with Wen. If she is in favor, I say let them go."

"You know where to find her." He nodded. "And they also have my support."

That night, Igua was restless. Gem's visit and their private conversation occupied her thoughts. *Season after season is the same in this land.*

It was different for Igua. Each new day was a blessing, no matter how ordinary.

Early the next morning, she made her way to the cove. The air was brisk, her mind uncluttered. The vessel was nearing completion, and Wen stood on its stern.

"Hello up there!" Igua shouted in a friendly voice.

"Good day, Igua!" Wen replied with equal warmth. "I'm coming down!"

The Zuku took a deep breath and waited.

"What brings you to the *Unity*?" she asked with a furrowed brow and then chuckled. "Are you here to enlist?"

"No." Igua shook her head and softly smiled. "However, I do have three candidates to submit for your approval."

"Wonderful, this will complete our crew. Who are they?"

"My son and his family."

"You are serious?"

Igua's expression did not suggest otherwise.

"Gem came to us yesterday. His reasoning was persuasive."

"There are expectations, out on the open sea."

"I realize with Harta and Mila, you lack a measure of skill. Yet because of Gem, you are more than compensated."

"Ram is in favor?"

"If you are?"

Wen broke into a big smile and blinked. "Kelp will feed them well."

* * *

After three days of maneuvers, the *Unity* was pronounced seaworthy. They would sail at first light—before that, a celebration and feast.

Mila playfully reminded Kelp, "Enjoy the meal. This will be the last one *you* won't be preparing."

"And *you*, fair Zuku," he scoffed. "How will you survive without your smelly warkin?"

Mila and Kelp were self-acknowledged outsiders, she with the blood of a Symlander and he the blood of a Tuz. And even though there were years between them, they easily became good friends.

Soon after Harta and Gem partnered they drifted apart. Mila was an early learner, and being guided by them both. Kelp felt insignificant and wallowed in self-pity. His good-natured humor turned disparaging. Mila searched his *truth* for an understanding. It was there she *felt* the animus.

THE VOYAGE

Ram and Igua held hands on an empty beach. The *Unity*, no longer in view. They were content, having been left there together.

* * *

The first six days on the open sea were mostly unsurprising, the exception being Kelp's culinary skills, which had vastly improved. The vessel was performing well, in steady winds from a helpful direction.

Gem approached Wen, standing alone beside the railing. "I've been wanting to ask you."

"Yes?"

"Your homeland, what do you miss the most?"

She stared intently at the gifted Zuku. "Five years have passed since I sailed from there. You tell me, Gem . . . my father? In my thoughts, he is ever-present. But you already knew that."

He turned and walked away.

* * *

The sun had reached the water's edge. Harta and Mila were resting on their bunks. Kelp was in the galley, preparing the evening meal.

"All crew on deck!" Wen commanded.

Without warning, the vessel was surrounded by a disruptive force. The sails grew taut and violently trembled. The wood planks creaked, and the rigging cried out. They were being assaulted by a northern wind.

Gem was already on deck and lowering the secondary sail. It took all of his strength to make those final pulls. The Zukus with him tackled the fabric and held it down.

"The main sail!" shouted one of the crew. "We're going to lose the mast!"

Wen fought her way across the deck, sea spray lashing against her face. Taking out the braided knot, she began to lower the sail. Four pulls down and the jute was ripped from her grasp. The sail was defenseless, pummeled by powerful gusts, the frantic rope striking out at anyone trying to control it. In an instant, a burst of swirling air wrapped it tightly around the top of the mast.

"Mila, stay down here," Harta insisted. "It's not safe."

"I am a member of this crew, and I want to help!"

She rushed to the top without looking back, pushing past Kelp on the way.

Wen shouted, "Someone must free the rope!"

"Mila!" Harta screamed out.

Gem stopped what he was doing and leaned ahead. A fierce wind was determined to hold him back. He looked up in time to see Mila disappear behind the billowing sail.

Conserve your strength, he said calmly.

I feel strong, Father.

Everyone watched for Mila to reappear, including Kelp. However, he was not in favor of her success. He wanted her to fail. If that meant for the *Unity* to be swallowed up by the sea, so be it.

Mila *felt* his negative energy and returned it tenfold. *Go away, KELP.* The relief was immediate, and she continued with her climb.

First one hand and then the other. There she was! Her shocking white hair shone as a beacon of hope. She reached up and uncoiled the rope, tying the end around her waist.

I will catch you.

Without hesitation, she released her hold and fell into Gem's waiting arms. They looked at each other with salt-stained faces.

"I only wanted to help."

"And you did, Mila . . . you did."

"Down below!" Wen commanded the crew.

Gem took the rope from Mila, and Harta led her away. He lowered the sail as fast as he could and secured it with the other.

"We are all here?" Wen asked with urgency. She searched the faces staring back at her. "Rini?"

"Here!" she answered, her hand waving above a shoulder.

She looked again at the faces. "Kelp?"

Mila said, "He's not down here."

Wen rushed up the stairs with Gem close behind.

"Kelp!" she called out.

"Kelp! Kelp!" the crew shouted and searched.

"Mother," she said softly.

Although Harta could not feel Mila's *truth*, she saw it in her misty eyes. "What is it?"

"The wind took Kelp, after—"

Wen and Gem came down the stairs, their faces withdrawn and defeated.

"Mila, what is wrong?" he asked.

Harta said, "She knows."

Father, it was me.

"The search is over," Gem said quietly.

Wen was alone and without comfort, precariously supported by the hardwood pillar. Sheltered on their bunks, the crew listened to voices in the wind. Kelp's spirit was present in the cool dark air. There would be little sleep that night.

* * *

When dawn arrived, a crew member suggested, "I'll prepare the meal?"

"Yes," said Wen, "we all must eat."

Harta was waking when Gem whispered in her ear, "I'll be back for food."

"Where are you going?"

"Up top, to inspect the damage."

The *Unity* was built for challenging conditions and required few repairs, its sails to be mended and planks re-fastened. Most importantly, the masts had survived.

There was a slight breeze, and the water was flat. The northern wind had moved on, to torment others in its path.

"Good day, Gem."

He looked up from what he was doing. "Wen . . . good day!"

"I made a wise choice."

"Yes?"

"Having you and your family on the crew. Without your skill and Mila's brave decision, would we be here now?" She raised her hand to silence his reply. "No is the answer."

"I was inspired by your leadership. There is something about you, Wen. Something hidden, deep inside your *truth*."

* * *

During the days that followed the air was still. Most of the crew were idle and listless. Not a moment too soon, the westerlies awakened. Encouraged by this, Wen gathered everyone around the main mast.

"A strengthening wind is at our back, leaving misfortune behind us. We will complete this voyage with togetherness."

She placed her hand on the resilient hardwood and encouraged the others to do the same.

"Unity!" Gem shouted out.

"UNITY."

Much to Harta's displeasure, and Gem's delight, Mila became the vessel's lookout. Most of her time was spent atop the main mast, searching—for signs of land.

"Birds!" Mila shouted. "Birds!"

The crew went to the bow and scanned the horizon. Sure enough, a small flock of pelicans flew in formation.

Wen walked up to Gem and dryly remarked, "Not what I missed the most, but a welcome sight."

"Good to know," he responded with a soft smile.

"Crew!" Wen loudly announced. "The Land of Tuz is within our reach!"

LAND

Early the next morning, Harta whispered, "You are going up?"

"Yes," said Mila, "before the sails are set."

"Be safe," she replied with sleepy eyes.

Mila climbed to her post and looked off into the daybreak. Beneath the glare of the rising sun . . .

"LAND," she shrieked with all her might. "Land! Land!"

Everyone rushed to the bow.

Land was in sight, and the crew had mixed emotions. The Zukus maintained their indifference. Gem and Mila were energized. Harta did her best to relate. Wen was uncertain and vulnerable. She had gone missing for years, only to return—without the others.

The *Unity* entered Tuz Harbor.

"Lower the sails and drag the anchor!" Wen instructed the crew. "Our arrival will cause interest. Expect to be greeted."

The Land of Tuz was a closed society, their two-class system strictly defined. Mortal stars were predestined to rule, all others obligated to serve.

* * *

A rowboat approached with five Tuz onboard.

Gem said, "Stand back, everyone, and let Wen be among her people."

"Nico!

"Wen!" he shouted back in disbelief. "Is it really you?"

"I've finally found my way home!"

Gem picked up the coiled rope and tossed it down.

"Permission to come aboard?" the officer requested with a warm smile.

"Granted!" said Wen, and lowered the ladder.

"Stay here," Nico instructed the enforcers, and climbed up the side.

He took one step onto the deck, and they shared a meaningful hug.

"We thought you were gone forever." His eyes misted over. "Your father"—he sighed—"has not been well without you."

"I've missed him so."

Nico composed himself and scrutinized the crew. *What are these people?* he wondered.

Mila shifted her position to get a better look.

"Symlander! Wen . . . how is this possible?"

She glanced over at Mila, awash in confusion. "This crew member is Zuku, with blood that is mixed . . . Nico?"

"Things have changed," he said bluntly.

Mila edged closer to Gem.

"How so?"

"Two years ago, there was a situation. Symlanders no longer live here."

"I will speak with my father."

"As you wish. But for now, she remains on the water."

Wen gathered the crew. "Tonight, I stay with my father. Tomorrow, we will dock and take on provisions. Rest well and blessings."

"Blessings!"

"Take me to the compound."

"At once, Wen Star." Nico, respectfully bowed his head.

Wen Star? Gem pondered.

* * *

Wen was the youngest of two children. Soon after she was born, her mother passed away. Her early care had been provided by the helpers of the house. Her father, Turk, was often missing. Matters of great importance kept him occupied. However, when they were together, a lasting bond was formed.

As Wen matured and gained independence, she gravitated to the docks. Her family laid claim to a variety of vessels, and she became proficient with each one. She favored the lifestyle and comradery of those dependent on the sea. Because of her abilities and pleasant nature, she was welcome there.

The ride to Bright Star Compound was not much more than a blur, with Wen's mind focused on her father's welfare. As they rounded another turn, the sun slipped behind the evergreens. The horses slowed and walked through the opened gate.

"There they are!" she joyfully shouted, momentarily absent of troubled thoughts.

Three aggressive purna dogs converged on the carriage. Wen had forgotten to be on the lookout for their greeting. Two of them she recognized, the third—a spunky overgrown pup—was new.

"Stop the carriage," she instructed the driver.

Wen opened the door and reached out her hand. In an instant, the excitable pup leaped into the carriage.

"Oh my," she blurted out with laughter. "It seems I have a new friend. You missed me, without even knowing me . . . is that right?"

An attendant waited in the foyer.

"Welcome, Wen Star. Your father—"

"I will go to him now."

After starting up the stairs, she was redirected. "He is out back, in a guesthouse. Follow me."

"Who resides in the main quarters?"

"Your Uncle Burg and his family."

This is curious.

"Here we are." The attendant opened the door.

"Father!" She rushed to his bedside.

"Wen Star. I do not believe my tired eyes. Come closer, my dear."

"If I were any closer—" She bent over with a warm smile and kissed his forehead.

"This is *not* a dream." He whimpered.

"Not a dream." She shook her head with happy tears. "But look at you, alone in this simple place. Can I never go off and explore again?"

They stared at each other in silence.

"What happened?" he gently asked.

"The vessel was destroyed in a most violent way. And by the slimmest of margins, only I survived. These past years, I lived with a tribe called Zuku, their culture far different than ours. I gained knowledge and was treated well. They made a fine crew. One of them is unique, with the blood of a Symlander."

"Oh, Wen Star." He paused to catch his breath. "Symlanders have been banished."

"Why?"

Wen did not want to provoke her father, yet was confused in so many ways.

Turk grimaced and gazed off into the past. "You had failed to return and we feared the worse. My health began to suffer. Your uncle took control of our responsibilities, with Luke at his side. In many ways, I felt relief without the burden. I had lost your mother . . . and then you."

For the first time that Wen could remember, tears flowed freely from her father's eyes, streaming down across the faded red star, inscribed on the side of his neck.

Turk's solid red star signified his level of importance. He was the Brightest Star, the highest honor for a Tuz. Wen's brother, Luke, was a level below, his star yet to be filled.

Wen looked around the sparse surroundings. "How did you end up here?"

"After Burg assumed complete control, the main quarters belonged to him. Apparently"—his voice trailed off into a whisper—"this is where you go . . . before."

"You're not going anywhere." She smiled and reassured him. "The Symlanders?"

Turk used his handkerchief to dab away the tears. "Luke traveled to the Dark Forest, everything prearranged with the matchmaker. He returned, with the most captivating Symlander. Her name was Solanze. I believed them to be happy—"

"Go on, Father."

"You know your brother well."

"I do."

"He is the same, if not worse—self-serving and violent. In the beginning, their relationship appeared normal. I was hopeful for a grandchild. Then one day, Solanze came to me on her own. She was frightened and trembling. I promised her . . . I would have a talk with my son. That was the last I saw of her."

"What was Luke's explanation?"

"'She got sick,' he told me, without a measure of distress." Turk shook his head and clasped his quivering hands.

"My brother is cold-blooded."

"Soon after her death, a proclamation was issued—all Symlanders ordered to leave our land. Many deep-rooted Tuz joined them . . . and rightfully so. Families and friends were torn apart. There were many sad farewells."

"Mila is a child," Wen passionately explained. "She appears as a Symlander, but with only half the blood."

"You and your crew can stay at the waterfront residence. Your cousin Alex is living there. She has partnered—his name is Kain. I believe them fair and open minded. The mixed Symlander is also welcome. Keep her covered until safely inside. I will send a messenger, and prepare them for your arrival."

"What about Nico?"

"I understand your history of friendship, but he is Burg's first officer now. I am sorry . . . he cannot be trusted. I will share more once you have settled. For now, let us enjoy a meal and be thankful." He gave her hand a tender kiss. "My daughter, we are together again."

* * *

"She is with her father?" asked Burg.

Yes, Brightest Star," replied Nico. "They have ordered food."

"What is her state of mind?"

"As before . . . strong, perhaps even stronger."

Burg raised his bushy brown eyebrow. "What does she know?"

"She is aware of the purge." Although staunchly loyal, Nico did not mention the Zuku-Symlander.

"And?"

"I did not share the details. However, I am sure that her father—"

Luke burst into the room. "Is it true what I've been told?" he snarled. "My precious sister has returned from the dead." His eyes darted between the men.

"She has," the first officer confirmed. "But not from the stars above. From a shipwreck that only she survived. Taken in by a tribe called Zuku. A unique people . . . you will see."

"This changes nothing!"

"Nothing at all," his uncle said laughingly. "Do not waste your energy. Let her catch up with the old man. He is close to the end, and their moments are precious. She enjoys the sea. We will send her out again. And this time, there will be no returning . . . from the dead."

* * *

The following morning, Wen rose early to leave for the docks. Alex and Kain had a boat waiting. The *Unity* would be towed in from her mooring.

"Sister . . . you are alive and well," said Luke, standing by the carriage.

She walked up and looked deep into his dark, narrow eyes. "Disappointed?"

"Why would you say such a dreadful thing?"

"My crew is waiting."

* * *

At the waterfront, her cousin happily greeted her, and they shared a warm hug. "Wen Star!"

"So good to see you, Alex . . . and call me Wen."

"Wen," she said with a cheerful exhale. "This is Kain. We have been together for over two years."

"It's a privilege," said Kain. "I have always admired your skills at sea."

"Why, thank you."

"Actually, we have met before."

Wen searched her memory. "I do not recall."

"I volunteered to be a member of the expedition . . . but wasn't chosen."

"As fate would have it," she said quietly, gazing up into the pale-blue sky.

"Excuse me for that reminder." He glanced over at Alex.

Wen took in a solid breath. "Only those wishing to be alone live in the past. We are together, and living for today."

"Here we are." Alex smiled with a nod.

"The Zukus are like no other," said Wen. "You will witness this by my crew. Male and female closely resemble. Gem is especially gifted, fluent in our language, and also . . . our thoughts."

"A wizard?" Kain suspected.

"Deeper than that," said Wen. "He can feel one's truth. The Zuku have a saying, 'To *feel* is to know.'"

Alex reminded herself, "The messenger spoke of a Symlander?"

"Mila is a young Zuku, but with the blood and appearance of a Symlander. She is also gifted, to what extent remains unknown."

"I was sad to see the Symlanders leave," said Alex. "One of my best friends, Solanze . . . was—"

"My father told me the painful story."

Kain spoke up, "Let us live in the present, and bring your crew to land."

"Agreed!" said Wen, then chuckled. "A warm bath will serve them well. We are grateful to share the residence. How long we will stay, I don't know." She sighed. "So much has changed."

"Yes . . . much has changed," Alex solemnly agreed.

* * *

"Welcome back!" said Gem as the crew gathered around him.

Wen smiled from ear to ear. "Ready to get your feet on solid ground?"

"Yes!" Mila sang out in a high-pitched tremolo.

Wen stepped to the side. "This is my cousin, Alex, and her partner, Kain. For the time being, we will stay with them."

Alex announced, "Welcome to the Land of Tuz!"

The crew was mostly silent and distracted, watching Kain's eyes as they moved from stern to bow.

"Your vessel requires assistance," said the Tuz. "This will keep you away from trouble."

"She'll tie-up over there." Alex pointed to a distant dock. "Who will help to row her over?"

The waterfront residence was older, yet spacious and well-thought-out. In years past, it was occupied by the mortal stars and bustled with activity. After the compound was built, it fell out of favor and was seldom used.

Two days passed.

Wen had unanswered questions and went to Alex and Kain. The engaging partners impressed her.

She looked intently at them both. "My father is not well. It appears Burg and my brother have taken full control. What can you tell me?"

"My grandfather has lost his mind to power," Alex said despondently. "He holds on to it with an iron fist. Ruling from a fortress hidden in the hills. Absorbed in luxury as his people suffer. He's taken away their freedom and left them with little hope."

Kain spoke up, "There is a large group of us, who strive for a better life. But even now we are watched and persecuted. They can ill afford to lose their youthful laborers. Our lives would be sacrificed, if we dare attempt to leave."

"I know a special place," Wen glowingly revealed, "to build a better life. It waits for us . . . to replenish our hope."

* * *

Mila rubbed her mother's belly. "I can't wait to have a brother."

"A child . . . a *brother*?"

"I am positive."

Gem walked in on the conversation. "How is everyone?"

Harta pointed to her midsection and dryly replied, "Including the boy?"

He stared over at Mila with an eyebrow raised. "Your mother is not well?"

"Both mother and son are doing very well." She beamed.

Rushing over, he placed his ear on the belly.

Boom-boom, boom-boom, boom-boom . . .

He looked up at Harta with joyful eyes. "I can guarantee this much. The child will be one . . . or the other."

CHAPTER 8
DARK FOREST TERRITORY

"How are you feeling?" asked Wen.

"Reminded of ten years ago, and Mila's introduction," said Harta with an empty face. "I had emotions on that day.

Wen exploded with laughter. "Harta!"

"I am ready."

"And I have an idea."

"Idea?" said Gem, barging into the room.

"You and your *gift*," Wen scoffed and raised an eyebrow. "You have read my mind."

He kept silent with a sheepish grin.

"Then, tell me," said Harta.

Wen explained, "I would like to get out on the water. Take the crew, including Mila, sail the Crescent Coast. It's a safe and scenic journey. With us away you'll have peace and quiet . . . before and after the birth. Alex and Kain will see to your comfort. What do you say?"

"I am in favor," said Harta right away.

"I am as well," said Gem. "And for Mila, better to hear from her."

"Let me first advise my brother."

* * *

At the compound, Luke said, "You've been avoiding me, sister? Or has it been me, preoccupied serving our people."

"I see how you and Uncle Burg serve our people."

"The land is prosperous," he gloated.

"I'm only here to inform you of my plans."

He stepped ever closer. "You've made plans?"

"I've become restless. My crew is not familiar with the coast. Now is the perfect time to sail along there. Two of our members won't be joining us. They have a newborn on the way. An allowance of space appreciated."

"Of course, dear sister." His stare grew colder. "One small favor."

"And what would that be?"

"Do not return with the Symlander."

* * *

"Yes!" Mila squealed, looking forward to her daily climbs.

"I believe she's all in," said Gem with a chuckle.

"And when we return, I'll have a brother to greet," she gleefully added.

Wen celebrated Mila's enthusiasm but was deeply concerned for her future.

* * *

Wen basked in the most satisfying of relationships: a vessel and open water. The freedom provided her joy, and always filled a void.

The coastline was interesting and well charted. The conditions were ideal. The crew welcomed the easy pace and absence of turmoil.

They would sail past the Land of Cantor, a place of natural wonders and advanced achievements. The Riveras who lived there were often uninviting. Wen had experienced it firsthand. She could easily imagine what the Zukus would face.

The Land of Sym was their destination. Wen and the royal family were friends. It had been seven years since her last visit. A courier was sent in advance, to announce their impending arrival.

"On my way!" Mila shouted, while climbing down the mast.

"Hungry?" asked Wen, though she knew the answer.

"More than ever."

"You've earned it. But leave some for the others."

Heading toward the galley, Mila came up with a song. "Soon . . . I will have a new brother. Soon . . . I will have a new brother. Soon . . ." She disappeared beneath the deck.

* * *

Later the next afternoon, Wen announced, "The Land of Cantor!"

The main sail was lowered, and they slowly crossed the harbor's mouth.

"Take us closer!" Mila pleaded, mesmerized by the sights and sounds.

Wen laughed. "We are close enough!"

They traveled a little farther, before dropping anchor for the night.

"Mila!" shouted Wen.

"On my way!"

"Do you ever get tired of being up there?"

"Never," she flatly replied. "Tomorrow, we will reach Sym?"

"Yes."

Wen envisioned, with great satisfaction, Mila surrounded by those who looked as she did.

* * *

At the royal residence of Sym, the messenger entered the dining room and read the note. "Be on the watch for a vessel of unique design . . ."

The lord and lady laughed freely, recognizing Wen's delightful style. They were anxious to see her again.

"Not to disparage the Symlander." Lord Martin snorted, finding humor to where his thoughts were leading. "However, won't it be refreshing? Visitors without intense opinions."

"Agreed, my lord," Lady Rook chimed in. "And those distracting eyes of theirs." She exaggeratedly opened her own.

"Excellent impression, Mother," Sir Hemeth blurted out.

"This tribe called Zuku"—Martin dramatically contemplated—"hidden away all this time. Apparently, no one found interest beyond the fisheries."

Rook displayed the last piece of bass on her fork and then ate it. "Apparently not—my lord."

LAND OF SYM

Wen pointed to the rolling hills in the distance, blanketed with tall evergreens. "Look over there."

"All those trees?" said Mila.

"Yes, the Dark Forest. I've been told it's a magical place. Can you *feel* it?"

"Let me try."

Wen watched carefully as the gifted Zuku concentrated with purpose. Her eyes shut tight, forehead furrowed, and lips pursed.

A few moments passed before she opened her eyes and sighed. "Just the salt air against my face. Should I have felt something more?"

"Maybe if we were closer." Wen blinked and gave her a hug.

* * *

"Mother! Father! Hemeth shouted from the balcony. The strangest vessel has entered the harbor. It must be them!"

"Down we go," said Rook. "Remember, son, not too much excitement. Let's not startle the Zukus. Be courteous and patient . . . we can surely manage that?"

An escort boat towed *Unity* to the dock.

Hemeth was not particularly adept at harbor life but could manage his way around a vessel. He would make every effort to impress the visitors.

"Throw me a line!" the young royal shouted.

His parents looked on with amusement.

Rook chuckled. "Next thing you know, he'll be wanting a vessel of his own."

"I'll check into that," Martin replied with a wink.

Once the bow was secured, Hemeth went to the stern. Mila had been watching and was fascinated by the young Symlander. Leaning farther over the rail, he caught notice of her, and she suddenly became reserved.

"You there!" Hemeth called out.

Wen came up from behind and shouted down to the dock. "Sir Hemeth?"

"Yes, I am Hemeth." He smiled and waved his hand.

"It's me, Wen . . . and this is Mila."

Mila's hand was slow to rise, when it did, she waved.

Wen and Mila stayed at the royal residence, while the crew remained on *Unity*. The Zukus were by no means neglected. Their bedding, clothing, and pantry were refreshed on a regular basis. An evening meal was delivered daily. And guides were provided to show them the area.

"The fish is well flavored . . . halibut?" Wen asked.

"Yes, it's been slow-baked," said Rook with a satisfied smile. "I'm glad you like it."

The young royal spoke up, "Mila, you're not completely Symlander, are you?"

"Hemeth!" Lord Martin reprimanded his brash son.

"My mother is Zuku," she acknowledged. "My father, I have never known. But he is of your kind."

She then gave in to an immature reflex and tested the capabilities of her gift.

Hemeth's feet began to tap. He stood up and hastily left the table. "I will return!" he shouted from outside the room.

Rook apologized, "Please excuse our son's misguided curiosity."

"It's normal for me," said Mila. "Growing up, I was the only fair Zuku in our tribe."

"We both were curiosities, weren't we, Mila," said Wen. "I was the mysterious foreigner, delivered from the cove. And you an obscure youngling, hatched from Mothers' Village." She paused for a moment and softly smiled. "As cultures blend, our differences will fade."

"Evolution," Martin spoke up with certainty. "My father and uncle founded this land because of it. However, their uniqueness was on the *inside*. Our true identity"—he pressed his fingers to his chest— "resides in here."

Mila lowered her head to hide her Symlander eyes. "There are Zukus," she revealed, "able to *feel* this true identity."

Rook impulsively asked, "Can you?"

"Most often, I can."

Hemeth returned and abruptly replied, "Yes!"

"To what?" Martin blurted out.

"Mila wanted to know if I felt relief."

The lord cocked his head in bewilderment.

"And there are also Zukus," she continued, "who can speak—"

Wen interrupted, "We are looking forward to the Dark Forest."

"A wonderful season to travel the Red Road," said Rook. "We will provide our finest carriage."

"The road is red?" asked Mila.

"It's in the rock," explained Hemeth, "volcanic."

"There's a glint of it." Rook nodded with a smile.

Martin spoke up, "You will visit my cousin Nord? I can make the arrangements."

"Yes, we plan to do so," Wen confirmed, "and thank you."

"His matchmaking has received quite the notice," said Rook.

"So I've been told."

"Father."

"Yes, Hemeth?"

"If our guests agree, I would like to join them. A chance to clear my head before Montro."

"This is true," said Rook, aware of her son's confusion. "Wen, would it be acceptable for Hemeth to tag along?"

She looked over at Mila. "What do you say?"

"Sir Hemeth, would you be asking the driver to stop for constant relief?"

"Not if *I* can help it."

118

* * *

"They are waiting!" Rook called out for her missing son.

"There he is." Mila flashed a knowing smile. "Last time," she whispered as he passed by.

Wen sat up top with the driver, while Hemeth and Mila shared the compartment below.

"You mentioned Montro?" she reminded herself to ask.

Hemeth's eyes warmed. "A very special place. Hopefully you can visit there."

"Tell me more."

"My grandparents developed the island as a retreat." He took a shallow breath. "They were lost at sea before my birth."

"Oh . . . I'm sorry." Mila thought back to what Gem had told her about the shipwreck outside the cove. "Where did they sail?"

"To the northwest, on uncharted waters."

I am familiar with those waters, she kept to herself.

"To honor them, a school was opened on Montro. I begin my studies there, soon after we return. You seem to have the required skills. When of age, you can apply."

"But I am not full Symlander?"

"The academy is open to all cultures."

"I believe your grandparents would be proud of this school."

"What about your land, Mila?"

Their conversation continued, down the Red Road.

The carriage slowed and then stopped at the final outpost.

Wen climbed down and poked her head through the window. "I'll be joining you the rest of the way."

Hemeth said, "Catching a chill up there?"

"The driver lacks personality." She sighed. "I fear of nodding off and tumbling down."

A hearty laugh was shared by all.

Mila asked, "How much longer, Hemeth?"

He pointed in the distance. "That smoke is from our lodge."

119

The royal lodge was well prepared for visitors: fresh-cut flowers, a well-stocked pantry, and seasoned wood for a crackling fire.

Dark Forest Village

"Good morning, Hemeth," Wen cheerfully greeted the young royal.

"Good morning, Wen."

"Have you seen Mila?"

"She stepped outside . . . through that door by the garden."

The first night did not go well for Mila. She slept poorly, if at all. Each time before drifting off, she was disrupted by her thoughts.

"Hemeth suggested I might find you here. How was your rest?"

She shook her head. "What is rest?"

Wen softly chuckled. "Maybe the fragrance in the linen?"

"I *felt* a presence . . . strangely familiar."

"Mila?"

"I don't know who, or why . . . just yet."

One of the attendants stepped out from the lodge. "A good night's rest for everyone?"

Mila rolled her eyes.

"Breakfast will be served on the sun porch."

"Let's have some food and plan our day," said Wen.

Hemeth was already at the table and nibbling on bacon.

"Would you like to go for a horseback ride?" Wen suggested to them both.

The young royal encouragingly looked over at Mila.

"Maybe so," she responded with indifference.

"There's a fantastic trail I know of," said Hemeth. "After reaching the top, all the territory is before you."

Mila perked up. "Actually, I do want to ride there."

"It's decided, then," said Wen. "But first, a visit with Nord. He is expecting us."

Although somewhat isolated, the wizard's hilltop lodge was not remote. The path leading up was wide and well maintained.

Opening the door was Elgin, Nord and Isa's highly independent four-year-old son. His Symlander eyes were similar in intensity to his grandfather's.

The boy spoke up with little inflection. "My name is Elgin, and follow me. I will take you through the lodge."

Wen was dumbfounded, to be directed in such a way. *What has the child been fed?*

Mila tried to search his *truth* but found it surprisingly sealed.

Elgin stared back at her. "Any questions before we begin?"

"Your parents . . . they are here today?" Wen inquired, her composure in the balance.

Mila covered her mouth and quickly turned away. Hemeth could not refrain. His laughter filled the entry.

Elgin glared at the young royal. "Of course, I am not alone. My mother waits in the study, while my father trades with Mona."

"What are they trading?" Wen thought out loud.

"Tea for mushrooms."

"Tea for mushrooms?" said Hemeth with a furrowed brow.

"The same black tea my mother drank, when I was still inside her, the source of my energy. Mona wanted the same for her child. She offered rare mushrooms in trade." He awkwardly giggled. "Even though Tulare's running up the path, she continues with the trade. Mona is determined to make her stronger than me."

Mila asked, "Does this bother you?"

"Not really," he scoffed. "I like the mushrooms."

She looked down and studied the wizard child. "I also have an *energy* . . . but my mother never drank this tea."

He ignored her and led the tour.

They finished in the study, where Isa sat in her favorite chair.

"Elgin insists"—she stood up and smiled— "showing our first-time guests around. His energy is never-ending. Constantly, we search for ways to burn it. His father could use some of that vigor." She sighed. "Last night he struggled to find rest."

"Likewise for our Mila," Wen chimed in and looked over to where she stood, her thick white eyebrows narrowed into one. "But she is resilient, and will go riding. Are you both ready?"

"I am!" Mila sharply replied.

"Me too," said Hemeth.

"Mother!"

"Yes, Elgin?"

"I could ride with them and burn some energy?"

Before she could answer, the young visitors were gone.

Hemeth gulped, "That was close."

Mila looked straight ahead and raced down the hill. "Faster!" she hollered, "and don't look back."

"I'm right behind you!"

They quickly made their way to the bottom and then stopped to catch their breath.

"There is *something* about that little Symlander," Mila decided.

Nord and Mona entered the study.

"I missed the others, didn't I?" asked Nord.

"Yes, dear, they went for a ride."

"You must be Wen." He smiled and stepped forward, gloved hands at his sides. "We've been expecting you. Welcome to the Dark Forest."

"Thank you, Nord."

Isa spoke up. "This is our friend Mona."

"Your son mentioned Mona, the rare mushrooms and black tea."

"Enjoy your time here," she spoke up. "I must be going."

"I'll see you to the door," said Isa with a nod.

Once outside, she took from her pocket a small drawstring purse. "Remember, not more than a grain."

"Only one," Mona confirmed with a sly smile.

She always added two.

"Your son is quite impressive," said Wen.

"Yes"—Nord chuckled—"he reeks of potential."

"Father!" Elgin blurted out.

Isa returned and prompted her son. "Say goodbye to Wen."

"Elgin, why don't you continue with your project?" Nord suggested. "He's been charting the stars."

"Goodbye," grumbled the wizard child.

"It is quite fascinating," said Isa. "I will leave you two alone and follow his progress."

Nord looked over at the wingback chairs in the corner. "Let's sit over there."

Wen observed with interest as he settled into the chair, the deep breaths he took, the way he rubbed his eyes.

She said, "I heard you slept poorly last night."

He tilted his head back and sighed. "Yes, an unusual presence."

"For Mila, it was the same. Could it be her Symlander heritage, and the nature of this place?"

"She is a wizard?"

"A wizard? I never thought to see her in this light. Is it even possible with only half the blood?"

"And the other half?" he asked.

"Zuku . . . they can be—"

"Gifted. Martin said so much. But for now, tell me, Wen, what is the main purpose of your visit?"

"My brother, Luke Star. I am here to know the truth."

"Your brother is a killer."

Wen did not anticipate his anger.

"It hurt when I learned of Solanze's death, the purge of Symlanders that followed, many of whom you must have known. Nord . . . what can you tell me?"

He closed his eyes and steadied himself. "Luke solicited me, with a desire to connect. By that time, I had performed a large number of ceremonies. Their popularity, at its peak."

"I understand the attraction," Wen said softly.

"His obsession with our culture was pronounced and disturbing. He met Solanze during the second day of interviews, and instantly was taken. Predictable, as she was exquisite."

"What went wrong?"

123

"For her, there was no attraction." Nord raised his voice in frustration. "They were not compatible!"

"Even so, they did end up together?"

"I performed the ceremony at Luke's insistence. It was pure insanity."

"Knowing all of this, you let him take her away."

Nord clenched his mangled fingers. "Let him? Your brother is very persuasive . . . when holding a knife to your throat."

"I am sorry."

"'She will obey and respect me!' is what he demanded." Nord looked deep into Wen's unwavering eyes. His tears flowed freely, as did hers. "What brings me the most pain? Luke's desire for Solanze was purely symbolic. He wanted *everyone* to know, the most appealing of all Symlanders belonged to him. Only the best for Luke Star! After refusing to be his treasure . . . she was silenced. Soon after, the Symlanders were banished. All those unfortunates who had truly connected."

"Nord," Wen spoke with the deepest sincerity. "I appreciate your openness and recognize your pain."

The deaths of his parents impacted Nord greatly, and he carried deep remorse. He honored them by committing to a life of righteousness.

"Come back to see me with the others?" he asked in a hopeful voice.

"Yes, Nord, of course we will." She smiled. "It's getting late. Tonight, rest well and without effort."

As she walked slowly down the path, her anger simmered.

Luke's cruelty had always been difficult for her to accept, given that their father was an honorable man.

* * *

Back at the royal lodge, Wen asked, "How was the ride?"

"Amazing!" Mila blurted out.

"Agreed," said Hemeth. "So much beauty."

"And your visit with Nord?" asked Mila.

Wen took a deep breath and slowly exhaled. "Sad, yet necessary. My brother is very dangerous. Mila, I must tell you now. He detests all

Symlanders. It isn't safe for your return." She smiled with confidence. "I have an idea, but it can wait until morning."

Mila said, "Good night, Hemeth. I enjoyed our time together."

"Me too." He softly smiled. "Good night."

They shared a gentle hug.

"Join us!" Hemeth encouraged Wen.

* * *

Later that night when the lodge was quiet and dark, Nord looked up—into a restless acceptance. The time had come.

NORD AND MILA

"I am here to speak with Wen," Isa informed the attendant at the door.

"One moment and I will let her know."

"Good day, Isa," said Wen with surprise. "What brings you here?"

"Nord . . . he would like to visit with Mila, alone, and today if possible?"

"Mila?"

"It's her abilities. He is curious for a better understanding."

"Once she's out of the bath, I'll ask her."

"Any time will do"—she smiled—"Goodbye."

"I will go there now!" said Mila.

Wen laughed. "Wait until you dry off."

* * *

Mila knocked on the door and waited.

"Nord?"

"I am . . . and you are Mila."

"I was expecting Elgin."

"He's out with his mother, burning—"

"Energy."

He chuckled. "That's right! Come with me. I want to show you the center."

"That sounds important," she said with sparkling eyes.

"It's where I work and also find comfort. Although, at times, the truth provides not so much—"

"Because of me?"

He explored her stare. "There is no need to search inside here." He pressed his gloved fingers to his chest. "After we are finished, you will discover all there is to know."

She followed him up the path and into the room. "What is that . . . a fountain?"

"An altar," the wizard reverently replied." He walked over and placed his hand on the round stone. "And this, a gift from our Maker. My father watched as it fell from the stars, a blaze of white fire behind it." He stared down into the basin. "When uncommon minerals are added to the water . . . mystic happenings are possible."

"Mystic happenings," repeated Mila as if in a trance.

"Perform an experiment with me."

"What kind of experiment?"

"One of understanding."

He took out the top drawer and set it on the small table near the altar. *Two pinches of truth, and one of connect,* he confirmed to himself. His gloved fingers sprinkled the blue and pink crystals, and they glimmered in the water around the gift.

"Beautiful," she whispered.

"I must warn you," Nord cautioned, "my fingers are disfigured. They have been this way for years."

He removed each glove, and she did not flinch.

"Now what?"

"Are you ready to know our *truth*?"

"I am."

"Then . . . hold my hands."

She did as he asked, and they lowered them into the potion.

The Mystic altar was forgiving and did not dwell in the past. The truth revealed was considerate and healing.

Mila said, "You are the Symlander in my blood, the reason for my hair and eyes."

"I am," Nord affirmed without hesitation.

She looked at him with care. "There is a Zuku I call Father. His name is Gem. He is with my mother, Harta, in the Land of Tuz. Very soon, I will also have a brother. They are my family."

"I am grateful to know of your family."

"Nord."

"Yes?"

"Would it be surprising if I told you, during our experiment, I heard a *voice*?"

"That would be unexpected. Are you going to tell me what—"

"No . . . I am going to show you. And your assistance is unavoidable."

He arched an eyebrow. "Listen . . . Mila, my abilities are not much more than matchmaking. My father, he was a true wizard."

"The recipe is quite simple."

"Oh?"

"Yes. We have nothing to lose." *Except your fingers*, she kept to herself. "Refresh the altar."

The bewildered Symlander did as he was told.

Mila examined the colorful minerals.

"One pinch of black . . . evolvement?"

"Yes," the wizard confirmed.

"And one pinch of pink . . . connect?"

"Right again."

"And finally . . . a few grains of the yellow?"

"NO. This mineral is forbidden."

"The recipe was clear. "Where is fury?"

"Not here."

"But it *is* close by," she said calmly while focusing through the wall. "It's there behind the rocks."

Mila went outside and returned with the box.

"A few grains of fury." She added the final ingredient.

"Now what?" he asked.

"Give me your hands and close your eyes."

She submerged them in the mystic water, and a transformation ensued. Nord's fingers started to tingle, sensitivity returning to his touch.

She let go and took a step back. "See what I see."

Nord looked down with discerning eyes and slowly raised his hands. All that remained was subtle scarring. The disfigurement was gone.

Oddly enough, there was a feminine quality about them.

"I have your fingers!" he joyfully shouted, wiggling them in amazement.

"Not *my* fingers . . . exactly." Mila chuckled. "But I do see a similarity. Would you like me to reverse the potion?"

"I only wish to help you and your family return home safely." He reached out his rejuvenated fingers and gently touched her face. "And I will do everything in my power to make this happen."

They continued their visit in the study.

Mila said, "I must be going now."

"Breakfast tomorrow?" he asked.

"Yes, we will see you then." She smiled and turned to leave.

"Wait! I have something for you." Nord hurried over to the small closet, where his most personal possessions were kept, and returned with a dark narrow box. He handed it to her with both hands. "Open it."

She undid the latch and lifted the lid. Cradled in deep-blue silk was a sheathed blade. She gazed upon it with fascination. "A knife."

"A Symlander dagger, forged with care in the Northern Frontier. It has been in our family since memory. It belongs to you now, and will serve you well."

She firmly took hold of the leather grip and immediately felt its worth. "I am honored."

Mila returned to the others exhausted yet deeply fulfilled.

"You are sure?" said Wen.

"Completely," Mila confirmed. "Nord is making the arrangements." She glanced over at the young royal and smiled. "Hemeth will also be there, until he's off to Montro."

128

"How impressive are you," Wen remarked with great affection.

"Agreed," said Hemeth.

Isa gasped, "Nord, your fingers! What magic is this?"

His eyes were imbedded with pride. "Mila, she has the blood of a wizard."

"The blood of a wizard all right," she thought out loud.

"More than that," he continued to gush.

"That . . . is quite enough," she insisted. A subsequent chill filled the room.

"They are leaving tomorrow," said Nord, "and I've invited them over for breakfast. There is a *situation* in the Land of Tuz."

Isa fidgeted with her bracelet.

* * *

At the lodge the next morning, Mila asked, "Alone again?"

"I am," said Nord, "and welcome everyone. Follow me to the dining room. Fresh fruit and warm muffins are waiting."

After settling around the table, Wen spoke up. "Mila has told us she'll be staying in Sym."

"It is safe for her there," said Nord. "Now, how else can I be of service?"

Wen stared into his receptive eyes. "There is a group of young Tuz, seeking to escape their oppression."

"What do you suggest?"

"We can seize a large vessel that is docked in the harbor. But two more are required of similar size."

"Those vessels will be provided." He abruptly stood up. "Excuse me for a moment. Enjoy the food. I won't be long."

He is going to the altar, said Mila to herself.

Nord returned with an abundance of energy. "I have a plan!"

The room fell silent as they listened.

"The vessels you request will follow sail barges loaded with salt, dropping anchor outside the harbor—hidden from view. The barges continuing to the docks with their cargo. Later that night, they'll provide transport to the waiting vessels. Your people will sail away before dawn."

"Free," said Wen with a sigh of relief.

"Well done!" Hemeth chimed in.

You are more wizard than you know, Mila said privately.

Nord looked at Wen. "The plan's success depends on you."

"We will be ready." She confidently nodded.

"And I am sure of it. However"—his eyes opened wide—"should this plan be exposed, we have a response."

"Show them," said Mila, aware of what he was thinking.

"Follow me." Nord led the way to the habitat.

"They are magnificent," Wen marveled.

"Yes," said the wizard with fondness, "and mighty when called upon."

"We need time to prepare. Next season . . . the first new moon?"

"The shipments will arrive accordingly, along with two supply vessels waiting for your return, laden with the necessities to support your relocation. Mila will be on one of them."

"Atop the main mast!" Hemeth blurted out.

Mila waited for the laughter to subside. "Where I come from, we express gratitude through blessings. This visit to the Dark Forest has been a blessing in my life."

LAND OF TUZ

Three rowboats came alongside the *Unity*.

"Let me take care of this," Wen informed the crew.

Luke stood up and shouted, "Let down the ladder!"

He climbed up with urgency and stepped onto the deck.

"Brother," she greeted him coolly.

"How was the exotic Land of Sym?" he asked with little interest.

Productive, she kept to herself.

Enforcers boarded the vessel and scoured it from top to bottom.

A friendly voice called out, "Good day, Wen Star."

"Good day, Nico," she respectfully answered. "My father?"

"He asks for you."

"Tell him I will be there soon."

"Of course."

The lead enforcer reported back and shook his head.

"Tow them in!" barked Luke.

* * *

"He looks like the both of you," said Wen (stating the obvious).

"His name is Koal," Harta announced.

"So soon to be named?"

"We are in the Land of Tuz," she coyly remarked. "What is the tradition here?"

Wen smiled down at the sleeping Zuku. "Wonderful to meet you, Koal. Your sister sings about you daily."

"Where is Mila?" asked Gem.

"At the royal residence in Sym."

Harta stared blankly. "Why there?"

"Because of my brother, and her Symlander blood. Mila is not safe here and understands the situation. She is also aware of our plan."

"Share it with us," said Gem.

To break free from here and return to the Land of Zuku.

* * *

The next day, Alex happily proclaimed, "The stars are shining bright for us! Until this moment, we held out little hope."

"Stay mindful," Wen cautioned. "All activities, normal in every way. Organize in small groups. There cannot be the slightest hint of an exodus. We mustn't get ahead of ourselves and become careless."

* * *

At the compound, Burg said, "Your sister has returned"—he arched his wild eyebrow—"with the Symlander?"

"Just the primitives," Luke snarled.

"It seems your resentment festers?"

"I don't care for her *popularity*."

"Keep an eye on her." Burg nodded with a knowing smirk. "She is not only popular . . . but powerful."

"She is nothing beyond an inconvenience," Luke fumed and left the room.

"Nico!"

"Yes, Brightest Star?"

"Stay close to them both, and keep me informed."

* * *

Alex and Kain conducted small meetings along the waterfront. Although efforts were made not to attract attention, an enthused atmosphere prevailed.

Luke paced the floor and raged, "Something is going on. I can feel it!"

Wen desperately wanted to confide in her father but dared not. The thought of him being interrogated was unbearable.

She turned to the sound of the opening door.

"He is sleeping?" her brother asked.

"Yes, he still breathes," she curtly replied. "And another day passes with your star incomplete. I will never understand your hate. Is it truly your calling to be a tyrant?"

"Strong words from such a personable Tuz. I'd rather consider myself . . . an assertive leader."

"You are no leader."

Luke inhaled deeply. "You have no idea how my life changed, the day you arrived from the stars. My destiny was in perfect alignment. Yet no matter how promising my light appeared, it could never shine as bright as yours."

Wen's eyes acknowledged his pain. "It was never my intention to take anything away from you."

"Oh, dear sister, you will *never* take anything away from me . . . again!"

THE EXODUS

Wen asked, "We are on schedule?"

"We are," said Kain, "and with a measure of guilt."

"Where does this come from?"

"From those who cannot join us," he said softly. "So many . . . to be left behind."

"It has been difficult," Alex spoke up, her words also lacking strength. "This land is not as you remember. Our people deserve better."

Wen put her arms around their shoulders. "Listen to me, my friends. We leave in two days' time . . . and we are ready."

* * *

Sailing with the flotilla was Nord, and two of his loyal falcons. He felt at ease in the barge's wheelhouse.

Staring out at the horizon, the wizard flexed his fingers—an acquired habit, ever since Mila restored them. "See you tomorrow, Luke Star," he said with contempt.

In the original plan, Nord was to witness the exodus from the altar and coordinate the falcons from there. As the time grew near, he changed his mind. Isa fiercely opposed his decision.

Straining their relationship even more, he noticed the missing fury. Isa was questioned without mercy, until she reluctantly confessed.

* * *

Burg remarked to Nico, "The waterfront is very active."

"There was an unexpected delay in deliveries. Now we have twice as many barges to manage."

"Interesting, everyone on their best behavior. Go down and take a closer look. Report back to me with your findings."

"At once, Brightest Star!"

As his barge was being unloaded, Nord stayed out of sight, down below with the falcons and sardines.

* * *

At the waterfront, Wen greeted Luke at the door. "You have a message from Father?"

"The messenger does not," he dryly replied. "Simply checking in on the primitives. They are well?"

"The Zukus. That is why you are here? They are very well, and enjoying Tuz hospitality."

"As they should."

Wen's eyebrows narrowed. "Move along, brother, and harass elsewhere."

He laughed in her face. "For certain . . . I have much harassing to do!"

Standing on a nearby corner was Nico and two enforcers. The first officer watched with discomfort as Luke approached.

"My uncle, he sent you down here to investigate the workers, or me?"

"Both," Nico openly disclosed. "Do you have information I can report?"

Luke tilted his head to one side. "You are familiar with the baby Zuku?"

"I am."

"Extremely gifted, and already with words."

"So I have heard."

"Apparently, the little primitive demands a star."

"Luke, I—"

"On his hindquarter." He nodded. "Though he hasn't decided on which side."

"I believe it best to be silent."

"Understandable, First Officer. However, you must report *something* of interest to the Brightest Star?"

"I've been up and down the waterfront. Activity is abundant . . . but nothing illicit."

Nico could feel the heat from Luke's breath. "You will find something illicit!

Harta asked, "Where are you going?"

"Out to check on the first group," said Gem. "Let Wen know of my purpose. I won't be long."

After walking a short distance, he *felt* an unwanted presence.

"Where are you going, Zuku?" asked the voice with disturbing intentions. "You know the rule!"

"Nico?"

"First Officer Nico!"

"It was only to get fresh air, First Officer! I will go back now."

As he turned to leave, two enforcers rushed ahead and stopped his progress.

"Gem!" Nico shouted. "Why the rush?"

"Where did he go?" asked Wen.

"To check on the first group," said Harta.

Wen's thoughts were troubled. *A Zuku without an escort on the waterfront. Enforcers lurking in the shadows. Any excuse to create a problem . . . Luke.*

She ran up the stairs to speak with Alex and Kain.

"Wen, what is it?" asked Alex.

"It's Gem, and he's gone outside. If I don't return before it's time, load the groups without us."

"This is unexpected," said Kain with rattled nerves.

"Everything will work out," she calmly assured them.

* * *

Wen gave one knock on the solid door, waited two beats, and then knocked once more.

"Yes?" said the voice on the other side.

"Wen Star," she quietly announced.

The door was cautiously opened. "We were expecting the Zuku."

"He hasn't been here?"

"No. But we are prepared. Will you be our escort?"

"It's not yet time, and it won't be me. Wait for either Kain or Alex. Be vigilant . . . your freedom awaits."

Where have they taken him? Gem? Feel my presence.

"How much longer are you going to hold me here," questioned the frustrated Zuku. "My mate is expecting me. We have a new."

"Luke! The primitive is worried about his *MATE*."

Raucous laughter was heard from the other room.

Feel me, Gem.

Wen! I've been detained and tied to a chair. Your brother—

Gem's predicament was dire. *Think!* she demanded of herself. *There needs to be a distraction.*

Luke stormed into the room. "You are not going anywhere, Zuku!"

"You have no reason to keep me here."

"My sister is my every reason."

"You should be proud of her."

"Grr . . ." Luke growled, his face flush with anger. "Why is she even alive?" He stepped ever closer and glared. "Because your tribe had to save her! And now once again, she desecrates my star."

"That star you claim is a myth."

The Tuz lunged forward and struck the side of Gem's face, with the full force of his open hand.

The enforcers were accustomed to Luke's violence and normally would be left unfazed. This time, however, the sound of his strike was especially impressive . . . and they winced.

"Leave the Zuku alone in the dark!" ordered Luke as he left the building.

He mounted his horse and rode to a nearby tavern, for an evening of food and drinks. After getting his fill he would return to the compound.

Harta had been waiting near the door. "You are alone?"

"Yes," said Wen, "Gem has been taken."

"Where?"

"A warehouse, not far from here." She looked down at the expressionless Zuku. "I will free him."

* * *

"One more, Luke Star?" the barkeep asked.

"For my sister!"

Wen waited for the second *knock* before she answered. "Yes?"

"It's done."

She cracked the door open. "Go back and make ready."

Wen called everyone together. "The vessel has been secured. Alex, escort the first group. Kain, once you see the flames—"

"Flames?"

"Our distraction. When you see the flames, take the second group. I will secure the others with Gem."

Harta looked on, with Koal in her arms. "And us?"

"Go with Kain." She smiled reassuringly. "Soon we will all be together."

The first group reached the docks and boarded the Tuz vessel.

Nord caught the flare-up out of the corner of his eye. "Fire?" *Something isn't right.* "GO." He launched a falcon.

Nico came to an abrupt stop and knocked firmly on the door. "Brightest Star!"

Some moments passed before the door was opened. Burg had been awakened and appeared with squinted eyes. "What is it, First Officer?"

"A fire at the dry dock. Vessels are in flames."

Burg tightened his robe and went to the balcony. In the distance was a red glow. Smoke, carried by an onshore breeze, settled above the compound. He stared up and saw the shadow.

The falcon streaked downward, piercing through the haze. In an instant, her razor-sharp talons flashed open.

"My eyes!" Burg screamed. "My EYES."

One of his eyes was completely ripped out.

Echoes of anguish and the raptor's screech startled the compound awake.

Down at the harbor Nord cursed the Brightest Star. "Live forever in darkness."

Blood spewed through Burg's quivering fingers. "What has happened? Nico—" He sobbed.

Only then did the first officer break free from the shock.

A group of enforcers swarmed in.

"Summon the physician!"

* * *

At the waterfront, Gem's senses were overloaded by chaotic sounds and the smell of smoke.

Wen arrived at the warehouse, supported by six Tuz and blades.

"Wen Star?" said the surprised enforcer. "Your brother is not—"

After a brief skirmish, the latch moved and the door opened.

"Wen!"

She rushed over to Gem and untied him from the chair. "The final groups are waiting."

"My family?"

"They are safe."

Luke arrived at the compound and slid down from his horse.

Nico came running out. "We must return to the harbor!"

"What has happened?"

"The Brightest Star, he's been severely injured. Dark magic has descended on this night."

The falcon returned to the harbor and circled high above.

Wait, directed the wizard.

The final group approached the barge. "Nord?" Wen called out. "You are here, and with a falcon no less?"

"I brought two," he said with a nod. "And how could I not be here?

"Blessings for your presence."

"What about this fire?"

"The vessels do burn well." She blinked.

The last of the Tuz boarded the barge. "Oars down!" shouted Nord. Luke, Nico, and a band of enforcers reached the docks at daybreak.

"We have to stop them!" Luke screamed out.

"That last one there," said Nico, pointing at the barge.

"My sister and . . . Nord! Take the cutter and bring them back."

"What now?" Wen asked.

Nord looked past the approaching vessel to a solitary Tuz on the dock. *Now*, he commanded the falcon.

Luke's body swayed from side to side, contemplating his sister's demise. (Nord's fate had been decided, beheaded on an executioner's block.) A high-pitched screech interrupted his gruesome thoughts. The falcon released something from its talons. Luke recoiled when it struck the plank, six paces from where he stood. It made an odd, sickening sound.

Some kind of fish? He walked over and bent down. "What is this?"

The glob was now discernable. A patch of short, coarse hairs and an eyeball. Luke's knees instantly buckled. His arms folded tight, and he violently convulsed.

"No, no, no," he repeated in denial.

The last barge was struggling to leave the harbor, and Nico was closing in.

"Stop them," Luke pleaded in a fractured voice.

"They are gaining on us," said Wen with uncertainty.

"So they are."

Nord opened the compartment where the second falcon emerged.

"What will happen next?" she asked.

"Wizardry."

He took the bundle of fury and tied it to the raptor's ankle.

"What is this?" said Nico, fixated on the approaching bird.

The falcon's tight circles captivated the crew, and disrupted the cadence of their oars. Then came the painful screeches, compelling them to cover their ears.

NOW.

The falcon glided down to the stalled vessel's waterline and then ripped the pouch open with its strong hooked beak. The volatile crystals created a caustic potion, that ate away at the hull. The cutter began to list.

"What is happening?" shouted Nico.

"We are taking on water!" an enforcer shouted back.

The stunned first officer looked over the side. *How can this be?*

"Abandon the vessel!" yelled another enforcer.

One by one, they jumped into the boiling fury. Sounds of their suffering could be heard on the docks, where Luke Star knelt on a sun-bleached plank, weighed down by misery. He raised his haggard face and watched in disbelief. The cutter was moments from slipping away. One loyal Tuz was all that remained, holding on to the mast in futile desperation. One familiar voice cried out for help, never to be heard from again.

Goodbye, Nico.

Luke returned to the compound, and immediately went to his uncle. He found him bandaged and heavily sedated. His injuries were grievous but not life threatening. Of primary concern was his sanity.

*   *   *

Mila sang her way up the mast. "Soon . . . I will have a new brother. Soon . . . I will have a new brother."

"She's up there." Gem chuckled as he *felt* she was near.

"Of course she is," said Harta, with Koal bundled to her chest.

Isa smiled with great relief, as Nord walked into the study. "You are safe." She rushed into his arms.

"Father! said Elgin, begging to be heard, "I was also waiting."

"Good to be home, *everyone.* But for now, I must go to the altar."

Isa sighed. "And you only just arrived."

"It's Luke, and I've had a premonition. I will share more once I find him."

Even though the youngest falcon lacked experience, Nord sent her anyway. Her speed and endurance were unmatched. She was routed along the coastline. He held out hope, the Tuz would not be sighted.

LUKE'S REVENGE

Luke intended to eliminate the wizard, and any Symlander in his way. He handpicked the most ruthless enforcers and commanded the swiftest vessel. They would drop anchor south of the Dark Forest. Once on land, the village could be reached in less than a day.

Nord stood over the altar and watched closely. *Perhaps he never left.* That thought was shattered when a vessel came into view, skimming along under a full sail, with something unusual on its bow. The falcon swooped down for a better look.

Could Luke be so mad? The head of his father.

The deck became a flurry of activity. One enforcer pointed at the falcon. Two others moved a weapon into place.

Return! Nord implored. But by then, it was too late. Lead shots were slung into the air.

The window become unsteady. Water was spinning and rising up.

"RETURN," he shouted helplessly.

A moment before impact, the window stabilized. The vessel returned to view, becoming smaller . . . and smaller. The falcon had recovered yet was flying at half her normal speed.

"She's been hurt." He sighed.

Disturbed by the commotion, Isa rushed to the center. Nord was in the corner, slumped over in a chair.

"Luke suffers from a vengeful rage," he muttered with little energy.

"What are you saying?"

He stood up and faced her. "Luke is on his way here with a band of enforcers, intent to silence us all. With me, his greatest prize. You and the others must go to Sym. They will not follow you there."

"You are coming with us!" she insisted.

The wizard's eyes were distant. "No . . . this is my fight."

"Nord—"

"Load the largest wagon, as if never to return. Include the altar . . . my father's legacy, its value beyond compare. Trust me, Isa."

"You have earned my trust, many times over."

"All is not lost," he assured her. Luke's incursion has been exposed. I will lie in wait, and cut the head off that snake."

"What about Tulare?" she reminded him. The child had been staying at the lodge, while her parents gathered mushrooms.

"When can we expect Mona and Jared?"

Isa's face reflected the answer.

"Take her with you."

He went to the altar and peered through its window. Blades of soft grass on a rolling hilltop was the falcon's final resting place.

A teardrop rippled the water. *She was courageous to the end.*

He sent her brother to retrieve the amulet and see her one last time.

* * *

"I believe we have everything," Isa said with a shortness of breath.

"Not everything." Nord handed her the amulet.

She looked at him with resilient eyes. "Slay that snake for us."

"See you soon"—he smiled—"and we will sail to Montro."

She smiled warmly in return as together they envisioned this pleasant thought.

* * *

Ten villagers were all that stayed behind, most of them original settlers, firm in their ways. Nord tried persuading them to leave, but they refused—no matter the cost.

The final holdout found a seat in the study, and Nord took the floor. "We can expect the intruders in two days' time, most likely arriving at dusk. Their numbers are greater, weapons more advanced. A leader . . . intently cruel."

"I'm not afraid!" shouted Shia.

Nord raised his hands to calm the room. "I honor your bravery. Despite our challenges, we do have an advantage. Their surprise is not as intended. However, time is a factor, and we must hurry our defenses."

"This is our village!" shouted another.

Nord cleared his throat. "Listen to me closely, Symlanders. Herd the livestock to high pasture. Take the items that you most value, and store them in Relics Cave. Keep the stoves lit in your dwellings."

"Why all of this?" asked Trundle.

"Because of the damage."

The room fell silent.

Shia spoke up, "What is our plan, Wizard Nord?"

"The falcons will warn us when the intruders are sighted. Two of you, welcome them with your spears. This encounter will provide clarity—their intent and our resolve. Four more of you, reveal your presence and then rush back to the lodge. By all appearances, everyone has sought refuge here."

Nord's lodge was the best strategic option, overlooking the village and surrounded by rough terrain. Sixty paces down from the front door would be their first line of defense. Clumps of dried leaves with a pinch of fury were arranged in a crescent shape, with a trail of lamp oil between them and fresh pine needles to mask the scent.

"Finally," Nord continued, "we require two brave fire starters. Their purpose is critical to our success, well blended and high up in the trees . . . patiently waiting. Once the spears take flight, they'll drop to ignite the oil, creating the toxic smoke."

"What will happen to us?" voices and mummers wanted to know.

"We will be protected," the wizard assured them.

Nord had filled a bucket with a special potion. In it soaked face masks, fashioned from cotton rags and strips of leather.

* * *

Two days passed.

The intruders had reached the Red Road.

The lead enforcer asked, "Over there is the village? Where the smoke rises above that hill."

"Yes, Renic." Luke gruffly chuckled. "It must be close to supper. Set the table, Nord . . . we won't be long."

"Take this, Wizard Nord." An old-timer handed him a leather sheath. "It's one of my favorites." He cackled with sparkling eyes.

Nord withdrew the knife and respected its qualities.

"I've managed a clean edge here," said another, twisting the blade back and forth, projecting the reflection of the sun's dwindling rays.

"Listen!" Nord silenced the room. "Our warning. Everyone, take a mask and go down to the lodge, except for you two." He placed a hand on each shoulder. "Be silent and strong. Now, up into the trees."

"Luke, the falcons!" said Renic, anxiously looking up.

"As all of the forest has heard," he dryly remarked. "Instruct the men to increase their pace."

As Renic issued the order, a spear landed in front of the group. Luke raised his hand to stop the advance and stepped forward to pick it up. He scrutinized the hardwood, from the shaft to the tip, resting its center on two fingers, gauging the balance.

"Perfect," he said softly.

A second spear sliced through the air and achieved its objective. The scarlet tip was visible to those in the rear.

Luke turned to Renic with an expressionless face. "Their spears are well made."

"Over there!" shouted one of the enforcers. Several Symlanders had appeared on the distant rise, standing tall with shimmering white hair.

Not timid, these villagers, Luke said to himself, *or another deception? What more magic do you have for us . . . Wizard?*

Nord asked the returning holdouts, "How was the greeting?"

"Meaningful," Trundle replied. "The range finder caught their attention. The strike . . . welcomed them to our forest."

"Well done, Symlanders! Prepare for battle."

Mona and Jared entered the village, each with a pull cart of mushrooms.

"So silent," said Mona, "and no one to be seen?"

A sudden uneasiness came over them.

"Tulare!" Jared blurted out.

144

They dropped their carts and started for the lodge.

"Wait." Jared lifted his hand and listened to the distant marching. He followed the sound to a clearing.

"Jared, what do you see?"

Tuz with weapons. He answered to himself.

"TAKE HIM," Luke commanded.

"Run, Mona!"

She stood there unable to move, until Jared spun her around. They ran from the enforcers as fast as they could.

"Spare them?" asked Renic.

* * *

The intruders lined up below the lodge, as the village smoldered behind them.

Luke shouted, "It's good to be back in the Dark Forest! You haven't been expecting us . . . have you, Wizard?"

"No one speak out," Nord quietly reminded them.

"There were two of your villagers who were not!"

A chorus of obnoxious laughter traveled up the hill.

Mona and Jared. Nord thought the worst.

Two enforcers stepped forward in the fading light, both with a Symlander spear. Posted on each tip was an anguished blue-eyed face.

It took immense self-control for Nord to harness his anger. "Do not forget this," he said between his teeth.

Ever suspicious of Nord's magic while most of the enforcers proceeded up the path, Luke stepped into the tree line and waited.

"Not until they are in range," cautioned the wizard. "Steady." Slowly he raised his hand. "Now!"

Spears were thrown in quick succession. Eight enforcers were hit, five mortally wounded. Up in the trees, the fire starters came down.

Waiting below one of them was Luke. "Did your plan include this?" He ripped the mask off the surprised face and then slit his throat.

"FIRE," Renic shouted.

Shia had been successful, but the other side was dark. She went there to supply a spark, only by chance avoiding Luke.

Ensnared by the poisonous smoke, the enforcers gagged and choked, one by one falling to the ground and struggling for air.

"Poison," was Renic's last word.

Luke tore his mask into pieces, giving them to the enforcers who survived. "Hold the cloth tightly to your nose. Do not breathe through your mouth!"

Nord took notice of the shadowy figures, finding their way up the hill.

"Follow me and grip your knives." He led everyone to the center.

The fury dissipated, and the air was safe to breathe.

The enforcers split up and surrounded the building. Sneaking up from behind was Shia, who struck out with her blade. She dismissed one enforcer and then engaged another. Two old-timers joined the fight. The intruders had lost their advantage.

"NORD," Luke shouted from the top of his lungs. "Where are you?"

"I am here!"

"Fight me alone! What are you without your magic?"

"A SYMLANDER," he thundered.

The wizard stood tall on top of the center, an anxious dagger at his side. He leaped down and, in one smooth motion, thrust the blade deep into Luke's gut.

The remaining enforcers unconsciously released their weapons. Motionless, they watched their leader bleed out.

"Take him," Nord demanded, "before the falcons have their way."

Demoralized and defeated, they lifted the body and left.

The wizard said, "Symlanders, come close to me." They came together in a tight circle. "We claim this victory for those no longer with us."

He looked up at the stars and silently prayed. *Peace for you . . . Solanze.*

* * *

Soon after Luke's failed incursion, the Crescent Coast Alliance was formed. It was a partnership between the Lands of Sym and Cantor.

Their first action was severing relations with the mortal stars of Tuz. The land's further isolation sowed seeds for a future rebellion.

Nord, with his victory over Luke now legendary, was formally titled a wizard.

CHAPTER 9
LAND OF RIVERA

Mila was halfway up the mast before Harta discovered her goal. "Climb back down here, now! And hand over your brother."

"Another time!" Gem chimed in with a burst of laughter.

Mila (reluctantly) placed Koal into her mother's outstretched arms.

Not far below Zuku Cove, the scout vessel waited—sailing ahead at Nord's request, in search of a favorable landing. The flotilla was led around the point, and into the Northern Sound. Across the mainland was an island harbor, where they anchored for the night. Early the next morning, one by one, they were escorted across the strait, secured to a seawall, and then off-loaded onto a windswept beach.

The Zukus were on migration, and the encampment deserted. Gem, Wen, Alex, and Kain managed the Tuz resettlement. Temporary living space was constructed, and the existing facilities improved. A permanent solution would happen later.

The general mood was festive, and a holiday declared. Once the initial work was complete, they would celebrate Freedom Day.

* * *

Before stepping up on the platform, Wen was reminded of Igua.

Though they struggled with shared feelings for Ram, their admiration for each other was clear.

"Blessings!" she proclaimed in a joyful voice.

"Blessings!" the small group of Zukus responded.

149

Wen urged her people a second time, with a brighter smile and wide-open arms. "Blessings!"

"BLESSINGS," the Tuz found their voice.

"We are all equal under the stars. *Stars* that reside above us and no longer among us. I renounce the stars that stain my body. My name is only WEN. Today, we celebrate our freedom . . . as one!"

The power of fellowship resonated throughout the encampment. Wen stepped down and immersed herself in the revelry.

SYM

Sir Hemeth's feelings were mixed. He felt privileged to be a member of the academy's first class, yet was troubled leaving Rachel behind. But without a serious commitment, they had agreed to go their separate ways.

He said, "I've made a decision."

"And?"

"Before leaving for Montro, we will formalize our relationship."

"Sir Hemeth," said Rachel with an eyebrow raised, "this is *your* final decision?"

"Yes," he foolishly stammered. "My . . . decision . . . for you to consider."

"I don't think we have the time, do we? That is—if I accept, and of course I will, and Hemeth . . . I do!"

"Wizard Nord! Wizard Nord! Rachel said yes!" Hemeth had fore-warned the wizard of his impending proposal and asked that he stay nearby.

Nord dramatically entered the room and feigned surprise. "Is it true what I —"

"YES," they shouted together.

"Well then . . . we must prepare the documents."

* * *

Nord and his family followed Hemeth to Montro, bringing with them the altar and falcons. He accepted a position on the academy's staff. Wizardry would take root on the island—and flourish.

LAND OF CANTOR

A place of seemingly endless opportunity, the Land of Cantor was experiencing a level of discord, unprecedented in its long and storied history. The youth from both royal families were bored and restless. Their once-resilient bloodlines had been diluted. Most of the desired positions were unobtainable. Only mundane openings existed, no better than where a commoner once began. For a lifetime, or so it appeared, they would be seated at the back of the room. One exasperated royal would have none of it!

Prince Gorsh was among those with a meaningless title. However, he was different from the rest. His strong presence and convincing words were those of a leader. He was also an opportunist with high aspirations.

"The way things are going, we'll be lucky to get on with *waste and cleanliness*," Prince Gorsh bemoaned. "Perhaps for you, little brother, this would suffice?" He paused and massaged his stubbled chin.

"What are you thinking?" asked Ivan.

"The Land of Tuz is ripe for an overthrow. I could be their king, and Ladesa their queen."

"Yes! Their sightless star has gone mad. Economy in shambles. You would be their savior."

Gorsh scoffed with amusement. "Who would ever want to rule a Tuz? At least those remaining in that decrepit land."

"Tell me again about the exodus."

"They simply vanished . . . out on the open sea."

"It was just like that, wasn't it?"

"With the help of Symlanders."

"Symlanders," Ivan repeated with disgust.

Gorsh was only warming up, and his impressionable brother enjoyed nothing more than his generous tirades.

"Remember this"—he raised a finger and held it straight—"always take caution with the Symlander."

"Always!"

Gorsh began to circled the room. "Evidence of wizardry and those obscene blue eyes. Confusing creatures they are. Never to be trusted."

"Unless shackled!"

An idea struck him, and Gorsh suddenly stood still. *It could be in our best interest, seeking out one of those blue-eyed*— His lips curled into a devious grin.

"What are you thinking now?" asked Ivan.

"The Cantors"—he shook his head—"custodians of our land."

"It hasn't been fair."

"No, it hasn't," said Gorsh. "But we do have good relations."

"Ladesa's brother—"

"Roland . . . a mature and honorable man, with stature far greater than our own. We've talked at length and agree on many things—controlling one's destiny, shaping history. However, to this day, I disagree with his choice of partners."

"A Symlander!" Ivan spat out.

Ten years had passed since Nord connected Roland and Jennifer. They had been years of joy and brought the birth of a son. Life for them was good in Cantor. Although the prince did confide in Gorsh. If the right opportunity availed itself, he would seriously consider it.

"One day for certain you will have your kingdom," said Ivan.

"And on that day, my brother, I will bestow upon you a prestigious title."

"You have always been good to me."

Gorsh walked over and gave his brother a generous hug. "Your loyalty is my treasure."

LAND OF ZUKU

They stood overlooking the encampment.

Gem shook his head in amazement. "What do you make of all this, Harta?"

"A wonder to my eyes."

There were twice as many dwellings, more land turned over for a variety of crops, additional livestock grazing, and Tuz in all shapes and sizes.

He turned to her with a soft smile. "The tribe will be here soon."

"And we have a youngling to present."

They pressed their foreheads gently together.

* * *

She was the fair Zuku, the odd one, with her crystal-blue eyes, unruly white hair, and wizard blood. After the tribe's return, Mila's uniqueness would stand out as before. She never questioned her acceptance yet at times felt alone. Unlike when she stayed in Sym, where she hoped to go back one day.

Mila excelled at almost everything she tried; guiding a horse was no different. Riding with her father, was a highlight to her day. He was taught from one of the best, and enjoyed passing down his knowledge.

As was her habit of late, she rode to the outskirts of the encampment. In the distance was an undulating horizon.

She encouraged her spirited horse. "Let's go!"

Sensing it was Mila, they galloped ahead of the tribe.

"Look at her ride!" Ram enthusiastically shouted. "She'll be a champion for sure."

Igua was equally proud of the special Zuku. She had missed her and the others very much. The wait was over—they were home.

"Mila!" Ram called out.

"It's Me!"

The horses converged and broke together, creating a cloud of dust. The ecstatic riders dropped to the ground and wrapped their arms around each other.

"She's looking down at us," said Igua.

"And her clothes," Ram remarked.

"Yes! We all have new and colorful clothes." Her eyes were wide open and sparkling. "There is so much more to share. But for now, I have something that cannot wait."

"Tell us that *something*," Igua smiled in anticipation.

"The encampment has changed."

"How so?" asked Ram.

"We returned with five large vessels, three with passengers and two with supplies. We had to make room."

In that moment, her presence was undeniable.

"Wen," Ram said softly.

"Yes!" Mila confirmed. "It was Wen's courage responsible for our safe journey." *Along with Wizard Nord*, she kept to herself.

"I will thank her at my first opportunity," said Igua.

Ram's feelings were torn. His partnership with Igua was natural, yet he also harbored a longing for Wen.

"Look who's here," Igua happily announced.

"Sym!" Mila knelt down and they rubbed noses. "I've missed you."

"He's also missed you." Ram nodded.

The warkin's canines were exposed and impressive, his silver coat lustrous.

"Oh, Sym," she chided the beast. "How you have grown up without me."

"Let Gem know we are here," said Ram.

"Lead the way, Sym. The Tuz are in for a surprise."

The warkin barked and bounded off.

They raced to the encampment and Mila swung down from her horse. "Father . . . the tribe!"

"Sym," Gem blurted out, after a second glance.

"Impressive, isn't he?"

"Very."

She gave his head a good scratch.

"Go to your mother, and I will tell Wen."

Wen spoke up before Gem could say a word. "They've returned."

"Yes," he replied, while she stared off into the distance. "Wen?"

"You asked, on the *Unity*, what I missed the most about my homeland."

"I did, but—"

"Everything is my answer. Because everything . . . was not as I remembered."

"This is where you belong."

She softly smiled. "Join your family, and I will organize my people."

* * *

Ram and Igua walked their horses into the encampment.

"Welcome back," said Wen with a blink.

They dropped to the ground and exchanged meaningful hugs.

"Welcome back to you," Ram said with an easy smile.

"Thank you for providing our family safe travel," added Igua. "Mila spoke of your courage."

The Tuz smiled broadly. "It was Mila the fearless one."

"And your father?" asked Ram.

"A blessing for our time together, before his passing."

Igua reached over and held her hand. "Oh, Wen . . . I am sorry."

"He must have found peace to see you again," said Ram.

"Yes—"

Wen's eyes began to brighten, and the Zukus followed them to where she was looking. Harta was carrying a sling.

"Koal!" they both called out, having *felt* his name.

Ram gazed down at the new with deep affection. "Welcome to our tribe, little Zuku."

"This is a most special day," Igua proclaimed. "Let us celebrate!"

Later that evening at Zuku House, Alex and Kain were introduced to leadership. Tradition was set aside, and shillig was served. Many toasts were made. Wen summarized the journey in passionate detail, the perils they faced, their triumphant exodus. They raised their cups to Wizard Nord and his valiant Mystic falcons.

Wen, Alex, and Kain took seats on the council, providing a voice for the Tuz.

155

* * *

Mila and Sym got an early start. They would spend the day at Sandbar Beach, where the open sea entered the sound. The scenery was rich, and wildlife abundant. Trails leading up to an overlook afforded panoramic views.

"Over there in the harbor," said Mila. *What vessel is that?*

Cautiously, she rode back down and got off her horse.

"Footprints," she whispered, peering through the natural blind. *See what you can find.*

With his sensitive snout slightly above the sand, Sym traversed the expansive beach to the waterline. Ears peaked and sitting up tall, he stared across the strait. They were alone. She walked over and joined him, and watched as the sails were set.

"Who are they, and what were they doing here?" she asked her silver warkin.

Sym pawed in the wet sand and cocked his head to one side.

"We have to leave . . . now!"

Mila communicated with a seriousness, her companion was not familiar.

LAND OF CANTOR

Prince Gorsh stomped his feet and berated the young operative. "I don't care so much its tranquility, or the uniqueness of the Zuku!" He lashed out with growing frustration. "This land is not for holidays, when the seasons turn to dark."

"Understood, my prince. If I could—"

"You were contracted because of your knowledge of this place, having sailed there with the Tuz. The only Symlander, if I'm not mistaken, lacking allegiance to Nord. Your services came with a price of course—gold!" He took a deep breath. "Your payment, contingent upon my satisfaction. Are you capable?"

"I am."

Gorsh folded his arms, and deadlocked his eyes with the Symlander's. "You have my full attention."

The operative started over, and provided the particulars he demanded. Much of her information had been obtained from an insider.

She befriended Herk as they traveled in the flotilla. The young Tuz was disillusioned and vulnerable. He spoke of the many disappointments in his life and lack of status. When they met that second time, he supplied a detailed understanding of the tribes, including what mattered most—their ability to defend themselves.

"This information will serve us well." Gorsh complimented the operative. "Your contact, the Tuz . . . you are positive he will not turn?"

"Positive, my prince. Herk looks forward to a position within your kingdom."

"Say that again, Symlander, the very last part . . . and slowly. I enjoyed the sound of it."

"Your . . . kingdom."

He smiled with contentment, and opened his eyes. "Herk will be provided a very important position. Supervisor of the royal couriers. A substantial upgrade from the stable work he's accustomed to."

"Herk will be most grateful, my prince."

Gorsh took a purse from his pocket. "Your payment."

The operative humbly accepted the gold, with a hesitant look on her face.

"There is something else?"

"Yes, my prince. At the moment our sails were set, a young Symlander was sighted across the strait."

"A Symlander?"

"She lives among the tribes . . . with a silver warkin."

"On your way," he abruptly dismissed her.

The prince walked down the hallway with fresh ideas and depraved thoughts.

"You are satisfied?" asked Ladesa.

"Yes," Gorsh replied. "The information is useful."

"This is good to know."

"A few more years of preparation . . . time for them to forget."

"What?"

"An unexpected Symlander witnessed our vessel. Their leaders, no doubt informed. I am not so concerned as to lose any sleep."

She shook her head and smiled. "Our newborn is responsible for that."

He looked at her with gratitude. "A son, to follow his father as king . . . King Nathan!"

"To follow his mother," she teased. "After all, he does have my nose."

"An unfortunate blemish that should correct itself over time."

Heavily influenced by the culture he grew up in, Prince Gorsh epitomized the superior male.

Ladesa, however, was merely an extension of him. Her extreme confidence and competitive nature mirrored his.

During Three Years of Time

The Tuz established their village less than a half day's ride north of the Western Encampment, located next to a large lake and nearby Coastal Jungle. On a clear day from the rolling hilltop, you could make out Zuku Cove.

While the tribe was away, the Tuz watched over their encampment, managing the livestock and turning over the fields.

Mila migrated the first two years and, as Gem predicted, became a champion. She led a team that second year, harvesting eight Lackland elk during an early round. Only Ram had accomplished such a feat, a long time ago.

"You're making me look bad," Gem scolded her in a playful way. "How does it appear to the others? Their leader, unable to match the youngest rider's tally."

Maybe with extra practice?

He laughed out loud. "Maybe!"

Once Koal took his first steps, Mila was often by his side. Curious, she searched his developing *truth*. His abilities impressed her. She came up with a memory game, and Koal did very well, yet not always perfect.

If forgetful, he developed a predictable response. It began by closing his eyes, then slowly opening them as wide as he could, while at the same time extending his tongue and pursing his lips around it. He held that *face* for as long as he could until losing out to laughter.

With the blessings of her parents, Mila did not migrate that third year, instead choosing to stay with the Tuz and live with Wen. Because of his value, Sym remained with the tribe.

Gem looked with care into his daughter's eyes. "You will not miss the hunt?"

"You know."

The question was a mere formality, as Mila's *truth* was clear. The hunt would be missed, but more so her family and Sym. She purely desired a change.

Something new. Gem privately understood.

Mila said to her mother. "Father knows—I will miss you both!"

"The time will pass." Harta smiled with a nod. "Before we leave, your father and I have treasures."

Mila's face lit up. "Treasures?"

Gem handed her a black oak box, smoothly finished, with a fine ribbon grain.

"This is well made."

"Look inside."

She lifted the lid and shrieked, "Rose pearls!"

Inside the box was a collection of matching necklaces. On each cord of supple leather hung a rare soft-pink pearl.

"Yes!" Harta exclaimed. "Your father searched endlessly for the perfect set, a reminder for our family . . . we are always together."

"They are beautiful and beyond special, I will cherish mine—"

"Mila?"

"There are five?"

"The largest one for the warkin," Gem blurted out. "We couldn't forget Sym."

* * *

During that third year, Kain and Alex welcomed their first child.

"Wen! The new is here. The new is here!"

Not surprisingly, Mila assisted with Dorin's arrival.

LAND OF CANTOR

"Prince Gorsh is at the door!"

"Rivera! Rivera!" his brother initiated the chant.

The charismatic royal strode to the center of the room.

"RIVERA. RIVERA."

Stepping onto the small platform, he smiled broadly and encouraged the demonstration. Then slowly he raised his hands and quieted the group.

He acknowledged his followers with determined eyes. "Rivera is the land of promise, and our mission continues on course."

"RIVERA. RIVERA."

He raised his hands once more. "We cannot take what is theirs without a fight. Our soldiers are restless, and hunger for battle."

"When do they sail?" shouted a voice in the crowd.

"During the season of change!"

"RIVERA. RIVERA."

LAND OF ZUKU AND TUZ

Mila rode to the outskirts of the encampment. Threading her way through the caravan, she saw Gem in the distance. He was sitting up tall and trotting toward her, with Koal tucked between his legs and holding the reins. The little Zuku wore a big grin, guiding the horse with flair.

"Who is the champion now!" he triumphantly screamed.

The two horses converged, and Mila dropped to the ground. Gem lowered Koal to her waiting arms.

"I can still carry you, dear champion."

"Put me down!" he demanded.

Gem slid off his horse and gave Mila an overdue hug. "It wasn't the same without you."

"The harvest?" she asked.

He looked into her unsettled eyes and smiled reassuringly. "Your numbers were not surpassed . . . if that was on your mind?" Not even close. But we did well, and blessings for that."

"How is Mother?"

"You are the keeper of her emotions. She felt an emptiness with you not there."

Mila's connection with Harta was deeply personal, and she longed to hold her tight.

"She's in a wagon with Rono, not so far behind. Surprise her."

"I'll go there now!"

On her way, she greeted Ram and Igua. They appeared happier than ever.

They were happy, and relishing their open partnership. It was, for them, as if they had always been together.

Three wagons farther back, there she was.

Harta instinctively stood up, and almost lost her balance. "Mila!"

They rushed into each other's arms and hugged for the longest time.

* * *

The tribes coexisted with little difficulty. Wen often serving as a bridge between the two. She understood their uniqueness, and similarities. A joint committee was formed, and she became its leader.

Tuz were welcome at all Zuku festivals. The Festival of Family was the largest yet, both tribes producing many offspring.

Mila and Koal arrived together.

"Follow me," the young Zuku insisted.

"As you wish, my leader," she complied with veiled amusement.

"You know, Mila . . . I can *feel* your insincerity." He made a face with wide-open eyes and a tongue stuck out as far as it would go.

"Some things never change, do they, little brother?" Mila laughed into the cool night air. "Let's find Dorin."

"But she can't do anything!"

161

"She doesn't have to—so precious."

"Only for a little while," he relented. "There are games I want to try."

Ram and Igua sat on a familiar bench, overlooking the festivities.

"Unimaginable, isn't it?" he said.

Igua smiled and turned to him. "You and me . . . up here on this old bench?"

He softly chuckled. "This encampment, our way of life. Forever changed, it seems—overnight. Could you have imagined that?"

"What has changed is my perspective . . . on everything. It's opened my understanding. Before Mila and Wen, I was purposeful to a fault, my true self abandoned."

"For the greater good of the tribe." He nodded.

"Yes, for our tribe, most of whom, are not *moved* one way or the other. But I felt obligated to make up the difference, carrying emotional burdens that never existed."

"You continue to make a remarkable difference, in their lives and in mine." He leaned forward and tenderly pressed his lips against hers.

FESTIVAL OF BLESSINGS

Standing on the platform were Ram, Igua, Gem, Wen, Stala, Alex, and Kain.

"Blessings!" Ram powerfully greeted the tribes.

"BLESSINGS."

"We are grateful for this generous land, and ever mindful of the Great Deep Sky."

Wen raised her arms and looked up. "Where the stars shine bright for us all!"

Before taking a turn, Igua flashed her distinctive smile. "Soon we begin our migration, a Zuku tradition since memory. For most of us, this will be our last."

She paused for the murmurs to settle.

"No longer returning to find changes made by the Tuz."

The commons remained indifferent.

She glanced over at Gem and he sympathetically shrugged his shoulders.

Commander Nader leaned against the vessel's railing, staring stoically across the strait. The young soldier, studying his moonlit profile, searched for clues to his thoughts.

"You see that distant glow?"

"Yes, Commander. The encampment is very active tonight."

"The primitives celebrate their blessings," he remarked with a seductive chill. "Let them enjoy. We will celebrate ours—soon enough."

The soldier was inquisitive yet hesitant to speak. "Commander."

"Yes, soldier, and your name?"

"If possible—"

"Your name?"

"Rork, Commander. My name is Rork."

"Go on."

He cleared his throat. "I am interested to know the qualifications of a commander."

Nader's eyebrows twisted and his forehead furrowed. "My answer is straightforward, Rork. With every effort, I am fully committed. It has been that way my entire life. I am trustworthy and allegiant without compromise. These attributes supported my advancement."

Rork was left in silence, captivated by the words and cadence. To his ears, transformative poetry. He absorbed it all and would follow him—to the end.

The reconnaissance soldier reported back. "We have our answer from Herk."

"Go on," said the commander.

"The Zukus leave in two days' time."

THE LAST MIGRATION

Igua and Wen were at the encampment, taking a final walk-through.

"How wonderful it has been," Wen warmly reflected.

"Agreed," said Igua. "And once we return, I look forward to every season here."

Gem walked up on the conversation. "Everything in order?"

"All in order," said Wen. "And Gem."

"Yes?"

"Do remember us?" She blinked.

"Of course!" He laughed. "We have Mila—your elk is guaranteed."

* * *

Herk lit the torches and anxiously waited. He brought four horses and flasks of fresh water, all that was required. His day had been filled with uneasy moments, time spent debating the invasion, pondering the extent of those who would suffer, the depth of his regret.

Prince Ivan joined the departing soldiers.

"Good fortune!" barked the commander.

"Oars down!" instructed First Officer Beanlin.

The sleek vessels skimmed along the water and through the patchy fog. They would reach Sandbar Beach at daybreak.

"Herk!" Beanlin called out for a second time.

The Tuz nervously stepped away from the overgrowth and onto the beach.

"Everything according to plan?" asked the skeptical officer.

"I believe so," he quietly replied.

Beanlin reached over and gave him a firm pat on the shoulder. "You have a simple task. Rest your thoughts."

Herk stared blankly across the strait.

"Keep together and stay alert!" ordered the officer.

Ivan and Beanlin rode side by side, behind the marching soldiers.

"The insider," observed the prince," he does not appear well."

Beanlin focused on the distant Tuz, leading the way on horseback. "No . . . not well."

The soldiers made camp in a wooded area, not far from their destination.

"Prepare your weapons. Then eat and rest," said Beanlin. "We move out under darkness."

* * *

At the Western Encampment, the Tuz shouted, "Who's there?"

"It's me, Herk!"

"Herk? What are you doing down here at this time of night?"

Without an answer he sat stiffly on his horse, warm blood rushing to his head.

"Herk?"

Run. Just as he thought to warn her, Rivera bolts streaked through the air. The Tuz was struck and rocked backward, guidance feathers protruding from her forehead. Herk twisted sideways and then fell to the ground, a glistening bolt six paces beyond his tremoring body.

"Change of plans," said Beanlin.

The soldiers moved in and executed the operation. All Tuz were eliminated, fifteen by bolt, five by blade, and one by a snap of the neck. The casualties were thrown into an open pit and buried without ceremony. A soldier returned to Sandbar Beach and went to the water's edge. He launched a fire-tipped bolt high into the sky.

Nader whispered, "It's over."

Early the next morning, the commander was ferried across the strait.

"That's a fine-looking horse."

"Yes, Commander," the escort replied, "the finest in their stable. We'll arrive by midday."

* * *

At the occupied encampment, Nader appraised the area with a discerning eye. "So here we are, the Kingdom of Rivera."

Beanlin pointed to the top of the rise. "We are situated up there."

"Zuku House," the commander presumed.

"In all its glory," Prince Ivan confirmed.

"Where is the insider?"

"He did not make it."

"Unfortunate." Nader's eyes continued to explore.

* * *

"We've heard nothing for two days," reported the messenger.

"Send someone down," said Wen.

She seldom visited the encampment, while the Zukus were away.

Mila rode up to the wagon with urgency. "I have to go back!"

"Go back?" said Harta.

"Sym's family pearl . . . I took it off to clean, and with everything else—I know exactly where it is."

"The pearl will be there when we return. Sym will not miss it."

"But I will, Mother . . . for two long seasons." She looked at Harta with sorrowful eyes.

"If something were to happen—"

"What could happen? I'll be with Sym. Let us go . . . now?"

"Take provisions and leave without delay. I will tell your father, if he hasn't felt it already."

Two days passed.

Wen asked, "Still no word?"

"Nothing," reported the messenger.

"Then, I will go there myself, with caution and spears."

She took five experienced hunters and stayed off the familiar road.

A wave of Rivera vessels had reached the Black Oak Bluffs.

Prince Gorsh stood on the bow and admired the billowing sails. *Almost there*, he thought with joyful relief.

Mila took notice of the panting warkin. "Yes . . . time for a short rest."

They were all tired from the furious pace, including her horse, standing beneath a large shade tree, grazing on late-season oats.

Prince Ivan confronted First Officer Beanlin. "The Tuz have lost communication with the encampment. They are not alarmed?"

Commander Nader calmly intervened. "Until our reinforcements arrive, we anticipate nothing more than an intrusive messenger."

The perimeter is well-defended," Beanlin added, "with orders to strike upon sight."

"I will breathe easier once my brother is here." The prince, did not share their confidence.

A Tuz hunter pointed through the trees.

"Two foreigners with weapons," Wen quietly confirmed. "Leave the horses and follow me."

Mila looked down and smiled at her majestic friend. "After we get your pearl, how about a quick dip in the cove?"

Sym's long bushy tail shook with excitement.

"I thought so!" she blurted out, laughing.

The warkin suddenly raised his snout, nostrils flared.

"Whoa!" said Mila, and got down from her horse.

"No," Wen gasped. *Why did she return? What is happening here?*

Startled by the sound, the soldiers readied their crossbows.

Wen is nearby—Mila sensed her presence—*and others.*

"Symlander!" the soldier shouted. "You are to come with us!"

Sym growled. His silver coat bristled, and amber eyes glared.

"Silence the warkin! That is a warkin?"

"Silver Warkin!" answered Mila. "And where are the Tuz who watch over this place?"

"No questions from you, Symlander!" shouted the other soldier. "Come with us and you won't be harmed."

"I am Zuku!"

The soldier taunted Sym with his crossbow. "This beast of yours, maybe our new king would like to give it a taste. Come with us willingly or I will skewer it for the fire." He steadied the powerful weapon.

"NOW," Wen commanded, and the spears were thrown.

The soldiers turned to the unseen shout. One of them was struck twice, the other unscathed and poised on one knee, releasing the bolt with a *whistling* sound that found silence in the hunter's chest.

The soldier had been trained to efficiently reload. However, no amount of training could have prepared him for a charging warkin.

Approaching top speed, Sym launched himself into the air. The helpless soldier was impacted with such force that five of his front teeth were uprooted.

"Get off me," he pleaded, struggling to breathe. Fractured ribs protruded through his bloodied uniform.

"Who are you, and why are you here?" Mila questioned the dying soldier.

She only had to ask the questions. Her access to his fading *truth* was unobstructed.

"What is it?" Wen asked the gifted Zuku.

"We haven't the time."

"Back to the village!"

"The foreigners?" asked one of the hunters.

"Take them with us," said Wen. "Everything must disappear."

Mila reached over and rubbed Sym's silver forehead. *You were brave my friend.*

* * *

At the Rivera Command Center (Zuku House), a disturbance along the northeast perimeter had been reported, the details yet to be disclosed.

"A minor incident," suggested Commander Nader, sitting at a table.

Ivan stood silently—staring out the window, thinking of his brother.

Officer Beanlin entered the room with urgency and Nader rose to his feet.

"What is it?"

"We have lost two of our lookouts, with evidence of violence."

"What evidence?" said the prince.

"Blood," the officer replied.

"And their bodies?" asked the commander.

"They are missing. We did find partial prints and hairs from an animal . . . thick and shiny."

"The silver Warkin," Ivan murmured.

"Most likely," said Nader. "Who did we lose?"

"Shayden and Rork."

"Replenish their positions."

"At once, Commander!"

"Before you go." Nader leaned forward, his hands pressed firmly on the table.

"Yes, Commander!"

"Select a handful of your most capable soldiers. At first light, go to their village. Take a look around . . . silently. We can ill afford another causality."

"Yes, Commander!"

* * *

At Alex and Kain's dwelling, Wen starkly announced, "We have been invaded. Mila discovered their intention"

"Who are they?" Kain asked in disbelief.

"Riveras, from the Land of Cantor. Soldiers, trained for one deadly purpose, with more on the way."

"Our children!" Alex cried out, holding Dorin close to her chest.

"The children and their families will be protected," Wen assured her. "You and Kain, organize a caravan. Travel east and join the Zuku. Load the wagons with all that we value. Take the Rivera weapons—they must know what we are facing. Work through the night, and be on your way by sunrise."

"And you?" Kain asked.

"I will stay here, with what hunters are able—"

"And us!" Mila insisted. "Sym and I will fight for what is ours."

"Your family is dear to me. I could not live with myself if something were to happen."

"We can be helpful . . . and we are staying."

Wen took a moment and studied the assertive Zuku. "Then, you will be at my side."

Mila firmly nodded. "Where do we go from here?"

"The Black Oaks."

* * *

At dawn, Alex confirmed to Wen, "We are leaving."

"Speak to Ram without hesitation. Explain all that we know. Once our camp is secured, we will send an escort to guide him there."

WAR

Riding ahead of the caravan, Alex and Kain sought out the Zuku leader.

"We've been invaded . . . forced to leave our village," said Alex with a shortness of breath. "The others, not far behind."

"Follow me," said Ram.

He led them through a cluster of tents before stopping to step inside.

Igua looked over in surprise. "What is this?"

"Foreigners on our soil!" Ram said angrily.

Feeling his turmoil was unexpected and confusing.

"Riveras from Cantor," Kain explained. "They seized the encampment and took each life that was there. We brought their weapons."

"Where is Mila . . . and Wen?" asked Igua.

"They are safe."

"Blessings." She sighed. "When can we expect them?"

Alex spoke up, "They won't be coming here."

"Why not?" said Ram.

"They've made camp in the Black Oaks with our hunters."

Gem rushed inside, his heart pounding. "Where is she? Those arriving were not sure."

"She is safe, and with Wen," said Igua.

"Is it true what the Tuz are saying?"

"Yes."

"We have to go back!"

Igua placed her hand on Ram's shoulder. *What must we do?*

He took a deep breath and collected his thoughts. "The matures will come with us. If recently partnered or with a new, they can stay. We will take most of the weapons, and all but one warkin. Those remaining . . . harvest what they can.

"Gem, communicate with the pack. They will be relied upon as never before. Igua, go to Stala. Her skill and healing aids are required. I will speak with Harta, about our food stocks and supplies. What is left they'll have to ration. While we are away, Rono will look after the tribe."

Gem spoke up, "Including Koal."

"Blessings for us all," said Igua.

"Blessings!"

* * *

Guided by the escort, Ram and Igua led the group westward. The general mood was pensive, yet resolute.

Gem and Harta had kept mostly silent, as the wagon rolled along.

"I shouldn't have let her go," she said softly.

"Mila can be very persuasive," Gem reminded her.

"She *is* resourceful."

He looked at her with a reassuring smile. "Very much so . . . and besides, she has Sym."

* * *

The vessels sailed around the treacherous point and into the Northern Sound. Prince Gorsh had finally arrived!

Later the following day at Zuku House, Commander Nader informed the prince. "The Tuz have abandoned their village."

"They simply packed up and vanished," Gorsh responded in dismay.

"No doubt traveling east, to join the Zuku," said Officer Beanlin.

"Actually, brother," Ivan stepped in, "we cannot be for certain of their whereabouts. Perhaps they watch us as we speak."

"Commander?" Gorsh snarled.

"Unlikely," Nader replied. "However, there could be elements nearby."

The prince began to pace, his agitation simmering. "I sailed past impressive bluffs that seemingly stretched forever. My first steps were taken on sparkling sand. The horseback ride through the countryside was sublime. Was this not my dream . . . finally to come true?"

"Brother," Ivan spoke up calmly, attempting to tamp down his surging anger.

Gorsh narrowed his brows and shook his fist. "Officers, explain to me this. How could your eyes be closed during such a critical time, allowing the Tuz to slip away, without one bolt released? Now, the Zukus have been warned!"

Ivan approached his brother and softly shook his head. "An unfortunate delay."

He stepped behind him and massaged his tense shoulders—while doing so, staring at Nader and Beanlin, to underscore his influence.

Gorsh's volatile mood was settling. "Your hands are therapeutic."

"With you here, my brother, we will complete our mission. This encampment is yours, and only the beginning. Welcome to the Kingdom of Rivera."

"Rivera!" echoed the military men.

"Commander Nader!" Gorsh silenced the room.

"Yes, my prince!"

"Go up to the village and burn it down."

"Look to the northeastern sky. It will reflect the heat from the flames."

Gorsh and Nader shared the same twisted mindset, their pairing natural from the moment they first met.

BLACK OAK FOREST

Wen welcomed Igua and Ram to the camp. "We are grateful for your arrival."

"A blessing to know you are safe," said Igua.

The two friends reached out and shared a strong hug.

"And Mila?" asked Ram.

"She is off with Sym on one of their walks."

Igua looked at Wen with concern in her eyes. "How is she?"

"Mila is well, and has become my closest supporter. She might seem different to you."

Ram's forehead furrowed. "How so?"

"Her fortitude."

"What can you tell us about the invaders?" asked Igua.

The soldiers are well trained and carry weapons that show no mercy. Their leader"—Wen reflected with bitter irony—"reminds me of my brother, as if his lifeless star has followed me here."

Drifting smoke from the smoldering village settled above them.

* * *

At the command center, Beanlin reported back with his findings. "They are nearby in a forest to the south. The tracks are fresh enough."

"Good work, Officer," said Nader.

"We can flush them out!" Ivan anxiously proposed.

The commander looked at the brothers with compelling eyes. "I recommend an alternative plan."

"Explain this plan," said Gorsh.

They sat at the table where the Zuku council would meet.

"The surprise will not be theirs," Nader concluded with a cold stare and curled upper lip.

* * *

"The soldiers are preparing to travel," revealed the Zuku scout.

"They believe we are in the east," said Igua.

"An opportunity." Ram nodded. "Similar to the elk, we will attack without warning."

"Riders, warkins, and warriors," said Gem, "engaging at close range."

"We cannot hesitate during this battle," Ram emphasized. "They will *never* hesitate."

"The warkins understand their task," confirmed Mila. "They will take the enemy down and leave their fate to us."

* * *

The brothers were with Nader, concealed on a wooded knoll.

"We will experience casualties," the commander reminded Gorsh. "The primitives must be convinced of our surprise."

"How many?" asked Ivan.

"Far less than on their side."

The soldiers organized at the base of the hill and then marched forward along the tree line.

"Here they come," said Gorsh.

One of the frontline soldiers asked, "They took away your crossbow as well?"

"And gave me this old spear." He sighed. "I'd be fortunate to hit a wagon."

"The commander said it's only temporary, and we won't be fighting for days."

"Good to know," scoffed another. "All I've got is this rusty old knife." He held up the crude blade, and together they laughed.

"How do you like it here?" one of them asked.

"So far, so good . . . but I miss my woman."

"We signed up to fight, and not be distracted. Gorsh will send for the women, once we finish up."

They continued to banter until one of the soldiers felt a searing pain, from a Zuku spear lodged in his shoulder. The velocity of the strike spun him to the ground. The soldier beside him lost his nerve and wildly searched about.

"What!" he screamed. The jaws of a warkin clamped on his ankle.

Both were finished off by the blade of a Tuz.

Impressive for a legion of primitives, Nader privately remarked.

Crouched in tall grass, the Rivera archers were on high alert.

"Wait until they advance into the fourth line," Beanlin instructed the lead archer, "and then let it rain."

The sequence of commands was initiated.

"Ready!"

The archers pulled back the strings until the proper tension was acquired.

"Aim!"

The bows were raised and arrows pointed skyward.

"Release!"

Fifty hardwood darts soared into the clear-blue sky. As they reached the apex of their deadly rainbow, fifty more, and then fifty more—one hundred fifty total—fell in one merciless downpour.

Many casualties were recorded, including a warkin.

Jerking his horse around, Gem was stunned to view the carnage. "Retreat! Retreat!"

"Stay here," she told Sym, before riding out to aid the warkin.

"The Symlander!" Beanlin blurted out with surprise. *My chance for glory.*

Mila knelt down next to the beast and pressed her hand against the wound. She sensed the approaching enemy—and his motivation. A great heat pulsated within her. She channeled the energy into an alarming sound, only to be heard by the aggressor's horse.

"Whoa!" Beanlin commanded. The spooked stallion reared and stomped, again and again! He held on with all his strength, until he was thrown to the ground.

Though his vision was not clear, her shocking white hair could not be mistaken. She stood over his broken body, glaring with contempt, Nord's dagger clenched in her hand. She knelt down and grabbed his hair, traced the sharp point across his neck, and then, in one smooth motion, drove it in and back across, releasing his final breath.

The execution was witnessed from both sides of the battle.

"Back to the forest!" Gem shouted.

After cleaning the blade with Beanlin's shirt, Mila stood up and sought her bearings. Lifeless bodies with crimson blood were scattered across the emerald field.

"Shall we submit our surrender to the Symlander?" Gorsh dryly proposed.

"She is a witch," fumed the commander. "And we will burn her at the stake."

After the interrogation.

* * *

Harta said, "I saw what you did out there."

"And now it is over," Mila cooly replied. "You are aware of my energy."

"Your energy . . . can be frightening."

Gem walked over, his face withdrawn. "We must learn to make those weapons."

"For more of this?" said Mila.

The suffering and death affected Mila in ways she could never have been prepared for. After the battle, she concealed her *truth*. Her privacy was respected, and reasoning not discussed.

"The blade you used?"

She stared into her father's curious eyes. "A gift that served me well."

Commander Nader gathered the troops and paid tribute to Officer Beanlin. "We lost a good man today. His absence will be felt throughout the campaign. We honor him, with the last breath of every primitive. One witch cannot deter our resolve. Rivera!"

"RIVERA."

Stala solemnly announced, "Another has departed," as the injured were spilling out from the tent. "We cannot meet them again in open battle."

"The reality is this," Ram said in a faltering voice. "Today . . . a great number of our people were struck down, lives ended in less time than a gull flies across the cove."

"We can attack in small, meaningful measures," Igua proposed. "Keep them off balance and disrupt their plans. If we are successful, there is hope."

"To stall their progress," said Wen, "and only that. Their strength and resources are far too great. However, if we can dilute their power and erode their confidence—"

"We can negotiate an end to the violence," Igua concluded. "Giving up what is rightfully ours is painful, but we have little choice."

Mila spoke up, "Explain the small, meaningful measures."

* * *

At the command center, Prince Gorsh and his brother were in conversation with Commander Nader.

"Come in!" said the commander.

A royal guard entered the room. "There has been another attack."

"And this time?"

"Six soldiers and their weapons."

Gorsh dramatically rose from his chair. "Will there be no end?"

"Guard, that will be all," ordered the commander.

"I have an idea," said Ivan.

"Prince Gorsh," Nader spoke up "Let me resolve this—"

"Commander! My brother deserves his say."

Ivan looked over at Nader and openly gloated.

* * *

The evening was cool and damp.

"Rivera hunting?"

Mila acknowledged her father with a firm nod.

"Be safe," said Harta.

Mila left camp with two experienced warkins. Unlike on the previous outings, Sym did not go along. A night of rest would serve him well. Even without him, she was as confident as always. The formidable beasts and her dagger were all that she required.

"Put that larger piece on the fire," instructed Ivan. "We can't let the mist get the better of it, can we?"

The soldier did as he was told, but in his thoughts, he questioned the reasoning. *And why were the others pulled?*

"You will refresh our checkpoint?" asked the only other soldier.

"Of course," the prince replied in a pleasant tone. "Relax and stay warm by the fire. It will be a quiet night."

As with before, the warkins would take the soldiers to the ground and then drag them to the blade.

However, on this occasion snipers were waiting, with three bolts sighted for each beast—two for the head and one for the heart.

Mila *felt* an instant chill. The warkins had been lost. Stepping backward, she tripped the line, releasing the weighted net. It took four soldiers to bind her hands and feet.

"This Symlander's got plenty of fight."

"Let's give her a toss!"

"Careful now, and don't harm the witch," Ivan gleefully reminded them. "Lay her gently between those warkins, while they still are warm."

The wagon pulled away, leaving the fire to dwindle under a dark and gloomy sky.

Harta softly asked, "You know something, don't you?"

Although troubled by the turn of events, Gem steadied his frayed emotions. "She has been taken."

"No—"

"But not for long . . . you have my word."

* * *

"Clean up the beasts and preserve them," Ivan ordered the soldiers, "suitable for display."

He hurried up the stairs and entered the room.

"We have a guest?" Gorsh asked with an eyebrow raised.

Ivan flashed a triumphant grin. "That we have, my brother!"

He strutted over and they shared an aggressive hug.

Gorsh slapped him on the back and laughed. "Sedated?"

"Heavily."

"Perfectly appropriate for a Symlander witch."

"It is late for you, brother?" Ivan asked with a smirk.

"Not too late."

"I'll let them know."

Meanwhile in the forest, Ram said to his son, "Bring her back to us."

"We will join you at the hunting camp,"

Gem set out to rescue Mila, with Wen, Sym, and two Zuku hunters.

"Enter!" replied the expectant prince, sitting in a chair by the bed.

Mila was assisted by a royal guard and a medical attendant. She was disoriented, yet aware of the circumstance. She was dressed in a sheer cotton robe, and Gorsh scrutinized her appearance as she was led to the chair that faced him.

"Finally, we meet . . . Symlander," said the fascinated prince.

"I am Zuku," she mumbled.

Gorsh turned to the attendant. "How long will she remain subdued?"

"A sound sleep would be required, before she regains full strength."

"Leave us alone."

During the height of Mila's violation, she summoned all the capabilities of her gift. The suffering she felt, captured and amplified, then transferred through her blood. The prince screamed out in agony, forced to stay committed.

"Enough!" He begged for the burning to stop.

Ivan rushed into the room. "Brother . . . what is happening?"

Gorsh was immersed in the most intolerable pain, and choking on his vomit. "Get the witch off me!"

Ivan was confounded by Mila's appearance as she was led out the door. She was calm, with no signs of physical abuse, whereas his brother was traumatized in every way.

"I regret my infatuation with this one," Gorsh weakly confessed. "Burn her tonight."

* * *

The Western Encampment was quiet and dimly lit. Most of the soldiers had been deployed in the forest. On the hilltop, the command center glowed. Snipers perched on its rooftop with crossbows.

Sym was deeply affected by Mila's abduction. Gem could *feel* the warkin's frustration, the way he prowled in circles, his amber eyes seething with rage.

Two dark figures appeared in the distance. Gem gave Sym a pat on the back, and the beast silently walked away.

Mila's *truth* awakened. *Father?*

I am here. Where are you?

Zuku House . . . but there is little time before—

Ivan charged into the room with eyes lit up. "What did you do to my brother, witch!"

He put his hands around her throat and squeezed. "You will suffer for this."

An outside disturbance caused him to release his grip.

A soldier came rushing in. "Men are down! A warkin has been sighted."

"The beast is not alone," Ivan thought out loud.

"I should advise the prince?"

"No! Let my brother rest."

Fresh from a successful mission, Ivan exuded an abundance of confidence.

The last patrolling soldier was successfully taken out. Sym's night vision, speed, and tenacity were indefensible. The snipers, however, were effectively stationed. If only they could better see their targets.

"Come with me and bring torches," Ivan commanded the royal guards. "We'll light them up!"

Despite being the military elite, those five guards with torches that night did not welcome their orders.

"They're coming down," Wen cautioned. "Follow me into the shadows."

"I see movement," the sniper informed his superior. "A small group, maybe four or five. I have one in my sights."

"And the warkin?"

"I don't see the beast."

The superior raised his crossbow and sighted the target. "Yes, that one there. I will keep an eye out for the warkin."

The now-familiar *whistle* preceded a sickening groan. The hunter collapsed to the ground.

"Well done," the superior commended the strike.

"It came from Zuku House," Gem quietly confirmed. "Snipers on top of us, aware of our location."

"Perhaps we can still make it there, but—" Wen stopped short of disclosing her true belief.

"The torchbearers," Gem whispered. "I *feel* a royal among them."

"I have an idea," said Wen.

The anxious snipers followed the light.

Gem looked over at the Zuku hunter, his spear cocked and ready to throw. "On my signal."

He raised his open hand—then made a fist. The deadly hardwood traveled forty paces without waver. Before losing consciousness, the guard pulled the tip from his breastplate.

Sym took advantage of the resulting confusion and sprung to a better position, silently poised above the enemy.

The fallen guard stayed motionless.

"He's been knocked out?" assumed Ivan.

A guard knelt down and checked his condition. Underneath the damaged armor was a pool of blood.

"He's gone."

Wen called out from the shadows, "Prince Ivan?"

"Who calls this name?" answered the voice.

Gem nodded. "It's him."

"Extinguish the torches," Ivan commanded the guards.

The frustrated sniper leaned forward. "Our light."

"We came here for Mila," said Wen. "Instead . . . we will leave with you!"

"You're not taking anyone—anywhere!" shouted back the defiant voice.

Sym anxiously waited for Gem's command. *Do not harm the royal.*

"Sound the alarm!" the soldier hollered. "Prince Ivan has been taken."

The prince was bound and carried to the nearby wagon.

"My brother will have none of this," Ivan snarled through his teeth.

"Tie him to the rail," Wen instructed the hunter.

The silver warkin leaped into the wagon and stretched out next to the prince.

"OW," Ivan cried out from the sharp pain. "Not so close."

Sym retracted his claws and rolled to the other side.

"That will be enough," said Wen. "Gag him!"

Gorsh was awakened by loud knocks on the door. "What is it?"

The royal guard bowed. "Your brother . . . he has been taken by the primitives. A warkin was with them, and—"

"Prepare my carriage!"

Harta said softly, "Mila should be safe by now."

"Yes, we will see her soon," said Igua in a comforting voice.

"I'll wait up for her."

"We both will." Igua softly nodded. "In the meantime, let us check on the others and make sure they are ready. Daybreak will be here soon." She reached over and held her close. It was ever so slight, but Harta was shaking. "Be strong."

The attendant had only finished dressing Mila when Gorsh burst into the room. Immediately, he paced the floor. "Witch!" His raised voice oozed with hatred. "This land of yours has become my nightmare. How inspired I was . . . and still would be. If not for the primitives, and a beguiling Symlander."

You will never rise above us.

He stopped and glared. "Rise above . . . us? Were those the *thoughts* you forced upon me? The primitives you claim as blood?" He twitched his fingertips around his chin. "Seriously, when was the last time you saw your reflection? Or better yet, looked at your mother. You bear no resemblance to a Zuku!"

Mila sat down in the chair, her eyes rolled up and she drifted away.

A guard announced his presence.

"Enter!"

"Prince Gorsh, your carriage has been prepared. However, I must inform you."

"What is it?"

"Most of the horses have been released."

"Go out and bring them back."

"At once, my prince!"

"Wake up, Symlander! There is no time for sleep."

A rush of energy jolted Mila awake. "I am not going anywhere without my property."

"That gaudy blade of yours?"

"I am as close to this blade as you to your brother. I will expect it during our exchange."

Gorsh was taken by surprise. *How does she know?*

* * *

Igua looked at Ram with determination. "Now?"

"Yes."

"Then, as we have planned." She nodded.

The tribes would break out at first light, and keep close to the forest. If necessary, they had the woods to find refuge. After reaching the hunting camp, they would organize a defense . . . and wait.

Igua met with the hunters. They, along with a pair of warkins, had been tasked with clearing the checkpoint. Stala's group, the largest and slowest, would go through first.

Once the breech was reported, a Rivera response was imminent. Ram, Igua, and the remaining hunters and warkins were responsible to disrupt their pursuit, providing separation for those already on their way.

The open carriage traveled with urgency.

"Faster," commanded the prince.

Mila was lying on the back seat, bound and blindfolded. She could *feel* a great disturbance but not decipher its meaning.

"Whoa!" The horses came to a stop.

Commander Nader rode up and issued his report. "They have broken through the far-eastern checkpoint. I am on my way there now."

Gorsh's face flushed with anger. "Will I ever wake from this madness?"

"Follow me, my prince!"

Mila's *truth* had cleared. They were in the heat of battle.

Ram emphatically reminded the hunters, "Strike, retreat, and move!"

Igua raced up beside him. "We've lost another."

"Into the trees!" he shouted.

"Wait for them!" Gorsh demanded.

"The tribes are safely away," said Igua.

"Yes," Ram agreed. "And we cannot stay here to be hunted." He looked at her with an open *truth*, and she *felt* the devotion he held there.

Lead the way. she instructed the beasts. "Hunters, follow the warkins."

"And keep your path uncertain," said Ram.

The warkins emerged from the tree line.

The soldier yelled, "They're coming out!"

"Target the leader!" shouted Nader.

Mila had never felt so incapable.

Take down the horses!" Gorsh bellowed.

Nader galloped to the front line. "Ready! Aim!"

Steady . . . Steady . . . Gorsh anxiously repeated.

"Release!" ordered the commander. No strikes. "Reload! Aim! Release!"

The horse collapsed from underneath her, and she tumbled helplessly on the ground."Igua!" Ram circled back against the bolts. "Stay down!" he pleaded.

Mila *felt* the rhythm of the sequence—so intense, at one point, she forgot to breathe.

"Take my hand!" he cried out.

Nader took aim with his crossbow. "Ram is mine!"

In the moment between the release of the bolt and its deadly strike, Igua had finished her climb.

"Go!" Ram commanded.

It was a relief to feel Igua's arms secured around his waist. They rode hard, and left the enemy behind.

Nader said, "The female was not my intent."

"Nevertheless, she was a prize." Gorsh nodded.

The commander looked over at Mila, curled up and without movement. "The Symlander?"

Gorsh chuckled. "She's had better days."

Igua spoke softly into Ram's ear. "Let me ride in front so you can hold me up."

Her arms were losing strength.

"Igua?"

She whispered, "I love you."

Ram slowed his horse and reached back. Igua had been struck and mortally wounded.

As the wagon neared the hunting camp, Gem *felt* a pronounced loss and dropped the reins.

Wen picked them up and took control. "What is it?"

"My mother . . . she has left us."

* * *

Prince Ivan's bloodied shirt was removed.

"There is risk of infection," observed Stala. "I should dress the wound?"

"Let it fester," said Wen.

Harta rushed inside the tent and caught her breath. "Where are they?"

"It's only Gem," said Wen, "and he is down at the willow."

"Mila?"

"He will explain."

Gem sat alone in the wagon holding a large soft blanket, waiting for his father's return.

"What has happened?" asked Harta.

185

He raised his head and openly wept. "My mother . . . is no longer with us."

"This cannot be true."

"It is."

"And our Mila, she is also—"

"No, she will be here tomorrow."

A horse and rider appeared in the distance. It was Ram, supporting a lifeless body. They hurried to meet him before he rode into camp. Igua was lowered into Gem's blanket-draped arms, where he held her with care . . . and sorrow.

* * *

"The prince has developed a fever," said Stala.

"Do what you can to keep it down," Gem replied. *For now.*

Ram asked "Are you sure this exchange will happen?"

"Yes," said Gem. "I have received their word, by courier."

Gorsh spoke in confidence with the commander. "What else is there to know about this exchange?"

"At daybreak, seek a clear vantage point. From there, you will experience a glorious happening. After your brother is again by your side, we will cleanse this land."

"I will sleep well tonight, comforted by this pleasurable thought."

THE HUNTING CAMP EXCHANGE

At sunrise, Gem sarcastically remarked, "You seem much better today, Prince Ivan. Perhaps you will recover."

"I remember when my mother took her last breath, and it wasn't because of a bolt."

Nader instructed the attendant, "Wash the witch's face before we take her back. We don't want those primitives to think she's been mistreated."

"My dagger," Mila insisted.

Gorsh handed it to Nader. "You'll get the old blade once we have my brother."

* * *

As agreed, they met on an open field.

The wagon and carriage approached from opposite ends. The drivers, stopping them twenty paces apart.

Commander Nader took Mila by the arm, and led her to the others.

She *felt* a strong and familiar presence. *Sym.*

"Prince Ivan!" Nader greeted the ailing royal. "Your brother has been beside himself without you."

"My daughter," said Gem as Mila held out her hand, "and the dagger."

"Yes, the dagger." Nader grumbled. *How did he know?*

She took the weapon and went to the wagon.

"Oh, dear Ivan." Sighed Gorsh with relief, as the carriage rolled his way.

Nader and Gem were left alone, the eyes of their people upon them.

"I must tell you," said Nader staring down at the Zuku, "it was never my intention to strike your mother. I was aiming for your father." He nodded with a half-smirk. "She made a poor decision."

"You are relieved of your duties, Commander." Gem's voice was cold and unforgiving.

The artery in Nader's neck began to throb. "That is highly unlikely, my primitive friend."

"I assume you are familiar with Mila's silver warkin? He is of a rare breed. Amazing beasts . . . warkins. Extremely impressive when you watch them in action—up close."

Courage would have no place at that moment, for there was nothing more frightening than the instinctive blood lust of an unrestrained warkin. Nader's screams would never be forgotten by those who were there that day, most of whom could not bear to witness his body dragged ruthlessly, around and around.

"Call them off!" Gorsh screamed at the top of his lungs.

Gem privately commanded it over.

Sym walked over with Nader's head between his jaws and dropped it next to Gorsh's shaking boots.

"Enough," the prince whimpered.

As a lasting reminder of the tribe's resilience, a volley of confiscated bolts whistled through the air, striking with precision Rivera's most skilled snipers, leaving them to fall in order, their eyes wide open and empty.

* * *

During their travel westward, the brothers were mostly silent.

"You are not feeling well?" asked Gorsh.

"I have a slight fever," Ivan replied, his forehead warm and damp.

PART I CLOSURE

Igua's life was celebrated during a five-day period of remembrance, her body set adrift and cremated on a river named in her honor.

Gorsh understood that continued strife would only delay the kingdom. Because of this, a peace accord was formalized. The tribes were granted a large tract of land, that included the Eastern Encampment. They named the territory, Truth.

With the exception of Sym, at Mila's insistence, the warkins were taken up to the Ancient Forest and released.

Prince Ivan succumbed to his infection and perished in his brother's arms.

Mila gave birth to a son and named him Wair. He had light brown hair, and eyes that were crystal-blue.

King Gorsh and Queen Ladesa welcomed their second child, Julia.

No longer able to cope with the pain during intimacy, Gorsh underwent a special procedure. Ironically, after the treatment, he related to the common Zuku.

At the king's invitation, Prince Roland and Princess Jennifer established the Principality of Marina.

The royal residence, Star Jasmine (built where Zuku House once stood), became the kingdom's crown jewel.

PART II

CHAPTER 10
MONTRO

In Forever Memory
of
Lord Crimion and Lady Tibene

The Academy for Special Studies—Montro

A school of higher learning and experiences.
Providing an exceptional opportunity
—for ALL—

STAFF:

Lead Administrator ········ Headmaster Pilar
Science ················· Professor Camden
Mathematics············· Professor Tic
*Cultures················· Professor Crystin
Leadership ·············· Professor Mwort
Abilities················· Wizard Nord

*Curriculum includes history and languages.

At the top of the island sat the academy's main building, overlooking the open sea. Before its expansion, it had been an elegant retreat house for the royals of Sym. Intricately engraved limestone, quarried from local deposits, framed the palatial entrance. An open-air atrium was nestled inside, well suited for special occasions, reflection, and study.

Located down in the basement were the main kitchen, housekeeping, maintenance, and storage rooms. A larger space for shelter was also there, though seldom used. On the first floor were administration, health, student services, dining, and library. The second and third floors housed classrooms and workshops. The top, fourth floor contained private residences, laboratory, and aviary.

Crushed stone pathways meandered through the manicured campus, leading to a modest orchard, flower garden, event area, and housing.

Forty students were members of the academy's first class, all of Symlander descent.

SYM

Stepping down from the royal vessel was an anxious Sir Hemeth, returning from Montro on his first-semester break.

"Welcome home!" Lord Martin warmly hugged his son.

"Finally," said Hemeth with mixed emotions.

His father sighed and softly nodded. "Sometimes the best of plans are not assured."

"It was difficult, not being here for Rachel and the birth of our first"— he shook his head in amazement—"children."

"Quite unexpected, all the way around."

Hemeth's eyes grew big. "TWO. How is that possible?"

Martin chuckled. "An ongoing conversation at the sailing club."

"Father," he gleefully asked, "which child announced themself first?"

"Lady Susan for sure, and all of Sym was informed."

They both broke out in laughter.

The lord caught his breath and cooled his tone. "In comparison, Sir Thomas was as quiet as a night possum."

"Father?"

"So much so, they gave him a shake."

Hemeth's stare was fixed and cloudy.

I should not have mentioned that, Martin scolded himself. "Of course the boy is perfectly fine."

"I have to see them now!"

They hurried to the carriage and then up the avenue, with Hemeth oblivious to the well-wishers along the way. Once at the residence, he rushed to the family's chambers, where Rachel and his mother were in conversation.

He barged into the room.

"Hemeth!" the startled women shouted.

"I'm here!" he ecstatically announced, landing on the quilt next to the infants.

The room fell silent and they watched the young father, his attention dedicated to the little girl and boy.

A sullen face appeared between the doors.

Ever satisfied to reside in the background, Tulare kept to herself, fidgeting. Challenged with pent-up energy, this activity provided her a measure of relief.

"Tulare?" Rook called out. "Come over, dear, and join us."

Without a word, she walked away.

"She's been struggling since the additions," Rook explained. "It hasn't been intentional, but the girl feels out of favor. We've done our best to include her . . ." She looked down at her grandchildren and smiled. "But with these little ones here."

"Tulare is fortunate," said Rachel. "To live in this grand place. You and Lord Martin have taken her in, adopted her as your own."

Rook sighed. "We've tried our best to improve her outlook."

"One day, she'll come to terms," Hemeth remarked with hopefulness. "A tragedy to lose one's parents at such an early age."

"May I join everyone down there?" Rachel did not wait for an answer and stretched out next to Hemeth.

He placed a tender kiss on her cheek. "I missed you, my lady."

"Now that you are here, let us enjoy every moment."

* * *

Later that evening, the family gathered at the dinner table.

Martin spoke up with an eyebrow raised. "Tell me, Hemeth, what news do you have of my dear cousin Nord. He is grooming you to be the next wizard?"

"Yes, Father, I am firmly on that mystical path." He laughed. "Cousin Nord would be the first to tell you I fit the mold of a proper student. The next wizard will be his son, Elgin . . . and a sinister one at that."

"Eyes in the back of your head, son," Rook chimed in.

Hemeth jumped up from his chair. "Wizard Nord is an amazing instructor! His dramatic presentations and elaborate wardrobe add to the magic of it all. Curiously though." He slowly raised his hands.

"Yes . . . those hands," Martin murmured.

"And the falcons, impressive creatures they are. He sent one off just the other day, to snatch a young kemit—a request of Professor Camden's, for dissection."

"You keep clear of those nasty lizards," his mother cautioned. "One bite may not take your last breath, but it will encroach upon it. They say the bacteria secures many sleepless nights, nights filled with pain and hallucinations."

"Mother! By the time the lizard reached the classroom, its head was nearly detached. Besides, the grounds are routinely swept for kemits. From what I've been told, there hasn't been a sighting in years."

Her eyes narrowed. "I don't trust those sweeps."

"They know where to hide," added Martin.

"Enough with Montro!" Hemeth admonished himself. "I promised Rachel not to dwell on island stories . . . and here I go."

"More bread—anyone?" Rook offered with a smile.

MONTRO

"A little farther!" the nine-year-old pleaded.

"You still haven't told me what you are searching for?" his exasperated mother reminded him.

196

Elgin was an ever-evolving wizard of dubious intentions. Causing Isa—at times, to question the decision she made, adding fury to the tea. She also thought about Tulare. What was to become of her, because of it?

"I am searching for a beetle," he falsely disclosed. "The bobo. It's missing from my collection."

The young boy had no intention of revealing the true prize: an egg from a kemit. The large lizards, native to Montro, were to be avoided at all costs. Elgin, however, relished the chance to acquaint himself. He viewed the reptile as misunderstood and was eager to document its habits. Mostly, though, it was the notorious bacteria that piqued his interest.

"You go ahead," she said. "I'll sit here on this rock and rest. Don't go venturing out of sight. I'll be watching."

He trampled through the knee-high grass, down to the edge of the meadow. "Where is that lizard?" Layered in earth-tone scales, they blended well with their surroundings.

His eyes lit up when he heard the rustle. *Between those rocks!*

Isa could tell he was on to something. His movements were purposeful.

"Elgin?" her voice rang out from across the field.

The young wizard bent over and then became completely still. Keeping his eyes on the mother kemit, he slowly raised one hand and acknowledged Isa's call.

What is happening down there? As she strained her eyes, he faded into a mash of underbrush.

"Elgin! I'm coming now!"

Before she took her third panicked stride, he reappeared.

"I've got you," he whispered, with the prize secured inside his coat pocket.

Isa walked briskly over to meet him. "Are we through here?" she asked while catching her breath.

"Yes," he replied with mock disappointment. "Unfortunately, not a good day for beetles. We can try again tomorrow?"

"Of course, son." She nodded. "Ask your father."

Elgin spent a great deal of time in the lab, often absorbed in the archives of his late grandfather, Kren. Inspired beyond compare, he hungered to produce his own magic. As he persevered, a voice provided guidance. It was the same voice his grandfather had come to know, one with a mantra: create and control.

The young wizard stepped over to the altar and onto a small wood crate. He rubbed his fingertips gently together, and the gleaming pink crystals sprinkled to the water below. He took the dark-gray egg from his pocket.

"Time to get wet."

He submerged it and carefully listened. Quietly at first, and then stronger, her heartbeat resonated within him. They were connected.

Four Years Passed

The royal family was elated to return to Montro. Tulare, unlike on previous visits, accepted their invitation and would join them, not because of the island's allure, or Hemeth's graduation, she merely was bored.

"Elgin?" Isa knocked on the bedroom door. "Elgin!"

"Come in," he grumbled.

Not surprisingly, the young wizard was lying on the floor, jotting down notes in his journal. The room was unkempt but not a disaster. Bec was curled up below the open window, bathing in early-afternoon sunlight.

"Please tidy up before they arrive."

Elgin responded in a low and steady groan, without bothering to lift his head.

"Your cousin Tulare will also be here. This is her first visit to Montro. You can help her feel welcome."

"Cousin?" He raised his head and glared at his mother. "And how are we related? Her parents harvested mushrooms."

Isa was awash in disappointment. "Elgin?"

"Yes"—he groaned once more—"I can help."

She smiled and said softly, "That's better."

"Father could allow us time in the lab and with the falcons? Tulare might find interest in that." It was less Elgin's willingness to help than the opportunity to work on his projects.

"Let me put in a good word."

Elgin dropped his head.

"Your room," she urged him before closing the door.

Again, Isa was reminded of the vast differences between her two children. Unlike Elgin, Quell was easy to please, her disposition open and friendly—his was guarded and often cold.

* * *

The *Royal Symlander CT*, the largest of the three royal vessels, was carefully assisted into the harbor. Hemeth waited on the private dock, overjoyed to reunite with his family.

"Father!" Sir Thomas screamed out.

"Father!" echoed Lady Susan.

"Father!" Sir Kingston chimed in.

Hemeth raised both hands and excitedly waved. "CHILDREN."

Being absent from his young family brought about loneliness and guilt. Hemeth was relieved to graduate and return to Sym—for good.

"Tulare." Lord Martin called out in a festive voice.

"Yes, my lord?"

He went to her with a warm smile. "We are happy to have you with us."

"Good," she simply replied.

"Sit with me on the ride up."

They loaded into the open carriages and slowly traveled up the hill.

"The breeze at times turns warm up here," said Martin. "Do you feel it happening?"

"Yes."

Tulare followed his pointed finger. "The air that flows from the Crystal Wash is heated. It cools over water yet up here maintains its warmth. This island is rich with natural wonders."

"And your parents, Lord Martin, you also feel their presence here?"

"I do."

He peered deep into her unflinching eyes, mystified that she could sense this.

"My parents," she said softly, "I don't feel anywhere."

* * *

"Elgin," his father instructed, "before we go down and greet the guests, put Bec in with the falcons."

"Why must she always be hidden away?"

"Let the visitors unpack and settle," said Isa. "Tomorrow would be better for an introduction."

The young wizard returned to his room. "Bec!"

There was no sign of the fully grown lizard. She wasn't on the balcony, or the other most likely places.

The carriages emptied, and everyone gathered in front of the main building.

"Cousin Nord!" Lord Martin reached out and greeted his dear friend.

"Very good to see you, my lord." Nord flashed a big smile and they shared a warm hug.

Tulare could not help but notice the uniqueness of the wizard's hands. They were oddly feminine.

"How was your sail, my lord?"

"Wonderful! Always a pleasure to be on open water. And sailing to Montro—what could be better? How fortunate for you, calling this island home."

Martin's grandchildren made their way beside him.

Nord took notice of the twins and little Kingston. "Oh my, how these Symlanders grow."

Hemeth nodded. "So fast."

"And Tulare?" asked Isa.

"She's here," said Rook.

Everyone glanced around to welcome her.

"Mmm," Rook contemplated. *A moment ago, she—*

"Over there!" Elgin shouted.

He pointed to where she was standing by the fruit trees.

"What does that girl have in her arms?" said Martin.

Tulare stepped closer and the twins cowered, clutching to their mother's sides.

"There she is!" Elgin blurted out.

"I thought we discussed this?" Nord admonished the young wizard.

"I couldn't find her."

Rook's eyes opened wide. "Is that what I think it is?"

"It's Bec . . . and she's *very* content." Elgin surprisingly acknowledged his joy.

Martin stepped over to Rook and whispered in her ear. "Have you ever seen Tulare with such a smile?"

She slowly shook her head in disbelief.

What a chance for them to have some fun, imagined Isa with delight.

"Elgin, take Bec up to the aviary," directed Nord.

The young wizard stared at Tulare with energetic eyes. "Follow me?"

She looked over at her adopted parents. "May I go with Elgin, Mother?"

"Yes dear," Rook replied without hesitation.

"Enjoy!" said Martin.

Tulare adjusted Bec in her arms and then walked away with Elgin. She shadowed him into the building and up three flights of stairs.

"Here we are." He opened the door. "Are you tired?"

She bent down and released the lizard. "Not at all . . . are you?"

"Never!"

Elgin was far from tired. Tulare had provided an unexpected spark.

"Let me take you on a special tour before the *family managers* have their way."

A muted chuckle escaped her inspired face.

Remarkably, Elgin found patience. He thoughtfully explained the history and function of the laboratory. Tulare's ability to absorb the information was impressive. He knew by the clarity of her focus she shared his fascination.

"The possibilities are endless," she marveled.

For the first time in her young life, Tulare felt purpose. Could it be she and Elgin were two of a kind.

"I can show you more before you leave?"

"I would like that . . . Elgin."

* * *

The royals hosted a special dinner in the atrium.

Lord Martin stood up and offered words of praise. "Divine Maker, we are most grateful for this memorable occasion. Family and friends gathered together to celebrate Sir Hemeth's graduation. Bless all at this table, and those less fortunate. We praise."

"We praise!"

Isa looked at the first-time visitor with an encouraging smile. "Tulare, what is your impression of this island?"

"It's magical," she cheerfully replied. "Wizard Nord's laboratory and the aviary, unlike anything I've ever seen."

"Beyond magical," Martin discreetly whispered to Rook.

They both were astounded by her newly acquired openness.

"Nord," said Isa. "Tulare is quite impressed with your facilities.

What is it with her? he silently wondered.

"Nord?"

"Yes, the facilities. However, are they mine or Elgin's these days?" He turned to his son and their eyes locked.

"Elgin is very knowledgeable," Tulare blurted out. "I've learned so much about—"

"Nothing!" interrupted the young wizard, while continuing to stare at his father. "In specific detail."

"Yes, that's right," she agreed.

Fury. It suddenly came to him.

* * *

Later that evening, Nord's weary eyes stared up from the bed. "You are aware, the similarities between them?"

"They are Symlanders," Isa replied with restrained amusement. "Young, adventurous, and—"

"Wizards."

"Of course they are wizards."

"Mystic . . ." he whispered.

And they both fell fast asleep.

* * *

The academy's first class graduated under a crystal-blue sky, a symbolic reflection of their Symlander eyes. The ceremony was well attended and enthusiastically received.

"Tulare, come with me!" Elgin insisted.

"To the lab?"

"Yes, before we are discovered."

The altar had been prepared. There was something Elgin wanted to know.

"An experiment between the two of us?" she asked with curiosity.

"Are you nervous?"

"Not in the slightest."

"Then give me your hands."

They joined hands and lowered them into the basin.

"Close your eyes," he instructed, "and I will do the same."

"What will happen next?"

"I'm not for certain."

The beat of Tulare's young heart quickened. "Open your eyes, Elgin."

They burst into laughter.

"Wait—wait," he pleaded for calm. "There is something else."

"I'm trying," she assured him and took a deep breath. "More magic?"

Elgin reached inside his pocket and pulled out an egg.

Tulare shrieked, "A kemit for me!"

"No—" He almost choked on her assumption. "A kemit egg does not have spots. *This* is from a falcon."

Tulare was no less thrilled, though somewhat unnerved by Elgin's snarky behavior.

"You would be laughing too," he suggested.

She sighed and rolled her eyes.

He eased the egg into the basin. "Hold it with me. Do you *feel* that?"

"His heartbeat?"

"His?"

She nodded.

Elgin focused on the rhythm. "Yes . . . his."

He placed the egg in her open hands. "Take this as a reminder of your first visit here. Keep him warm and soon you will have a special companion."

"And I can name him—now?"

"If you like," he said with a big smile.

"Pino!"

"Why Pino?"

She grinned. "Pineapple is too long."

* * *

After returning to Sym, Tulare slept with the incubating egg. Several days passed, and then the first crack appeared. She was prepared for his arrival.

Leery of Tulare's temperament, Nord provided the basic requirements of a first-time handler.

"Father."

"Yes, Elgin?"

"Could we send a falcon to check on Pino?" It was Tulare and not the recently born falcon he yearned to see. "Father?"

Although hesitant, the wizard was not in the mood for conflict. Falcons had been sent to Sym on numerous occasions, whether to correspond with the royals or to look in on the Dark Forest.

"Yes, son, first thing in the morning."

Nord's relationship with Elgin was not what he had hoped for. It was respectful yet far from close. Meanwhile, Elgin's relationship with his mother was solid. He energized her with his unyielding tenacity, as she motivated him with her ardent support.

PASSAGE OF TIME

Tulare and Elgin kept in regular contact, by means of her reliable falcon. They fit what they could inside a bamboo canister, then attached it to his talons. Besides letters, they exchanged drawings, dried flowers, and polished stones.

As the academy's enrollment increased, so did its diversity. Students from the Land of Cantor were accepted. A Tuz living in the Territory of Truth was also being considered.

Wizard Nord continued to lead the abilities program. The relatively benign potions and falcon stunts were no less popular. At Isa's urging, his wardrobe was enhanced. Elgin also contributed to the makeover, coaching him up to a more *mystical* presence.

Truly, Elgin was the progressive wizard. As he approached the age of fifteen, his understanding of the minerals and their properties was far superior than his father's. During the academy's most recent break, they sailed to the salt flats together.

"Why do we ignore the yellow, Father?" Elgin knew the answer but never grew tired of asking.

"Again with the fury." He sighed. "The mineral is not required. We have no use for it." *Unless absolutely necessary*, he concluded to himself.

Based on his grandfather's writings, Elgin was confident where the fury could be found. He promised himself that, one day, he would bring a sample home. His father would never allow it. However, without fury, his magic was suppressed.

Isa and Quell had fallen ill, and the trip to the flats had been cancelled. Until they recovered, Nord was not going anywhere. Elgin proposed to go himself. He had been well behaved of late, and surely his father would agree.

"I trust you will stay within the guidelines." Nord searched Elgin's intense blue eyes for signs of disobedience.

He replied with an engaging smile. "Yes, Father, you can trust me."

* * *

The young wizard finished the note and sent it back with Pino.

See you Soon!

your Elgin

SALT FLATS

Tulare crossed the shallows and beached the skiff at the predetermined location. Sitting down on the warm sand, she looked out on the open sea. Pino circled high above, keeping watch. Shortly before sunset he screeched.

Elgin anchored the vessel and rowed to shore in a dinghy.

"Good to see you, Tulare."

They reached out to each other and shared a warm hug.

"Of all places to meet."

Laughter filled the balmy air as they strolled the water's edge, leading them back to the skiff and their bed for the night. Where they cuddled beneath a star-laden sky, content to go no further than that.

"You mentioned a dream," Tulare softly reminded him. "Our future?" Her eyes wandered the twinkling lights.

"There were two special wizards . . ."

Soon after the story was over, they fell asleep in each other's arms.

* * *

The first full day, they extracted the commonly used minerals. For each color, Elgin explained their purpose. Mostly, though, they opened themselves to each other.

* * *

Later that evening, Elgin asked, "What of your dreams? Do you have one to share?"

Tulare closed her eyes for some moments in silence. "It's there—but faint," she whispered.

"Try harder," he playfully coaxed her.

"I have it now, and it's very clear." She opened her eyes and turned to him. "There were two special wizards . . . *Mystic*."

"Tulare."

"Yes?"

"I wish to spend every night with you."

* * *

Early the next morning, Elgin belittled himself. "I am the most incompetent wizard!"

Once again, their search had brought them to the beginning.

"Let's take a closer look at the notebook," Tulare suggested. "This landmark." She pointed to one of the drawings on the page.

"That rock," he thought out loud.

She swiveled her head and scoured for clues. "I believe it's over there."

Elgin followed her to a windswept basin. "And?"

She stared down at the exposed crown. "Here." Dropping to her knees, she cleared away the sand.

The sought-after boulder was almost entirely submerged.

"Yes!" Elgin's mind proceeded to calculate. *It came from . . .*

Tulare stood back and let him solve the puzzle.

"It came from over there."

He led her up a crusty slope. In the near distance were weathered cottonwoods and desert scrub.

"You've done it!" Tulare rejoiced. "The fury should be under that fallen tree."

They ran down with high expectations.

Elgin walked over to the uprooted trunk. "We'll know for sure after I get down in there."

"I'm tingling inside." She vibrated her hand rapidly to express the sensation. "And you?"

"Only slightly . . . but there is a *tingle* as you describe."

Tulare's chemistry had been jolted by its origin.

"Elgin, I can't help you. It's too much for me."

"Step away, then, and let me take care of this."

He worked his way through the brush, and soon enough, the glimmering minerals were found.

Tulare looked on with a sigh of relief.

"And how are you feeling now?" he gently asked. The pouch of fury did not seem to affect her.

"It has passed."

* * *

Pino performed one last maneuver as the vessel's sail was set.

It had been difficult for the two young wizards to say goodbye.

MONTRO

"You did well, son," said Nord.

"As if you were there guiding me, Father," Elgin embellished. "How are Mother and Quell?"

"They have regained their strength," he said with a smile. "The healing power in the tea is remarkable."

Some days passed. Elgin had become distant. His level of energy was lower than Isa could remember.

"Why so down, Elgin?" she asked. "Is it the academy, your father . . . me?"

"It's Tulare."

"Tulare?"

Isa was aware they kept in contact. They were close friends, but surely nothing more than that.

"She was there at the flats . . . waiting for me. Those days and nights we spent together—I did not want them to end."

Isa was astonished. Elgin spoke as if possessed. The raw display of emotion betrayed his prior existence.

"Tulare will visit us before you begin your studies?"

His eyes opened wide and his eyebrows lifted. "I was hoping for this, but father would never approve. He mustn't know about the flats."

"That meeting never happened." She nodded. "You are my son, and I will help you through this. Tell her she is welcome."

* * *

Nord, anticipating Tulare's arrival, arranged to spend the day with Elgin. They would sail around the island—a time or two.

"Lord Martin and I often sailed these waters." He turned to his son and smiled. "Out here without boundaries . . . our thoughts were free."

"You have always been fond of open water."

"This is where I find comfort."

"And I desire the same."

"Your studies, their importance . . . Elgin, I cannot stress enough. You are gifted. Take your fresh ideas and make constructive use of them."

Nord placed his soft hand on Elgin's shoulder.

He pulled away. "You have concerns, Father?"

"It seems to me, there is an element of distraction. Your interests . . . lack stamina."

"My interests are evolving, and"—his voice began to rise—"I have discovered something else."

"What is this *something*?"

209

"Passion."

Nord was left unbalanced. "These feelings for her are not too much?"

"I've been connected with Tulare for years, and our feelings have never been stronger.

"Elgin?"

"You cannot simply disconnect. We wouldn't if we could."

"My son." He reached out to hold him.

"Don't touch me with *those hands!*" His words cut as if a blade. "I shouldn't have said that."

The young wizard closed his eyes, wanting nothing more than to be with Tulare.

They returned to the harbor in silence.

Isa was waiting for Nord, when he haltingly entered the study.

"Your *talk*, did it go well?" she asked with reservation.

"No." He walked over to the window and peered outside. "Elgin's edgy temperament has always been pronounced. A consequence of fury I suspect."

"Nord?"

He turned to her with a cold stare. "I witnessed Elgin as a never before."

"He is merely trying to find his way."

"He is lost. And I am hopeless to know him otherwise."

"You are talking about our son."

"His preoccupation with Tulare. You were aware of their connection?"

"No . . . only of their mutual care."

"Care? It is their chemistry! And I will do all that I can to reverse this madness of fury."

Nord's intent to neutralize their son's behavior was shocking. Isa could not—would not—let this happen.

* * *

"Do you believe the potion will work?" asked his mother.

"Without a test subject, I'm not exactly sure. And to what extent the damage? Initially? Permanently?"

"Elgin!"

"Our objective of course is a harmless and agreeable wizard, not a raving-mad one."

She reminded herself to ask, "The bacteria?"

"Solved." He grinned. "The odor and bitterness no longer exist."

Isa gazed warmly upon her son. "Tomorrow, I will add this to his tea."

* * *

"Where is your father?" asked Tulare.

Isa interjected, "He is resting, dear."

"So much lately," she quietly remarked.

"Yes, he requires much rest these days," said Elgin. "All these years of wizardry seem to have taken their toll."

Tulare played along with the ruse; however, she was clearly not convinced. Privately, she would have a discussion.

Later in the laboratory, she said, "You've applied a potion to your own father."

"He does not approve of us," said Elgin. "But all that is forgotten."

"You've also removed his memory?"

"Selectively."

"Elgin," she said while shaking her head. "It must be difficult for your sister, to know him in this way?"

"My mother and I are helping her adapt."

"So fast—these changes."

"Our relationship—that is what matters most . . . today and forever."

Tulare leaned forward and pressed the side of her face against his chest. "Together—always."

He kissed her forehead and then jumped back. "Not only that."

Her eyes opened wide. "Tell me, my wizard."

"The laboratory is ours! My father has officially retired. His letter of resignation, accepted by Lord Martin himself. *Everyone* was saddened to learn of his condition."

"What will become of his program?"

"Professor Mwort will fill in and finish up the semester. I have also been approached."

"A first-year student?"

"Strictly falcon workshops. Headmaster Pilar would like them continued."

"That's something to be proud of."

"I suppose." He sighed. "I would have preferred Bec be involved. But the feedback for a kemit workshop was not encouraging."

"Restart the full program after you graduate. Add the lizard then. Imagine the possibilities with a bounty of test subjects."

"Tulare, your vision . . . disturbingly brilliant."

* * *

"Time for tea," Isa said cheerfully. "We must get your strength up!"

Nord lay still on the bed, his eyes staring blankly above. Attempts to speak discernible words resulted in lowly mumbles. He shut his eyes and tightly pursed his lips.

"I know you are frustrated, Nord. But with rest and your daily tea . . . you'll get better. Let's not give up." Isa put on a smile, should his eyes reopen. "I'll be back, after I serve Quell her breakfast."

Instead of this, she went straight to the laboratory.

"Elgin! We must do something about that recipe. Your father's head . . . it's almost completely empty."

"I'm working on it."

* * *

Elgin looked over at Tulare, the canister in her hand. "Pino has returned."

212

"With a brief and encouraging message." She nodded. "They understand and support my extended stay. Their thoughts are with Nord. Wishing him a full and lasting recovery. And those items I asked for will be on the next supply vessel."

"You are one crafty wizard."

"Yes," she said with a shameless smile, "I believe I am."

Adjustments were made to the special tea. Though Nord remained lethargic, he was able to communicate in simple terms. His memory retained what he was told.

Quell closely followed her mother into the bedroom.

Isa announced, "Someone wanted to visit you!"

"Father?"

Nord turned his head to the sweet voice. "My dear, how you have grown."

"I just made seven."

Isa gestured for her to move closer.

"Then we will go for a sail and celebrate. But first, I must recover my strength."

Tulare stepped into the room with a breakfast tray.

"Speaking of your strength," said Isa. "Look, Nord, something for you."

"Biscuits with honey?" he optimistically inquired.

"Yes, Wizard Nord," Tulare brightly replied. "Sweet clover honey from the meadow."

She set the tray down and left.

"Isa."

"Yes, Nord?"

"We must thank the royals."

"And what would that be for?"

"For sending dear Tulare to help with my recovery. I've always been fond of that girl." He favorably remembered.

"We are all fond of Tulare . . . especially our son."

Nord's heavy eyes opened as wide as they could. "Perhaps one day they'll engage."

"Isn't that a pleasant thought." She reached behind his back. "Up we go!"

PASSAGE OF TIME

Elgin joined his parents in the garden.

"Here we are after two years of study." Isa softly shook her head. "Time is fleeting."

The young wizard glanced over at his father. "For those aware of time."

"By the way, Nord's new roller chair is exceptional. The light weight and larger wheels make it a breeze to maneuver."

"The next one—even better." He winked. *If needed.*

"What plans do you have for sol break?" she asked. "What magic will the wizard conjure?"

"We will continue to work on our theory."

"That is good news, son," Nord remarked with a crooked smile.

"Yes, very good news," Isa agreed.

"Work hard, son."

"I will, Father, I will. Now, let me take you back."

"That would be good of you," said Isa with a subtle nod.

"Elgin! Tulare shouted from the laboratory's balcony.

"She sounds frantic," said Isa. "I'll roll your father from here."

Nord looked up as best he could. "That Tulare . . . very helpful."

"Yes, my dear. How could we manage without her?"

After Nord was settled, Isa hurried to the lab.

She gasped and startled the wizards. "What is that?"

Tulare opened the sack and quickly disposed of the carcass. "A rabbit, more or less."

"Another test subject—lost." Elgin sighed. "Maybe it's time to reconsider—"

"Never!" Isa sternly blurted out.

"Elgin!" Tulare echoed the sentiment.

"We are running out of rabbits," said Elgin. "Mother, would you like to volunteer?"

Tulare spoke up, "Actually, we *have* made progress. The core minerals of our theory, evolve and fury. The origin of our evolution."

"You were the one, Mother," Elgin emphasized. These minerals—this energy, provided by you."

"Share with her our vision," said Tulare.

"Mystic wizards, conceived and nurtured through chemistry. Powerful rulers, destined to create and control."

Isa's heart began to pound. "I can *feel* it!"

A reverent silence came over them.

*　*　*

Later that evening, Elgin rushed into Tulare's bedroom. "I have an idea."

"Should I dress for rabbits?"

He laughed. "Only if stew is on the menu . . . and it's not! Let's go outside, and I'll tell you under the stars."

THE ACADEMY WELCOMES A ZUKU

The Territory of Truth was bustling with excitement. Gem and Harta's son, Koal, had been accepted to the academy. The mood in Montro was far less ecstatic.

Isa asked, "And what do you make of the Zuku?"

"I'm undecided," Elgin casually replied. "However, I have heard disparaging snippets, from the students already here."

"That should tell you something?"

"It happened before with the Tuz. She was also an outsider, yet eventually absorbed."

"But Elgin . . . a *Zuku*."

"Yes, a most peculiar breed. A select few . . . surprisingly gifted.

"Not so close, then, son."

He left the room chuckling to himself.

215

* * *

"Today is orientation?" asked his mother.

"Yes," confirmed the young wizard. "I will join staff for introductions and welcome the new students. Because of the falcons, I have status."

"Don't forget to wear your father's robe."

As anticipated, the Zuku sat in the corner isolated from the others. During questions and answers, Elgin *felt* his presence. After they made eye contact, it turned personal.

Elgin whispered to Professor Crystin. "The primitive, he is trying to read my thoughts?"

The professor was knowledgeable of their culture.

"Yes," he whispered back. "They call it *feeling one's truth*. This could create a problem here."

"I will stay guarded."

Headmaster Pilar sat behind an expansive cedar desk, her Symlander eyes sharply focused on the gifted Zuku.

"Welcome to the academy, Koal."

"I am grateful to be here, Headmaster."

"We appreciate those students among us with surprising capabilities. You, for one, can access the thoughts of others. We call it *mind reading*. While here on the island, you will refrain from such practice. Feelings can be misunderstood . . . and Koal?"

"Yes, Headmaster."

"I do not wish to arbitrate a misunderstanding. Are we clear?"

"Perfectly clear, Headmaster Pilar. It's a natural reflex, and I will do my best to restrain it. I want nothing more than to fit in."

"And you will, Koal." She nodded. "You will."

Elgin was waiting outside the main entrance. He decided now was the perfect opportunity to get acquainted.

"Every is good?" he asked in a friendly voice.

"Yes, Professor Elgin, thank you."

The wizard looked down at the much-shorter Zuku and smiled. "Call me Elgin. And actually, I'm a student, as you are."

"Pleasure to meet you, Elgin. My name is Koal. But the robe and your position?"

He shook his head. "My father's robe, Wizard Nord. Have you heard of him?

"The name is not familiar."

"An original member of the faculty. He became quite ill, and reluctantly retired."

"How unfortunate."

Elgin stared off into the distance. "To see my father humbled in this way . . . is difficult. He has shown improvement but will never be the same. I watch over the falcons in his absence. Next year, you can apply for the workshops."

"I have every intention to do so."

"In the meantime, perhaps you'd like a preview?" He winked.

"Sure!"

* * *

A few days later, Koal visited the residence. After the preview, he drank tea with the wizards on the balcony.

Elgin closed the parlor door and turned around "So tell me, what do you think of our Zuku?"

"*Different*," said Tulare. "But once you get past the anomalies."

"Not a Symlander by any stretch," he dryly remarked. "Yet of all things . . . a mind reader."

She pressed her fingertip against her forehead. "He'll be staying out of here."

"And he's been warned."

"What about the—"

"Experiments?" asked Elgin.

"Yes."

"He is eager to assist us."

She walked over with a provocative smile, kissed his lips, and said, "The eager Zuku will assist us in more ways than he could ever know . . . no matter if he were to browse our minds."

* * *

"Wizard Elgin."

"Yes, Koal."

"The black tea."

"Our special blend." He winked.

"Remember my first sip?"

"You nearly spat it out."

Koal shook his head. "The taste! I still can't explain it."

"And now?"

"Would there be another cup?"

* * *

Tulare's frustration was evident in her tone. "Again, the results are in-conclusive. We know little else than his affection for the tea."

"We agreed to take it slow," Elgin reminded her in a calm voice, "and limit our exposure. Nothing radical to stir up a scandal. Koal's first-year studies have always been the priority."

She took a strong breath and slowly released it. "You understand it's in my nature, wanting to skip tomorrow, then on to the next day."

He said to her with a reassuring smile, "We have accomplished more with this one Zuku than a colony of rabbits."

PASSAGE OF TIME

Tulare and Koal were alone in the lab, cleaning and organizing.

"How does it feel to be in your second year?" she asked.

He took a moment to reflect. "Actually, it feels like a fresh start. Last year, if it weren't for you and Elgin, I would have been lost. Your friendship and support, the time we spent together. Then again"—he softly chuckled—"it could have been the tea."

"Speaking of which," she suggestively offered, "would you care for a cup?"

"Sure!"

* * *

Two days later, Tulare quietly asked, "Koal is still in bed?"

Elgin's unsettled eyes held the answer.

The despondent wizard leaned her body against his. "I lost my patience."

He rubbed her back, in a slow, circular motion. "I am working on a remedy."

* * *

Elgin and Tulare delivered the breakfast.

"Good day, Mother, Father."

"Good day, son," she warmly replied.

Nord's head moved slowly, up and down. His dry lips parted as if to speak.

Isa said, "I hear we have good news?"

"We do!" Tulare happily confirmed. "Koal is recovering."

MORE PASSAGE OF TIME

Koal rededicated himself for the remainder of his studies. Though no longer a test subject, he and the wizards stayed on friendly terms.

The special tea was never implicated as cause for the mysterious illness. Headmaster Pilar, however, did have her suspicions. Regardless, the Zuku no longer indulged.

During his third year, Koal met a first-year student from Sym, a royal by the name of Lady Susan. As their relationship blossomed, Elgin was asked to perform a connection. Surprisingly (but not to them), their natural attraction was a match.

During that same year, Quell began her first evolvement.

"You are confident to proceed?" asked Tulare.

"Yes," said Elgin, "with her, there is little risk."

* * *

Isa said, "Your sister . . . she spends a great deal of time with you and Tulare."

"And a very good helper she is," said Elgin.

"How much help do you require?"

"It's not only the lab but the falcons and Bec."

"At first sign of illness, I will end your supervision. Quell's chemistry is unlike yours and Tulare's, and not to be tampered with.

"We would never compromise my sister's health."

"Why is it always 'we' with you, Elgin? Have you misplaced your identity?"

Isa's words had teeth that found their way beneath his skin.

"My identity?"

By this time, the impassioned sounds had escaped the chamber. Drawn to it, Tulare listened outside the door.

"There is a reason I include Tulare." Elgin's voice continued to rise. "We are connected." His piercing blue eyes locked with hers. "And this will be forever!"

Tulare was profoundly moved, and her bottom lip quivered.

He took a deep breath. "Mother . . . we are one."

CHAPTER 11

TERRITORY OF TRUTH

Once decimated by the brutalities of conflict, the tribes' numbers recovered and grew. Over time, a cultural overlap emerged. Partnerships between the Zuku and Tuz became natural.

Mila's life and aspirations had been abruptly assaulted, her dreams of adventure replaced with the reality of raising a youngling. Never did she resent the birth of her son, who was cared for unconditionally.

* * *

As Koal approached the riverbank, Sym lifted his head and snarled.

He laughed at the silver-and-gray-haired elder beast. "You can call off your old warkin."

Sym!" Mila feigned admonishment.

"That's better."

Wair, knee-deep in the River Igua, was intensely focused with his spear.

"You do know," Koal mockingly suggested, "there is an easier way to catch fish?"

Sym responded with a low, rumbling growl.

"My son is being taught in the traditional way, as I was at his age. He enjoys the history, challenge, and satisfaction. Casting a net is easier, but for *this* I have no lesson."

Koal kept silent and shook his head. Debating his gifted sister was senseless. Her opinions were well-considered, and oftentimes relentless.

"I *feel* your excitement, little brother, and also hesitation."

He took a measured breath. "I am leaving the security of family."

"Keep us with you always," she reminded him.

"I will."

She shouted over to Wair, "How many now, son?"

"Five more makes twenty!" he excitedly counted.

"That should do it!"

"See you tonight, sister."

"See you there."

Before Koal turned to leave, he called out to the old warkin. "See you too . . . Sym!"

The beast's tattered ears perked up, and his matted tail swung gently.

* * *

Later that evening Harta asked, "What can you tell me?"

"Later," Gem said softly, "here she comes."

Mila walked up to the small group, Wair by her side. "Mother?"

"I was only—"

"There is no reason to be uncertain. I am happy for Koal." She reached over and gave his shoulder a firm squeeze. "This is a special occasion . . . for all of us."

Mila smiled over at her father. His *truth* was open, and she welcomed the familiar warmth.

"Someone speared all the fish today!" announced Stala.

Wair's face wore a wide grin. The sack he carried nearly filled to the top. "Not *all* the fish. I left the little ones to grow."

They sat on the overlook, surrounded by radiant rock formations jutting into a magenta sky.

"We should be down there," said Wen.

Ram leaned forward and tenderly kissed her lips.

* * *

"There they are!" shouted Wair.

Wen presented an easy smile. "Here we are."

"How many toasts are we behind?" Ram cheerfully asked.

Gem handed his father a large mug of shillig. "Start with this one. And Wen, for you."

"Speak to us, Koal!" Urged the group. "Yes, Koal . . ."

For a moment, he found himself awkwardly mute—but only for a moment, as a purposeful energy lifted his voice.

"Blessings, everyone."

"Blessings!"

The group listened intently.

"Earlier today, I was down at our beautiful river. My sister was also there. We spoke of family." He brought his hand to his chest. "I will keep you *here* . . . always. Mila—"

Wair tugged at his mother's clothing and whispered, "Uncle Koal is talking about you."

Koal continued. "Is my inspiration. She has taught me more than words could ever describe. Because of her, I am off to the academy." He shook his head. "A Zuku . . . who would believe it?"

"Zuku!" everyone celebrated.

His eyes were glistening. "My sister has always been selfless and mindful of others. Much in the same way as Igua . . . never to be forgotten."

Wen held Ram's hand tightly as he allowed his emotions to flow. She, too, was weeping, as were the others (who were able).

"I will represent the tribe to the best of my abilities. I am proud to be from Truth."

Koal went to each person, and shared a meaningful hug, saving Mila for last. He *felt* the warmth of her innermost self, a warmth that was never-ending.

Wen and Ram walked quietly to their dwelling.

"How are you?" she asked.

"There are times I relive those final moments . . . and it hurts."

* * *

"See you at break!" shouted Mila.

Koal waved back to the dock. "See you then!"

She continued to watch the vessel until it disappeared around the bend.

Shortly after Koal began his studies Sym passed away. He lived much longer than the average warkin. In the end, he gave Mila one last nuzzle and then swam away in the River Igua.

KOAL RETURNS

Two seasons passed. Koal stepped down to the dock. Mila was there to greet him. They indulged in a big hug and pats on the back.

"I was sad to hear of Sym's passing. Our friend will truly be missed."

"It's not the same without him." She gazed down the waterway. "He left us in this river."

"A beautiful way to depart."

They turned to each other in silence.

"Now!" said Mila. "Let me take a good look at you." *Have you changed in any way?*

Koal undoubtably answered her thoughts when he bulged his eyes and extended his tongue.

"Same brother!"

They burst into laughter.

Her crystal-blue eyes opened wide. "Before we go and see the others, tell me something about the island."

On rare occasions, Mila imagined life outside of Truth.

"I have made friends, with a wizard and his family."

"Symlanders, no doubt."

"Yes, with a royal bloodline."

Mila's interest was stirred.

"Next year, Elgin will connect me with the falcons."

"This family . . . is familiar."

She raised her hands and displayed them—front to back.

"Wizard Nord!" Koal blurted out. "You are related?"

"I believe we are of *distant* relations."

He bowed his head, "The wizard would not be as you remember."

"And because he has aged as I have."

"More than this, I am saddened to say. He came down with a terrible illness. It took his mind and made him . . . simple. He is barely able to walk, and spends his days in a roller chair."

"This is tragic." Mila shook her head. "I've only known him as vigorous and brave."

"Elgin is the energetic one."

"He was remarkably so when we first met.

"Sister, you *must* come to Montro."

"Watching the sunset, with a bowl of fresh pineapple on my lap? Tempting." She sighed. "But leaving here would be difficult."

"And how is Wair?"

"He is good, from what I've been told. I continue losing time with him. His guide sees to that."

"Father!" Koal blurted out.

"Wair's greatest desire is to be a champion. The Zuku in him remains strong."

"A champion as his mother . . . the greatest of them all."

"Tales from the past can be exaggerated," Mila modestly suggested. In an instant, her expression turned somber.

"What is it?" Koal asked.

"Stala . . . she is gravely ill and will leave us soon."

"This is for certain?"

"By her own words . . . and who would know better?"

"She has been the leader of wellness since before I can remember."

"And provided me valuable knowledge. I will take her position when—" Mila's sadness interrupted her words. "Ram has been with her much of the time . . . for comfort."

"I would like to see her."

They went to the clinic, where their parents were in the waiting room. Without words, Koal hugged them both. Ram appeared in the hallway, walking toward them in a daze. He had witnessed Stala's final breath.

"She called me 'brother.'" His voice filled with sorrow. "How did I not know?"

PASSAGE OF TIME

Koal returned home after his second year of studies. Once again, Mila was at the dock. His unsettling appearance caught her by surprise.

She said, "You've lost so much weight."

"I know—I know, I still look sick." Koal furrowed his brow. "But what about this?" He stuck out his tongue in a distinctive way. *Same brother*, he added to her thoughts.

"Blessings," Mila responded with relief. "We depend on your resilience. One day, you will be a leader."

* * *

Soon after he was back on the island, Koal sent word to Truth. He had met someone of interest, and his free time belonged to her. Although their reunions would be missed, Mila was busy at the clinic, and without time to dwell on disappointments.

The territory was going through an early stage of mourning. Ram's chronic cough had progressed beyond that. Mila provided the harsh prognosis.

The Zuku leader had a personal request, with what little time remained: return with Wen to where it all began. Knowing of his condition, King Gorsh afforded the kingdom at their disposal.

THE KINGDOM

The Zuku's former encampment had been dramatically transformed. Below Star Jasmine was an extravagant public square named after the queen. Surrounding Plaza Ladesa were outdoor cafés and popular shops. Artwork was on display in every corner. Theatrical performers roamed the interlocking bricks. In the center of it all was a magnificent fountain, where colorful birds gathered and bathed.

"There is a word for this beautiful place?" Ram thought out loud, his eyes enlightened at every turn.

"Sophisticated," Wen suggested.

"Truth is far from that." His chuckle led to a cough.

"The beauty of our territory transcends the physical." She blinked.

"True beauty . . . is here with me now."

Holding hands, they continued their stroll.

Soon after she asked, "Would you like to go back and rest?"

"No, I am fine." He stopped and looked down. "It could have been here, that Igua spoke of change."

"With a smile more brilliant than the brightest star."

"Always. And her words of wisdom, I will never forget."

Wen understood his contentment and encouraged him on. "What were those words?"

Ram's eyes drifted into the clear-blue sky. "'As the seasons change, so, too, will our tribe. Change is a natural progression. We will adapt and find balance.'"

* * *

With the help of Gem and others, Truth's clinic was significantly improved. Treatment and recovery rooms were added, the waiting and work areas enhanced. In one of those new rooms, Ram shared his final thoughts.

"It is my time," said the proud Zuku.

Wen's eyes were filled with endless tears. "I don't want you to go."

"I know how you feel, my dearest, yet I am grateful to leave in this way. Too many with deep meaning have passed before me. Having you here . . . is a true blessing."

Susan and Koal

It had been over a year since Koal returned to Truth. On this visit, he would not be alone.

Mila stared across the water with a furrowed brow. The vessel was close enough, and she was struck by her appearance.

"Over there on dock, waving . . . your sister?"

"That's her," said Koal, waving back.

"A Symlander?" said Susan.

"I left that out?"

"I believe you did," she curtly replied. "Is there anything else?"

"Her *Zuku half is* gifted," he said with a smirk.

"You're not being fair."

Mila helped his guest down to the dock, Koal an afterthought.

She smiled and shook her head. "It seems my playful brother anticipated our confusion. And by the surprise on our faces, he succeeded." Turning to Koal, she scowled.

Same brother, he privately reminded her with bulging eyes.

"I am Susan," the royal introduced herself.

"Lady Susan, actually," Koal muttered.

"No need for formality."

"A pleasure to meet you, Susan. I am Mila. Sit up front with me."

They walked over to the open carriage and climbed up inside.

Koal loaded the belongings and sat with them in the back.

"Only a short ride now," said Mila, grabbing hold of the reins. *Go,* she silently commanded the horses, and the wheels began to roll. She looked over at Susan and smiled. "We knew it had to be someone special, keeping my brother away so long."

"It's wonderful to finally be here."

"I must say, you remind me of someone."

"Hemeth?"

"Hemeth," Mila repeated with fondness.

Susan was stunned. "I just said my father's name, and for what reason—I can't explain."

Koal blurted out with laughter.

Mila pulled back on the reins. "I know your father.

"How—"

"It was unexpected, but we became close friends. Your grandparents provided me with shelter. Sym is a glorious place."

KOAL'S GRADUATION

In Montro, Koal said, "You may recall my sister."

Elgin cocked his head to one side. "And why would I—"

"Her name is Mila. You were very young at the time."

Elgin's memory was impressive, and he tried to place her.

"She traveled to the Dark Forest, with Wen and Sir Hemeth. You led them on a tour of the lodge."

"I gave a lot of tours," he said dryly. "I do know Sir Hemeth, and vaguely remember Wen. This girl you speak of was a Symlander?"

"Mila appears a Symlander but is equally Zuku. The blood from her mother we both share. She is coming to my graduation," he revealed with a happy eyes.

Elgin was not prepared for this. Mila could not find Nord in his present state of disorder. He would increase his stamina and nudge his memory.

"Careful, Elgin," Tulare warned. "We have come too far."

"I'll simply water it down."

"No more than this?"

"You tell me, my Wizard."

"Add a hint of the *blue* for good measure. To better his social skills."

"Only a hint." He nodded. "Mila is exceptionally gifted. We must stay guarded, yet—"

"Friendly," Tulare wickedly concluded. "After all . . . she *is* family."

* * *

The newly commissioned *Stala* eased away from the dock.

"She is a fine vessel," said Gem. "And with no better name."

They meandered down the River Igua, until it merged with the mighty Sucrene, where placid aqua waters turned dark and energetic.

"Look!" Wen pointed downriver. "Our new sail barge."

Keeping pace with the kingdom's demand for minerals, a large cargo vessel was procured from the Land of Sym.

Everyone stood against the railing and admired the fully loaded barge, as it was deftly guided up the expansive river.

* * *

Isa stood on the balcony and watched the workers below. "Every year, we add more chairs."

"This is great," said Wizard Nord, sitting next to her.

She considered his state of mind. "You are feeling well?"

"I believe I am . . . I believe I am."

"Well then, you're ready for the party."

His thick eyebrows narrowed, as he searched for thoughts not easily found. "Isa . . . about this party?"

"Tomorrow, a graduation ceremony. Visitors from your past."

"A grand party with Mystic falcons—" his eyes fluttered shut.

Isa rolled him back inside, where her son and Tulare were standing.

"A miracle . . . isn't it?" Elgin's voice resonated with sarcasm.

"Nothing short of a miracle," his mother dryly agreed.

Tulare cleared her throat. "Because of Elgin . . . Nord is much better, and so are we."

Isa ignored the *stare* and faced her son. "When do we expect our dear friends from Truth?"

"The Zuku waits for them now."

* * *

"KOAL" they shouted, as the *Stala* approached the dock.

"Welcome to Montro!" he hollered back.

The vessel was tied off, and everyone disembarked.

Koal and Mila shared a vigorous hug and pats on the back.

"How was your travel?" he asked.

"It was fantastic."

She took a deep breath and glanced around, settling her eyes on the largest vessel.

Koal said, "The royals arrived yesterday."

Isa reminded Elgin, "Bec is to stay in the aviary until the guests have left the island . . . no exceptions."

"As you wish, Mother."

Hemeth caught sight of the carriages and rushed down the stairs to meet them.

"Mila!" he shouted with joy. "My favorite Zuku-Symlander."

"Hemeth!"

Elgin, standing on the top-floor balcony, observed their joyful embrace.

"Enjoying the view?" asked Tulare from the room.

He kept staring without an answer.

Sir Hemeth," Wen greeted the royal.

"Wen—"

"Up there!" Mila silenced the group.

All eyes were led by hers.

Who is that? Gem wondered.

"Elgin!" she called out.

The wizard begrudgingly waved his hand.

Surprisingly, Nord stood up next to him, dressed in full wizard attire. A Mystic falcon perched on his handler's glove.

It was Elgin's idea, presenting his father in such a way.

"Wizard Nord!" Mila shouted, with unrestrained happiness.

His hands slightly tingled with an awareness.

"Now! commanded Elgin.

Nord launched the falcon into the air.

"Oh my," said Mila.

High above in the light-blue sky, Pino screeched and performed dazzling maneuvers.

Gem stared up in awe. "Incredible."

The visitors were captivated.

Return.

And the loyal falcon did so.

Later that night, the royals hosted a fine meal in their residence. Sixteen friends and family members gathered around a large oval table. Tulare arranged the seating and kept Mila apart from Nord. Even so, there was an energy between them, familiar and warm.

Bottles of vintage shillig were brought to the table and generously poured.

Lord Martin stood up and the others joined him, except for Nord, embedded in his roller chair at the opposite end.

The lord raised his glass. "A toast . . . to the graduates!"

Glasses were raised. "To the graduates!"

"And to Koal," Hemeth smiled with a nod.

"To Koal!"

"What a party," Nord said, his words smothered by laughter and happy chatter.

Elgin tapped his glass with a spoon, and the room quieted.

"A friendly reminder to our guests from Truth—on this island, we do not read the thoughts of others."

"I advised them on the dock," said Koal.

"Your restraint is appreciated."

Though perplexed by the youthful wizard's disposition, Gem was also fascinated.

Dinner had finished, and Nord was expedited to his room.

Isa made the announcement. "A good rest for the wizard will build up his strength for tomorrow."

As the others mingled, Elgin showed Gem to the laboratory.

"I *feel* a presence here," said the Zuku, his eyes adjusting to the freshly lit lanterns.

"The essence of my grandfather, a brilliant man, and the first Mystic wizard."

"And that over there?" asked Gem, pointing to the center of the room.

"The Mystic altar."

As Elgin prepared the experiment, Gem went over and explored it, slowly walking around the basin, tracing his fingertips along the volcanic rim.

Leaving the items on the table, the wizard reverently placed his hand on the round stone. "A gift from our Maker. My grandfather was the chosen one, told by a voice of its arrival from the stars.

"And you have also heard this *voice*?"

He stared at Gem with his Symlander eyes. "I understand my purpose."

"If all that you say is—"

"True?"

"Yes."

"Tonight, you will bear witness to a truth beyond belief, a method of energy without limits."

Gem had fallen under the spell of the wizard's entrancing tongue. "Show me."

Elgin looked down at the small pine box. "Once an improbable theory, now . . . revolutionary magic."

He unfastened the latch and lifted the lid. Inside, six copper-clad orbs nested in a bed of white cotton. He picked up an orb with bamboo tongs and submerged it in the basin, carefully adding a few grains of fury. Soon after, the orb was placed in a beaker of water.

"Watch," he whispered.

The beaker was capped, and the water began to boil. Soon, the glass became cloudy. A small hole in the cap produced a steady whistle.

"Steam," Gem uttered.

"Yes," confirmed the wizard, while attaching a pinwheel to the cap.

The Zuku watched in amazement. The wheel effortlessly spun.

"Elgin, you have created the future."

"Let us drink some tea to that."

* * *

233

Headmaster Pilar welcomed those in attendance on a warm afternoon beneath a cloudless sky. Royals and professors sat on the stage behind her. The graduates in the garden awaited their cue. Their lavender robes and white headbands had been custom made from Symlander silk. A string quartet began to play, and they slowly processioned to their seats.

"Koal!" Susan stood up and shouted for all to hear.

The program proceeded as scripted, culminating with the grand finale.

All heads turned to the top-floor balcony, where Wizard Nord presented himself in his finest robe and headdress, one at a time releasing four Mystic falcons. The performance was epic. After every screech and precise maneuver, the ecstatic audience begged for more. Wing to wing in a climatic formation, the falcons swooped down above the delirium, leveling off to glide gracefully above the outstretched hands.

Headmaster Pilar made the announcement. "Celebrate the graduates!"

* * *

At Montro Harbor, Susan and Quell were among those sailing back to Truth. Susan's trip coincided with solar break and was previously planned. Quell's inclusion was not anticipated.

Mila shared her thoughts with Isa. "This island is all your daughter has ever known, a special place for sure but without compare. I can promise you this, she will return with treasured memories."

"I am thankful for your care," said Isa, reaching to grasp her hands.

She did so and took pause—their shape and texture were uniquely familiar. Mila sensed her overt curiosity and tactfully eased them back.

By all appearances, it was Mila's persuasion—in actuality, Isa's intent. Quell had to be separated. The secretive young wizards had become cause for concern. Elgin was always on his guard. Tulare was never to be found. Everything would be resolved while her daughter was away.

Quell's evolvement was disrupted, yet complications not to be feared. Absent of fury, her chemistry remained intact. Elgin's portrayal of the supportive older brother would continue. He could ill afford to validate his mother's suspicions.

"I will keep my end of the bargain," Gem assured him.

Elgin accepted the Zuku's sturdy hand, and they shook on it.

"The falcons will keep us informed," said the wizard. Then he whispered a warm reminder. "Do take your supplements. One tablet every four days will suffice."

* * *

Once out of the harbor, Mila approached her father. Although unsettling, it was not for her to question his concealment.

"You have bonded with the young wizard," she remarked.

"It's clear our cultures blend well." He nodded. "Look at us."

Yes . . . look at us, she kept to herself.

They left the Sucrene and entered the River Igua.

Quell gazed upon the water with wonderment, "The color is peculiar."

"Peculiar?" Koal chuckled.

"She is interested in everything," whispered Harta.

"And not surprising," said Mila. "All those years on that island. Could you even imagine?"

"Never."

"She will acquaint herself."

Harta walked over to the naive young Symlander. "Quell."

"Yes."

"If you have any questions, about anything . . ."

"Harta."

"Yes?"

"I was wondering—"

"No . . . I cannot read your thoughts."

"She is a kind one," Mila reminded Koal. "Help her to learn without judgment."

Territory of Truth

Several days passed.

Harta called out, "How was the ride?"

Mila looked back at the young Symlander, who lagged behind with a slight limp.

"Amazing!" Quell shouted. "To sit up high and move as the wind."

"You galloped on your first ride?"

"Not quite that fast." Mila chuckled.

"Fast enough to water my eyes," she boasted.

Harta simply shook her head and then suddenly remembered. "Gem was asking for Quell."

"He was?" said Mila with surprise.

"Special visitors have arrived from the kingdom. Something regarding trade, but I'm not aware of the specifics. Tomorrow night, there is a gathering, and she is invited."

"I will find out the specifics."

Quell was distracted by a lingering discomfort. "I am sore from where I sat," she thought out loud.

Soon after, Mila confronted her father. "What is the meaning of this? Subjecting our guest to a business gathering."

"It's a social reception. The business happens later. Another chance for Quell to discover something new. Wen will be with her the entire time."

"I am against this."

"And I understand your position," said Gem with care in his eyes. "Trust me, she will be safe."

"If anything were to happen—"

"Mila. Why let one king poison you?"

"Yes . . . he poisoned me."

Later that day, Wen sought to reassure the young Symlander. "You'll be fine. Remember, we won't be staying long, only to exchange greetings and taste the food. I have a friend who is a seamstress. She has samples in her shop. Let's go there and see what we can find."

Quell chose an outfit and tried it on.

"You look wonderful!" said Wen. "The clothes were waiting, just for you."

Her eyes sparkled in delight.

* * *

Trade officials from the kingdom entered the room.

Gem said, "Good to see you again, Prince Nathan."

They shared a firm handshake.

"And you as well, Gem. We have a full house tonight."

"A surplus of food required extra mouths."

The young prince wore a satisfied smile. "We have come a long way, haven't we?"

"Our commitment to peace and cooperation has revolutionized the territory."

"That is a powerful statement."

Gem raised his glass and called for a toast.

"Raise your glass with me," said Wen.

"To our friends from Rivera. Providing a better future for us all. To the kingdom!"

"The KINGDOM."

Gem whispered into Nathan's ear. "Later, I have something to show you . . . in private."

"And Wen?" the prince whispered back. "You know better than to make a move without the Tuz."

"She's occupied, a family guest from Montro."

"That's a shame," he responded with disappointment.

"They are over there."

Nathan's eyes followed Gem's. "The family guest is a *Symlander*," he remarked with interest.

"She shares Mila's bloodline."

"Introduce me."

Montro

The young wizards relaxed on the bed. Tulare's fingernails scratched the back of Elgin's neck. His mood was uncommonly subdued.

"Tulare, you do realize we'll be harvesting the fruit ourselves this season."

"Pity that."

"Stop where you are!" the voice rang out from the edge of the orchard.

"Listen," Tulare whispered.

Isa shielded her eyes from the midday sun and stared up at the top-floor balcony. "Elgin!" she shouted, hoping he would appear. "Elgin!"

"Your mother calls for you," Tulare said softly, her long fingers combing through his thick white mane.

"Drop that basket!" she demanded.

The defiant lizard continued to weave through the trees. The basket's handle was locked between her frothing jaws.

"You'll be banished to the roof for this!"

Elgin sat up and convincingly explained, "It's happened before, wild creatures with their natural instincts."

"And Bec?"

He leaned over and kissed Tulare. "There is an island to explore . . . and no more eating from bowls."

"Where did she go?" said Isa, looking up from the abandoned basket. *Over there.*

The lizard was climbing the rock border—almost to the top. An uninviting marsh percolated on the other side.

"Bec!"

Her thick studded tail was all she could see, until it, too, disappeared.

Tulare launched herself from the bed. "Ready or not!"

"Has anyone seen my lizard?" Elgin cried out in mock distress.

The rejuvenated wizards laughed their way down the stairs.

Isa bent down and picked up the basket and then started walking back. Suddenly she stopped. *What . . . is . . . this?* There was a large kemit in her path.

Sounds of movement all around indicated there were others.

* * *

Quell returned to Montro with mixed emotions. She had experienced a personal awakening during her time away, inspired by an independence she had never known. On the island, she was often overwhelmed by the dominant forces surrounding her.

Susan and Quell stepped down to the dock, Tulare there to greet them. "Welcome home."

"Thank you, Tulare." Quell softly smiled.

"Your brother . . . is anxious to see you."

"There is something wrong?"

Tulare's face revealed compelling grief. "There has been a tragedy."

"What has happened?"

"It is your mother. Elgin did all that he could to save her."

Quell's eyes glazed over and her knees buckled. Susan rushed forward and kept her from falling.

Elgin was waiting when the carriage arrived.

"Mother!" Quell's trembling voice cried out.

She sought comfort in her brother's open arms.

Tulare stayed out of the way and savored the drama.

"It is true," conceded Elgin with a sigh. "And why wasn't I there to prevent this?"

"I know . . . you tried, brother," said Quell within the sobs.

"I tried everything," he said softly while rubbing her back.

She took a deep breath and exhaled. "I am tired."

"Your room has been prepared. I'll send Tulare up with a cup of hot tea."

Elgin's voice was soothing, and she would go there.

Later, at Quell's bedside, he asked, "You were able to find rest?"

"Yes, the tea was helpful."

He looked at her with caring eyes. "Tell me, sister, your time away?"

"An adventure for all my senses," she said with a soft smile. "You remember it was Mother encouraging me to go. I only wish that she were here . . . so I could—"

He reached over and held her trembling hands. "We still have each other."

Isa was laid to rest among the roses in the garden. Nord stared at her headstone, from a table nearby. He would do so daily, until his final breath.

* * *

Nord finally finished his biscuit and slowly took a sip of tea.

"Father seems so tired of late," Quell remarked.

Elgin despondently shook his head. "Mother's death has taken its toll, and sadly he has regressed."

"Very unfortunate," added Tulare.

"Sister, tell us more about your travel."

"Yes, Quell, share all the details."

"The color of the River Igua . . ."

The wizards listened quietly to every word.

She continued, "The royal reception was completely unexpected. If not for Wen, I would have *never* survived, especially when introduced to the prince."

"Nathan?" Elgin blurted out.

"Yes." She blushed. "We had a conversation."

Tulare's interest was piqued. She glanced over at Elgin, and he reflected the same.

Nord wore a crooked smile, and his eyes flickered.

Quell spoke up. "I'll take Father to his room. Better for him to sleep in his bed."

* * *

Later that evening in the laboratory, Elgin took out the tray from the drying rack.

"Tablets for your sister?" asked Tulare.

"Yes. You might as well get her started."

"One per day?"

"With or without food," he dryly replied.

"And your invention?"

"I continue to make refinements. The kingdom, I've been told . . . intrigued."

"The diagram you showed me, the vessel with the wheel. You can build it before graduation?"

"I believe I can."

"Imagine this, Elgin . . . after the ceremony, steaming our way up to Truth."

"That would make quite the impression, wouldn't it?"

SUSAN'S GRADUATION

Just prior to the celebration of graduates, Prince Nathan sailed to Montro, tasked by his father to reach an agreement with the academy. Although a staunch critic of the Symlander, the king respected the institution. He was envious of the other lands, where graduates contributed to their success. There were those well qualified in the kingdom, unable to apply. Nathan would make sure they were no longer excluded. He was also eager to reacquaint himself with Quell.

* * *

Elgin spoke with Tulare and confirmed the arrangements, "Everything is set."

"And your degree of certainty?" she asked.

"High."

* * *

In the headmaster's office, Prince Nathan said, "The tour was very insightful."

Headmaster Pilar smiled and engaged her Symlander eyes. "We look forward to your applications."

"They will be delivered soon after my return."

"Is there anything else, Prince Nathan?"

"The top floor here . . . I am curious."

"Private residences, and falcons."

"Falcons?" He tilted his head to one side.

"Mystic"—she cackled—"tomorrow, be on the alert."

Before returning to his bungalow, the prince took a walk around. Quell was in the garden, head bowed and hands clasped together. He stood there unsure if the moment was right, until she looked up and waved him over.

"Quell," he said warmly.

"Prince Nathan, there was talk that you were here."

"Conducting research"—he glanced over at the headstones—"this might not be a good time."

"Stay. I am happy to see you." Her mood was lifted by his presence. "This research?"

"There aren't any students from the kingdom here. My father, adamant I open the door."

"And you must," she insisted with a smile. "Tell me, what is your impression of this island?"

He gazed off into the surroundings. "There is a *magic* to this place."

"You think so?"

"Yes." He returned to her smile. "Gem has suggested, privately, your brother is a wizard."

"He is." She giggled.

"I must confess, my father, the *king*, is not fond of wizards."

"Then my brother is a scientist," she decided.

"And this scientist . . . communicates with birds?"

"He does." She nodded. "A process better for him to explain."

Quell's refreshing personality was endearing to Nathan.

"This all seems so far-fetched, but—"

"Would you like meet the falcons?"

"I would."

"Follow me."

Into the main building and up the stairs they climbed.

"Almost there!" she cheerfully assured him.

They entered the residence and caught their breath in the parlor. The spacious room was warm and inviting. She led him down a wide hallway, to the laboratory at the end, with the door cracked open and the wizard inside.

"No need to interrupt," Nathan discreetly suggested. "The falcons?"

"It's fine. My brother is expecting you."

He whispered, "What have you told him?"

"Everything." Her laughter carried into the room.

"Come in!" the wizard called out.

Quell pushed open the door. "Brother—"

"Prince Nathan! Welcome to Montro."

"Good to be here, Elgin."

"We have a mutual friend."

"Gem, a fine Zuku," said the prince. "He has briefed me on your project, and we can schedule a demonstration?"

"This can be arranged. But for now, let us explore a more personal magic."

Nathan raised an eyebrow. "Are you asking me to volunteer?"

"The both of you."

Quell was taken by surprise. "Brother, really . . . *not* what I am thinking?"

The wizard flashed a clever smile. "This exercise was first developed by my father. He became well-known because of it."

The prince said, "Clarify this . . . exercise."

"A test of compatibility. The results can be interesting . . . or only wet hands."

"What do *you* say, Quell?" Nathan cautiously asked.

"Actually, I'm not quite sure of what to say."

The prince took a shallow breath. "We'll do it."

"Then it's settled," said the wizard. "Join me at the altar."

Soon after, Tulare anxiously asked, "How did it go?"

"Their connection was instantaneous."

She grabbed Elgin by the shoulders and shook him madly. "I began the special blend this morning. Tonight is our night!"

* * *

The next afternoon, Koal and his family arrived from Truth. That evening, Susan's parents hosted a special dinner in the atrium. Music played softly in the background, and the stars twinkled above. It was an exceptional event, diverse cultures gathered around one table, sharing their traditional food and drink.

Sir Hemeth stood up and provided a welcome. "At this table, I see familiar faces, and also those that are new. Welcome, everyone, to the island of Montro! My parents founded this academy so that all cultures could gain knowledge. This year's graduates honor their vision. Among them is my daughter."

Rachel stood up and raised her glass. "To Lady Susan."

"Lady Susan!"

* * *

At the celebration of graduates, Mila looked over at Prince Nathan, who sat on the opposite side. She was tempted to search his *truth* but refrained. However, she did observe his mannerisms, thankful they were unlike his father's.

The students were lined up in the garden, waiting for their cue. Once those familiar notes were heard, they slowly processioned to their seats.

Koal stood up and shouted, "Susan!"

She adored the attention and blew him a kiss.

"And one for me?" asked Gem.

Harta leaned over and gave him a peck on the cheek.

* * *

The celebration had finished, and all was quiet. Chairs were stacked and stored. Everyone had gone their separate ways. Suddenly, the ground trembled and shook.

"What is happening!" shrieked one of the students.

Panic prevailed throughout the buildings as objects crashed to the floor. Those who scrambled their way outside, stared blindly in disbelief.

The falcons in the aviary, were making unusual sounds and excitedly flapping their wings.

"Sister!" Elgin called out. "Are you here?"

Quell hurried into the parlor. "Everything was moving!"

"It's over?" questioned Tulare, her eyes shifting about.

Cautiously, they went to the balcony.

"Again!" Quell shouted.

Tulare pointed across the bay. "Over there!"

The sea is angry, thought Elgin.

The wizard's mind was overloaded, with theories and calculations. Despite being well versed with the properties of nature, this was unprecedented.

"Find Nathan and bring him here," he instructed his sister.

Moments later, the prince rushed into the room.

"He was already up the stairs," said Quell.

"I'm sending a falcon across the bay," the wizard explained.

More magic, assumed the prince.

Elgin attached the amulet to Pino, the fleetest of them all.

* * *

Everyone surrounded the altar, watching and waiting.

"She is approaching the peninsula," said Elgin.

A collective gasp filled the room. Pino had reached the devasted shoreline.

"We must deliver a message to my father."

245

"Write your words without delay," said the wizard.

Even though Montro was spared from serious damage and injuries, an uneasiness prevailed. Would the ground continue to shake? Was open water safe for travel? All vessels remained harbored until further notice. During this time, Elgin completed the steam-powered prototype. Once travel was restored, it followed the *Stala* on her way back to Truth.

TRUTH

GENERAL COUNCIL:

Gem · · · · · · Leader of the Territory
Taku · · · · · · Leader of Finance
Koal · · · · · · · Leader of Justice
Rubin · · · · · Leader of Farming and Hunting
Rono · · · · · · Leader of Education
Kure · · · · · · Leader of Building and Services
Mila · · · · · · · Leader of Wellness
Wen · · · · · · · Leader of the Arts and Culture

Truth's form of governance was based on the Zuku model. The Department of Justice had been added with Koal in mind. Its primary function was the settlement of disputes.

Koal showed Susan around the office. "The space is small, but for now, it's enough."

"So many changes since last I was here."

"Zukus and Tuz working in harmony," he said with a wink.

She smiled and brought him close. "I am grateful to be here with you."

* * *

The falcon arrived with a message from the kingdom.

Elgin took out the note. "It's from the prince."

"What does it say?" asked Gem.

"Marina has suffered enormous loss. The Harbor District—swept away. Prince Roland and Princess Jennifer, so many others . . ."

He's not coming, Quell thought with disappointment.

"See you as planned." Ended the note.

Elgin was relieved; the demonstration of the prototype would go on as scheduled. Quell was even more so—the prince's absence had become intolerable.

Gem and Elgin toured Truth's main district by carriage.

"It's not Sym," said the wizard, "yet clearly a place to be proud of."

"The benefits of our resources downriver. As the kingdom expands, so do our exports."

"I admire your commitment, Gem. Together, we will accomplish great things."

"How can I be of further assistance, my wizard?"

"You and the prince are close."

"Close enough."

"He and my sister yearn to be together. We want the same."

"Their partnership will bring us all closer together," suggested the Zuku.

"Very much so," said Elgin in a soothing voice.

"They have my full support."

"Once again, we are in agreement. Before I leave—the supplements, you are content?"

Gem impulsively nodded.

The wizard smiled. "I have brought you a fresh supply."

THE KINGDOM

"Something is troubling you, Nathan?" the king asked. "It's not the girl—"

"Quell! And yes, I miss her."

"We've gone over this."

"And every time I've tried to explain . . . Quell, is *not* as you imagine. She has all the qualities I could ever ask for."

Integrating with other cultures, Symlanders in particular, the king had spent a lifetime loathing the very thought. His royal bloodline forever tainted, with white-haired, blue-eyed—never!

However, he did realize his ideals were from an earlier time, and not of his son's generation.

Nathan was trustworthy and greatly admired, a role model for the youth. Their positive relationship could not be jeopardized. After all, he was the heir to the throne.

"Bring this Quell to your mother and me, and let us get to know her."

"Thank you, Father." The prince respectfully bowed and left the room.

TRUTH

At the wellness clinic, Mila said, "You haven't been yourself."

"Perhaps the travel and lack of rest?" Tulare suggested with a forced smile.

"Or because you carry a child."

"You are certain?"

She stared intently at the wizard. "His presence is undeniable . . . and strong."

CHAPTER 12
FICUS

"This is everything!" Elgin raved.

"Mila told me the child is strong."

"And this is surprising?"

* * *

The prototype performed flawlessly, and afterward a meeting was held.

"The energy is capable of diverse applications," the wizard explained. "Not only over water, but also over land. No longer wagons being pulled by oxen."

Nathan said, "I will speak with my father and make the arrangements."

"Do so without delay."

* * *

"You are taking a tablet daily?" asked Tulare.

"Yes, and the difference is remarkable. I have an abundance of energy, and my sensitivity—" Quell became bashful.

"I understand," said the wizard with a subtle nod.

"Prince Nathan has invited me to the kingdom . . . to meet his parents," she haltingly divulged.

"And you will be welcome."

She smiled with sparkling eyes. "Nathan said the same."

"Elgin and I will be sure to visit, once you have settled in."

"Do you believe I can be a princess?"

"Of course, dear Quell. But do not neglect your supplements—they provide an incentive for your prince."

* * *

Tulare looked over at Elgin, steering the prototype down the Sucrene.

"Quell is on her way to the kingdom," she remarked with hopefulness.

"My sister will make a fine first impression. She epitomizes not only the alluring Symlander but also the pleasant Zuku."

"Elgin!" snapped Tulare, with a knowing grin.

"Soon enough, the blood of our chemistry will leech into the kingdom . . . the blood of wizards."

"We control the destiny of Rivera," she said firmly in the cool morning air.

To create and control, he silently concluded.

Unconsciously, Tulare touched the inside of her ear. There was a slight wetness. On her fingertip was a red-translucent fluid. She wiped it off and touched again. This time, nothing was there.

* * *

"She is quite charming," remarked the Queen.

"Charming enough," said the king, with surprisingly little discomfort.

"Did you notice the delightful way she and Julia got along?"

"I did."

"And how our son only had eyes for her."

"I did."

"Let it not be us to deny *their* happiness."

"I agree, my queen . . . I agree!" Gorsh emphatically waved his hands. "I was straightforward with Nathan beforehand. The Symlander, hmm— Quell, would have a fair review."

"And now that she has?"

"They have my blessings."

* * *

Shortly after returning to Montro, Elgin referenced his grandfather's notes and created the potion of truth.

"Drink this first," he instructed Tulare. "Then place your hand on the gift."

They intently watched as the water darkened. After a few anxious moments, an image appeared.

"Our son," she quietly announced, "Ficus."

Elgin stared down at the pulsating water. "The clarity is amazing . . . the energy."

"Even now his strength."

The following days were troublesome for Tulare. She had become anemic and bedridden.

"Sit up and drink this," said Elgin, and helped her with the tea. The formula had been adjusted with hope to improve her condition.

* * *

"Elgin!" Tulare called out.

He rushed to her room with uncertainty. When he arrived, she was standing up in her daytime clothes, smiling from ear to ear.

"I woke up feeling much better. What changes did you make? I am invigorated!"

"Fury," disclosed the wizard, "progressively . . . more and more."

"Only that?" she had her doubts.

"And a touch of pink," he revealed with an eyebrow raised. "I was told—thought—a better connection would be helpful. It seems that Ficus was merely trying to get our attention. Taking your air was extreme. But the child was desperate. Are you aware of his satisfaction?"

Tulare closed her eyes—then smiled. "Yes."

"I've sent for Quell. She'll be here for the birth and provide us extra help."

* * *

Meanwhile in Truth, Koal took Susan to a popular vista. It was there, overlooking the River Igua, he envisioned their ceremony.

"It's perfect," she said with heartfelt satisfaction.

Mila was very much involved in the event's preparation. It seemed all of Truth would be there. Not to mention Susan's family and friends, expected from the Land of Sym.

"We must post signs of warning," Gem teased. "Symlanders are coming. Do not stare into their compelling eyes."

"Very clever, Father," said Mila, taking exception.

THE BIRTH OF FICUS

Tulare's labor was extremely difficult. It took a delivery team of four to facilitate the birth. Quell was also there, to assist as best she could. Elgin chose not to be present and sequestered himself in the lab.

"Push, Tulare!" pleaded the medic. "PUSH."

Elgin heard the primal screams, anticipating nothing less. He understood Ficus's intense desire to remain inside the womb, his unwillingness to leave its comfort and mystic nourishment.

Quell spoke up with urgency. "The blood in her ears."

"More gauze," ordered the lead medic.

The loss of blood was alarming.

"What is happening to her!" Quell cried out.

Tulare's condition turned critical. Her mouth gaped, and her eyes rolled up.

* * *

The exhausted lead medic entered the laboratory.

"My son?" Elgin anxiously asked.

"He is stable."

"This is good to hear."

"However, his transition was abnormal, and there are remnants of shock. We have done our best to calm him."

"And Tulare?"

"She gave everything for this child . . . and asked for you, before—"

"I will go to her."

But first he went to Ficus, who by now was sound asleep, his little chest heaving up and down. Standing over him, he gently swept his fingertips across the fuzzy white scalp.

Bending down, he whispered, "You were very selfish, my son."

Quell was standing next to the lead medic when Elgin entered the room.

"Brother . . . it was horrible," she stammered, tears streaming down her face. "There was so much blood and—"

Elgin studied Tulare's ashen face.

"She is in a coma," the lead medic explained. "It is too early to know for sure, yet I am afraid there has been damage."

"To what extent?" he asked.

"First, she must wake up. If and when she does, we can make that determination. Until then, she receives the best of care."

Several days passed.

Quell introduced the newborn to his grandfather.

Nord reached out his quivering hands. But Ficus screamed when they first touched, as if dropped into scalding water. She lifted him away and the hysterics fell silent.

Nord looked up with a sorrowful face. "Ficus," he moaned and reached out again. "Ficus . . ."

"He's been restless." She softly nodded. "You can hold him another day."

"Ficus . . ."

* * *

Quell rocked the unquenchable boy, with a bottle of fresh goat's milk and minerals in his mouth. He could see clearly now and was well adapted to

253

his surroundings. Once the bottle was dry, she laid him down and found her brother.

Elgin placed his hand on her shoulder. "Thank you for being here."

"It's hard to believe she's gone."

"Dear sister . . . Tulare hasn't gone anywhere." His soothing fingers massaged the tension away. "She lives on in Ficus." *More than you can imagine.*

A ROYAL UNION

"Cast off!" ordered the captain, and the vessel's sails were set.

Quell leaned over the railing and waved goodbye.

"See you soon!" shouted Elgin.

Walking the streets of the kingdom was one thing, but a Symlander on the royal court? Unthinkable. Although, in many ways, it was another sign of the times. The youth of Rivera had turned progressive and tolerant, similar to the Cantors.

Ladesa's eyes opened wide. "The kingdom is energized!"

Gorsh sighed. "They must think I've gone completely mad."

"Most likely." She snickered.

* * *

Birma rocked Ficus in her sturdy arms.

To assist with the child's upbringing and Nord's daily care, Birma had been hired away from the academy. Before leaving Montro, Elgin provided her final instructions.

"The supplements are stored in the side pantry. They are well organized and labeled. The note in this envelope will provide greater detail." His piercing eyes narrowed, and a chill came over his voice. "Do not deviate from my son's daily routine. I will know if this should happen."

"Understood," she obediently replied.

"My father's care is purely incidental. He will do what he does, which is very little. After breakfast each morning, roll him out to be with Isa.

There he can drink his tea. Do remember to bring him back by midday. And one more thing . . . he'll want to spend time with his precious falcons."

"I will make sure he is able to do so."

"Expect my return when the moon turns full."

* * *

Elgin paddled up to Truth in the steam-powered vessel, relishing the stares and double takes he encountered along the way. Gem met him at the harbor, and they traveled to the kingdom together.

The demonstration took place at Star Jasmine, in the presence of the royal court. It was a spectacle without precedent, a miniature rail coach compelled to move effortlessly around a metal track.

"You have done it!" shouted Gem.

The royals clapped their hands in unanimous approval.

"What magic is this?" King Gorsh blurted out. "A small metal ball producing energy."

"Not magic!" Elgin asserted, his crystal-blue eyes sparkling from across the room. "A testament to natural forces . . . and only that."

Elgin would not validate the king's outspoken perception, nor the whispers of others. Symlanders were wicked. In the Land of Rivera, he would be less a wizard and more a man of science.

"We have witnessed the impossible!" declared the king. "Elgin, provide us your terms and we will formalize a partnership."

* * *

"How did the meeting go?" Quell asked with nervous excitement.

"Excellent." Elgin confirmed with a brash smile. "Tomorrow, I will shop for property along the cove."

"Brother . . . I am beyond happy for you."

He walked over and reached inside his pocket, then handed her a drawstring purse. "Mother took an identical formula. To give us strength before our birth." (This was only a half-truth.)

255

Her fingertips traced the tablets through the thin fabric. "When the time comes, I should take one per day?"

"Yes . . . and the time has arrived."

"In the blink of an eye," she quietly reflected.

They shared a warm embrace.

* * *

Nathan presented Elgin's proposal to his parents.

"Initially, it's a lot to provide," admitted the prince. "However, our future returns will be generous and long-lasting."

"We are listening," said the king.

CONCESSONS:
- *Deed to the Territory of Lackland.*
- *All mineral rights, above and below.*
- *A fully supported camp for three hundred laborers.*
- *Ironworks factory and sawmill.*
- *Sixty-percent ownership of all railway assets.*
- *Fifty-year exclusive mineral agreement, between the kingdom and the Territory of Truth.*

"This Symlander," the king bellowed, "is not a wizard or scientist . . . but an extortionist!"

Ladesa sought to diffuse the tension. "Gorsh, my dear, let us think openly. What we have here is a rare opportunity."

"Mother is right," Nathan agreed. "Elgin's invention, we cannot yet replicate. Its value is immense. He has leverage."

The queen said calmly, "We will agree to his terms with two conditions."

"Listen carefully, Nathan, and learn. Your mother is shrewd in matters of business."

"Firstly, once the railway is profitable, all financial burdens revert to Elgin. Secondly, equal partnership is expected for export transactions."

Gorsh smiled over at Ladesa and then instructed his son. "Take this information to your Symlander friend."

Later that evening, Nathan met with Elgin at a Cove District pub. Over toasts of shillig, they discussed the pending agreement.

"Let me guess, your mother added the conditions."

"*She* is the one to watch out for."

"One more toast!" Elgin called out to the barkeep, in between their laughter.

"Do we have an agreement?" Nathan reached out his hand.

Elgin grabbed it, and they firmly shook. "Yes!"

"One more toast!!"

The next day, the king said, "I've been thinking."

"Yes, Father?"

"From where will Elgin contract the laborers?"

"I believe from the Land of Tuz."

Gorsh shook his head bewildered. "A Symlander, capable of this?"

"He has contacts in Truth who will provide them."

Later that afternoon, Nathan sat with Elgin at a café in the plaza.

"My father insists you are a wizard."

"Your father is the king, and can imagine as he wishes."

The prince smiled briefly and then looked down.

"What is it?" asked Elgin.

"Quell . . . she is happy?"

"Very much so."

"In two short days, our union will be official."

"A cause for celebration across the land."

"You are returning to Montro, directly after the ceremony?"

"Yes . . . before my son has forgotten me."

"Do not isolate on that island of yours," said Nathan as a brother. "Visit us as often as you like."

I will always be present.

* * *

The wagon rolled eastward on the grasslands toward Truth.

Gem said, "I *felt* your sister's sadness as we were leaving."

"Did you also *feel* her joy, when the vows of their union were exchanged?"

Elgin was encouraged to leave the kingdom—his sister and the deception.

Two days passed.

"Look there." said Gem, pointing to the movement up ahead.

"Cantors, I suspect." Elgin shielded his eyes from the sun. "What's left of them."

"Whoa!" The Zuku pulled back on the reins. "They should appreciate the elk. Their trail eases the journey."

"Go up to Sucrene and introduce yourself." The wizard smiled with a nod. "Spare them a wagon of salt and get them started."

Soon after arriving in Truth, Elgin met with Alex and Kain. They further discussed the acquisition of Tuz laborers, and the plan for their escape.

"Tylot is our contact," Alex confirmed. "He understands your requirements and the two-year wait. They are anxious, yet patient." Her voice became impassioned. "They have known nothing but patience . . . and pain . . . and anger. These were the children left behind."

The wizard thought with satisfaction. *These Tuz, will do very well under my control.*

Elgin made a final stop at the clinic. "I heard Koal and Susan welcomed a child."

"Yes," beamed Mila. "Caus . . . at long last, another fair Zuku."

"Congratulations for *that*."

"And your sister obtained her title?"

"The princess is living her dream. Although"—he sighed—"she is the only Symlander there."

"Yes . . . but for how much longer, brother?"

"In the meantime, I've gifted her a falcon. A faithful companion an courier." He looked at Mila with a knowing smirk. "If she should ever feel alone."

258

ONE YEAR PASSED

Elgin steamed into Montro and tied up the vessel. He had been away on a scouting trip to Lackland.

"Welcome back, Wizard Elgin!"

Something was not right. He brushed past the worker without a word. The ominous *feeling* grew stronger around each bend. Daylight was fleeting, and a soft glow illuminated from his father's room.

As he was about to turn the knob, the door opened. Before him stood a disheveled young boy. By all appearances, his care had been absent for days.

"Welcome home, Father."

"Ficus." The confused wizard bent down to hug his son. As he did so, the smell of neglect enveloped him. "Where is Birma?" he asked and then quickly straightened up.

The boy pointed to the light and ran toward it.

Elgin entered the unkempt room, greeted by a stale chill. Nord was sitting in the roller chair, facing a picture window. His slender hand rested on Ficus's shoulder.

"Birma is not here?"

"She is," Nord replied in a raspy voice.

"Where?"

"With the falcons. Ficus, show your—"

"No!"

The boy spun around. "Father!"

"Ficus—" Nord mumbled.

Elgin locked eyes with the disturbed young wizard. "Stay here with your grandfather. I won't be long."

"Father!"

He looked back through the doorway. "Yes, son?"

"We missed you."

On his way to the aviary, Elgin stopped by the pantry. When he pulled aside the curtain, the shelf was bare—the supplements gone.

He turned and bumped into Ficus. "You were *not* to leave that room."

His son stared up with an empty face. "Grandfather told Birma to feed the falcons."

"Stay with him while I finish this."

"Yes, Father."

The falcons were sent into a moonless night, each one with a bag of bones, releasing them over the open water, to settle deep down, into darkness.

Elgin rehearsed his explanation. "A family crisis in Sym, and she urgently left the island.

Mystic falcons would not act with aggression unless commanded to do so. Nord's faculties, though severely diminished, were capable enough. Elgin adjusted his father's formula to ensure it would never happen again.

Ficus was brought to the altar, and engaged with vision and truth. What transpired was then made clear. The disturbing imagery, however, failed to answer the question, why? Why did he compel his grandfather to take such grave action?

* * *

Nord was laid to rest next to Isa. Elgin and Ficus were the last to leave.

"Only you . . . and me, Father?" asked the disoriented young wizard.

"Only you and me."

Ficus's impairment was serious, but not permanent. His evolvement would have to be postponed. That following year, Elgin remained on the island and focused on his son's recovery.

TRUTH

"Orientation went smoothly," Nathan commended the wizard.

"Yes, it did," said Elgin. "The Tuz will make fine laborers. Once they are up in Lackland and properly trained, we can establish full production."

"My parents look forward to traveling—on those rails of yours."

"In their special coach, my prince."

"You have keen eye for the details."

"And what about you," said the wizard with a wink. "Quell informs me the best she can, considering her hands are full. Sienna, a wonderful name . . . you must be proud."

"Extremely—and where to begin? Her development has been impressive, walking and communicating in half the normal time. Wait until you see her."

"Yes." Elgin envisioned his erroneous surprise.

"And then there is my sister." The prince softly chuckled. "You must have seen *them* together."

"I pass by Julia now and again. Most recently, yes, with a Symlander. Kingston, I believe, Hemeth's youngest child."

"What were the odds." He chuckled some more. "Surely my father's health will suffer."

"At least he's not a wizard."

"Thankfully not!"

"Be grateful for this," Elgin said dryly.

After an awkward moment Nathan asked, "And how is your son?"

"Strong."

LACKLAND

Dark's dwindling sunlight offered little relief.

A shivering Ficus looked up at his father driving the covered wagon. "It's so very cold back there."

"Wrap an extra blanket around you." He nodded with a smile. "It won't be long and we'll have a warm fire."

Lackland's iron and lumber factories were the first to be built. Skilled operators from the kingdom were brought in to start them up. They stayed on after completion to train and manage the Tuz. The labor camp was located nearby.

Elgin's modest cabin sat on the far end of the camp. It was prepared for his arrival, the wood stove radiating a comforting heat.

"Here we are, son." He carried the sleepy boy to his bed.

Early the next day, Elgin called out to the stocky foreman, "Tylot!"

"Good day, Wizard Elgin!" he enthusiastically replied.

"Everything is well?"

"Very well, my wizard! Each new day, we become better equipped for the weather."

"I've brought a special supplement, to provide energy and a positive mood. I am depending on you for its distribution."

"Understood, my wizard."

Elgin displayed a coarse brown tablet. "The supplement is concentrated, only one required per day. Simply drop it into the barrel of drinking water. Every Tuz under your command—hmm, supervision—to have a full cup with the midday meal. This also includes you."

"I will log each serving, my wizard."

Tylot was fully aware of the surveillance, with eyes and ears imbedded among the laborers—loyal falcons that circled and screeched. The Mystic wizard was ever present.

THE KINGDOM

The prince asked Elgin, "How is everything in Lackland?"

"Cold!" Ficus blurted out.

Nathan laughed. "But here in the kingdom, you are good and thawed. Quell is upstairs with Sienna. Go there and surprise her."

Elgin glared down at the sleeping child and mockingly *gasped*. "She is of our bloodline? Brown hair, straight as if ironed . . . eyes—"

"They are undecided," said Quell.

"They are brown," insisted Ficus, "and always will be."

"Her *appearance*," suggested Elgin, "has brought the king a measure of contentment."

"He does seem rather fond of her."

"Your next one will add a blue-eyed to the court."

"Or before that . . . depending on Julia."

Princess Julia's union to the Symlander, Kingston, would take place during the academy's next break.

"By the way," Quell continued, "I mentioned the supplements, and she's interested . . . when the time comes."

Elgin whispered in her ear. "Do not mention the supplements again. They never existed."

She stared at him with restrained desperation. "Then for me, my supply is—"

"I know."

*　*　*

They walked down the hill to Plaza Ladesa.

"Father, is everything all right?"

"Yes, Ficus, all is normal. Tell me, do you like this place?"

"I do! It's very active."

"One day, my son . . . this will all be yours." He bent down and gave him a hug.

TRUTH

Gem extended a hearty greeting, "Welcome back, Wizard Elgin."

Ficus jumped from the wagon. "And Ficus!" he shouted in midair.

"And Ficus!" the Zuku said cheerfully.

"He just now woke up," explained Elgin.

"With a surplus of energy, I see."

"I feel strong!"

"And your strength, my wizard?" asked Gem.

Elgin took a deep breath. "The travel provided much time for thought."

"The Tuz?"

"Yes." He sighed. "Yet we had little choice in the matter. If only their productivity matched that of the commons."

While the common Zuku were extremely productive, it was more about convenience and control. Unlike the Tuz, they were scarcely intuitive, and naturally subordinate. Their chemistry would not have to be altered.

Elgin asked, "Was there a problem with the Tuz being excluded?"

"Initially . . . but the issue has been resolved."

"How so?"

"My last visit to Sucrene."

"Go on."

"After we signed the expected agreements, I learned of their future plans. Major endeavors—mine shafts, pipelines . . . a castle on Mount Golder. To complete all of this, they had one serious problem . . . lack of labor.

"Imagine that," said Elgin.

"I offered a large number of Tuz, to satisfy their needs. They have since been hired. Their employment is guaranteed for years."

"This could not have happened at a better time."

"And to you, my wizard, our territory is greatly indebted.

"The future is bright. Let me share our progress."

Elgin updated the status of the Trans Rivera Railway (TRR).

"Lackland's stockyard has reached capacity, and the materials are being delivered. Rails are to be laid simultaneously in Lackland, the kingdom, and Truth, converging at a hub on the Central Grasslands. Three engines and two personal coaches are being assembled on the island. The academy has partnered in their development. The kingdom is responsible for the standard coaches and containers."

Gem shook his head in amazement. "How do you manage all of this?"

"Symlander blood and supplements." The wizard winked. "Which reminds me, I have brought you a fresh supply."

Gem's reformulated tablets included trace amounts of fury, enough to enhance his anger—if provoked.

MONTRO

When Ficus was not occupied with his studies, he enjoyed helping his father in the lab. It was there he felt most satisfied.

"Am I a Mystic wizard?"

Elgin's eyes became brilliantly alive. "Do you believe that you are?"

"I do!"

"Sit with me, my son, and I will tell you why."

Early the next morning, while his father was at the engine yard, Ficus went to the lab. One by one, he brought in each falcon.

Tracks were being laid across the land, and the falcons provided watchful eyes. Some time ago, Elgin had taken the gift's fragment and quartered it, crafting an amulet from each piece. The altar's basin was equally divided with removable copper panels, each amulet connected to a *window*.

Shortly before sunset, Elgin returned to the lab.

"You've been working here all day?"

"Most of it." The young wizard nodded. "Father—"

"Yes, Ficus."

"I want to send a falcon."

The wizard was aware of his dabbling, and the request came as no surprise.

"Choose one, and we'll attach the amulet."

"Let me attach it, Father."

Elgin observed with satisfaction his son's supple dexterity. "Where to?"

"The kingdom."

"And the falcon is aware of this?"

"Yes, he knows."

Elgin looked deep into the Ficus's confident eyes. "Send him off."

The mighty falcon *screeched* and climbed, up into the fading light.

"I did well?"

The wizard smiled with pride and clutched the back of his neck. "Yes, son . . . very well."

Ficus crowed "Tomorrow, we will wake up in the kingdom!"

They laughed and extinguished the lanterns.

* * *

Elgin got out of bed and put on his full-length morning robe. It was dark purple in color and plush.

Ficus was fully dressed at the altar and viewing the kingdom's sunrise.

"You were up with the sun?"

"Father!" The young wizard snapped to attention. "Both times." He grinned.

Elgin stood at the doorway, his thick white mane flowing down past his shoulders.

"One day, I wish to have hair so regal as yours."

"And you will, my son—you will," the amused wizard assured him.

Ficus returned his focus to the window.

"Your attraction to the kingdom never gets tiresome?" asked Elgin, walking over to join him.

"The kingdom energizes me. Aunt Quell has good fortune, to be a princess there."

"Her good fortune is your destiny."

His father's voice was soothing.

They stood together, watching the view over Star Jasmine, its impressive walls bathed in the sun's early rays.

Elgin's eyes narrowed. "Remember this, my son. The Symlander makes the king nervous—a wizard . . . beyond that."

"What is beyond that, Father?"

"Dangerous."

"Are we to make him dangerous?"

"Not if we are careful, and let our patience outlast his fear. The transformation of the kingdom has begun. For now, we create—in time . . . control."

"And the Zuku, Gem," Ficus asked with an envious curiosity, "he is of great importance to us?"

He looked at his son with an understanding. "Gem is no more than a useful tool, forged from our mystic chemistry."

FIVE YEARS PASSED

Lord Martin's remembrance was the largest event Sym had ever known. For over fifty years, the royal patriarch had ruled the land. Faithful mourners lined the avenue and grieved as the procession passed by. His body was sailed to Montro. Its final resting place, a majestic mausoleum.

Classes at the academy had been suspended. Students were instructed to pack their belongings and leave the island. Accommodations would be required for those attending the entombment.

These names were among the invited guests:

Land of Sym
Lady Rook
Sir Hemeth and Lady Rachel
Sir Thomas and Lady Rosa (Sir Graf, Lady Twila)

Territory of Truth
Mila
Koal and Susan (Caus, Mote and Raye)

Kingdom of Rivera
Princess Quell (Princess Sienna)
Princess Julia and Prince Kingston (Prince Lent)

"Are you prepared to apply your magic?" asked Elgin.

"Yes, Father."

"Very well . . . let us make our way down and welcome the guests." He gave him a firm pat on the back.

Elgin had not seen his sister since her infuriating breech of confidence. "How dare she discuss the supplements with Julia!" After that, he modified the formula, She felt a measure of relief, but not the same euphoric satisfaction. Because of this, she struggled with an unresolved emptiness. A similar, though less disruptive condition was present within her daughter.

Quell stepped out of the carriage and immediately went to her brother. "How long has it been?" she asked with a nervous smile.

"Some years," he cooly replied.

"How fortunate we have the falcon."

"The bird can be trusted." An uneasy moment of silence passed. "A shame Nathan could not be here with his family."

"He is deeply committed to your projects."

Sienna emerged from behind her mother. "Are we going to get settled?" she asked.

Elgin smiled at the young princess, looking up at him with lazy brown eyes and a droopy mouth.

"She is tired," said Quell, justifying her disposition.

Elgin was distracted by familiar faces and walked away to greet them. "Welcome back to Montro . . . where it all began, endorsed by the Mystic altar."

"So true!" Prince Kingston happily remembered.

"Yet unlucky Julia had to forego her studies."

"Nothing happens by chance." She smiled over at her son. "One day, Lent will attend the academy and fulfill my promise."

"Indeed he will," agreed the wizard. "His eyes are those of a successful Symlander."

Quell hovered ever closer. "We can talk later?" she asked with subtle urgency.

He forced a smile. "Of course we can."

Elgin anticipated Quell's edginess. Consequently, he developed a temporary formula to smooth her mood. Once she returned to the kingdom, the formula would revert. The wizard did not dispute the cruelty of his manipulation, the reasoning kept only to himself.

* * *

Ficus led the children into the laboratory.

"Your father is a wizard, isn't he?" asked Sir Graf—age fourteen, and the oldest.

"Yes, a very fine wizard," said Ficus. "But what is disclosed here, we do not share with others . . . agreed? Everyone?"

They all agreed, except for Lady Twila, the youngest at age four. "I'm not familiar with the wizard?" she said with a furrowed brow.

"My dear cousin, let me show you one."

He went over to a dark-oak closet and opened its doors. Inside hung a custom-made robe and a matching headdress—gifts from his father, after connecting with the falcons. With his back to the group, he transformed himself and then, slowly, turned to face them.

Impressive, Graf privately gushed.

Ficus stepped over to the altar. "Join me."

The group obediently complied and formed a tight circle around it. They were entranced by the young wizard's words and gestures.

"This ceremony was brought to life by my Grandfather Kren . . . the first Mystic wizard."

Ficus closed his eyes—and soon after, a falcon perched on the balcony railing.

"Oh, look—" Twila started to say.

"Shhh." Graf silenced his little sister.

"That falcon on the balcony?" said Ficus, his eyes remaining closed.

"How did you know?" Twila blurted out.

"Because we are *connected*, and I am speaking to her now."

"Amazing," Lent whispered.

Ficus opened his eyes and acknowledged each child. "To form a connection is why we are here."

Caus spoke up with reservation. "And become wizards?"

"I would rather not be a wizard," Lent confided, looking at the others for support.

"Not wizards," Ficus assured them.

"What then?" Caus anxiously asked.

"United," he said proudly. "United in body and mind. We are young and the future is ours, not as wizards but as loyalists. Are we together?"

"Yes!" Sir Graf avowed. "We are with you, Wizard Ficus."

The others were cautious yet did not disagree.

Ficus instructed them in a soothing voice, "Place a hand in the water and close your eyes. Everyone . . . repeat after me. We are all together."

"WE ARE ALL TOGETHER."

The room became quiet.

Twila's eyes sparked open. "I feel a tingling!" she shrieked.

"I feel it too," said Raye. "First my fingertips . . . now, everywhere else."

"My connection . . . was pronounced," said Graf with halting breath. Sienna gazed at him befuddled. "Mine, equally so."

The others, unsure of what they felt (or continued to feel), stared blankly in confusion.

* * *

Elgin and Tulare's bloodline was mutated by fury, a mysterious and volatile mineral, altering their history—forever. They shared a vision of a new age, created and controlled by wizards. Ficus was at the forefront of this vision.

Elgin worked tirelessly to complete his son's evolvement, an arduous yet satisfying process. While away on business, the young wizard studied and practiced on his own. There were guidelines, targets, and goals.

The railway was completed, and Elgin traveled by private coach. He boarded in Truth—on his way to Lackland, where he spent the majority of his time. He avoided the kingdom, instead meeting with Nathan at the Rivera Transit District.

The district was located in the Central Grasslands, an integral hub linking the kingdom, Lackland, and Truth. It was a unique place, where all cultures lived and worked together. Travel into the kingdom from there was restricted, and required a certified permit.

TWO YEARS PASSED

Elgin entered the residence and dropped his bags.

"Welcome home, Father!" Ficus greeted him with a warm and familiar hug. "Lackland was pleasant without a heavy coat?"

"Indeed." He chuckled. "Solar is a fine season for travel. So tell me, do you have good news?"

The young wizard flashed a confident smile. "You will always be the judge."

Elgin raised an eyebrow. "Should we wait, or—"

"If you are too tired, old wizard?"

Elgin was now for certain Ficus had discovered the missing link. He said, "Sleep can wait."

"Good . . . everything is prepared."

They went to the laboratory.

Elgin sat down in his large reading chair. "Remember, son, don't put me to bed without a bath."

"I'll make sure the water's warm. But before that, let me place these drops in your ears. To improve your hearing."

Interesting twist, thought Elgin.

He adjusted his position and Ficus applied the drops.

"Close your eyes, Father," he said softly and stepped way.

Some moments passed.

"Would there be a falcon in this room?" asked Elgin.

"Open your eyes and see."

A Mystic falcon perched atop the gift, its powerful wings spread wide. *Impressive.*

Ficus stood in the corner by a lantern, its flickering light reflecting off his fine silk robe and headdress. Elgin watched with heightened anticipation as the young wizard's arm slowly rose. A steady finger pointed at the posturing raptor.

"What is your name?" he commanded.

As instructed, she waited until asked a second time.

"Tell us your name."

"Reya!"

* * *

"Ficus, do make yourself available to Sir Graf. He has been asking about you since he arrived."

"Father, you know how difficult it is for me to leave my work."

"Difficult as it is, you cannot be a total recluse. Hiding away only fosters speculation and rumor. Take away the magic of the falcons—our work must be perceived as strictly academic. The Academy's demographics

271

have changed. Symlanders account for less than two-thirds of the student body. Wizards are often misunderstood, and feared by other cultures."

"I'll clean up and take a look around."

Soon after Ficus left the building, he spotted the first-year student walking down the path.

"Sir Graf!"

The royal spun around and enthusiastically waved.

He's a perky one, thought the wizard while shaking his head.

Graf ran up the path and reached out his wanting hand. "Great to see you again, Ficus!"

"Has it really been two years?"

"It has! And ever since then, I worked hard to receive my acceptance. It's all come true, and here we are." He took a deep breath and smiled. "I hope to know you better."

"And you will Sir Graf, providing your studies come first."

"Absolutely!"

"Let me speak with my father, and we'll have you up for supper."

Being the grandson of Lord Hemeth included privileges. While most of the students were housed in a dormitory, Graf had his own private residence. The royal guesthouse was spacious and well appointed. Off the kitchen was a garden patio. From there, the falcons could be seen—flying in and out. And also Ficus, should he step onto the laboratory's balcony.

"How was life on the *outside*?" asked his father.

"By coincidence, I happened upon our dear friend, Sir Graf. We will have him over for supper. In the meantime, I would like to continue with my work."

"Of course," said the satisfied wizard.

Elgin was very close to his son, and open with his thoughts. However, there were plans kept only to himself. Ficus required a confidant, a person of his generation, loyal to his bidding. Sir Graf was the ideal choice. He was intelligent, well connected . . . and motivated.

Several days passed.

"I've never tasted this before," Graf said. "The flavor . . . maybe oxen?"

"Not oxen," replied Elgin. "It's a local delicacy."

Ficus's lips were sealed, suppressing his chagrin.

Graf raised an eyebrow. "Tell me?"

"Filet of kemit."

He chuckled with sparkling eyes. "That was to be my second guess."

Elgin asked, "More tea, Sir Graf?"

"Please! Each cup is better than the last."

"I'm glad you favor it." He smiled." Our family has been brewing this blend for years."

After the meal, Ficus led Graf through the residence. The royal followed closely, lingering on the wizard's every nuance.

"The laboratory!" Graf joyfully blurted out. "My favorite place."

"Working here is my passion," said Ficus.

"And the altar," Graf smiled into the wizard's eyes, "where we connected."

"A powerful commitment, shared by us all."

"My studies are weighted in science. I could be of some help for you here?"

"If not with my father, I am accustomed to working alone."

"I could be of service . . . and companionship."

"The falcons are available for that."

"Mystic falcons," Graf said warmly.

Ficus was reminded of his father's wishes. "Perhaps a small amount of assistance. But we cannot have you obsessing over this place. Your parents would be highly disappointed if your studies were to suffer."

"I will only do as I am told."

"Then we are in agreement." Ficus reached out and firmly shook his hand. "Good night, Sir Graf."

"Good night . . . my wizard!"

* * *

Elgin's voice was steady and to the point. "Sir Graf has value. Go easy, manage his feelings with care."

"He aspires to be one of us."

"Wizards evolve from inception, and he is far too late for that."

"We can provide an incentive?"

"He can earn a title . . . associate wizard. I will order a robe"—he nodded—"but not a headdress."

Passage of Time

The specially blended tea tempered Graf's inquisitiveness but not his intelligence. Because of this, the wizards proceeded with caution. He was kept occupied with harmless studies, developed without a solution yet worthy of academic credit.

Elgin walked into the lab and shared the news. "I have spoken to the headmaster."

"The program?" Ficus assumed.

"She is confident we have the votes."

"Congratulations."

"An elective, and less intensive than before. Same requirements, high marks in science—"

"We can discuss this over supper?"

Later that evening, Ficus said, "Father, tell Sir Graf the news."

"It's still not official"—he tapped the table twice with his knuckles—"but the abilities program has been revived."

"This is excellent news!"

"Agreed," said Elgin.

"Get to the point, Father."

"Your name, Sir Graf, has been mentioned to lead the program."

The royal was flabbergasted. "I have no formal training to instruct."

"We can manage around that," he assured him. "The program's re-instatement is conditional. The first year requires my full support."

Speechless, Graf looked back and forth between the wizards.

"I've thought it out," Elgin continued, "and the situation is ideal. Ficus's early enrollment has been approved. This frees up my time to guide you."

"I am equally honored and perplexed."

Elgin stood up. "Before you go, I have something to give you."
What could it be? wondered Ficus.
The wizard returned with a silk robe and leather-bound notebook.
"These are for you . . . Professor Graf."

PROFESSOR GRAF

Soon after his appointment, Graf moved in with the wizards. It was a matter of convenience, as most workshops took place in the laboratory. His cousin from Truth, Caus, would occupy the guesthouse. The half-blooded Zuku favored his Aunt Mila, appearing as a Symlander—and gifted.

"Congratulations, *Professor.* Mother mentioned you added a title."

"An achievement, no doubt," Graf responded with a wink. "Considering my father never studied on this island."

"You said it." Caus nodded. "Susan was always the more gifted of the twins."

Graf's thick white eyebrows converged. "Did you just peer into what I was thinking?"

"It happens," he awkwardly conceded.

"Cousin, you will not last long doing such a thing. The island's policy is straightforward. Do not explore the thoughts of others."

"It won't happen again."

"I am not the sensitive one, but there are those extremely so."

Later, during supper, Ficus asked, "Your cousin, he has settled in?"

"He has, and—"

"What else?"

Graf nervously glanced at them both and took a shallow breath. "I had to remind him of the policy."

Elgin groaned with displeasure. "The policy is underlined in the packet."

"No reading of minds," said Ficus. "While father and I can shut him out, most cannot. If compelled, I'll probe the imposter myself."

"How can—"

"Our connection!" he blurted out.

Elgin grimaced, dismayed at his son's disclosure.

"And . . . me?" Graf said softly.

Ficus leaned forward and stared deep into his eyes. Graf was for certain his well-kept secrets were being processed. He sat motionless, paralyzed by discovery . . . and waited.

Ficus replied in a low, ominous voice, "Nothing there."

Elgin burst into laughter.

Graf took a very deep breath. And as he did so, his eyes rolled up and disappeared.

* * *

True to his word, Elgin spent a great deal of time mentoring the young professor. While doing so, they closely bonded. Graf became as a second son. Unlike Ficus, who was often cold and calculating, Graf was engaging and personable. This provided mixed feelings when the wizard prepared his tea, knowing Graf's essence was progressively slipping away.

They cruised in calm water, under steam-generated power.

Graf said, "The Dark Forest . . . tell me more."

He listened attentively whenever Elgin shared stories from the past, marveling at his attention to detail and his recall from an early age.

"A magical place—that forest. I often wandered into its depths. Somehow . . . never losing my way."

"And your mother?" he asked with uncertainty. She was rarely mentioned.

"My poor mother." Elgin sighed. "How she tried to manage my energy. It was often difficult for her to keep up. Yet she never complained. She was devoted."

"I don't mean to pry, but—"

"It's not discussed. The wizard gazed off across the water.

"Forgive me."

"Take down these notes, Professor."

"I am ready."

"Integrate more history into next year's program. Important! The *factual* story of our culture."

"Got it!"

They stared into each other's Symlander eyes.

"There are those, Professor Graf, that would have you believe wizards eat the hearts of young children and sleep with the dead."

TRUTH

A small gathering of family welcomed Caus home for solar break.

"Share with us the latest from Montro!" Susan anxiously asked her son.

"The dwelling is comfortable enough," he said with a listless chuckle. "But other than that—"

An unexpected silence filled the room.

"Caus?"

His eyes despondently glistened. "Even though we share the same appearance, to *them*, I am not a true Symlander. I hear the name . . . imposter. If only I resembled my father and brother, the Zuku I truly am."

"I understand," said Mila.

He glanced over at her and then his cousin Raye (Wair and Dorin's son). "It can be difficult when you are isolated and alone. The island's beauty is deceptive. Next year will be different." He nodded. "Raye will be there with me."

"What about your cousin?" asked his mother.

Caus shook his head. "Sir Graf? Professor Graf? Wizard Graf?"

"And now—a wizard?" she scoffed.

"He lives among the wizards, and our paths seldom cross."

"Speaking of wizards," Koal spoke up. "What is your impression of Ficus?"

"I don't' trust him. His *truth* is cold and concealed."

* * *

Caus spent much of his break at the clinic. His younger brother, Mote, was training there.

"How is she today?" asked Caus.

"Awake and talking," Mote replied. Mila and Gem are with her."

The Zuku leaders provided Wen comfort until her final breath, sharing memories, meaningful and deep.

THE FOLLOWING YEAR

Ficus respected his father's wisdom and valued his beliefs. He listened carefully.

"Never trust one drop of gifted Zuku blood. The nature of their chemistry is elusive . . . lacking explanation." For each word, he aggressively shook his finger. "Not . . . ! One . . . ! Drop!"

"Not one drop, Father."

"True . . . most Zukus are common. Not so primitive as first perceived, yet no concern of ours. The gifted such as Gem, however, are capable of silent communication and mind reading. All without the mystic minerals that we require."

"And with the minerals?" asked Ficus.

"Their behavior can be modified."

And controlled, the young wizard privately determined.

"Now . . . take a Zuku with Symlander blood."

"Mila!"

"Yes." Elgin's eyes, roamed freely. "What might the possibilities be, if *she* were to drink a special blend?"

"Unlimited." Ficus believed.

"Not so, my son." He shook his head. "Instinctively, she would fight the intrusion, potentially with her final breath. No . . . Mila's departure will take its natural course."

"Father."

"Yes, Ficus."

"When will you share more of our future?"

"Have patience."

"I am learning."

"And very well." He looked with pride into his son's impressionable eyes. "We must take great care of our future."

"Yes, Father."

"Those imposters in the guesthouse—be cordial, but do not invite their interest. Graf is vulnerable, and we must protect him."

* * *

The cousins stepped out on the patio and sat down.

"This is perfect," said Raye with a slow exhale.

"It's much better with you here in that chair," said Caus. "Better still if we were on the other side."

"And why is that?"

He raised his eyes. "Up there, they watch over us. If not the wizards, their falcons. Be mindful of their presence. Ficus lurks in every shadow."

* * *

Graf was into his third week of a newly formulated tea, an enriched recipe with transferable qualities. Once absorbed by the recipient, additional supplements were not required.

"I haven't been myself lately." Graf shook his head in frustration." My thoughts are unsteady."

"Let me tweak the blend," suggested Elgin.

Graf's pale-blue eyes reflected a measure of despair. "Can we simply stop the tea?"

"No," he replied, in a firm yet compassionate voice.

Later that evening, Ficus joined his father in the study.

Again, the young wizard listened carefully. This time, the magnitude of their actions was revealed. Instead of unsure and anxious, he was enthralled.

Elgin stared intently at his son. "We understand our purpose. It is Graf's directive that must be realized. You are his inspiration, encourage him with your support."

"After this is over, his condition will improve?"

"For both of you."

"I will speak with him now."

He walked into the laboratory and greeted the professor with a smile.

Graf looked up and his eyes opened wide. "Wizard Ficus, this is a surprise."

"The breeze is warm and the stars are bright. Join me on the balcony."

Early the next morning, Ficus woke up with his father standing over him.

"Get dressed and join me in the garden."

Elgin sat on a bench, overlooking the headstones of his parents and Tulare.

"Good day, Father."

"Yes, son, it *is* a good day." He nodded. "And you slept well?"

"Very well."

Elgin's thick eyebrow lifted. "You and Graf were on the balcony . . . in conversation."

"We drank tea under the stars."

"And?"

"He is capable and prepared."

Later that evening in the laboratory, Elgin was dressed in his father's ceremonial attire, the altar's basin refreshed and specialized—a final potion before their travel.

"Welcome, Wizards!" Ficus and Graf were boldly greeted. "Join me here."

Reverently, Elgin placed his hand upon the stone. "A *gift* from our Maker, delivered from the stars in a blaze of white fire. Its limitless power rages eternal. Close your eyes and absorb the supernatural. Let it provide all that you require."

When they submerged their hands, a pulsating energy surged within them.

Something unusual is happening, thought Caus, observing the shadows from below.

* * *

Caus had accepted the inevitable: Montro was never going to be a place of comfort. For Raye, it was different. He was immune to self-doubt. His sparkling character was attractive, and he made friends with little effort. Invited by classmates, he had already left for Sym on solar break.

The wizards would attend Sucrene's celebration. They planned to meet with Gem and travel there together. The Zuku was familiar with the valley, and he knew the royals well.

"Professor Graf!"

He watched with curiosity his cousin running up the path. "Caus, why so urgent?"

"You . . . are traveling to Truth?" he asked with a shortness of breath.

"Yes, with Elgin and Ficus."

"I am by myself . . . without transport. Would it . . . be possible to join you?"

"I don't—" Graf became flustered, his thoughts easily traced. "We have responsibilities, and . . . much is on our minds."

Elements of a sinister plan had been exposed.

Caus was shocked by what he discovered. *I have to warn Gem. The wizards must be stopped!*

Graf rushed away in panic. *Elgin is going to be livid.*

Later that night, the wizard stood over the altar as Ficus entered the room.

"What are you preparing, Father?"

"A gift."

"Our plan?"

"Has been revised."

On the way to the guesthouse, Ficus mulled over his father's disposition. He remained composed, undeterred by Graf's disclosure. How was their plan not compromised?

Caus answered the door. "Ficus?"

"I am here for my father. Pack your belongings and join us at daybreak."

"Tell him I am grateful."

* * *

At Montro Harbor, Elgin said, "Wait here."

Graf did as he was told, staying out of sight in the vessel.

Elgin walked over to Ficus and Caus. "It seems we require a minor repair."

"I can help with that, Father?"

"Yes . . . and for you, Caus, I've secured passage on a cargo vessel. There is no reason to delay your travel."

He said, "Are you sure?" then privately asked, *Something else?*

As they stared at each other the wizard nodded. "One small favor."

"Of course."

"This gift is for Gem. It's not to be opened until received . . . understood?"

"I will handle it with care."

Caus took hold of the small copper-cladded box (cool to the touch, sealed and latched).

"Let our friend know we are close behind."

"I will tell him . . . and safe journey to you."

And to you, Caus.

They went their separate ways.

"We have an issue with the vessel?" asked Ficus.

"No."

Caus climbed aboard and sat next to the captain. The waters were calm, the smell of ripening fruit in the air.

"What's inside that box?" enquired the captain.

"I have no idea," said Caus with equal curiosity. "It's a gift."

"Maintain our distance," instructed Elgin.

"Yes, my wizard," Graf replied, with both hands firmly on the wheel.

The cargo vessel entered the Sucrene.

"Increase our speed, Professor Graf." *I want a better view.*

"Yes, my wizard."

Caus's thigh had become exceedingly warm.

He handed the box to the captain. "Do you feel that?"

"Heat," he confirmed. "Why don't we open it. The fresh air might help to coo—"

"No . . . I was told not to."

"We won't look inside," the captain said with a shrug.

There was a brief pause before the latch was pressured by his thumb.

"NO," Caus cried out.

A thunderous sound was heard.

Upriver, a plume of dark-gray smoke slowly began to rise.

"Steer the vessel over there." Elgin pointed to a nearby inlet. "Debris and high water are on the way."

"Wh-what was that?" Graf stuttered.

Ficus spoke up for his father, "The imposter's final breath."

CHAPTER 13
SUCRENE'S CELEBRATION

E lgin reached to the sky and emphatically declared, "We are the Mystic wizards. We are the chosen!"

* * *

Gem smiled broadly and shouted, "Throw me a line!"

The vessel was tied off and Elgin stepped down to the dock. "It's been far too long, my friend!"

They shared a generous hug and patted each other's back.

"Your travel went well?"

"The trip upriver always inspires," said the wizard with an easy smile. He glanced around the surroundings. "And the changes that I see here."

"We've expanded and made improvements," acknowledged the Zuku. "Including your new guesthouse."

"We'll make good use of that tonight."

Gem looked off into the distance and took a deep breath. "The railway has changed everything."

"And soon, Sucrene will experience the same," said Elgin. "They can't stay isolated forever."

"For now, I have fresh horses and a dependable wagon."

Later that evening, the overnight guests attended a small dinner gathering, hosted by Susan and Koal.

Mila walked over to the wizards. "Good evening," she cordially greeted them.

"Good evening, Mila," Elgin replied, and Ficus nodded.

She raised an eyebrow. "You have been avoiding us?"

"Not at all." He stared back into her probing eyes. "I've been occupied at the academy, assisting Professor Graf."

"Where is the professor? Gem mentioned he is here."

"Resting at the guesthouse before our travel. End-of-semester finals got the best of him.

Graf was held back at the guesthouse for a reason. Elgin could ill afford another breach of confidence. Mila's abilities were exceptional. She had the potential to know one's *truth*—at its core.

"Ficus."

"Yes, Mila?"

"My nephew, Caus, was expected back on his break. Were you aware of his travel plans?" She studied the young wizard as he replied.

"I believe he was waiting for space on a cargo vessel."

Elgin abruptly spoke up. "From what I can tell, your nephew is quite gifted."

"Uniquely gifted," she replied, stepping ever closer to the wizard. "Although not unexpected considering his bloodline. What is your opinion . . . *brother*?"

The siblings stood face-to-face, their matching eyes locked in a battle of understanding.

Elgin was not interested in meaningless debate. His position was firm. The naturally gifted were emotionally unstable, weak, and susceptible to harm—incapable of challenging a Mystic wizard, an all-powerful creation of pure Symlander blood and fury.

Soon after the dinner was over, Mila searched for Gem outside. She found him there—alone, staring into the night sky.

"Father," she said tenderly, "what are you looking for among those stars?"

She looked up at the twinkling lights and asked herself the same.

He sighed. "Answers."

She reached over and placed her arm around his shoulder. "I *feel* your distress."

"The king will be there."

"And your thoughts belong to him?"

On occasion, Gem would call Mila by her childhood name. "Fair Zuku"—his eyes narrowed in anguish—"Gorsh had no right to violate you as he did."

"We cannot undo the travesties of the past. But if we could, would I be here? Would Wair? The king has been punished. And I have no thoughts of further retribution."

I have! Gem silently fumed.

He ran off without a word, and Mila called after him, her voice, growing faint—then silent. He was at her doorstep. Once inside, he knew where she kept it.

* * *

Two days passed.

Gem drove the four-horse team steadily up the grade, with Elgin next to him and Graf and Ficus in the back. Behind them were two large kegs of fine shillig reserved for the banquet.

"Something familiar about this elevation," Elgin muttered.

"Lackland," Ficus blurted out.

"A beautiful time of the year, early solar," said Gem.

"Those peaks over there"—Graf pointed to the Red Vein Mountains—"they have snow year-round?"

"All year round," confirmed the Zuku.

They reached the crest and the valley came into view.

"Sucrene!" Gem announced.

"There's a carriage down there," said Ficus. "It appears to be from the kingdom."

After two turns, Gem pulled the horses to a stop. "You have trouble there?"

"We have broken an axle!" a voice underneath the carriage replied.

There was movement inside the compartment and the door opened.

"Prince Nathan!" Elgin warmly called out.

287

"Wouldn't you know it? We drew the weakest of the lot."

"Traveling alone?"

"My father's continued on, and left us to the warkins."

"I wouldn't worry about those bloodthirsty beasts," Elgin said dryly, "unless the sun goes down,"

"Warkins. Father!" cried out the voice inside the carriage.

"No need for concern, Sienna," Nathan assured his daughter.

Sienna, thought Graf.

The driver shimmied out from underneath the carriage and informed the prince, "It's only a temporary fix. We'll have to lighten the load to make it there."

"We can help with that," said Gem. "Our wagon has room for one more and belongings."

"I can ride with them, Father."

"You will follow us?" asked Nathan.

"All the way to the castle," said Gem.

"It's settled, then."

Graf approached the young princess. "Let me help you."

"Those two pieces up there," she said with an eager smile.

On the way over to the wagon, there was a lightness in her step.

"My sister . . . she is tired from the travel?" asked Elgin.

"Yes, she is." Nathan sighed. "Just tired."

Quell's mental state had become precarious. It angered Nathan as he tried—but failed—to find a remedy. Powerless, he watched her endearing personality erode. Why? Over and over, he asked himself. Was it the pressure of her appearance? Was it him? The answer would not come from her.

Elgin walked over to the carriage and peered inside. Quell was leaning back in the corner, her blue eyes glazed and distant, her slightly parted lips pale and dry.

"Ficus!"

The young wizard rushed over. "Yes, Father."

"Bring me a flask of our water."

Elgin sat down beside her. "I have something for you," he whispered.

"Here, Father."

He took the flask, then placed a small tablet on her tongue. She took a passive sip and swallowed it down.

The wizard gently kissed her cheek. "Happiness awaits you."

Soon the carriages were on their way, down the serpentine road.

"Professor Graf," Elgin spoke up. "Ask the princess if she would care for a cup of tea."

"I would like that," she said before he could ask.

Graf sat between Ficus and Sienna, their thighs pressed together, absorbing each bump and turn. The princess was content beyond measure.

Sienna's imagination was in full bloom, reunited with her childhood connection from Montro. The professor's purpose was clear, inspired by another.

"More tea?" Graf offered.

"Please." She softly smiled.

He smiled in return and placed his hand on hers while at the same time pressing his thigh firmly against Ficus.

I am doing this for you, he revealed, if that someone were to listen.

They rolled into Sucrene, and reminders of the celebration were everywhere—large colorful banners, festive music, and villagers dancing in costume.

Sienna pointed to a man on stilts, wearing an exaggerated smile. "To be so happy!"

"So . . . happy," Ficus uttered beneath his breath.

Straight ahead was Mount Golder, rising up from the valley floor.

"I will say this much," Elgin remarked. "The Cantors made a bold choice, building on that volcano."

They slowed to a stop at the western gate and waited behind the royals. Sitting next to one of the attendants was a four-legged beast, its sensitive ears perked and amber eyes darting about. Another of its kind circled the carriage with nostrils flared.

"Warkins," said Graf.

"Royal warkins," Gem clarified. "Prince Roland's prized possession."

The carriage cleared, and they were motioned forward. Elgin waved their invitation, and the attendant came around. Ficus kept an eye on the approaching warkin. Gem leaned over and lowered his hand. The beast nuzzled the rugged knuckles and gave them a lick.

Good to see you too, the Zuku privately agreed.

The warkin backed away and then lunged up against the side board. Glaring at Ficus, it released a low, menacing growl. Sienna's mouth gaped open, and she clutched Graf's supportive hand.

"That's enough!" the attendant ordered, causing the warkin to retreat. "It's the Symlander blood," she explained.

A basic potion will remedy that, Elgin silently decided.

"Welcome to Castle Golder," the attendant concluded. "Enjoy the celebration."

The young royals were on the lookout for visitors entering the spacious courtyard below.

"Symlanders!" Robert shouted. "We should go down."

Sara was transfixed by Ficus's magnetic presence. His steady gaze slowly climbing the jagged rock, until reaching the balcony where they stood.

"That one there," noticed Robert, "is staring up at us."

Impulsively Sara raised her hand and extended a wave.

Ficus returned the gesture. *A pleasure to meet you, Sara.*

"Yes, Robert, let's go down." And together they hurried away.

"Sienna wasn't much trouble, was she?" Prince Nathan asked the group.

"The princess," said Graf, "was delightful."

A rejuvenated Quell stepped from the carriage, encouraged to join the others.

The castle's reception area provided welcome relief. Attendants carrying trays of refreshing beverages and appetizing food greeted the long-distance travelers. Royal representatives and porters provided escort to the guest rooms. Celebration packets had been left there with a layout of the castle and schedule of events.

The princess exhaled with disappointment, "We have missed them."

"Missed who?" said the wizard, appearing from around the corner.

"Oh!" Her eyes lit up and she caught her breath.

"I am Ficus from Montro, son of Elgin." He bowed his head.

"I am Sara . . . and this is my brother, Robert."

The princess had long admired her parents' relationship. The devotion between them was special. The passion burning in their eyes—undeniable. As Sara matured, she dreamed of that same passion. Ficus embodied the essence of those dreams.

The Symlander lightly chuckled. "It seems I've been forgotten."

"We'll help you find your way," Sara cheerfully assured him.

Upstairs in the guest room Elgin asked, "What is it, Gem? I sense your turmoil."

"You know me too well, my wizard."

"It is Gorsh, isn't it?"

"I don't want to jeopardize our relationship with the kingdom."

"And you won't—my friend, you won't."

Gem pressed his fingers to his chest. "The king incites a vengeance inside me that impairs my better judgment. I fear what would happen if—"

"We are all here for the same reason, to celebrate Sucrene's success." He put his hand firmly on the Zuku's shoulder. "A good night's rest will calm your anger."

* * *

A parade the next day was the celebration's first event. It would begin and end at the village square, passing twice through the castle's courtyard. A viewing stand was erected there, for the royals and their guests.

"Are you sure?" Quell asked.

"Yes," Sienna replied. "There is so much excitement among the locals."

"And Professor Graf will provide your company?"

"At all times."

"Do return, well before the banquet."

"Yes, Mother."

Instead of going to the central square, they ventured off and explored the grounds. As they distanced themselves from the castle, the festive sounds began to fade. Reveling in her independence, Sienna walked briskly ahead. Graf's mind strayed elsewhere.

From behind a group of trees, Sienna's voice rang out. "Graf! See what I've found!"

She had discovered an oasis of fruits and nuts, and a spring-fed pond with lilies.

"There you are," he said with a warm smile.

"Try one of these?" She handed him a deep-orange apricot.

He held the fuzzy fruit beneath his nose. "It smells wonderful."

"And delicious," she marveled, after tasting her second bite.

"The rich flavor will go well with a toast." He opened the flask and took a generous drink.

The shillig was specially prepared by Gem, at Elgin's request. He did so without questioning the motive.

Sienna accepted the flask and took a drink. "A perfect combination!"

"As we are . . . together? said Graf with an inviting smile.

"I am profoundly attracted to you," she confessed. "It has been that way since the altar.

"I was moved there as well." His eyes looked up—and wandered away.

She reached out and pulled him toward her. "Lie down with me."

* * *

The parade long over, most of the guests were in their rooms, resting before the evening banquet.

Nathan was slowly pacing the floor.

"She'll be here soon enough," Quell assured him.

Just then the door opened.

"Sienna!" her mother happily called out.

"It's not too late, is it?"

"No," said Quell, glancing over at the prince.

"Not too late," he agreed.

She smiled warmly at them both. "May I take a short rest?"

"Yes," said her father. "Now that you are here, we will do the same."

Sienna stepped away and closed the door behind her.

The young princess lay still on the bed, choosing not to bathe until the last moment, treasuring the intimacy as long as she was able.

"Her mood is the best that I can remember," said Quell.

Nathan kept silent, occupied in thought.

She went to him with a flirtatious smile. "We have been rewarded. The decision to make this travel has stimulated our desire."

The prince gazed longingly into her Symlander eyes.

THE BANQUET

Gem made it clear to those responsible that they were not to be seated near the king.

Earlier that day, unbeknownst to the Zuku, Elgin managed a short conversation with the Gorsh and Ladesa. They exchanged pleasantries and discussed the railway. The royals were in high spirits and indulging in Cantor hospitality.

Halfway through the reception line, Elgin tapped Gem's shoulder and quietly confirmed, "He's been seated."

The edgy Zuku took a slow, deep breath.

"We're almost to the front," said Graf, looking back to where the line formed.

"He's on his way," replied Elgin.

"It is good to see you, Gem," said the prince reaching out his hand.

"And you, Prince Jordan . . . and your family."

Princess Mirasol spoke up, "Our *family* is short one member. The fit of her new dress"—she shook her head—"untimely alterations."

"I am Elgin, from Montro. And this is Professor Graf, of the academy."

The princess smiled and took hold of his hand. "Welcome to our valley."

"We are delighted to be here," said the wizard. "Congratulations on your many achievements. My vision for Lackland has been reimagined."

"Your railway is the talk of the land," remarked the prince. "There are plans for a station here?"

"Yes, is the short answer," he said with a wink.

Ficus entered the hall and excused his way to the front of the line. "Forgive my delay. I got involved in conversation and lost awareness of the time. Your castle is most impressive."

"My son, Ficus," Elgin proudly acknowledged.

The young Symlander respectfully bowed.

"Hello again," said Prince Robert, staring up with a big smile.

Ficus smiled in return. "Hello again to you."

"Please excuse Sara's absence," Prince Jordan apologized. "She will greet you at your table. Enjoy!"

Toasts of fine shillig made their way around the hall.

King Gorsh stood up and commanded the floor. "It is unfortunate the queen's brother is not here with us tonight."

A chorus of sighs filled the air.

"I know Prince Roland would have been honored to lead this celebration. Nevertheless, through the strong efforts of his son, his legacy lives on. To Prince Jordan!"

Glasses were raised high. "PRINCE JORDAN."

The king waited for the room to settle. "Twenty years ago, this was an isolated and little-known valley, home to resilient miners, trappers, and wild beasts. Its hidden resources largely untouched. Today, it is a region of wealth and opportunity. A safe haven for growing families . . . and royal warkins!"

Raucous laughter ensued.

"To Sucrene!" Gorsh shouted.

"SUCRENE."

"This is the Land of Rivera! "A glorious land! Where even the primitives have been tamed. See how they benefit from civilized living. Together, we celebrate evolution. We celebrate . . . prosperity!"

Elgin looked over at Gem and studied his simmering rage.

"To Rivera!" Gorsh roared.

"RIVERA."

"This king has not tamed me." The Zuku's voice was loud enough to be heard at the nearby tables.

Elgin handed him a tablet, and he washed it down with a mouthful of shillig.

By now, many of the guests were influenced by the fermented beverage. King Gorsh in particular was unwilling to limit his toasts. His voice grew louder, his opinions without restraint. Although seated at the other end, Gem could discern his obnoxious behavior.

"You must be Sara." Elgin stood up and greeted the young princess.

"Yes . . . and finally, I've made my way to your table."

"I am Elgin of Montro. This is Professor Graf and my son, Ficus."

"Good to meet you, Elgin and Professor Graf." She glanced over at Ficus and smiled. "I have already had the pleasure."

Gem stood up and greeted the princess. "Good to see you again, Sara." Over her shoulder, he could clearly see the king, his flushed face contorted in laughter, his arms flailing about, saluting himself and boasting of exploits.

"Good to see you . . . Gem?"

"Excuse me for a moment," the distracted Zuku replied.

Elgin alerted the others, "Stay here and remain calm."

"King Gorsh!" Gem shouted, his glass raised high.

Anticipating a toast, the inebriated royal did the same. As his glass went up, the Zuku's vengeance was swiftly delivered.

"This is for my mother!" He thrust the blade deep into the king's lower abdomen.

"Argh!" he groaned in pain.

Ladesa fainted, and toppled off her chair.

"And this—for Mila!"

Once more, the blade disappeared, this time into the bent-over king's lower jaw.

Gasps, shrieks, and cries reverberated off the walls.

Gem's face was mapped in a mixture of blood and fury.

"King Gorsh!" one of the guests screamed out. "Someone help the king!"

The assault would have continued, if not for Prince Nathan's blade.

The hall was soon cleared. Stunned guests returned to their rooms. Gorsh's body was prepared for travel.

Elgin stood over the Zuku leader lying face down on the floor. "Turn him over," he instructed his son.

Underneath lay a bloodied dagger. The wizard picked it up and brought it closer to his eyes, slowly turning the handle back and forth, scrutinizing its crimson blade.

Ficus asked, "It is familiar?"

"The iron was forged in the Northern Frontier. This dagger belonged to my father."

CHAPTER 14
MYSTIC WIZARDS

The mass desertion was staggering. Most of the guests left the valley by sunrise. Limited information filtered out from the castle. Something terrible had happened. The mood in Sucrene transformed from jubilant to somber, all elements of the celebration immediately removed.

"By order of the royal family," one of the workers replied.

Castle Golder became dark and silent.

THE KINGDOM

The king's initial viewing was private.

"Why?" the prince asked in disbelief, standing beside the hollowed-out body.

"Vengeance," his mother answered, from the shadows of the dimly lit room. "Vengeance for the invasion, the loss of his mother . . . and Mila."

Nathan turned to the voice.

The queen came into the light and approached her son. "Gem cared for Mila as if she were his own daughter. Your father assaulted her innocence. You have a brother."

"How long have you known?"

"Long enough."

Queen Ladesa abdicated her right to the throne, and Nathan was crowned the new king. Despite in poor health, she remained influential until her final breath.

Truth

Elgin stopped to see Mila on his way back to Montro.

"Gem was overtaken by anger," said the wizard, "and simply lost all control. No matter Truth's progress, he could not let go of the past. The theft of your land, death of his mother . . . your personal sacrifice."

"How dare you speak of that!" Mila bristled with indignation. "You find it within your rights, knowing one's *truth* yet concealing your own?"

"Concealing the father we both share? Ironic, isn't it? The king's life taken with his dagger."

"What are you saying?"

Elgin handed her the blood-stained blade. "You haven't missed it?"

"I am only missing Caus. He hasn't returned."

* * *

On a peaceful day beneath a clear-blue sky, Gem's ashes were spread among the evergreens.

"Mother, you have made tears," said Mila.

"Yes, on this day I have."

Harta adapted to her emotional limitations. A gifted Zuku would never live a life so pure. During the season of darkness that following year, she reunited with her mate.

Lackland

"She will be here," Graf assured the wizard.

Soon after this was said, Sienna arrived at the district hub.

The princess abandoned her family and dedicated herself to Graf. The king was incensed with his daughter's decision. The queen was apathetic. Elgin's reformulated supplements had kept her in a placid state of mind.

The private coaches were pulled through the turntable by an engine bound for Lackland. Tylot would be there waiting with the wagons.

"Welcome back, my wizard!"

"Good to be here, Tylot," replied Elgin with a subtle nod. "You have been well?"

"Very well, my wizard, and all is in order!"

An impressive stone wall now surrounded the camp, twice the height of an average Tuz. Elgin's original cabin expanded in three directions. The Mystic altar was placed in the largest room. The falcons perched on the roof.

* * *

The next day, for those preselected Tuz, this was their moment of commitment.

Elgin said, "Lead them in."

The young conscripts followed Tylot to the altar, one by one submerging their hands in the mystic minerals and wizard blood.

The transformative potion was progressive. When combined with aggressive training, the desired attributes—strength, endurance, high tolerance for pain—were acquired.

* * *

The training ground was located in a nearby forest, well hidden from those outside its timbered walls. Elgin and Graf entered through the secured gate and joined Tylot at its center.

On a raised platform, Graf addressed the enforcers, two hundred strong. "I am your commander. It is here you will prepare. Tylot is your guardian—follow his every word. His guidance comes from me. My guidance, from the Mystic wizard. Together, we are united. Together, we are family!"

"United!" Tylot shouted.

"United!" the enforcers answered back.

"Family!" Graf shouted.

"Family!" the enforcers answered back.

"Family!" the Mystic wizard powerfully declared, his tight fist raised up high.

"FAMILY." The enforcers erupted, and thrust their fists to the sky.

Elgin reveled in the outpouring of allegiance.

* * *

Sienna was isolated in a wing of the cabin, bedridden and cared for by birthers. In the beginning, Graf was also there. Once the potion took hold (and she lost reason), he left. Even though the princess appeared lifeless, her womb was fortified and vital. She survived the toxic delivery, only to be discarded without her memory. She was placed in a Lackland factory, and absorbed by the Tuz in their village.

The child would come to know Elgin as her adoptive father.

SUCRENE

As with Sienna's pregnancy, Sara's came as a complete surprise. The identity of the father, however, she refused to disclose.

Ficus had captured the princess's imagination. In her thoughts, he was always there. Before Jasira's birth, she wandered the halls of Castle Golder, inevitably ending up in the guest room where her fate was sealed. As she lay upon the bed they shared, the wizard's enchanting presence surrounded her.

"Someday," she whispered.

* * *

"There is blood there," her brother noticed with concern.

"Only an inconvenience," Sara replied. Taking a piece of cloth, she dabbed the fluid from her ear.

"Does it hurt?"

"Not at all . . . everything is fine."

The royal physician sat with Sara's parents and explained the grim reality.

"Your daughter's condition is extremely unusual. She is dangerously weak, yet the child grows ever stronger."

Mirasol cried out, "There must be something you can do?"

"What if . . . we take the child?" Jordan reluctantly asked.

"We lose them both."

MONTRO

With his father and Graf in Lackland, Ficus maintained the abilities program. It was a watered-down version, consisting of mundane lectures, a temporary solution until the altar and falcons returned. A future replacement to lead the program would also be required.

Prince Lent fulfilled his mother's promise and followed her path to the academy. He was the perfect candidate for the position. Although of mixed cultures, he took after Symlander (a wizard prerequisite).

The first-year student stepped down from the vessel.

Ficus reached out his hand. "Welcome, Prince Lent, to Montro and the academy."

"Thank you for being here to greet me."

"My father was emphatic I do so. The loss of your grandfather remains unsettling."

"It is true, the kingdom still mourns. However, we have found comfort with my uncle on the throne."

"King Nathan, an honorable man."

The prince glanced around the surroundings. "To be here on this island . . . is a breath of fresh air."

"Your room has been well prepared." The wizard smiled. "Its spacious balcony will provide much of what you speak of."

"I look forward to the pleasantries absent during my travel."

"I am familiar with this sacrifice."

They both broke out in carefree laughter.

* * *

Raye returned from solar break to find himself living alone. Caus's death had been confirmed: a tragic accident without explanation.

He answered the knock on his door. "Ficus."

"Hello, Raye."

"This is unexpected."

"I am here for myself, and also my father. We were saddened to hear about Caus. If we can assist in any way."

"Very considerate of you both."

"Yes . . . of course, and—"

"There is something else?"

A friendly reminder.

"I understand."

Ficus turned and walked away.

"You're back so soon," said Lent.

"It was nothing more than a courtesy call," the wizard dryly replied.

"How is he?"

"As before, a blue-eyed imposter. But here we are, and a brilliant sunset on its way. Let's sit on the balcony and have that tea!"

Lent's early dosage was similar to Graf's—mild and deceptive.

The prince gazed out across the water. "I could never get enough of this. The colors are ever-changing. The sea has many moods."

Ficus raised his cup and smiled over at Lent. "To us . . . a wizard and a poet."

A note from Ficus:

Father—

Greetings from Montro.

Lent's markers are solid, and he is progressing according to plan. Raye continues to be a nuisance. Lady Twila should provide a diversion. As promised, the minerals have been secured.

I feel strong and energized—because of you!

—*Ficus*

LADY TWILA

Twila had committed to one year of child care. After this, she would begin her studies.

She walked out on the balcony, with Ficus close behind. There was a *presence*—familiar.

"Who stays down there?" the young royal asked.

"A past acquaintance of yours."

"I certainly feel that."

"It's Raye, from Truth. He's entering his fourth year."

Yes . . . Raye, Twila thought happily to herself. Then she shouted, "Raye!" waving down to the guesthouse, not certain he was there.

"Let's have some tea," the wizard encouragingly suggested.

"No, but thank you," she said with a smile. "Is it true you have lived here all your life?"

"I have, with travels in between."

"My brother wrote of you with admiration."

"Sir Graf is held in high regard. You do know he's in Lackland?"

"I wasn't exactly sure."

"Working for my father, as an overseer, a very important position."

"I'm glad to hear he's doing well. We haven't been in touch."

"You can always visit him. Travel by rail is quite efficient."

"Perhaps," she said without much thought. "The newborn, tell me more."

"An orphan, adopted by my father. Her mother was single. A supervisor at his factory. Shortly after the birth, he was called to the clinic. Before she passed, he promised her the child would be well cared for."

"Very sad."

"Yes, very sad."

Twila took a deep breath. "I would like to go outside, reacquaint myself with the campus."

"Naturally." He smiled. "But do be mindful of our lizards. There was a sighting just the other day."

"I promise not to wander."

Her sole intention was spending time with Raye.

* * *

"That was you on the wizard's perch."

Twila grinned. "Good to know my energy wasn't wasted."

"Not a measure!" Raye laughed. "We can visit here or take a walk?"

"I'd prefer to walk."

"Let's go."

"Tell me, Raye, what have you been up to?"

"I recently traveled to Sym."

"I wish I would have known."

"Friends from the academy, they asked me to join them."

"What was your impression of Sym?"

His eyes grew big and he shook his head. "Amazing!"

"And what is it like in Truth?" she wondered.

A tribal territory"—a subtle smirk crossed his face—"but not so backward."

"I'm ready for a change." She abruptly stopped and turned to Raye. "Take me there and show me around."

Twila's enthusiasm stirred the gifted Zuku.

He smiled broadly. "Let's get you through the academy first."

"How well do you know Ficus?"

"Not at all, really. I don't think anyone does, except his father. He is a *wizard*, this much is clear . . . and suspiciously so."

"Why do you say that?"

"For one, he conceals his thoughts."

"Raye! You are a *mind reader*."

"And you . . . a Symlander royal."

"And YOU . . . a Zuku wizard!"

Their banter was interrupted by laughter.

"When is Elgin expected back?" he asked after catching his breath.

"Ficus mentioned in three days' time."

"We can still visit?"

"I'm sure we can manage that." She reached out and offered her hand. "But for now, I must be going. It was good to see you, Ray."

While walking up the path, she heard his distant voice.

"Tomorrow, we can have breakfast . . ."

Ficus sat in the parlor, anticipating Twila's return. "You were visiting with Raye?"

"Yes," she confirmed, somewhat surprised. "Mostly, we discussed the academy. I am inspired to study here."

"Of course you are. However, the child remains our focus. Her first year is critical. We must have confidence in your commitment."

"I can assure you of my commitment, Wizard Ficus." They shared a deep stare. "The child will have my focus."

Twila was confident in her abilities yet did have reservations. The situation was unusual.

* * *

The next morning, at sunrise, Raye opened the door with a sleepy-eyed smile. "You must have left without notice?"

"I was hungry," she said, "and slipped away."

"Follow me to the kitchen. I have fruit and plaka."

Twila sat at a small table, while Raye sliced up the pineapple.

She shook her head and sighed. "Ficus is ever-present."

"Caus said as much, before . . ." He paused in remembrance and then sliced another round of fruit. "Careful with your thoughts, Twila."

She took a bite of the Zuku bread and slowly chewed.

"Here." He handed her a cup of coconut water and sat down.

"What about your thoughts, Raye?"

"My thoughts?" He gazed warmly into her receptive eyes. "They've been occupied by you."

Two days passed.

The falcon *screeched* the vessel's sighting. Lent and Twila joined Ficus in the largest wagon, and they rode down to the harbor.

Elgin stepped down to the dock, a blanket-draped basket in his hand. "Everyone is here!"

"Welcome back, Father!"

"Good to be back, son."

He gestured for Twila to come closer and lifted the fabric away. "This is Kendra."

The baby was wide awake and staring up at her.

Blue eyes? she kept to herself. Then she blurted out, "So much energy."

"Fury," said Ficus under his breath.

"Prince Lent! We are delighted to have you with us."

"The pleasure is mine, Wizard Elgin. The island's fresh air is most uplifting."

Once the altar and falcons were secured, everyone gathered around the table. Elgin stood, as the others sat and listened.

"Kendra's schedule will be posted in the nursery and updated from time to time. Twila."

"Yes, Wizard Elgin."

"Never deviate from the schedule. I have an awareness if this should happen. Also, do not be perplexed by the child's rapid development. Enjoy and encourage her progress. Questions?"

After a moment of silence Twila spoke up, "I am ready to begin."

"Good . . . you can check on her now."

Elgin followed Ficus into his room.

"Yes, Father?"

"Freshen the altar. We will connect with Lent—tonight."

KENDRA

Kendra's advancement was everything Elgin had foreseen, and more. By the end of two seasons, she walked without wobbles and readily asked for things. Although not articulate in complex conversation, she understood much of what was said around her—and bluntly expressed herself.

"Happy Birthday, Kendra!" Twila enthusiastically greeted the child.

"Happy Birthday to me," she replied, sitting up tall in her bed.

"How does it feel to make one year?"

"The same." She shrugged.

"This is your day. What would you like to do?"

Twila watched with amusement as Kendra mulled over the possibilities.

"Look for a kemit," she ultimately decided.

"You know . . . that is the last thing we should be doing."

"You said it's *my day*."

Twila's caregiving was coming to a close. It was Kendra's birthday, and she would indulge the child.

"Don't be gone for too long," Elgin reminded them. "We have planned a special lunch."

Twila chuckled. "Only long enough to find what she's looking for."

"I'll have Ficus prepare the fire," he said with a knowing wink.

Kendra pointed to the orchard, and they went off in that direction.

"What's the rush!" Twila shouted. Ignoring her, Kendra picked a low-lying peach and continued on her way. "That's far enough!"

The defiant child kept going, until she was stopped by a border of rocks. "I know you're over there," she said firmly and started to climb.

"Kendra! Come down from—AHH." She grimaced in pain. Her foot had twisted in a rodent hole. Unable to walk, she eased herself to the ground.

"There you are, my kemit . . . fruit?"

"Kendra—" Twila cried out in frustration, her injured ankle swollen and throbbing.

A little hand reached over the rocks. "I'm here!"

"There you are," she grumbled. "And what is that?"

"He's very heavy."

It can't be.

The wizard child had a young kemit by the tail.

Ficus's voice rang out. "Are you down there?"

"YESSSS," Kendra shrieked. "And Twila is hurt!"

He came down and picked her up and then carried her back upstairs.

Elgin said, "Lift your leg." He wrapped her ankle with a cloth soaked in minerals. "This should help."

Almost immediately, Twila felt relief. "Much better." She looked at the wizard and smiled.

Ficus called out from the kitchen. "Roasted kemit, anyone?"

* * *

Later that evening, Twila responded, "Come in," to the knock on her door.

"I hope it's not too late?" said Elgin, his eyes gleaming from across the room.

"Not . . . too late," she replied with curious hesitation. "Just now thinking of sleep."

The wizard stepped forward with a soothing voice. "I won't be long."

"What is on your mind?"

"You are released from your obligation." He said with a smile. "And I am here to express my gratitude."

"How thoughtful."

"Throughout her first year, Kendra has thrived. Your positive influence has not gone unnoticed."

"She never really required much care . . . perhaps in the beginning."

"Will you be staying at the guesthouse with Raye?"

"He did offer, and there is plenty of room."

"Quite suitable for your studies," suggested Elgin. "And of course you are always welcome here. Do find the time and visit us . . . especially Kendra."

"I will make the time, Mystic Wizard."

"Good to know. Sleep well, Twila."

"Good night."

On the way to his room, Elgin shared a moment with Ficus.

"You had your talk, Father?"

"Yes."

"And she is moving in with Raye?"

"Everything according to plan. Our work will proceed without distraction. I will concentrate on Kendra—and you, the academy and Lent."

The wizards shared a strong and meaningful hug.

PASSAGE OF TIME

Raye returned to Truth and became the leader of finance. Once graduated, Twila joined him and they partnered. Nev was their firstborn; Riker arrived three years later.

Elgin continued to monitor his assets, by means of the Mystic falcons.

* * *

Ficus took out the note and handed it to his father. He watched him read it twice, make a flame, and burn it.

"Father?"

Elgin's fingers flexed in and out, as he stared down at the floor. "Her fertility. She carries a second child . . . a wizard, tainted with the blood of a Tuz." He lifted his head and faced his son "Look after Kendra while I am gone. Arrangements must be made."

Elgin packed his warmest clothes. At daybreak, he left for Lackland.

Commander Graf was waiting at the station. "Good to see you, my wizard."

He brushed past the commander and continued to the carriage.

Graf was deeply disturbed, feeling somehow responsible for his unhappiness.

Elgin sat with his eyes closed, as the wheels began to roll.

"It was unexpected," the commander explained, "and only by chance discovered. I happened to be at the factory. A woman fell to the ground . . . Sienna! She was examined on the spot. It was obvious to her condition."

The wizard took a deep breath and opened his eyes. "The blood of this child cannot elude our control."

"She will disappear?"

"No . . . the village cannot be disrupted."

"What can I do for you, my wizard?"

"Find another at the camp with a similar gestation. Isolate and sedate them both. Induce their labors, and switch the newborns at birth. Kendra will have a sibling."

"And the mother from the camp?"

"*She* will disappear."

ONE SEASON PASSED

Elgin carried Murn to the laboratory, while Kendra and Ficus followed close behind.

Kendra asked with a hint of annoyance, "Who is this one?"

"You will find out soon enough," replied Elgin. "Ficus, has the altar been prepared?"

"It waits."

After the ceremony, Ficus asked, "Were you confident of their connection?"

"I wasn't for certain," Elgin confessed. "Murn appears as a Symlander yet is equally a Tuz. She will never be a wizard, but they are sisters—close enough."

"Look there, Father . . . Kendra won't leave the baby alone."

"Something favorable after all." He nodded.

"What about Sienna?"

"She has been *corrected* and returned to what she remembers.

* * *

At the kingdom, Nathan said, "It does not bring you discomfort, the continued absence of our daughter? For all we know, she's been dead for years."

"Nathan . . . don't say that," Quell stammered.

"Actually, did she ever exist?"

"Sienna's instructions were specific."

"We've given her more than enough time!"

"Time becomes lost, when one finds contentment," she said softly before walking away.

* * *

In Montro, the falcon had long since taken flight, yet Elgin remained fixed on the balcony, standing there in solitude, pondering his mortality.

The Mystic wizard was long aware of his fate, disclosed in a series of stark dreams, as revelations that would provoke fear in most—but not him. He understood and accepted his purpose.

LACKLAND

Graf opened the canister, surprised to have received a message so soon.

Commander Graf—

King Nathan is traveling to Lackland, alone and unannounced.
He is searching for his daughter. Encounter him as we discussed.
Do not deviate from the circumstance of her condition.

—WE

"I'm going into the village," Graf advised Tylot. "Secure the perimeter with our best defenders.

"At once, Commander!"

"The camp is sealed until further notice."

* * *

311

Graf returned to his seldom-used dwelling. He lit the lamps, dusted the furnishings, and sparked the kindling in the stove. *The pantry and icebox?* "Relax," he muttered.

Darkness descended and the commander grew weary. He settled into the cushioned chair and drifted off.

When he was startled by the sound of a halting carriage, his eyes flashed open. *Mystic Wizard, be with me.* He went to the door.

"You were expecting me?" asked the king, his anxious face exaggerated by the flickering light.

"Tonight was not for certain," Graf calmly answered. "But yes, I was expecting you."

"Where is my daughter? Where is Sienna?"

"I regret to inform you, she is not here, my king."

Nathan lunged forward and took Graf by the throat. Offering no resistance, the commander dropped to his knees.

"Let me explain," he begged.

"Explain!" demanded the king.

"Sienna left me, soon after we arrived."

"How could this be? She gave up everything for you and this hideous place."

"I acknowledged my true self and—"

The king let him up, and they stood face-to-face.

"What are you suggesting?"

"A personal preference . . . difficult to explain between most men."

A moment passed as they searched each other's eyes.

The king said, "Where is she?"

"Here, in the village."

"Take me to her now!"

"Before we go . . . I must forewarn you."

"What is it?"

"After my disclosure, the princess became unstable. She spoke of hurting herself . . . and we feared—"

"Who shared this fear?"

"The Mystic wizard," Graf revealed. "He produced a remedy to cleanse her anguish."

"And this remedy did so?"

"Yes . . . and also her memories."

"My daughter, will remember me!"

They traveled a short distance, to the other side of the tracks.

Graf pointed to a small brick building. "That dwelling over there."

Nathan strode up to the front porch and took a slow, deep breath. "Announce our arrival."

Sienna's partner, Holden, opened the door.

"Bow before the king!" Graf demanded.

The puzzled Tuz did as he was told.

"We are checking on the welfare of workers and their families.

"Karin is feeding our child." Sounds from a baby could be heard in the background.

"We won't be long," said Graf.

The king's daughter appeared, with an infant in her arms. She greeted the men with lazy eyes and a crooked smile. There were no signs of recognition. She simply stood there and rocked the baby boy.

Nathan lowered his head and stumbled off the porch.

"We must be going," said Graf. "Good night."

The King sat stoically in the carriage, pondering his daughter's condition. *Elgin.*

"Have him send a falcon to confirm the date."

"Yes, my king."

THE KINGDOM

"You saw Sienna?" asked the queen.

"Yes—and you were right. She is content."

"I imagined this," she said with a warm smile. "Come to my bed?"

"Not tonight."

The next morning, Quell was kept occupied far from her chamber.

Nathan said, "The queen has misplaced her medication. Be thorough in your search."

Before long, a guard called out. "Under here . . . I found something!"

The king inspected the drawstring purse. "That will be all."

Two days passed.

"The falcon has brought us a message?" asked Nathan.

"For you," said Quell despondently, and handed him the parchment.

"I've been expecting this."

As he read it, a smile formed on his face.

"You are pleased?"

"Your brother and I will meet. Loose ends that must be tied."

"I see."

Nathan looked over at the royal guard. "The courier has been released?"

"Not yet, my king. She was fed and now is resting."

"It is good, taking care of the falcon as we do." He turned his attention to the queen. "Tell me, is there something I can do for you?"

The queen was not well. Without the supplements, her chemistry was confused and destructive.

Quell silently shook her head and started for the door.

"Would this help?" said Nathan.

She turned around. "Those are mine!"

"Yes, I believe they are." He held out the purse and taunted the ailing queen.

"They are important . . . to my health."

"They are yours with a warning. Take them sparingly. By doing so, you may survive the pain of their absence."

She stepped forward and swiped away the purse.

"Sequester the queen until further notice," Nathan commanded the royal guard.

* * *

In Montro, Elgin had left the island before the young wizard opened his eyes. Later that morning, he found the note in the laboratory.

Ficus, my son—

I am traveling to meet the king. The time has come, and I leave you with these final words.

The mystic blood flowing through your veins is rich and powerful. Your ascension to the pinnacle of our culture is a testament to the will of our Maker. It is your destiny, to create and control.

I will be with your mother, and together, always, with you.

—Father

CENTRAL GRASSLANDS

"Everything is ready, my king!" confirmed the guard.

"Let us be off, then."

At the district's hub, they transferred to wagons and rolled eastward alongside the tracks.

"This is the place!" announced the king.

One wagon stayed next to the rails, the other concealed behind a weeping willow tree.

As the engine slowed, Elgin opened the window and peered outside. Up ahead were a supply wagon and workers. Soon after the coach stopped, the engineer came to his door.

"What is the meaning of this?" asked Elgin.

"The track is under repair. I was told it won't be long."

"Then I will stretch my legs."

The wizard stepped out in a fine cotton robe. The delicate, cream-colored garment had been saved for this day.

He has dressed for the occasion, thought the fascinated king.

Elgin walked over to the workers.

"Wait," the lead sniper instructed.

Four deadly bolts were readied and aimed through the willow's branches.

Elgin was engaged in light conversation until, suddenly, everything turned to silence.

"He knows we are here," whispered the king. "Steady . . . steady."

The Mystic wizard looked up into the sky. His long, white tousled hair shimmered under the midday sun. He extended his arms, and the flared sleeves waved in the gentle breeze. His body stiffened and slowly began to rise.

The lead sniper spoke out in disbelief, "He is levitating."

"Not for long," the king cooly replied. "Deliver."

They gathered around the fallen wizard. His fine cotton garment was patterned in blood.

"Pull the bolts," ordered the king, "and send him back to Montro."

Chapter 15
KENDRA AND JASIRA

"Mila!" the messenger called out.
"What is it?"
"The Wizard Elgin, he returns without life!"
Mila and Mote hurried to the station.
"We will preserve his body and take the stains from his robe."
"But, Aunt Mila."
"We will return my brother with dignity."
"He is deserving?"
"Remember this . . . Elgin was born deprived of free will. His thoughts were predetermined, and influenced without consent."

The wizard's body was placed on red cedar shavings, inside a simple pine box. Mila was among the few who gathered to watch the vessel steam away.

Reclaim your truth, my brother.

Proclamation from the kingdom:

Elgin of Montro has been felled.
A reckless wizard with a destructive nature.
His actions threatened our land.

The king said to her with distant eyes, "Your reality does not allow an understanding of why this was done.

Later that night, Quell swallowed the last of her supplements.

* * *

"Is there anything that I—"

"In due time, Professor Lent," Ficus said. "In due time."

According to Elgin's wishes, his ashes were scattered above the open sea.

KENDRA

Elgin's mystic influence flowed without mercy through the child's veins. How would his death affect the developing wizard? Ficus would see to her well-being.

Kendra searched the star-filled sky. "And he is up there?"

"Yes," Ficus assured her in a calming voice. "Look closely at that brightest star and you will feel his presence."

She focused intently on the light. "He *is* there," she whispered.

"Your father listens from this star. Be open with your thoughts. He will provide you comfort and strength. One day, you will join him there. Until then . . . I will care for you.

JASIRA

As the cries of the newborn echoed throughout the castle, Sara's eyes rolled up into darkness.

Jasira appeared as her mother, a brown-eyed Cantor. Although mystically enhanced, she was not irreversibly compromised, unlike Kendra, who was plied with fury after her birth.

By age four, she was a daring improvisor. Playing the game of *you can't find me*, she balanced on a narrow ledge, outside her bedroom window. Free as the breeze blowing through her hair, she looked down and smiled at the valley below.

"Jasira—oh, Jasira," Uncle Robert sang out. "Where are you?" *Where did she disappear to this time?* "Jasira!"

318

Preceded by giggles, she skipped into the kitchen, where Robert sat waiting for his meal. "You gave up!"

"Not fair, searching for someone who can vanish . . . just . . . like . . . that!" He snapped his fingers with each word.

"I do know a few tricks, but not that one."

Her befuddled uncle could only shake his head.

"Maybe one day." She giggled some more.

"Are you hungry?"

"Very!"

"Sharing the extras with those dirty warkins, I suppose?"

The royal warkins had lost favor and were mostly neglected. Jasira, though it was frowned upon by her grandparents, visited their enclosure as often as she could. The older warkins were not partial to her attention. The juveniles and pups, however, enjoyed her playfulness.

* * *

In Truth, Raye and Twila were at the clinic. In a few days' time, they would travel to Montro. The Academy was celebrating its fiftieth anniversary.

"You are for certain?" asked Mila.

"My grandparents are expecting us," said Twila. "My brother, Graf, will also be there. I haven't seen him in years."

"Your Aunt Susan won't be going?"

"No . . . she will not travel that river. The memory of Caus remains too painful."

"Everything will be fine," Raye chimed in with a nod.

"Do not limit your gift," Mila reminded her grandson.

"I will stay mindful of the wizards," he assured her. "You should reconsider and come with us. Your gift is still reliable?"

Twila softly chuckled.

"Quite reliable," Mila confirmed with a sly smile. "But Mote would be left here alone. Express to your grandparents my disappointment, and encourage them to visit. What a sight that would be, the *Royal Symlander* docked in our harbor."

The Academy's Golden Anniversary

Commander Graf was summoned to Montro. He had not been on the island since before the birth of Kendra.

Graf stepped down to the dock and searched the immediate surroundings, hopping that somehow Ficus was there to greet him. It was another, however, who walked toward him along the planks. *The new professor*, he assumed.

"I am Lent! Welcome back to Montro. King of Lackland, is it?" he said in jest.

"You can call me this if you like," replied Graf, looking over at the distant carriage.

"He's with the falcons, rehearsing. You can surprise him."

The commander slowly curled a smile. "The wizard is aware of my presence."

"Of course he is," Lent meekly agreed.

"And the sisters?"

"Here at the harbor . . . until the island returns to normal."

"Well then, let's be on our way."

When they arrived at the residence, Graf went straight to the aviary.

"Good to see you again, Commander!" said Ficus, his back facing the doorway.

"Always a privilege to be in your presence, my wizard. The harbor is at capacity, with vessels moored in open water."

Ficus turned around and smiled. "I have viewed this from the altar. The *Royal Symlander* . . . an impressive sight."

"They do travel in style," Graf dryly remarked.

"You are eager to reacquaint yourself?"

"I have little interest in my royal family."

"Nevertheless, Raye will be here, and we can discuss the extension."

Years of potions and training rendered Graf to identify as a wizard, his true nature eliminated. Only externally did he resemble the person he once was.

"There is something troubling you, Commander Graf?" Ficus understood his despondence.

"I cherished your father as if he were mine. An emptiness resides in me, with him no longer here."

Ficus appreciated Graf's sentiment; however, for him, his father lived on—similar to the presence of his mother, yet even more intense.

Ficus stepped ever closer, with a stare that did not waver. "There is no need for emptiness, Commander. The Mystic wizard is here with us now. Before his body burned to ashes, I created a special potion from instructions written in his hand.

The more Graf listened, the stronger he *felt* Elgin's presence.

"I added the minerals and blood to the basin, and the water glowed deep-red. Our father's face materialized . . . and he spoke to me."

"What did he say?"

"Drink."

Graf imagined this, and it thrilled him to do so.

* * *

In Montro Harbor, Raye caught a glimpse of the main building atop the lush hillside. "Do you ever wonder about that day as I do?" he quietly asked.

"The ceremony," said Twila, "when we were children?"

"Yes."

"As if our partnership was prearranged?"

"It bothers me to think that way . . . but—"

She pulled him close. "Let us be grateful."

The academy's commemorative program included a tribute to Ficus's grandfather, Nord. Two full pages were devoted to the "Wizard of Montro," and his celebrated achievements: defender of the Dark Forest, master of connections, professor of abilities, and maestro of the Mystic falcons. Elgin received barely a mention.

"Our father deserved much more!" Graf angrily denounced.

"When the embers of this school no longer glow," Ficus ominously predicted, "our father's legacy will rise from its ashes. But for now"—he smirked—"I will give them their precious falcon show."

"The greatest of them all, my wizard."

"Professor Lent!" shouted Ficus. "Join us on the balcony for tea."

Under a canopy of sparkling stars, they drank well into the night.

* * *

The royals of Sym hosted a private luncheon the day before the assembly. It was a relaxed affair, held in the academy's atrium.

Graf was forewarned by Ficus. "Stay guarded and cloak your thoughts. Do not be fooled by the *friendly voices*. Beware of Raye—his skills are worthy. He will try every trick he knows."

"Is that your brother over there, walking in with Ficus?" asked Raye.

Twila abruptly got up from the table. "Follow me."

Wearing a broad smile, she approached her much-older sibling.

"Twila," said Graf, with little emotion.

They reached out to each other and shared a brief embrace.

"I've been told you are still up in Lackland . . . so far away."

"Not so far by steam, sister. And haven't you heard? I've been crowned the king of Lackland." He raised an eyebrow. "It seems royalty is in my blood."

"I never knew you with such high aspirations."

Ficus interceded, "What the *king* aspires to most is the expansion of our railway. Sucrene clamors for our services."

Raye spoke up, "A most impressive endeavor."

"And yet incomplete." The wizard softly smiled. "We could use your assistance, Raye."

"What do you have in mind?"

"Your next meeting with Prince Robert . . . Sir Graf may join you?"

"This can be arranged."

Ficus gave him an assertive nod. "It would be in everyone's best interest to expedite this project."

Back at their table, Raye leaned over and discreetly asked, "Your brother, he has always behaved in this way?"

"Not that I can remember. What did you *feel* on the inside?"

"It was strange . . . empty."

"I am not comfortable with you and him working together. His relationship with Ficus is peculiar."

"I respect your concern but I can handle this. The extension is old news, and you understand the benefits."

Their conversation was interrupted by the server.

"This soup is very tasty," Twila remarked. "What is it?"

"An island delicacy . . . kemit, with creamed mushrooms."

* * *

The outdoor venue had overflowed its capacity, leaving those in the back to stand.

Despite getting on in years, Lord Hemeth and Lady Rachel were quite spry. They welcomed everyone enthusiastically and provided the opening remarks.

A poignant moment came toward the end of the program, when Hemeth spoke again. He reflected on the influences in his life. He began with his grandparents, tragically lost at sea, and then his parents, who had founded the academy in their honor. He warmly acknowledged his family and their daily inspiration. Ultimately, he paid homage to a friend from long ago.

The lord browsed the faces before him, the majority with white tousled hair and crystal-blue eyes.

"Before my studies here"—he smiled in reflection—"the academy's very first class. It amused me to remind her. Although she appeared to be, she was *not* a true Symlander. No, my friends . . . Mila was much more than that! She showed me strength and shared her wisdom, well beyond her years. She reminding me to cherish what is meaningful in life.

"My parents envisioned a school, open to all cultures. Today, we announce with great pleasure the Mila Scholarship, awarded annually, to a deserving student from Truth."

Everyone stood and warmly applauded.

Twila looked at Raye, with proud tears streaming down his face.

He leaned over and whispered in her ear, "She can *feel* this."

Ficus grimly stared down from the balcony. He had little patience for heartfelt nonsense and was anxious to release the falcons.

SUCRENE

Soon after the academy's celebration, Raye secured a meeting at the castle.

"Let me . . . remind you." Graf's words were jostled by the ride. "Travel on polished iron will provide comfort, and take less than a day."

"What about Ficus," said Raye. "There has been no setback, without his father to guide him?"

"It is better to hear this from me," he said sternly. "There has been no *setback*. The wizards have merged. The combination of their abilities, unlimited. It would be wise to contain your curiosity, and appreciate our progress . . . from a distance."

Conversation was limited throughout the remainder of their journey. Once at the castle, Prince Robert introduced his parents. The exchange was cordial but brief. Their once exuberant personalities had also passed with Sara.

They sat at a table in a private room.

"The section over the river should be our only challenge," remarked the prince.

"Yes," said Graf. "Progress will be steady after reaching the trail."

"Two years," Raye answered Robert's unspoken question.

"That is realistic," Graf confirmed, avoiding eye contact with the Zuku.

We are not in Montro, Raye privately reminded him.

"Is there anything else?" asked Robert.

"Yes," Graf spoke up, "the warkins?"

"They are kept down at the stables. If you're interested, stop by and see them before you leave."

The following morning, Graf found his way to the enclosure. He brought strips of treated elk meat and fed the receptive beasts. When called upon, they would answer to the wizards.

* * *

For two years after his father's death, Ficus maintained a low profile and seldom left the island, spending much of his time in the lab and at the altar.

Lent served as Kendra and Murn's guardian, though mostly the sisters watched over themselves.

Graf supervised the extension. The project was running on schedule. When not in the field, he met with Prince Robert at the castle.

"Before too long," Graf reminded the beasts, "you will have your space to roam."

They raised their snouts and howled.

What is it with the warkins? wondered the prince.

* * *

The final bolts were tightened on the railway's missing link. An iron-and-wood-trestle bridge, that spanned a narrow gorge. It was intentionally last to be completed. Enforcers, in the guise of laborers, occupied the work camp.

"Tomorrow will be a wonderful occasion," said Tylot. "The Mystic wizard, steaming across the divide."

Graf admired the bridge. "He will be very pleased."

The valley was abuzz with anticipation. The railway's grand opening was a historic occasion. The economic and social benefits were enormous. Local officials would be on hand and issue a proclamation.

Aside from Princess Jasira, the royals were more restrained. Prince Robert planned a brief appearance, but nothing other than that.

"The Wizard Ficus . . . he arrives today?"

"Yes, Jasira," the annoyed uncle replied, "and I won't be telling you again."

"Might he visit the castle?"

"Most likely not."

"Why can't I go with you?"

"Because your grandfather disapproves."

For reasons Jasira was unable to process, her attraction to the wizard was

pronounced. A burning energy grew within her, the closer he approached.

The mighty engine rumbled north to Sucrene. Coupled behind it were two personal coaches, two containers with fresh pineapples, one container with kegs of sweet (coconut) water, and two empty livestock haulers.

It was midday, and all those in the valley had flocked to the station. The engine's whistle sounded in the distance. Small children climbed up on shoulders to gain a better view.

Billowy white steam appeared on the horizon. "I can see it!" shouted the exhilarated boy.

The gleaming engine was a sight to behold, coated in an emerald-green lacquer. Black-lettered **SUCRENE** was boldly displayed across its front. The engineer gave one last tug, and the whistle blared triumphantly. The pulsating crowd erupted in delight!

The engine slowed and then came to a stop. Without delay, Graf emerged from the coach. He walked with purpose to the center of the platform.

"People of Sucrene!" he announced with vigor. "I present to you, Ficus, the Mystic wizard of Montro!"

The captivated crowd held their collective breath and stared at the opening door.

The dynamic Symlander smoothly stepped down, then stood there as if he were deity. He was dressed in a splendid deep-red robe, his snow-white hair flowing just past his shoulders. Smiling broadly, he went to the platform's very edge.

"Greetings, Sucrene!" His powerful voice resonated with strength and influence. "You are now connected . . . to the Trans Rivera Railway!" He grasped his hands together and shook them victoriously above his head.

Prince Robert submitted to the euphoria and hurried across the platform. "Mystic Wizard!"

They reached out at the same moment and shook each other's hand.

"Congratulations on your railway"

Ficus smiled broadly. "Finally . . . your valley has been rewarded."

Graf said, "How good of you to be here, Prince Robert.

"The royal family would be remiss not to show their gratitude."

"Speaking of gratitude," said Ficus, "we have brought a fine selection of fresh pineapple and sweet water, reserved specifically for the castle. Would it be possible to personally deliver them?"

"In appreciation of our partnership," Graf added.

"That would be an excellent surprise. I'll arrange the transportation. Tonight, you will stay at the castle!"

"Your offer is considerate," said Ficus. "However, we will return to our coaches."

"We could stay long enough for a light supper?" Graf suggested.

During the festivities, Tylot led the enforcers into the valley. The large wagons were driven to a wooded area on the outskirts of the village. There, they would eat, rest, and wait for darkness. Graf had provided a layout of the castle. Their mission was well rehearsed.

After the accolades and before the crowd dispersed, sweet water was served and pineapples handed out.

The villagers would fall asleep that night and not wake for two days' time. When they did, their memories were selectively confused.

The carriage approached the gatehouse and slowed to a stop. Prince Robert handed the attendant a flask of sweet water. "Compliments of the Mystic wizard."

Jasira watched from an upstairs window as her uncle arrived with his guests—it had been eleven years since her mother witnessed the same. She rushed out of the room and scrambled down the stairs.

Graf opened the crate with a smile on his face. "These pineapples are uniquely delicious."

"Jasira!" Robert scolded his niece as she burst out from the doorway.

"May I . . . have one of those?" she asked while catching her breath.

"Of course, Princess Jasira," said Graf. "Does this one look good to you?" He handed her a medium, well-formed pineapple. "Give the bottom a sniff."

Ficus chuckled. "I can smell it from here. There is someone to help her with the others . . . and the sweet water?"

"I can carry more than one!" the princess strongly asserted.

"Jasira," her uncle groaned.

"Here, take these." Graf stacked two more in her open arms.

"Two more," she insisted.

The pineapples never touched her arms, hovering ever so slightly above them.

"Jasira."

"Yes, Uncle."

"See that the keg is tapped and everyone is served . . . beginning with your grandparents."

"Right away!"

He then turned to the guests. "Follow me."

They went to a small dining area adjacent the kitchen, where a simple meal was served.

"The sweet water is refreshing," said Robert after taking a drink, "And for you?"

"Thank you—no, we've had our fill," Graf replied.

The sweet water brought to the castle was less potent than what was served at the station. However, deep sleep was imminent and would last long enough.

The prince yawned (yet again). "Excuse me, but with all the excitement I've become uncommonly tired. You can find your way out?"

"Yes, and thank you for your hospitality," said Graf.

"Sleep well, Prince Robert."

"And you the same, Wizard Ficus."

* * *

The royal staff was systematically extracted, their sedated bodies loaded onto racks in the wagons. At the platform, they were revived and packed into the haulers. Their memories scrubbed, a new life awaited them in Lackland.

Ficus placed his hand firmly upon Graf's shoulder. "You did very well, Commander."

"Anything for you, my wizard." He closed his eyes tightly and absorbed all that he could.

"I will see you at the station."

Ficus took possession of his sleeping daughter and some of her belongings. The remaining royals were left undisturbed in their beds.

As if in a trance, Graf walked across the dimly lit hallway and down the switchback stairs. At the enclosure was the leader, up on hind legs, paws against the mesh, his bushy tail vibrating madly. The warkins behind him were anxious and drooling. He unlatched the gate.

The Mystic wizard stood alone on the platform, feeling closer to his father than ever before. Gazing up at the full moon, he basked in its radiance. The peacefulness of that moment was interrupted by the howling.

At the trail hub, Graf's coach and the haulers were coupled to an engine bound for Lackland. Ficus and Jasira continued on to Truth.

The altar was prepared as the princess slept. Fury and wizard blood were added to the potion.

She opened her eyes and slowly sat up. "I am so tired and confused."

"For certain it was sudden," Ficus responded in a soft caring voice. "Your grandparents saw us off at the station. You don't remember?"

"Nothing."

"After you are settled, they promised to visit."

"I look forward to that."

"It will be special for sure. But for now, let me show you something."

After their connection, the princess smiled and drifted back to sleep. She would not recall the abduction, nor the future family reunion (or family, for that matter). Soon enough, she would know only Montro.

* * *

Tylot and the enforcers stayed in Sucrene, tasked with transforming the royal castle into a wizard's fortress.

Valley residents woke up from their extended sleep and continued with everyday life. The principality was dismissed into fable, tales of royals who once were, whispers of their bones buried by warkins.

The kingdom turned a blind eye to the Cantors' demise. Sucrene's elected government was unanimously accepted. Most importantly, trade agreements were kept intact, and payments continued without pause.

Royal assets were transferred to Sucrene Valley Holdings, a secretive business created by Ficus. Libby, a former member of the royal staff, managed the operation.

The Mystic wizard's wealth and influence were on the rise.

Passage of Time

Kendra and Jasira shared a larger room near the laboratory, away from the everyday distractions. Murn's room was at the opposite end, next to the kitchen.

Murn received training in the academy's culinary and housekeeping departments. A quick study, she developed into an accomplished domestic. Her low-dose supplements ensured contentment and productivity.

The evening meal was brought out and served.

Kendra said, "Smells and looks wonderful."

"How kind of you to say, sister. Although, I believe the curd was finished a tad too soon."

Professor Lent put a spoonful in his mouth. "The curd is perfect."

"The meal has been well prepared," said Ficus. "That will be all, Murn."

"Good night, everyone."

The table fell silent and waited.

"What about their skills?" asked Ficus.

"We have made wonderful progress," replied the professor. "They both have chosen and connected with a falcon."

Their faces beamed with accomplishment.

"Maneuvers?"

"Nothing technical—yet—but an encouraging start."

Ficus looked around the table. "Schedule a demonstration . . . technical maneuvers included. Good night."

Before the young wizards went to their room, each drank a small cup of tea, a normal routine for them.

Kendra's toxic chemistry was receptive to the minerals. Her vital organs stored them, their influence progressive and lasting.

Inside Jasira the minerals flowed free and discharged without permanence.

* * *

Kendra said, "Let's practice without the professor over our shoulders.

"Down at the garden?" suggested Jasira.

"I'll get the gloves!"

Ficus observed from his balcony as the young wizards readied their falcons.

Jasira launched hers in the air. "Stay on my tail if you can."

The impressive raptors soared up into the sky, their distinctive screeches heard down at the harbor.

"The falcons are out!" shouted the dockworker.

Kendra's bird gave close chase as together they continued to climb. The leader veered sideways and pulled its wings in tight.

"Try to follow me now," said Jasira, her falcon becoming a blur.

"You'll have to do better than that."

Good progress, thought Ficus. *Now let's see what she makes of this.* He pointed his finger and took control.

"Not so close!" shouted Jasira.

"It's not me!"

No longer a participant, Kendra stepped back and kept silent.

Her possessed falcon extended its beak and latched on to a cluster of tail feathers. The ensnared falcon lost velocity and struggled to maintain flight.

Jasira felt a surge of heat, deep within her chest. It ignited a pulsating energy, and her arm began to rise.

331

She twirled her finger and the bird spun free. *Return!* she implored. *Return!* But there was not enough separation, and the falcon was forced to climb. Making a fist, she stalled the ascent and sent it streaking downward. The moment before impact, its deadly talons locked. Ficus commanded the same. There was a violent collision. Feathers shot out in every direction.

The heat subsided and Jasira's arm fell limp. Powerless, she watched her courageous falcon plummet to the ground. The survivor was injured yet capable of flight. It returned to Ficus and perched on the railing. The wizard with his fingertip, gently rubbed its bloodied crown.

Kendra said, "You should have known better than to challenge the Mystic wizard."

Rather than being despondent, Jasira took solace. Her abilities had been exposed, her confidence empowered.

COMMITMENT

Hiking to the meadow was a favorite pastime of theirs. It was a special place Jasira believed enchanted.

"Jasira?" Kendra called out.

"I'm right here," she whispered.

"Jasira! You were nowhere to be found and then suddenly behind me?"

"I jumped out from that bush over there." She laughed. "You really must practice your awareness."

*　*　*

Lent returned from a short visit to the kingdom.

"Your family is well?" asked Ficus.

"Everyone except King Nathan."

"Oh?"

"He became quite ill before I left."

"Do they know what ails him?"

"They haven't a clue."

Lent had brought a special seasoning to the kingdom. Indistinguishable from salt, the poison was sprinkled on his uncle's daily meals. The royal chef was to be compensated in more gold than he could fathom—riches to last a lifetime. The chef was last seen trolling for sardines in Zuku Cove.

"Your mother will soon be the queen, which leaves you first in line . . . King Lent!"

The prince respectfully bowed. "You—my wizard, are the true king."

Ficus stepped forward and placed a hand on each shoulder, pressing down with an easy firmness. "The time has come to expand our family. Tonight is my commitment, and tomorrow will be yours. The future of our culture . . . begins with us."

* * *

"Kendra is well?" Lent asked.

"Yes . . . everything as planned," said Ficus.

Jasira was unaccustomed to sleeping alone, and Lent went to her room.

"What has happened to Kendra?"

"No need for concern," he reassured her with a smile. "She is resting in the guest room."

"Why there?"

"She committed—"

"With the Mystic wizard."

He gently nodded. "And we will make the same."

To say Jasira was not attracted to Lent would be untrue. Yet there was a clear boundary. He was her professor. However, when he looked at her and spoke of commitment, she saw him in a different light, heard a different voice.

"What is next, and what is required?" she asked.

"Tonight, we will go to the altar, and from there . . ." His warm gaze did not waver. Taking her receptive hand, he raised it to his lips.

The laboratory was transformed back in time, with soft lights and a glowing altar. But instead of Wizard Nord, it was Ficus, dressed in his grandfather's most opulent robe.

They arrived holding hands, and the Mystic wizard was pleased.

"The connection ceremony"—he reverently explained—"cannot forcefully unite. A level of comfort must preexist. If dormant, it will awaken."

A cozy bungalow had been set aside, stocked with provisions to last one week.

* * *

Lent asked, "She will be separated from the child?"

"Nothing has changed," said Ficus, in a cool and steady voice. "Kendra and Murn will raise the girl in Sucrene. The boy stays with me on the island."

"I can bring Jasira to the kingdom."

The wizard stepped closer and stared into his wanting eyes. "There will be another, Prince Lent. A connection everlasting."

* * *

Arnela and Daniel were born two days apart.

Both mothers had been abused by the delivery. Ficus had held out hope that Jasira would not survive. But she was too strong.

"Our baby," Jasira weakly pleaded. "I want to hold our baby."

"She is well and being cared for," said Lent. "Close your eyes and rest." He tenderly pressed his lips against her damp forehead.

Ficus reminded Lent in the hallway, "She must be kept sedated."

"Mystic Wizard," he passionately requested, "let me take Jasira out to sea. Be alone with her before . . ."

"Is this not asking too much of yourself?"

"I know what to do, my wizard."

"Enlighten me."

"She will wake up in open water, disoriented and alone. There will be a small copper box with a note attached, written in my hand. She will unlatch the lid and open it. And I . . . will continue to the kingdom."

Ficus searched Lent's persuasive eyes for a deeper understanding. "As you wish, then. Let this be your final night together."

* * *

It was early dawn, and they traveled down to the harbor in the darkest shade of light. Lent used one arm to guide the carriage, the other to hold her close.

"Where are we going?" asked Jasira with confusion.

"To the kingdom."

"And what of our baby?"

"I will explain later."

"Our baby," she whispered with heavy eyes.

He placed the box in the dinghy and then returned to the steam-powered vessel.

"Stay down there," he said firmly. "Trust me."

"I will—I do," she softly replied.

Safely outside the harbor, Lent looked back at the island's vague silhouette. He imagined Ficus on the balcony, as always feeling his presence.

Jasira said, "I'm regaining my strength."

"Don't move from where you are."

He cut the rope and set the dinghy adrift, and then lowered himself to her.

"What now?" she asked.

"I need you to perform one of your *tricks*."

"Which trick?"

"Move something with your finger."

"Where is it?"

"In the dinghy . . . a latch, on a small copper box."

She closed her eyes for a moment. "I see the box . . . and there is a note."

"For your ears." He handed her two pieces of fabric. "Now, move the latch and lift the lid!"

She closed her eyes and focused. "Almost there."

Ficus stared out on the distant horizon, his hands firmly on the rail.

There was a brilliant flash, followed by a loud clap—startling the falcons into flight. One of them soared away from the others.

"That was quite the gift you left for me. Can I come up?"

"No, it's still not safe."

Lent was aware of the falcon above but did not acknowledge its presence.

Soon after entering the River Igua, he took from his pocket a small crystal vial. It contained a deep sacrifice, first created by Elgin.

He handed it down. "This is for you."

She put the crystal to her lips and drank.

Before they closed, he gazed deep into her warm-brown eyes.

Their connection was real, and Jasira's essence would always be with him.

Ficus scrutinized Lent's every movement, from Truth's harbor to the station. Once he boarded the royal coach, the falcon was instructed to return.

The prince slumped down on the seat and closed his eyes. He took a slow, deep breath and reached inside his pocket. It calmed him to massage the purse filled with supplements.

A burst from the whistle and the wheels began to roll, the engine steaming westward, to the Kingdom of Rivera.

* * *

Tuz and Zuku children were exploring on the docks.

"Is she alive?" one of them asked.

"I don't want to get too close."

"I think she moved!"

"A Cantor?"

The stranger slowly climbed out of the vessel, Her eyes squinting from the late-afternoon glare.

"Are you all right?" asked the young Zuku.

"I believe so." She glanced around. "Where am I?"

"You are in Truth."

336

"Truth?"
"Yes. What brings you here?"
"I don't know."
"What is your name?"
She rocked precariously back and forth.
"You don't look well."
Suddenly, she collapsed on the dock.
"We need help."
"Go to Mila!"

CHAPTER 16

EVOLUTION

Through his diverse business holdings—transportation, manufacturing, real estate, and mining—Ficus amassed great wealth, providing the means to build and support his growing empire.

The kingdom remained indifferent as their coffers continued to be filled.

"The treasury has received another shipment of gold," the lead accountant announced.

"Lent, express our gratitude to Ficus," Queen Julia reminded her son.

"The gold is always welcome," Prince Kingston chimed in. "However, the *wizard* makes me nervous."

Truth was also wary of the wizard but did not have the resources, or firm desire, to confront him.

MONTRO

Ficus connected with both Daniel and Arnela immediately after their births—Kendra with Arnela soon after. That first season, the children were plied with fury and evolve. Receptive to the mystic minerals, they developed accordingly.

"The time has come," said Ficus to Kendra.

"I am ready, my wizard."

"Yes, you are."

Before leaving for Sucrene, Pratt was brought on to watch over Daniel. A former student of Lent's, he was knowledgeable of wizard culture, and respected it. The child was administered a potion of dormancy. Rendered almost lifeless, he would stay that way until his father's return.

SUCRENE

During the carriage ride from Truth's harbor to the rail station, Arnela became disturbed.

Murn looked down at the child in the carrier. "What is it, little one?"

Kendra said, "Pick her up."

"Let her be," objected Ficus.

She began to shift wildly from side to side, froth oozing from the corners of her small mouth, her pale-blue eyes frantic.

Ficus relented and took hold of the raging child. He brought her flushed face to his chest. Her breathing was rapid and shallow. *What do you know that I don't know, Arnela?* He closed his eyes and listened.

"Mila!" Mote called out. "Come quickly!"

"She is awake?"

"Not awake . . . something else."

Mila reached over and held the stranger's hand. It was fraught with tension. *Ficus.* She *felt* his presence.

Unbeknownst to Mila, the Mystic wizard was not the explanation.

As the carriage approached the station, Arnela had quieted down.

Ficus said to Murn, "Take her."

Soon after they boarded the private coach, the child fell asleep.

* * *

The engine slowed to a stop, and Ficus looked out the window. Tylot was hobbling across the platform. His physical impairment and absence of vigor were concerning.

"Welcome back to Sucrene, my wizard."

Ficus slightly nodded.

Before continuing to the cottage, they walked over to Sucrene Valley Holdings. Libby was expecting them and gave a brief tour.

After Libby was hired, she was introduced to a milder form of control, a diluted potion allowing most of her identity to endure. Those familiar with her past behavior never noticed a difference. Yet she had transformed. The Mystic wizard commanded her total allegiance.

The cottage had three bedrooms, and a study for training. Murn was thrilled with the kitchen.

"Everything is in order," Kendra confirmed.

Ficus was satisfied with Kendra's assertiveness. He understood her to be in balance, evolved into a fearless wizard.

Murn stood to the side with Arnela in her arms.

"We will return in time for supper," said Ficus.

"I will have it waiting to be served."

Kendra spoke up with surprise, "Through the closet?"

"Yes," said Tylot.

A pocket door at the back of her closet hid a staircase, descending to an underground passage that led to the fortress basement.

"It won't take long," the guardian assured them and limped ahead.

Although dimly lit, the straightforward tunnel appeared well constructed. It was six bodies wide with ample headroom. The air was fresh and well circulated.

The lights flickered.

"We're working on that," said Tylot. "It's the flow of gas . . . a valve."

Half the lights went out.

"Tylot!" A perturbed Ficus barked.

"What is that sound?" wondered Kendra.

Coming toward them was a small mass of rapidly moving shadows.

"They're harmless," said Tylot, "but crouch down and shield your eyes."

"What is harmless?" she asked.

"Bats."

The winged intruders streamed past them, carrying a blanket of warm, distasteful air. They held their breath for an extra moment, then slowly stood up.

"Interesting," Kendra remarked.

"Resourceful creatures," said Tylot. "They made their way through the vents. The grates are being replaced, and they'll be gone by morning."

Not only the bats, thought Ficus.

They reached the basement and followed Tylot to the lift. The open platform would take them to the observation deck, where Commander Graf was waiting.

"This transport is powered by steam," observed Ficus.

"Yes, my wizard," confirmed Tylot. "A vertical rail system, replacing the ropes and pulleys."

"A substantial improvement," he replied. "You put the orbs to good use."

"Developed by a Zuku."

A chill came over the wizard. "A Zuku?"

"Roman, promoted from the mines."

"Clever," Kendra blurted out.

Ficus in that instant, felt the presence of his sister.

Despite Kendra's essence being ravaged by potions, traces of Quell's once-pure and charming personality lived on—deep inside her.

"Yes . . . very clever," Ficus agreed. He distrusted the gifted Zuku, but this one had value. "That will be all, Tylot. We can manage from here."

The lift traveled steadily through the different levels, until it reached the top.

"My wizard!"

"Commander!"

They grasped each other's forearm.

Graf briefly turned his attention to Kendra. "Welcome to Sucrene. I hope the cottage is to your liking?"

"It is," she curtly replied.

Kendra accepted Graf with reservation. Privately, she had read the notes His loyalty to the Mystic wizard, it appeared to her, transcended obligation. Ficus believed Graf's intimate reverence a consequence of mystic chemistry, and nothing more than that.

Standing on the volcano's rim, they looked out over the valley.

"Down there!" Graf pointed to the trampled-down trails. "Your pack of warkins."

"They've added to the family," Ficus remarked.

"Yes, those pups over there. Only the strongest, my wizard."

Good for them, Kendra grumbled to herself.

"Now, let me show you around!"

The commander led a tour of each level. Especially impressive was the armament factory, where the lead enforcer, Kip, demonstrated the latest crossbow.

Excluded from the conversation was Kendra, who obediently tagged along. Once Ficus returned to Montro, she would have her say.

TRUTH

At the clinic, Mote asked, "Are you any closer to bringing her back?"

"She isn't ready," said Mila, who then softly smiled. "But her fever has passed."

"Maybe if—"

"In her time."

Mote looked on with admiration. Mila was tamping the stranger's forehead with a cool compress. He said, "The stranger is blessed to have your care."

"She is *gifted*."

"How so?"

"I came into this room, and the bed appeared empty. Where could she have gone without my notice? I turned to leave, and then glanced back. She was there."

SUCRENE

Two messages had been sent to the commander, each one unanswered. It was highly unusual for him not to reply. A falcon was sent to view the circumstance. It glided around Mt Golder for the majority of the day. Puffs of smoke rose from the cottage. Tylot was out feeding the warkins.

Roman had joined Kendra on the observation deck. Yet as the falcon continued to circle, Graf was nowhere to be found.

Ficus's private coach was expedited through the turntable.

Murn rushed to the window. "Kendra!"

"Yes," she calmly replied, "he has been expected."

"The Mystic wizard!" Arnela blurted out.

"No *tricks*," warned Murn.

Ficus stormed into the cottage.

Murn grabbed Arnela's little hand, said, "Let's go outside."

"He's not here," confirmed Kendra.

"I know that much. Follow me."

Ficus walked briskly through the tunnel, with Kendra keeping pace.

"I was waiting for the right situation and didn't want to trouble you. We did everything to save him. His injuries, beyond repair. I realize how disturbing this must be, considering how close—"

"Not so close."

"This way," said Kendra, and he followed her to the lift. She stopped and looked all the way up. "The commander fell from there."

"To where I stand," he murmured, staring at his feet.

"Roman has considered every possibility. The cause of the accident remains unclear."

"And his body?"

"Given a proper burial."

"Perhaps we should call your Zuku and have him read your mind? Seek clarity from there."

"If you so desire, my wizard."

He stared hard at her expressionless face. "There is only so much one can prepare for."

"Very true," she replied with a subtle nod.

"If it were not enough raising a young wizard, but also to command a fortress?"

"It feels natural . . . doing all of this."

"Summon the Zuku."

They waited in silence until he arrived.

"Greetings, my wizard!"

"Greetings, Roman. I am here because of Commander Graf."

The Zuku flashed back to the commander's final moments: the fear on his face, an empty lift descending without him, his tortured body hanging from the end of a rope.

Kendra abruptly spoke up, "This won't be necessary!"

"Go on, then," said Ficus.

"I fed his shattered body to the warkins."

* * *

The Mystic wizard returned to the island and monitored Sucrene from there. For the time being, he was content.

Kendra became known as a healer, diagnosing and treating a variety of modest ailments. Her association with the castle remained a well-guarded secret.

TRUTH

Mila sat next to the stranger and held her hand. She listened closely. This time, it was different. The stranger's hand clutched hers!

"Where . . . am I?" she whispered. Her reborn eyes struggling to open.

"Truth, and my name is Mila. Your determination is remarkable."

"I have no memory."

Mila looked at her with a warm smile. "You will stay with me, and we will work on that."

* * *

"The position is yours."

"Am I ready, Aunt Mila?" asked Mote.

"Have I not prepared you well?"

"Yes, but—"

"Nev's internship is almost complete. Truth will have the best of care. If called upon, you know where to find me. For now, I will help the—" Mila paused without explanation, her eyes distant and disturbed. She could no longer call her in this way.

"Stranger," Mote reasoned.

"Our *guest* . . . and she will reclaim her name."

* * *

A tranquil environment would provide the best opportunity. Mila had great faith in this therapy. They took long and gentle horseback rides. She shared stories of the Zuku.

"Your culture is beautiful," the guest glowingly remarked.

"And yours?" asked Mila.

"Wizards?"

The silence was deafening—finally, a breakthrough. Her *truth* had been revived.

Sensing an opening, Mila did not hold back. *Your name is.*

"My name . . . my name is . . ." Her eyes closed ever so tightly. Pent-up tears forced their way through the seams. "Jasira."

"Blessings, Jasira!" Mila shouted with joy.

Jasira's recall did not flow effortlessly, and gaps of understanding prevailed. Unlike memories of Sucrene which were often vivid, Montro lingered in the dark.

* * *

At the clinic, Mote's forehead furrowed. "She is a Cantor from Sucrene?"

"A princess," Mila replied, "and the only surviving royal. She asked about her family, believing they were well."

"You told her of their disappearance?"

"I did, and she fell silent for two days . . . not a word."

"How is it possible to identify with wizards?"

"As I do, with their blood."

Mila rarely mentioned that aspect of her heritage.

"She must have lived in Montro."

"Most likely but not for certain."

"And her child?"

Evidence of Jasira's motherhood was discovered during her first examination.

"This hasn't been discussed."

PASSAGE OF TIME

Kendra had left the cottage earlier that day, to perform another healing.

"Arnela!"

"I hear you, Aunt Murn!"

"Don't be gone for too long!"

"Only for forever!" she shouted back with laughter. And down her favorite trail she went.

Kendra glared down from the observation deck. "Once again, wandering off on her own accord."

"Arnela?" Roman assumed.

"She'll visit with the creatures, on her way to Sara's beach. Adopt an odd piece of driftwood for her collection. Not returning—until after dark." Kendra stepped away from the wall and faced the gifted Zuku. "There will come a time when I clip her wings. And during my absence, I am counting on you, Roman."

"Yes, my wizard!"

MONTRO

Unlike the freedom Arnela enjoyed, Daniel was suffocated by authoritative rule. Each new day, he was subjected to a regimen of supplements and training.

Ficus looked down at the ever-developing wizard, an instrument of the future—the ultimate sire.

"Together, we will complete a masterwork of evolution, where exists a culture groomed by Mystic wizards."

Daniel could not fully translate the meaning of those words yet *felt* their purpose.

TRUTH

"Mila is here?" asked Jasira.

"Yes," Mote replied, "washing up. We have a delivery and she was able. There is time, if you want to see her."

"She only came to visit, and you put her back to work?"

"Nev and Cray are still in Lancaster. Searching for that last butterfly, I suspect."

Cray was a member of the railway's maintenance crew, and injured while working in Truth. Nev provided his care at the clinic. It was during his recovery they developed a close relationship.

Down the hallway were sounds of labor. As Jasira passed through, her heart quickened.

She said to Mila, "The parents are gifted?"

"Common. Why do you ask?"

"I *felt* an energy."

"Something you have felt before?"

"Yes."

"In Montro?"

Montro

"Take your time, Jasira," said Mila before leaving the room.

The sounds of labor grew more intense.

Maze was born on this day, a healthy new and the son of commons. That he was gifted was evident to Mila—from his first breath.

NEV AND CRAY'S CELEBRATION OF PARTNERSHIP

The ceremony overlooked the River Igua. Four generations of Mila's bloodline were present. Cray's family, unable to attend, remained in the Land of Tuz.

Before the vows were exchanged, Mila shared her thoughts. "My parents partnered when I was an early learner. They were the first of our tribe to do so. Today, we celebrate this joyful ritual. Blessings to Nev and Cray!"

"BLESSINGS."

Ficus viewed the event from above. "Look at the primitives." He scowled.

"What exactly are they doing?" asked Daniel, standing next to him on a box.

"Celebrating nonsense."

Closer, he instructed the falcon.

The pronouncement was made and flowers tossed in the air.

"What a special day," said Jasira, her voice sparkling with emotion.

"Yes!" Koal ecstatically agreed.

The reception line began to move, and Jasira was bumped from behind.

"Excuse me," the Tuz apologized and shook his head. "I misjudged the distance. My name is Tiller. I worked with Cray."

"I am Jasira, a friend of Mila's."

He chuckled. "It seems everyone in the territory is her friend."

Wair was at the front of the line and presented the couple with necklaces.

"Rose pearls!" Nev gushed. "They are precious. Thank you, Grandfather."

"Very special," said Cray.

The elder smiled warmly at the Tuz. "Welcome to our family."

Tiller raised his hand to shield the sun. "What do you see up there? That bird? Beautiful creatures . . . falcons. They would circle above us from time to time, when we were working on the rails."

Her focus on the falcon did not waver.

"Jasira?"

She raised her energized finger and took control of the winged intruder, forcing it to climb.

Ficus's powers were elite, but at this close range, she held the advantage.

Dive! demanded the wizard, confounded by his loss of control.

Daniel was bewildered, witnessing his father disturbed in such a way. "DIVE."

"What's wrong?" the boy cried out, his little heart pounding.

The hijacked bird continued to climb, the gathering below—becoming smaller and smaller.

Tiller watched in awe. The falcon, merely a speck, had reached the edge of the sky. The doomed raptor gave one last thrust.

Jasira's arm—slowly came down to rest.

The altar's window dissolved into swirls of blues and greens.

Ficus quietly told Daniel, "Go to your room, and I will join you later."

The tumbling falcon slammed viciously into the river's aqua waters.

Tiller looked at Jasira with eyes wide open. "You did that?"

"Yes."

Most of the bird floated downstream, as the amulet sank to the bottom, and a bed of soft mud.

The wizard peered through the darkening window, until it went black. "Jasira," he despondently exhaled.

A note from Ficus:

Lent—

I was disappointed to find Jasira, alive and well in Truth. Regretfully, her skills have not diminished. Because of your carelessness, I have lost a falcon and an amulet. Another lapse in judgment would not be wise. As a reminder, your supplements have been amended.

—MWF

* * *

"I wish I could share more," said Jasira.

Tiller studied her every movement.

She shook her head. "You are staring."

"Yes"—he smiled—"I am."

MILA

"The wagon is ready?" asked Mila.

"It is," said Jasira.

"Let the journey begin!"

Mila sat up front with Koal at the reins, with Jasira and Tiller behind them. Their first destination was the hunting camp. It was early rebirth, and the herd was returning from the south. Riker had recently become a champion. His great-grandmother grew anxious to see him in action.

The hunts had progressed into a test of skill. Long gone were the warkins, and the elk only to be tagged.

After spending two nights at the camp, they traveled north and into the Ancient Forest. Mila had been secretive as to why she chose to go there. They arrived just past midday.

"Let's make camp over there." Mila pointed to an area near an easy-flowing stream.

That's the spot!" Jasira enthusiastically agreed.

"Brother, you will be catching tonight's meal?"

"I'll give it a stab." Koal laughed and extended his tongue. "Where might you be off to?"

"Looking around."

Mila left the group in conversation and disappeared behind the tree line. A short distance from there, she entered the meadow.

"I am here!" she announced—then listened.

It had been over fifty years since Mila last saw a warkin. She often thought of Sym and imagined where his bloodline flowed.

A few moments passed in silence.

"There you are." She smiled and gestured with her hand. *Come closer.*

Sitting down on the lush grass, she waited. But the warkin stayed still and softly growled. Almost immediately, an overgrown pup jumped into the open, a striking young beast with silver highlights.

Mila was overcome with emotion, and tears flowed freely. The mother warkin walked over and gently nuzzled against her neck. The pup looked on with large amber eyes, its bushy tail vibrating madly, in an instant pouncing into Mila's open arms. She held him close, and they absorbed each other's scent.

"I almost called for a search," said Koal with a knowing smile. "Anything of interest in there?"

Mila softly nodded.

* * *

Soon after their return, Jasira and Tiller were partnered. Although in poor health, Mila attended all the events, most often holding Pearl, Nev and Cray's newly born, and her great-great-granddaughter.

At Mila's request, Jasira stopped by her dwelling.

"This is for you," said Mila.

Jasira took the dark-oak box and opened the narrow lid.

"Symlander?" she asked, admiring the blade.

"Yes . . . a gift from my true father. When called upon, it will serve you well."

Later that night, the fair Zuku closed her crystal-blue eyes, one final time.

Mila's ashes were taken to the Ancient Forst and scattered in a particular meadow. Truth spent the season of solar celebrating her exceptional life. A vast prairie was named in her honor. Tributes arrived from far and near. She had touched so many, in unique and everlasting ways.

Ficus zestfully rubbed his hands together. "This is the best news I have heard in years."

During Three Years of Time

Truth mourned another loss, as Dorin passed away without warning—Mote would later determine there had been a blockage in her vein.

Raye replaced his father as Truth's leader, while Wair continued to advise. Riker became leader of farming and hunting.

Before the mineral agreement expired, Sucrene Valley Holdings brokered an extension. The terms were highly favorable to the kingdom.

First Evolvement:

Years 1–4
Fundamental studies: cultural history, math, science.
Physical and mental well-being: strength, endurance, focus.

Years 3 and 4
Mystic abilities:
Arnela (telepathy, telekinesis).
Daniel (chemistry/potions).

* * *

Arnela reached her eleventh birthday with high expectations. First evolvement had arrived. She would develop her abilities and bond with her mother.

"Are you ready, Arnela?" asked Kendra.

"Beyond ready."

"Then, let's begin with a walk."

Kendra kept a moderate pace, with Arnela just off her shoulder.

"Your friends . . . are quiet?"

"Yes." Arnela chuckled. "They are accustomed for me to be alone."

The wizard stopped with an eyebrow raised and surveyed the surroundings. "They will have to get used to this."

"I will let them know."

"I already have."

*　*　*

Ficus nudged the sleeping young wizard. "Get up."

They left the harbor and set a course for the flats. Once under a full sail, Ficus handed Daniel a notebook and pencil.

"There will be situations when words and actions find importance. Write them down."

"Yes, my wizard."

"These minerals that we seek were first revealed to my Great-Grandfather Kren. Their purpose, a voice described in detail. Applying this knowledge, he created the foundation of our culture, the Mystic blood that flows within us."

*　*　*

Arnela listened closely as her mother continued to speak.

"He was the chosen one, foretold of its arrival, watching in amazement as the white-hot stone streaked across the sky. A *gift* from our Maker. The altar's source of power."

"Mystic altar," Arnela thought out loud.

"After your studies begin at Montro, you will come to know the altar well. Until then, we will revisit the history of our culture. Gain an understanding of our origin and evolution. Appreciate the contributions and sacrifices made by those who came before us."

Those walks around the Zone enlightened Arnela. Each new day, adding a meaningful layer to her being.

YEARS THREE AND FOUR

Daniel connected with the falcons at the beginning of his third year. Soon enough, he was adept at preparing the altar and communicating with the loyal birds.

Tasked with acquiring a training resource, he sent out another falcon. Trusting unlike the first attempt, the small kemit would be delivered unharmed.

Ficus looked over at the reptile in the corner, finishing a leafy green. "Does she have a voice?"

"Not yet, but she is receptive to mine," Daniel proudly confirmed.

"Perhaps by tomorrow."

"Yes, my wizard."

* * *

Kendra asked, "How was your run?"

"Not so much today," said Arnela. "Down to the river and only half-way back."

"Continue where we left off?"

"Have they been rearranged?

"You tell me."

Arnela stared down at the three overturned bowls, with a different-colored stone under each one. "Red under that one."

Kendra lifted the bowl and exposed the red stone. "Good start . . . and the others?"

"Mother, this is obvious."

"Is it?"

"Those stones are in your possession."

Kendra reached out and opened her hand. The green and black stones dropped to the table.

"Your turn?" the young wizard suggested with a sly smile.

"Why not!"

"Close your eyes." Arnela placed a stone under each bowl and shuffled them madly. "You can open them now."

Kendra firmly tapped the bowl. "Under here is the black one."

"Are you sure?"

"Positive . . . lift it."

Arnela raised the bowl, but nothing was there. "Guess again?"

"Turn it over, Wizard!"

Slowly, she turned the bowl over. Trapped against its bottom, the black stone was revealed.

"Now, let it go."

Arnela did so, and the stone released.

CHAPTER 17
SECOND EVOLVEMENT

TRUTH

"He has departed." Mote acknowledged his father's final breath. Susan raised her head and softly smiled at those around her. "Koal was my special partner, a gifted and humble leader, a Zuku with a lighter side"—she bulged her tearful eyes—"we all had the pleasure to know."

Laughter, hugs, and stories were shared by all.

* * *

Leader Raye opened the meeting and quieted the murmurs. "Council members, disturbing information has arrived from Sucrene. Rube has been inside the castle and will provide us with the details."

"Welcome, Rube," said Wair.

"Welcome, Rube!" echoed the others.

She spoke to the leaders in a steady voice. "I labored in the mines for two seasons—"

"You are a Zuku," Mote interrupted. "This is not unusual?"

"There aren't many of us. Yet because of our strength and smaller size, we can do jobs that are challenging for others."

"Understood . . . go on."

"In the beginning, I never left the camp. That changed after meeting another miner, a family man who lived in the village. He invited me to share his table. I did so, and on more occasions after that. We became good friends.

"Four days he went missing. I was concerned and stopped by his dwelling. His partner told me he had taken a job in Lackland, for the same company but with better pay."

"Sucrene Valley Holdings?" Wair suspected.

The Zuku closed her eyes and nodded. "He said goodbye to his family . . . and never—"

"Some water," Raye offered.

She took a drink and collected her thoughts. "More time passed without a word. His partner asked the company for an explanation. They said he was working in a remote location. She thought this to be true, as his payments continued to arrive.

"I decided to apply for the same job. They were somewhat skeptical and questioned my interest. I said there was *talk* in the mines. The clerk stepped away . . . and I waited. He returned and confirmed an opening. But before considering the transfer, a physical was required."

Wair spoke up, "They did not suspect you to be gifted?"

"No . . . they believed me to be a common."

"Listen carefully, leaders," said Raye.

"I was prescribed a tonic, to clarify their findings. From what I was *feeling*, this was not the liquid's intent. I absorbed just enough to understand its design . . . a loss of one's identity.

"Instead of Lackland, I was brought to the castle. They issued me clothes and assigned a bed. I was introduced to a manager and followed his instructions. He led me to a large room, filled with machines and laborers—methodic in their work. The noise was deafening and the air sour."

"What were they doing?" asked Wair.

"Making weapons."

Riker spoke up from the edge of his chair, "Did you see your friend?"

"Yes . . . in the dining area. He stared through me as if I wasn't there."

The furious Zuku jumped up and shouted, "What madness this wizardry!"

"Riker!" Raye put out his hands and motioned for calm, then returned his focus to Rube. "Describe your escape."

"I isolated an enforcer and spoke to his *truth*. He believed me to be a transport officer, in need of urgent support. He led me out of the fortress, to the stables where I put him to sleep. Claiming a horse, I galloped past the western gate and never looked back, waiting at the first water station for a rail coach to jump."

"Rube, your bravery is to be commended," said Raye. "We would be grateful to have you join us."

"Will you join us?" shouted Riker.

"I will!"

Raye recognized each leader with steadfast eyes. "I have discussed this with my father, and we must prepare for battle."

Wair stood up and the room fell silent. "Leaders, there are eyes in the sky. Outwardly, let us reflect an illusion of normalcy, shielding the aggressor from our resolve."

Raye would direct the effort, with his father by his side. Riker co-ordinated the defenses. Rube was second-in-command. Tiller quietly procured metals from Lackland, through his contacts there, fabricating in Truth what was critical for battle.

"Maze!" Raye called out to the gifted Zuku.

"Yes, Leader!"

"You are well qualified to attend the academy. When of age, I will sponsor your application. We must be clear as to the wizard's intent."

"I will search for that answer."

Raye emphatically declared, "We begin here and now!"

Montro

A note from Ficus:

Kendra—

Tylot's services are no longer of value. Dispose of him by the apple trees. The green ones were his favorite.

—MWF

Tylot's replacement, Kip, did as he was ordered.

* * *

First evolvement was over, and for the moment, an opportunity to reflect.

Ficus sat alone in the study, sipping tea from his favorite cup. As the sun began to rise, he stepped out on the balcony and went to its edge. He took a slow, deep breath and gazed across the water.

Truth, he contemplated its future.

The wizard was forever leery of the gifted Zuku, and all but a few would be spared—for research. The Tuz could be modified with little effort, as much was learned in Lackland. The commons were harmless.

* * *

Though Ficus was absent during Arnela's upbringing, Kendra and the falcons provided him with insight. The young wizard's abilities were impressive, and she channeled them with little effort. Troublesome at times were her voracious curiosity and penchant for mischief, attributes passed down from her mother.

Ficus fully understood Arnela's temperament. She could be influenced yet not commanded. Her natural defenses were necessary to augment Daniel's caustic chemistry—once combined, producing mystic majesty.

In preparation for Arnela's arrival, the royal guesthouse was thoroughly renovated. She would not only be educated but also comforted, for it was in her womb that the most sacred of them all would be nourished.

"The vessel is outside the harbor," said Daniel, peering through the window.

"Go down and greet her," directed Ficus. "Make a good impression . . . everything as we discussed."

"Yes, my wizard."

Although Daniel lacked creativity, his attention to detail was impeccable.

It was a warm day on the docks.

"Arnela?"

"Yes!"

"Welcome to Montro. I am Daniel." He reached out to help her down.

She accepted his hand, oddly cool to the touch. "Good to meet you, Daniel."

He simply nodded. "How was your travel?"

"Long—but inspiring. I hesitated to close my eyes!"

"This island is my home, and I know it very well."

"You are also a student?"

"I begin my studies this term."

"Then we have something in common." She smiled.

Besides being wizards, he kept to himself. "Let me help you with your belongings. The carriage is waiting."

Daniel accompanied her to the guesthouse and opened the door. "Your residence."

Arnela's eyes darted about. "All of this!"

"The arrangements were made by . . . the Mystic wizard."

"I wasn't expecting—"

"Where should I place your things?"

"Anywhere is fine, and I am thankful for your help."

"Registration is in the main building, on the first floor."

"And where do you live, Daniel?"

"I will show you." He led her out to the patio. "Up there."

"With those birds?"

"Falcons."

"Impressive."

"I must be going." He reached out and they shook hands.

Ficus watched from above with calm satisfaction.

Daniel hurried to the main building and up the stairs. Once inside, he went straight to the lab.

"You did well, Daniel."

"As you instructed, my wizard."

"Invite Arnela for supper. We will introduce her to the altar."

No matter that rest was long overdue, Arnela's mind would not let her. It took everything she had to stay anchored above the bed.

"YESSSSSS," she roared, throwing her arms out wildly.

A note from Ficus:

Kendra—

Daniel met Arnela at the harbor today. I am pleased.

—MWF

The next morning, Ficus said to Daniel, "She has left the guesthouse."

The young wizard scrambled down the stairs and out the door.

"Arnela!"

She searched through the glare. "Daniel?"

He walked down the path to join her. "How was your first night. You slept well?"

"Finally . . . but before that"—she laughed and shook her head—"another time."

Daniel stood there for a moment awkwardly mute, evaluating her expressive face. "You're adjusting."

"I've arranged my things, come see!"

He entered the guesthouse and looked around. Displayed on a shelf along the far wall was a collection of small objects.

She noticed his attention. "Driftwood, from Sara's Beach. Their natural shapes . . ." Her memories returned to that special place.

Daniel stepped closer for a better look, and she followed him there. After inspecting each one he asked, "You find them interesting?"

"Very much so." Her infectious smile persuaded even him.

"If not too soon, join us for supper . . . tonight?"

"I would like that."

"I'll return at sundown, and take you up the stairs."

"See you then . . . Daniel."

Ficus paced the floor in thought, *should I make it less formal?*

* * *

The solar sun approached the glimmering horizon.

"This way, Arnela . . . to the study."

She rushed past Daniel and straight through to the balcony, stopping with her hands against the rail. "Oh my . . . the view!"

"Hello, Arnela."

"Oh, hello! You startled me."

His crystal-blue eyes sparkled in the distance.

"You startled me." He smiled on his way over to greet her. "Welcome to Montro, I am Ficus."

Daniel watched in silence, with one foot on the balcony.

Arnela respectfully bowed. "It is an honor to be here . . . with you, a direct descendent of the Mystic Wizard Kren. I spent many days with my mother, exploring the history of our culture."

"From what I've been told, it is *you*, the special wizard,"

She modestly laughed. "I am motivated to explore that rumor."

"Daniel is also very gifted." Ficus glanced over and acknowledged the somber wizard. "We have been working closely together. And now, I have the good fortune to advance you both."

She looked over at Daniel to gauge his response—there was none.

His relationship with Ficus remained unclear to her.

"Arnela, would you be willing to experience the history of our culture firsthand?"

"Yes!"

At the entrance to the laboratory she felt a presence, a warmth, emerging from the depth of her chest.

Ficus said, "The Mystic altar calls to you both"—though he was drawn to Arnela. "You feel it, don't you?"

Her eyes misted over. "I do."

"It makes you weep?"

The wizard did not anticipate a reaction he had never witnessed before.

"I don't know for what reason," she said—just above a whisper.

Daniel stood opposite Arnela, confused and waiting for instruction.

Ficus spoke to the young wizards in a comforting voice. "Your second evolvement begins with this simple ceremony, a ritual, from the beginning of our culture. Hold your hands together and rest them in the water. Close your eyes . . . and free your thoughts."

After the ceremony and a light supper, Daniel saw Arnela out of the building. Standing under a moonlit sky, they shared a soft embrace.

She stepped back and looked into his eyes. "I don't mean to intrude, but I've been wanting to ask. the Mystic wizard is also—"

"My father?"

"Is he?"

"Our relationship is not like that."

"I don't understand."

"Next time"—he took a deep breath—"the falcons."

"Yes, we neglected them, didn't we."

* * *

A note from the kingdom:

My wizard—

The queen has taken a turn for the worse, and I am often at her side. Overcome with grief, the prince has joined her in distress, the elixir well conceived. They are both under watch with a bleak prognosis. Preparations have been made.

The Kingdom of Wizards will soon be yours!

—Prince Lent

* * *

Daniel helped to load the wagon. Among the items was a large crate bearing a special gift.

"Your friendship with Arnela continues to grow," Ficus said on the way to the harbor.

"As you predicted, my wizard."

"While I am gone, welcome her to the residence. Impress her with your wizardry. But remember, listen to her with care. Unlike you, she is a sensitive one."

"She is weak."

Ficus gazed off into the distance. "Do not be misled by her passionate nature. Her strength, I am confident, is no less abundant than yours."

Nothing more was said until the vessel was loaded.

"And her curiosity . . . about us," Daniel asked as he untied the rope.

"I am your father, and you are my son. There you have it! He caught the rope and coiled it up.

The young wizard stood alone at the end of the dock, Remaining there, until the vessel was no longer in sight. Fury simmering in his veins.

The Kingdom

At Star Jasmine, Lent's exhilarated mood was enhanced by the fresh supplements.

"Your robe and headdress, very regal!" said the king to the guest of honor.

"Custom made by a family in Sym," replied Ficus. "They have provided our special garments for years. The fabric and detail are of the highest quality."

"I feel undervalued."

"Not in the least."

They smiled at each other—then openly laughed.

"Unbelievable." Lent shook his head. "Two blue-eyed wizards stepping out on the central balcony, a throng of adulation below them. King Gorsh was ever fearful of this day."

"Your grandfather was a visionary," Ficus concluded. "And we are fast approaching his prophecy."

The expansive doors swung open.

"It is time, my king," said the royal guard.

"Join me, my wizard!"

Lent stepped up to the railing and delivered his opening remarks.

Ficus stayed back, respectfully unnoticed, until he was announced.

"Loyal citizens of the kingdom, it is my privilege to present a very special guest!"

Riveras had long been entranced by the Symlander. Ficus's striking appearance that day reinforced their fascination.

The Mystic wizard came into view and eloquently waved to the crowd. As he did so, a young boy emerged from behind him with a box in his hands. Everyone was curious—notably Lent, who had no prior knowledge of the spectacle. Ficus took the box and lifted the lid. Inside was a well-worn handler's glove. Effortlessly, he slid his hand into the thick, yet supple, hide. With his other hand, he pointed up to a falcon circling the cloudless sky. Making a fist, he thrust it down. The glistening raptor screeched and collapsed its wings. The captivated audience watched

366

breathlessly as it streaked toward them, catching their voice when it swooped back up.

Perch. The falcon gracefully glided to his glove.

The boy returned with a similar box and presented it to the king.

"For me?"

"Put it on and rekindle your skill," said Ficus with a wink. "But not with this one."

What haven't you told me? Lent wondered.

Ficus raised his hand to silence the murmurs. "To commemorate this historic occasion, I have brought a special gift!" He pointed in the direction of Zuku Cove. "The Northern Frontier falcon, an ancient and treasured breed. Behold! The Mystic falcon—RIVERA."

A high-pitched screech preceded the young raptor's arrival. The amazed crowd oohed and aahed, then shouted their approval!

The king raised his gloved hand and Rivera perched upon it.

"Treat her with care," Ficus said with a subtle nod.

"She is to be cherished," Lent glowingly replied. "Her offspring will flourish in our land."

Both falcons were raised up high and dramatically displayed, their crisp golden eyes flashing from side to side.

TRUTH

On his way back to Montro, a messenger spoke to Ficus at the rail station.

"Tell them I am on my way."

The doors were latched and everyone seated.

Leader Raye brought the meeting to order. "Mystic Wizard Ficus, good of you to come with such short notice."

The wizard stood up. "It is an honor to be here with the council."

"The stability of our region is in question," said Raye, his voice serious and clear. "An operation has been discovered in Sucrene . . . with military implications."

"A military operation?" Ficus responded with pronounced surprise.

"We have knowledge of body armor and weaponry."

"That valley is a peaceful place. I have observed nothing to suggest otherwise."

"It is happening inside the castle, with support from Sucrene Valley Holdings. You have a relationship with this company?"

"I assure you, only the transport of their commerce."

He lies. Maze privately insisted.

The gifted young Zuku had been asked to join the meeting and sat quietly in the back. Although Ficus was well concealed, he could assess his truthfulness.

"Council members . . . your concerns are understandable. I will travel there during our recess and investigate the situation. We can meet after this?"

"I am in favor!" said Wair.

Ficus glowered at Maze. *Is that acceptable to you . . . mind reader?*

The wizard is aware of my presence.

Raye looked over at Ficus.

The wizard's disdain was clear, his voice low and ominous. "Where I come from, attempting to read one's mind is a punishable offense. If we are to meet again, personal privacy is mandatory."

He left the room without another word.

MONTRO

Daniel's wizardry was more advanced than Arnela's, an advantage gained by supplements, the altar, and heavy-handed instruction. However, naturally, she was the pure wizard.

She continued to pressure Daniel, "Why won't you share the recipe?"

"It's not—"

Ficus would not allow it, and Arnela could never know.

"What?" she scoffed. "And who needs a potion to speak with the birds anyway."

He shook his head, befuddled. "You're not making sense!"

She softened her expression and warmed her voice. "Let's go out on the water?"

"If you like."

"And it's my turn," she playfully reminded him.

Daniel preferred taking the steam-powered vessel, while Arnela enjoyed being moved by the wind.

Halfway around the island, the steady breeze abandoned them.

"This is the reason I do *not* enjoy sailing," said an irritated wizard. "Being at the mercy of anything . . . is never good."

Arnela was teetering on the edge of laughter.

Once again, she would conjure a breeze to fill the sails.

"You see, Daniel, everything . . . including the wind, must take some moments for rest."

A note from Ficus:

Kendra—

The coronation was successful, and the kingdom is secured. As expected, Truth has been told of the operation. Do not deviate from our mission, and remain vigilant.

—MWF

* * *

Not long after sundown, Ficus went to the guesthouse with a pot of hot tea. He would visit with Arnela in her surroundings, away from the lab and Daniel.

She continued with her questions. "Your grandfather, Nord, was also a Mystic wizard? Mother was not clear about that."

"Grandfather never claimed to be much of a wizard, giving himself less credit than deserved. But he was more than competent, with potions and connections."

"The bloodlines he has influenced," Arnela imagined out loud.

"This is true." Ficus nodded with a warm smile, admiring the way she thought.

369

"I was told—that sadly . . . he succumbed to an unknown disease?"

"No." The wizard stared deep into her eyes. *He was poisoned by my father.*

Why are you telling me this? she questioned his inner-voice.

Because you are family.

Arnela lay awake that night, shackled by a lingering conversation. Ficus's words were personal, leaving her alone and confused. She wished her mother were there.

* * *

Ficus traveled to Sucrene, but not under the pretense Truth's leaders were told.

"Ship a small assortment to the kingdom. I will assure the council there is no cause for alarm. The armaments have been commissioned, and strictly for self-defense. Assign ten enforcers to provide security. Lent is aware of the deception."

"Yes, my wizard," said Kendra.

Enforcers accompanied subsequent deliveries. However, those well-sealed crates were empty.

Two Years Passed

The Academy for Special Studies

STAFF:

Lead Administrator · · · · · · · · Headmaster Wembley

Science · · · · · · · · · · · · · · · · · Professor Coy

Mathematics · · · · · · · · · · · · · Professor Wrike

*Cultures · · · · · · · · · · · · · · · Professor Reno

Leadership · · · · · · · · · · · · · Professor Stubin

Abilities · · · · · · · · · · · · · · · · Professor Lipit, Mystic Wizard Ficus

*Curriculum includes history and languages.

The abilities program was expanded and the curriculum revised. Professor Lipit, recruited from the Dark Forest, instructed from a second-floor classroom. Her students were denied access to the wizard's laboratory. Daniel and Arnela would study there in the afternoons, privately tutored by Ficus.

* * *

As was customary, first-year students arrived before the others, a full-blooded Zuku among them.

Headmaster Wembley smiled broadly from across his large desk. "Welcome to the academy, Maze."

"I am grateful to be here, Headmaster."

Wembley looked down at the paper in his hand. "Your scores are impressive."

"Thank you, Headmaster."

"And your *connections* . . . even more so."

"I have been blessed."

"Let us have an understanding."

"Yes, Headmaster."

"On this island, intruding into the thoughts of others is strictly prohibited."

"I am aware of the policy."

Wembley leaned forward with penetrating eyes. "We are committed to providing a positive experience, for everyone here. Mind readers will be expelled without recourse."

"I have worked diligently, in advance, to suppress my natural instincts."

Later that afternoon, Ficus stormed into the headmaster's office.

"This application was to be rejected!"

"My wizard, I assure you, if not approved by Lord Hemeth himself, Maze would not be here."

"You can appreciate my uncertainty?"

"The Zuku will be kept under tight observation. I am confident your plans are secure."

"Do not disappoint me."

Wembley traced his fingertips along the polished desktop. "Is there something else, my wizard?"

Ficus reached inside his pocket and took out a small silk purse. The headmaster's eyes intensely followed its travel.

"I believe these . . . will be to your liking."

* * *

Arnela could no longer restrain her frustration.

"Why is it, my wizard, I share in the results but *not* the preparation? She took a deep breath. "I also have an aptitude for potions."

"I trust that you do, Arnela . . . and you *should* be more involved. Let me think on this tonight."

"I want to experience everything!"

He looked deep into her absorbing eyes and privately presumed. *She is tampering with my chemistry.*

Later that evening, Ficus sat alone on the balcony, sipping a cup of hot tea.

She could focus on the properties of vision. What harm could there be in that?

Arnela became responsible for the altar's daily upkeep. She did not prearrange the falcons' flights but communicated with them and monitored their travel. Kendra was warned to cover her activities.

THE MEADOW

Daniel said, "It will be only us today."

"He is down at the yard," Arnela supposed.

"Yes, the second engine has final testing."

"What will we do?"

"Contribute to a potion."

"A potion!" The young wizard rejoiced.

"An influencer of perception. The recipe calls for a natural fragrance. We will go to the meadow and gather it."

There was a sensation that came over Arnela every time she entered the meadow, an energy that welcomed her magic. Daniel was accustomed to her abstract episodes. He was the clear and orderly one. Arnela admired those traits, unaware they were not inherently his.

While she traversed the wide-open space, Daniel gathered the lavender.

He shouted from the other side, "I've got all that we need!"

The spirited wizard frolicked her way to him. "Can we stay a little longer?"

"Not too much longer. We must be back before he walks through the door."

"Over there!" Arnela reached out and took his hand, ever cool to the touch.

She led him to an old oak tree. They sat underneath its canopy of sturdy limbs and whispering leaves.

"What are you thinking?" he asked.

"Time"— she sighed—"and where has it gone? We are almost to graduation."

"Time passes," he remarked without much thought.

"It seems not long ago, you met me at the harbor. Your greeting was unexpected, and helped me feel at ease. You introduced me to kemits . . . breathing or not!" Her bright laughter filled the meadow. "You brought me here"—she gazed about—"to this enchanted place."

"I do remember all of this." He smiled the best he could.

"And your future, Daniel?"

"Nothing changes for me," he said quietly. "I'll continue working with my—"

"Father?"

"Yes, my father." He lowered his head and stared at the ground. "And you?"

"Return home, of course . . . but for how long, I cannot say. I might travel to the kingdom. The altar has piqued my interest. Could you imagine living there?"

He looked up to find Arnela's captivating eyes. "It's not something I've considered . . . until now."

And as he said this, his hands started to warm. Instinctively, Arnela reached out and held them.

"Daniel, what just happened?"

* * *

Ficus asked, "Why so quiet this evening, Daniel?"

"I must be tired."

"The cuttings will do very well. Tomorrow, we finalize the recipe."

"Arnela, she can participate?"

The wizard abruptly turned away. He sensed a change in Daniel's chemistry, a dilution—Arnela most likely to blame. "No. She will be occupied elsewhere."

Daniel understood. The conversation was over. "I will go and rest."

Ficus went to the laboratory. He worked with urgency long into the night. It had to be done.

* * *

The following morning, Arnela said, "I haven't seen Daniel?"

"He has taken ill," Ficus coolly replied.

"This is unexpected."

"Yes."

"Only yesterday he was in the best of moods. He was going to ask you—"

"The fever came late last night, and I stayed with him until it passed. He is sleeping now."

"When it is possible, I would like to see him."

He stared into her troubled eyes. "I have a task for you."

"Yes, my wizard."

"A falcon has been sent to Sucrene, and carries an important agreement. Go to the altar and confirm its delivery. I will take care of my son."

Instead of an agreement, the canister contained the newly developed potion. Libby would see to its delivery.

After a meal and short rest, the falcon began its journey home, soaring above Granite Gorge and headwaters of the mighty Sucrene. Half aware of what lay below, Arnela was suddenly moved. Impulsively, she diverted the falcon's route.

"Truth," she whispered.

"What is it, Jasira?" Nev asked her distracted companion.

"Another falcon . . . but this one is different."

Nev looked up and found the bird in flight. "How so?"

"It's not here on hostile terms." She pointed at the circling falcon. *I am Jasira. What is your name?*

Arnela. You know who I am?

Jasira became quite shaken. *I'm not sure.* Then she shouted, "I'm not sure!"

"What is it?" Nev blurted out.

"Was the delivery made?" asked Ficus from the doorway. "Arnela?"

She kept staring through the window without an answer.

"Arnela!"

"Yes . . . what? I was distracted." *I have to go.*

Nev said, "The falcon is leaving."

"Was the agreement delivered?"

"Yes, my wizard . . . everything according to plan."

"Follow me."

Ficus stood to the side, and Arnela entered the room. It was dimly lit, and the air was thick. The chill that once gripped Daniel's hands now enveloped his surroundings. Heavy and aggressive, it challenged her every breath. She stepped closer to his lifeless body.

CHAPTER 18
ARNELA'S HOMECOMING

TRUTH

The disruption of the territory was in full progress, with increased railway costs, delays, and restrictions, and slashed mineral purchases and furloughed Tuz laborers. Truth had become isolated, fractured, and vulnerable!

Council of Defense:
Raye · · · · · · *Leader*
Wair · · · · · · *Senior Advisor*
Jasira · · · · · · *Special Forces*
Riker · · · · · · *Lead Warrior*
Rube · · · · · · *Logistics*
Mote · · · · · · *Wellness*
Maze · · · · · · *Intelligence*
Tiller · · · · · · *Weaponry*

Maze stood up and reported back from Montro. "Meaningful information has been impossible to obtain. They judge my every movement. However, there is an opportunity."

"Go on," said Raye.

"The wizard, Arnela, is returning to Sucrene. She travels the old way through Granite Gorge. The *truth* she carries could be insightful. I suggest we seek her out."

"Assemble your team and go through the hardwoods," Wair advised. "This will bring you to her path. Leave now, under the full moon's light."

"We'll be off without delay.

Raye then asked, "Have we heard from the king?"

"The *king* remains elusive," responded Riker with growing frustration. "'Do you have an appointment? He's not here. Try again tomorrow.' Documents that bare your seal mean nothing!"

THE KINGDOM

A note from the kingdom:

> *My wizard—*
>
> *Today, we turned away another courier. Should we continue in this manner? Truth is nervous, and their patience waning.*
>
> *—Lent*

A note from Ficus:

> *Lent—*
>
> *Invite the leaders to Star Jasmine. Explain the legitimacy of the armaments. Ease the travel restrictions. Make an additional purchase of salt. If the migrants are mentioned, provide words of encouragement but no guarantees.*
>
> *Calm their thoughts and eliminate the speculation. We have made strong advancements yet require additional time.*
>
> *The supplements are enhanced. They will provide clarity and comfort.*
>
> *—MWF*

Lent took the silk purse from the canister. In it was a generous supply of bold-yellow tablets. He could feel his temperature rise and his heart begin to flutter. These new supplements would take him to a place of extreme contentment, a precarious place where he was intimately familiar.

Down the stairs he walked with purpose, his hand gliding along the polished rail. The basement was warm where the incinerator burned. He opened its heavy door and threw the misery inside.

Although Lent was forever connected to the elements of fury, he would no longer be dependent.

* * *

Not long ago, Lent set out on a relaxing sail. It was to be a day of leisure, a respite from the rigors of royal duties. Early on, the sleek vessel was seduced by a favorable wind. The aggressive conditions inspired the crew and their captain.

"Let her fly!" the king shouted.

Racing atop white-capped waters, the crew found their skills especially tested. Lent joined their effort and was exhilarated to do so.

The wind suddenly vanished, and the sails fell in despair. They began to drift. The horizon from where they came was but two shades of blue.

Stranded and deprived of supplements, the king's body violently rebelled. The anxious crew had no other choice and forcibly restrained him. On the fifth day, when they returned to land, he was unresponsive.

"No word of this to the Mystic wizard," Lent insisted, his voice struggling to be heard.

"Not a word, my king," the royal physician promised.

It was Nardine who, as an apprentice, had witnessed a similar condition. Those experiences helped to guide her treatments. Because of this, Lent escaped the snare of addiction and recovered.

SUCRENE

"Time for me to go."

"Must you, Hendrick?" said Arnela with disappointment.

"Your mother insisted. I was to report back as soon as we reached the valley." He spread his wings and flapped away.

"CAW. CAW."

Hendrick entered the cottage through the kitchen's open window.

Kendra's eyebrows narrowed. "You can tell me, can't you?

The crow nodded. "She's a talented one."

"Murn!"

"Yes, sister."

"Warm up the stew."

"Now, something for you." She held out a cloth pouch, filled with dried fruit and nuts.

"Thank you, my wizard," said the famished crow.

"Find somewhere peaceful and have your fill."

Arnela approached the shadow of Mount Golder. Stopping for a moment, she took a look around. *Almost everything is the same. Yet for me . . . so much has changed,*

At the doorstep, she smelled the stew.

"Welcome home, my dear!"

"Aunt Murn!"

They shared a joyful hug.

"Your mother requested garden stew. You must be hungry."

"Beyond hungry." She laughed. "And with nut bread?"

"Yes, Arnela!" answered Kendra from her bedroom. "As much as you can stomach."

"Mother!" Arnela rushed to the voice she hadn't heard in years.

Kendra was astonished by the wizard's appearance. Ficus's updates did not fully convey her transformation.

"Is Hendrick close by?"

"Hendrick?" Kendra raised an eyebrow.

"The crow you sent to watch over me. My surprise companion," she said with a big smile.

"Yes . . . the crow must be resting. Somewhere in the woodlands, I suppose. Let's eat!"

THE KINGDOM

The three Truth leaders approached Star Jasmine.

Raye looked at the others and said, "Impressive, isn't it?"

"Very," she replied.

Riker stayed silent and preoccupied in thought. *Royal guards without expression, impeccably presented at their stations. An impressive saber holstered at their sides. Snipers with crossbows discreetly positioned above them.*

Lent reviewed the spacious room, bathed in an abundance of natural light. At its center was an oval-shaped table made from hard maple. The chairs surrounding it were cushioned in red velvet. Alongside the back wall was a table with specially prepared food and beverages.

"Is everything to your liking, my king?" the royal attendant asked.

"Yes, the room is in order. Welcome our visitors and see to their comfort. I will return once they are settled."

Lent was well rehearsed and obliged to his directive.

"Welcome to Star Jasmine!" The royal attendant extended a hearty greeting. "Please—follow me." He led them up the stairs to the second-floor meeting room. "Help yourself to our regional tastes. The washroom is through that door. I will announce your arrival to the king." He bowed his head and left the room.

"Excuse me for a moment," said the leader.

"We won't begin without you," Raye assured her.

Lent took pause before entering the room, distracted by an unforeseen remembrance.

The royal attendant opened the door. "King Lent of Rivera!"

The leaders respectfully stood up.

"Welcome to the kingdom," Lent warmly greeted the visitors. "Excuse the delays, unfortunate timing, and by no means intentional."

"We are thankful for better timing," Raye responded in a straight-forward manner. His relationship with the king was nothing more than cordial. "One of our members has—"

The door opened and his words fell silent.

She looked over at the king. "Please excuse my absence."

"This is Jasira," said Raye, "leader of special forces."

"Special forces?" Lent quietly repeated, his head slightly cocked to one side.

Though relieved, he was also baffled. *How did she acquire her name? What else does she remember?* Once again, he felt vulnerable to her influence.

"And this is Riker, leader of our warriors," Raye concluded.

As Lent acknowledged the Zuku, he could feel her stare.

Do I know you?

"Please be seated," said the king, ignoring the inner voice.

The meeting proceeded as planned. The armaments were presented and explained, concessions provided, and agreements signed. The king was attentive and understanding. He was extremely convincing.

Lent stood up and commended the leaders, "We have accomplished much today."

"That, we have," Raye agreed, and the leaders rose to their feet.

"Let us celebrate!" said the king with satisfaction. "Tonight, on the waterfront with fine Shillig."

* * *

Lent and his guests occupied an intimate room at the kingdom's most popular eatery, their table overlooking Zuku Cove.

"Let us toast as one." The king reached for his glass and the others followed.

"To our gracious host," Jasira proposed with a brilliant smile.

Samplings of fresh seafood and savory side dishes were brought to the table, the ingredients and presentation unlike anything found in Truth.

Jasira sat beside the open window. From her vantage point, the trendy district was in full view. Oil lamps, hung like teardrops, illuminated the waterfront with a warm glow. Diverse eateries, shops, and galleries lined the spacious boardwalk.

"The nightlife is very active," she remarked. "What are the chances of encountering a Zuku along their namesake cove?"

"That would be rare," said the king. "However, there is a colony that lives in the nearby jungle, most likely harvesting the fruit you ate earlier today."

She silently stared into the cove.

Raye spoke up, "The fish was very good."

"Everything well prepared," added Riker.

Lent looked over at Jasira and, in that moment, was not reluctant to linger.

I would like to speak with you alone, she said privately, before turning to face the table.

"Jasira," the king spoke up, "an art exhibit just arrived. If you have interest . . . and there are no objections?"

"No objections," she responded for the others.

They said good night to the leaders and strolled down the walkway. Engaged in conversation, without notice, they had reached the end.

"The exhibit?" she reminded the king.

"We must have missed it." He chuckled. "We can sit over there."

"On those rocks?"

"I've spent many nights alone on those rocks, getting to know each one of them."

She gave him a curious look.

"*Alone*," he emphasized.

"There is to be no queen in your court?"

"My queen is Rivera . . . and you?"

"I do have a partner."

The revelation of Jasira's attachment did not come as a surprise. Much time had passed since she was abandoned at the harbor. Yet Lent felt an emptiness, an undeniable regret.

"And you are content?"

"I believe I am."

"Have you lived in Truth all your life?" he was compelled to ask.

She stared off into the darkness. "No, but my memory suffers. If not for the help of a dear friend—"

"Jasira?"

She brought her eyes to his. "Why do I *feel* a closeness with you?"

Lent very much wanted to be open with her—perhaps one day.

SUCRENE

Three days had passed since the crow was last seen.

Arnela yelled back at Murn, "I won't be long!" and continued down the trail. "Hendrick! Hendrick!"

A red-faced rabbit hopped out from the underbrush. "You are calling for the crow?"

"Yes!"

"Follow me."

Arnela was thrilled to reunite with her oily-feathered friend.

"He's in here."

She stepped over a moss-covered log and went to where the rabbit was sitting. There, on a bed of leaves, were the remains of Hendrick and a family of mice. Beside them sat a pouch with dried fruit and nuts.

"Poisoned?"

Arnela would return to the cottage and confront her mother. The Zone could wait another day. Considering the warkins, one could ill afford a distracted thought. But she changed her mind, no matter her misgivings.

After a deep breath, she swung up onto the oak, where Cleo in her memories led the way. Up high in the middle, she sat against the weathered bark. The castle loomed in the distance, with a disturbing energy overflowing its volcanic walls.

She jumped down and ran across the buffer and then waded into the waist-high grass.

"Silver warkin!" she called out, and then vanished alongside the trail.

The leader appeared with nostrils flared.

Arnela steadied her finger, and cast a spell from deep inside.

"Where did you vanish to?" the beast snarled, with her newly acquired voice.

The wizard let go of the grass. "Over here."

"Mmm," she rumbled. "Gifted as your mother."

"You are familiar with Kendra?"

"Not her!" She shook her head. "Your true mother."

"My true mother?"

The warkin approached with a menacing growl. "It could never be Kendra. She is without warmth. It is Jasira, fondly remembered by our kind."

CHAPTER 19
RECOVERY

K endra asked, "Not feeling well?"
"Not so well," replied Arnela. "Maybe something I caught along the trail."

"Murn will prepare a special broth. This and rest will provide your remedy."

A note from Ficus:

> *Kendra—*
>
> *We will gather the minerals and then join you. The time has come. Keep a watchful eye on Arnela, and make the arrangements.*
>
> *—MWF*

TRUTH

Some days passed.

Raye asked, "What do you bring us, Maze?"

The gifted Zuku stepped forward and briefed the council. "Ficus is leaving the island and travels in a flotilla."

"Why so many vessels?" Riker thought out loud.

"Cargo," he replied. "Rail engines and a private coach, sealed containers—except for one.

"What does it hold?" Raye asked.

"Pineapples."

"Pineapples!" Riker blurted out.

"We will confront him at the harbor," said Raye.

Jasira closed her eyes and could see the wizard clearly now, standing tall on a balcony, with wild white hair and an elaborate robe, his piercing blue eyes staring down at her. A bloodied falcon perched upon the rail.

Riker implored the leaders, "Let us arm our warriors with the newest weapons. Give Ficus a taste of our strength!"

"Not yet!" Wair responded in a commanding voice. "This is not an invasion. Our *strength* is the perception of our weakness."

"Agreed!" said Raye and settled the discussion.

* * *

"Remember, Daniel, this is only a courtesy visit. We roll out the engines, say a few words, distribute the pineapples . . . and wave goodbye. For all they know, we are relocating to the kingdom."

"Why so many pineapples?"

Ficus gazed up river and smiled. "We must extend our kindness, to every mouth in Truth. Their leaders would be foolish to disrupt our generosity."

"You are masterful, my wizard."

He looked down into his son's wanting eyes. "Your offspring will be all this and more. However, before our glory, the people must be prepared, able and eager to embrace a new order. They must be—"

"Controlled."

"That's right, Daniel."

A Zuku spotter reflected the signal.

"The vessels have entered the Igua," the messenger confirmed.

"Everyone in position," Riker instructed Rube.

The warriors scattered among the growing crowd.

"All this excitement over a pineapple," Raye grumbled. "Including the commons."

Falcons had dropped leaflets earlier that day, promoting the delectable fruit.

"The wizard is cunning," Wair acknowledged.

The flotilla came into view and blared their horns. Waving straight out above the lead vessel was a gold-embossed rendering of the Mystic altar, set against a vibrant blue background—the color of Symlander eyes.

"He travels with his own flag," Wair dryly remarked.

Two at a time, the vessels offloaded their cargo, lowered to the tracks by steam-powered cranes. Lined up and coupled, the new engines pulled them to the nearby station.

The private coach slowed to a stop, and the door opened. Ficus stepped down and presented himself, in a regal robe and headdress. His magnetic eyes appraised the crowd and sparkled in the midday sun. He strode across the platform, smiling along the way. At its center, he extended his arms in a symbolic embrace.

"Good day, my friends!" his powerful voice rang out.

The Tuz responded enthusiastically.

"Each time I return, there is something new for me to see. The wonders of Truth are endless! In all the Land of Rivera, your independent territory is respected."

"Once again," Maze confided to Tiller, "the wizard fills the air with lies."

He shook his head in disgust. "I'm ashamed to be a Tuz. We honor him, as if he were our king."

Ficus stepped to the very edge and absorbed the admiration.

He pointed to the front of his coach. "Behold our latest engine . . . stronger and with more speed. Delivering to the kingdom your valued resources—in two days' time instead of three!"

Raye and Wair weaved their way closer to the platform, while Jasira stayed back and vanished against an elm tree.

"Enough talk of engines and commerce," teased the wizard. "Before my son and I depart for the kingdom, we have brought a favorite delight . . . Montro pineapples, the sweetest I have ever tasted!"

Right on cue, Daniel appeared on the platform with a large, well-formed pineapple.

"Father!" he called out with confusion, the pineapple floating above his hands.

Nice trick. Ficus anxiously searched the crowd. *Where are you, Jasira?*

The leaves on the elm rustled wildly, even though there was barely a breeze.

I am here inside your memories . . . Father.

The distraction had left him unguarded.

Get out! he demanded.

After I restore what is mine.

Ficus angrily spun around and almost knocked Daniel over. "Get rid of the pineapples!"

Raye hurried back to where Jasira sat against the tree, depleted.

"What was that all about?" he asked.

"Reclaiming what was stolen."

"What?"

"My life," she whispered, and closed her eyes.

SUCRENE

The private coach was diverted at the hub, coupled with an engine bound for Sucrene. After they were on their way, rail traffic was suspended.

"Father, your tea."

Ficus bristled to hear Daniel refer to him that way.

* * *

"Running off to practice your tricks?" asked Murn.

"Most likely," said Arnela.

"Have you come up with something new?"

"Nothing new"—she laughed—"only a refinement."

"Oh?"

"I haven't dropped a rabbit in three days!"

"Lift me a little?"

"Just a little."

Slowly, Murn rose up and wiggled her suspended toes.

* * *

At the fortress, Ficus instructed Kip, "First the altar. Follow it up to the laboratory. Then summon Kendra to my quarters."

"Yes, my wizard!" He respectfully bowed.

Kendra went to Ficus as soon as she was told. He sat in a corner chair, head down and motionless.

"It was to be no more than a brief appearance." He sighed. "A simple gesture of friendship. We would distribute the pineapples and be on our way."

"What happened there?"

He stood up and made a fist. "Jasira is what happened there."

"Jasira?" Kendra was stunned to hear that name.

"She not only lives . . . but thrives. I was lapse in the moment, and she pried herself inside me."

"Arnela! She will come looking for her."

"Let her dare behind these walls."

Kendra asked, "The potion is ready?"

"It simply needs to be heated."

"Then tonight?"

"Yes. And her cycle?"

She flashed a wicked smile. "Receptive."

"I will prepare his tea."

After the final evolvement Daniel would be served the tea, a special blend with a toxic level of fury. Breathing would be difficult at first, and then impossible.

Ficus approached Kip and spoke to him in confidence.

"I have an idea."

"Yes, my wizard?"

"A way to achieve an early advantage . . . a decisive advantage. Sten will travel to Truth, cloaked in darkness and bearing a *gift*."

Kip listened closely to every detail.

* * *

Later that evening, Kendra said, "Serve this new blend to Arnela. Highlight its benefits, undisturbed slumber with vivid dreams. And Murn—"

"Yes, sister?"

"Do remember your smile."

* * *

"Ficus instructed Sten, "Have her carried up to the room."

"I am impressed," said Kendra. "Only one sip . . . and then . . ." Her words fell silent as he walked away.

The wizard appeared a short while later, high above on the observation deck. "Raise the flag!" he commanded.

TRUTH

After two full days of sleep, Jasira woke up at the clinic.

"Here, drink this," said Mote.

She sat up and drank the tonic, a blend of hibiscus water and powdered banana.

"Do you feel like talking?" asked Raye.

"Yes, and I have much to say. But only to you and your father." She looked over at Mote. "I hope you understand?"

"I do, and will bring him here."

Jasira was resting comfortably, when Wair entered the room.

"What led to this?" the senior elder asked.

"It was personal." She took a slow breath and arranged her thoughts. "Ficus is my father. I have a daughter—her name is Arnela. She will be sacrificed . . . as the wizard intended for me."

"We won't let this happen," said Wair. "Where is she now?"

"Sucrene."

Raye spoke up with urgency. "The council will meet at once."

The instant they left the clinic, a circling falcon screeched. Jasira instinctively raised her finger.

"Leave it alone," said Wair. "He already knows."

CHAPTER 20
RESOLUTION

TRUTH

Raye opened the meeting without them.

"I'm here!" Riker barged through the door.

Wair called out, "What do you know?"

"Ficus has traveled to Sucrene, and enforcers occupy the hub."

"Where is Rube?" asked Jasira.

"She jumped the wizard's coach, and intends to take his life."

Tiller stood up and shouted, "This is reckless!"

Wair put out his hands and motioned for calm.

"It was," Raye agreed, "and I fear she will be lost."

"Let me go there," Tiller said firmly.

Raye was surprised by his request. "You have a plan?"

"A small band of warriors. An elusive presence causing confusion, and holding them to the castle."

"Giving us time," said Wair.

Although Jasira endorsed this plan, she never expected Tiller to lead the effort.

SUCRENE

At Fortress Golder, the grueling travel and abuse from her captors had rendered the Zuku incoherent.

"We found her outside the station . . . carrying this!"

"A mind reader with a blade," Kendra said cooly.

"Let me take her to the Zone," suggested Kip.

"Not this one," said Ficus, with uncharacteristic amusement. "This Zuku has purpose. Imagine our good fortune, to be delivered such a distraction. Because of her, Officer Sten can travel without concern, and make the exchange unnoticed."

Kendra said, "I will begin the process."

"And do so immediately."

"When I am finished, she'll be as gifted as a pineapple."

"Kip!"

"Yes, my wizard!"

"Alert our contact."

The falcon carried two messages, one for Truth's leaders and the other for the operative.

TRUTH

Riker held up the parchment. "This was received at the station."

"Go on and read it," said Raye.

> *Leaders of Truth—*
> *The Zuku will be returned tonight.*
> *Her condition, a warning.*
> *Submit to the Mystic wizard,*
> *or risk unnecessary harm.*

* * *

Later that afternoon, Jasira insisted, "Take my dagger."

"Are you sure?" said Tiller. "Mila gave this to you . . . for *your* protection."

She looked deep into his eyes. "I trust the dagger in your hands. Promise me you'll take it."

"I promise."

She brought him close and lightly kissed his lips. "The council waits. Be strong and well."

He smiled with a nod. "See you soon."

* * *

The altar's window had lost most of its light. Only hints of steam rose from the stack below. Ficus was undeterred and followed the engine's progress.

"Riker, go to the boundary as we discussed," said Raye. "I will be at the station, with Jasira and Mote."

The leaders stood at the far end of the platform, backed by a team of warriors.

Jasira closed her eyes. "It's through the boundary."

"Rube is almost home," said Mote.

A distant rumble grew louder, and the ground began to shake. With a squeal from its brakes, the engine slowed and then stopped. The coach door opened, revealing a dimly lit space. The station's senior guard cautiously entered.

"Deliver this to the dwelling," said Sten. "Display it as you would for your partner. The seal must not be broken."

"The Zuku does not look well," commented the guard.

"No . . . not well. Take her and complete your task. The Mystic wizard extends his gratitude."

The operative accepted the pouch, then escorted Rube to the leaders and slipped away.

"No loud voices," Mote reminded them.

"Rube?" Raye said softly.

The Zuku stayed silent with empty eyes.

Mote said, "I'll take her to the clinic."

"Tiller!" The warrior banged on the door. "The wagons are loaded, and the horses are fresh."

"Coming!" the distracted Tuz shouted back.

He grabbed his bag of belongings and rushed out to join the others.

"YAH. YAH." the drivers ordered, and the wagons rolled away.

Lurking in the shadows was the operative, with a small copper box in her hand.

Where to put this . . . ? Over there! She placed it on a side table, next to a sheathed blade.

"Turn the wagon around!" Tiller reached over and took hold of the reins.

"What are you doing?"

"I've forgotten something important"

"Jasira!"

She stopped and turned to the voice. "Maze?"

He hurried up to her. "Can we talk?"

"I'm beyond tired." She sighed. "Tomorrow is better, bright and early."

"I understand, but I *felt* something at the station."

"Something?"

"An intense and unstable energy."

"That is a strange feeling to have."

"Even stranger, I *feel* it now . . . close by."

In that instant, Jasira also *felt* it.

"Whoa!" the driver pulled back on the reins.

Tiller jumped to the ground and entered the dwelling. He reached for the dagger and then hesitated. "What is this?"

"Run!" Jasira screamed at the top of her lungs. RUN.

A flash of light escaped the altar.

"Tiller!" she cried out. "Get Mote!"

Ficus recalled the falcon, and went to Kendra's chamber.

"There is something on your mind?" she asked.

"Jasira opened her gift. Truth has lost its wizard."

Her lips curled into a smile. "We will strike as they mourn."

Mote arrived and cared for the driver, thrown from the wagon when the horses were spooked. His injuries were not serious, and he explained what he knew.

Through the haze was Jasira, kneeling over the lifeless body.

Mote entered the dwelling and found what he was searching for.

He said, "This violence was meant for you."

She looked up with tearful eyes.

"Tiller came back for this." He handed her the blood-stained sheath.

She withdrew the dagger and stared at the blade. "Go to Raye. We must meet at once."

VENGEANCE

Truth warriors and supplies were loaded into rail coaches and then pulled to the boundary by oxen.

Raye brought the meeting to order, Jasira standing by his side. "My father and I will stay here and reinforce the territory, while Jasira and Riker lead our attack."

She spoke up, "The wizard believes me dead, and must remain convinced of this. In due time . . . I will prove my passing otherwise.

"Our warriors have been mobilized. An engine sits idle at the boundary and will take us up to Sucrene."

"And the enforcers at the hub?" asked Wair.

"They will serve to sharpen our skills."

A tussle at the door disrupted the meeting. "This Tuz is a traitor!" shouted the warrior. "She is responsible for the death of Tiller!"

"What is this?" said Wair.

"Our suspicions led us to her, and a stash of Sucrene gold."

"It isn't what it seems," the guard insisted.

"Bring her here," said Raye.

The Tuz stood in front of Jasira and Maze with her head hung low, a futile attempt to shield her *truth*. Some moments passed—without a sound.

"Shackle the assassin!" Jasira demanded. "And take her to the boundary."

Maze asked, "Who is Kendra?"

Fragments of her history were evident in both Jasira and the guard.

"An old friend," she whispered.

Maze *felt* Jasira's inner struggle. "Your memories are complicated."

Resolution will come, she privately assured him—before concealing herself.

"Forgive my intrusion."

* * *

Truth was a peaceful territory. The violence that occurred during King Gorsh's conquest had largely been forgotten. Unlike the enforcers, Truth's warriors were not emboldened with fury. It would take the actions of their leaders to inspire them.

Forewarned of impending trouble, the engineer applied the brakes.

Sten peered out the windows. *What is this?* Both sides of the track were lined with torches.

The engine slowed—then stopped in front of a wagon filled with rock.

"Secure the coach," Riker instructed the warriors. "I will replace the engineer." A trusted Zuku took over the controls.

Jasira arrived and sought out Riker, finding him walking toward her. He could tell by her stride she had taken command.

"How can I assist you?" he asked.

"Clear the track and extract the escort. I will return with the assassin and meet you outside the coach."

"At once, my leader!"

"Honorable Jasira," the operative pleaded, "that gold has been in my family for years. I know nothing of this Mystic wizard. I am loyal—only to Truth."

"Unshackle her."

Jasira forcefully took hold of the assassin's arm and vanished.

To those at the boundary, the Tuz walked alone. However, the steps she took were uncertain.

Sten watched with his back to the coach as the operative stumbled his way. Captivated by the fear that occupied her face.

I was your target, wasn't I? asked the mysterious voice.

"Jasira!" Riker called out. "The track has been cleared. Where are you?"

The warriors rumbled in amazement, as suddenly she appeared from nowhere.

"Tell me!" Jasira demanded. "Wasn't I the one?"

Sten's forehead beaded cold sweat.

She took out the blade and raised it high. "This is the dagger of Mila! This is the dagger of Truth! This is the dagger of JUSTICE."

Glaring down into the assassin's eyes, she privately told her, *Where I am sending you, gold has no value.*

The galvanized warriors edged closer to view the wizardry. The shimmering blade left on its own, twirling in the smoke-laced torchlight, slowly drifting downward, until it stopped with the tip pressed firmly against the assassin's taut chest.

Jasira rallied the warriors in a commanding voice. "The Territory of Truth shall *never* submit!"

The assassin's eyes burst open. The unforgiving iron driven straight through her heart. She relaxed but did not fall. The wizard's magic kept her upright.

Withdraw the blade.

Sten did as he was told. Then, although not his intention, he brought the blade to his neck.

"Forgive me," he stammered, "I came here . . . simply to return the Zuku."

I, too, have an operative, Jasira said privately. *Perhaps you are familiar with their kind?*

Sten imagined a silver warkin, and quivered.

* * *

Truth's warriors were prepared for battle, in the ways of the Zuku hunter. The progression was clear: respect, engage, and finish!

* * *

401

At daybreak, the engine slowly approached the trail hub. Truth's warriors were perched on top of the coaches with their crossbows at the ready. The unsuspecting enforcers were quickly overwhelmed. Those who avoided the deadly bolts, were hunted down and silenced.

"We are all accounted for?" asked Jasira.

"Yes," confirmed Riker. "Two were injured . . . one, will not survive."

SUCRENE

Later that afternoon, the wizards stood on the observation deck and looked out over the valley.

"There!" Ficus pointed to a distant puff of steam. "And with—"

"Coaches," Kendra blurted out.

"Send Roman to the station."

"At once, my wizard!"

The engine came to a stop.

Jasira vanished behind Sten, holding on to his arm with one hand while gripping the dagger with the other.

"Remember this," she whispered, "perform as instructed and your life will be spared, only your memories sacrificed. *Open the door.*"

"Roman!"

"Welcome back, Sten."

"It's good to be back. Come in!"

"You have returned with unexpected cargo?"

The tip of the dagger pressed against his lower spine. "Somewhat unfortunate, but there was little choice."

The gifted Zuku studied the officer, unable to *feel* his *truth*. "Go on."

"They insisted I return with the laborers. There was little time. The gift had to be delivered."

"Odd," he muttered. "However, Jasira was our priority and the Mystic wizard is pleased."

"A fair trade, for a horde of migrants," Sten concluded with an uneasy laugh.

"I'm here!" Maze announced himself at the door.

Roman was taken by surprise. "A Zuku?"

"Their foreman," said Sten.

"Gifted, no less, and able to shield his thoughts. Why stoop so low, Zuku, as to manage a gang of Tuz?"

"By chance you can relate?"

"You're not a foreman. Sten! what is the meaning of—"

Maze jumped into the coach and broke the Zuku's fall, Sym iron lodged in the side of his neck.

"The body?" asked Maze.

Jasira withdrew the crimson blade. "Let it drain over there, on my father's bed."

"Yes, my leader."

She turned to Sten. "About this fortress."

"I will explain . . . everything," he said with hesitation.

"What is it?"

"I beg of you. If my information enables your victory, do not take away what I know of myself. Leave me whole to live in the Land of Tuz, never to be heard from again."

"You and your gold?" Maze scoffed.

He emphatically shook his head. "I am merely a secondary officer and receive but a token. It is Kip, the lead enforcer, the one they call Guardian. He is the most rewarded."

"Your request will be considered," said Jasira.

Riker was brought in and questioned the officer.

"I have told you all that I know."

Maze nodded in agreement.

Unbeknownst to Sten, what remained unspoken had also been revealed to the gifted Zuku.

"Now, those wagons we asked for," said Riker.

"In the supply yard behind the station."

* * *

"We are ready to move out," confirmed Kendra.

"Yes . . . ready," Ficus said softly.

She stepped closer to the despondent wizard. "Is it Jasira? I realize you were fond of her."

He grimaced and closed his eyes. "This should not be happening. It is as if she were here, in this valley . . . suffocating me."

"What you sense is her blood, flowing through Arnela. Let us take a moment and drink some tea. Roman and Sten will be here soon enough."

"Yes"—he sighed—"it must be only that."

* * *

Wagons filled with Truth's warriors converged on the cottage. Jasira and Maze sprang to the ground and dashed into the dwelling.

"Jasira!" said Murn with astonished eyes.

"We are here for Arnela."

"She's been taken to the castle."

"Will you help us?"

Murn was riddled with guilt. She was the one who put Arnela to sleep. Helping Jasira was a chance for redemption.

"Yes!"

Riker barged into the room. "Excuse the interruption," he said with uncertainty.

"This is Murn"—Jasira smiled warmly—"and she is with us."

"There's been movement, a patrol of enforcers heading to the station."

"We are in position?"

"Yes."

* * *

Jasira huddled the leaders and provided their instruction.

"Maze, go into the Zone and seek out the warkins. Speak with the one who wears a silver coat. Tell her our purpose, and ask for their support." *My truth is open for you.* She privately assured him. "Riker, take out the guard post without delay. Then go to the main entry. Engage the enforcers and persuade them to seal it. When they do come out, it must be through the tunnel. I will take Sten into the fortress and finish my business there. Blessings—for us all!"

"Blessings!"

Maze located the first vent and climbed the carved-out steps to reach it. He gave a solid push, and then another, but the grate would not budge.

"Warkins!" he called out, pressing his ear to the iron.

Their presence was announced by a blast of warm wet air.

"No reason to shout, Zuku. We could smell you from a distance.

"Help me through here?"

The warkins dug with their thick claws and dislodged the grate. Maze pushed it to the side and climbed through.

They sat together in the tall grass.

"Jasira mentioned your silver coat."

"The mother of Arnela has returned?"

"Yes . . . she is our leader."

"Where is Arnela?"

Maze pointed to the top of the fortress. "Up there, and we are here to free her. Will you join us?"

The silver warkin conferred with the pack. Symbolically, they flared their nostrils and raised their snouts, and then howled in agreement.

The distinctive sound could be heard throughout the valley.

"Now it's the warkins!" Ficus lashed out and then sighed. "What is becoming of this day?"

Kendra charged through the door. "The fortress is under siege!"

"TRUTH"

He darted to an overlook. Down below lay four or five—then eight to twelve—enforcers, fallen by bolts. To the side of the road were remnants of a bloody skirmish and more casualties. Victorious Truth warriors scrambled away from the carnage.

"Where is Kip?" the wizard raged. "What is our response?"

"We have retreated to the courtyard and barricaded the entry. I am going there now."

Ficus never thought of defending the fortress. His enforcers had been developed to be hunters, not the hunted.

Jasira and Sten were halfway through the tunnel.

"Faster!" she pushed him along. "And remember, no idle talk."

"I understand." He winced, feeling the tip of the dagger between his ribs.

She gripped his arm and vanished. They urgently moved across the basement, but not suspiciously so.

"Sten!" an enforcer yelled out. "There you are."

Don't look back, and get on the lift.

The enforcer shouted up, "Go to the courtyard! The Guardian is there. We are organizing . . ." His words grew faint as they continued to rise.

Take us to the wellness room.

"Why are we going—UGHH."

The butt of Jasira's dagger struck him just above the eye. Blood gushed from the gaping wound.

Because you have been injured by a warrior and require immediate attention.

Jasira *felt* a familiar presence, approaching from above.

"Sten!" Kendra shouted as the lifts slowly passed each other. "What happened?"

Repeat these words . . .

"We were ambushed at the station," Sten moaned. "I have important—"

"You there!" said Kendra, after reaching the courtyard level.

"Yes, Commander!"

"Seek out the Mystic wizard and deliver this message. Sten has returned but is injured."

"At once, Commander!"

Kip's voice resonated from the far end of the courtyard.

"The primitives have made a grave mistake! Tonight, it will be their blood that spills without mercy!" He took his hands and dramatically choked the air in front of him. "*Their* last breath we take! Together, we are united. Together . . . we are family!"

"FAMILY." The enforcers shook their fists and stomped their feet.

Kip walked across the stone floor to where Kendra was waiting.

She said, "The Mystic wizard is disappointed. We have no answer for this assault?"

"Assure him our retreat is only temporary, and not an indication of our courage."

"The warkins, where is their loyalty? Have they turned?"

"A gifted Zuku could have managed that"

"And?"

"They will also be silenced."

"And what of our snipers?"

"We have managed an occasional strike. But Truth is well positioned in the dwindling light.

"Continue to launch the random volley," she insisted, "enough to hold their interest."

"Yes, my wizard." He stared back with resolute eyes. "The enforcers hunger for battle. Tonight, they will feast."

Half of the enforcers were kept on the alert, the others afforded rest.

"Sten!" The physician came rushing out.

Having experienced a significant loss of blood, the officer was weak and confused.

"Hep me . . . the Wiz—rd Ja—"

"Save your strength, and let me take care of that wound."

Sten was helped inside and laid down on the table.

A strong sedative is required, the un-seen Jasira persuasively suggested.

Yes, for the pain, the physician privately agreed.

Now!

He hurried off to the supply room.

Jasira turned Sten on his side and covered his mouth. Then she severed his spine—in an instant.

"Traveling anywhere will be difficult for you."

She heard voices approach the room.

Kendra said, "I know nothing more than this, my wizard."

Jasira backed herself into the corner and vanished.

Ficus whirled into the room. "Sten, can you hear me?"

"Something isn't right," Kendra thought out loud.

Ficus inspected the room, his Symlander eyes ablaze.

"It's Jasira—" Kendra hissed. "She's here."

"Yes."

The physician returned with a loaded syringe. "My wizard," he said with surprise.

Jasira summoned the extent of her energy. Lunging forward in one fluid motion, she snatched the syringe and plunged it deep into her father's neck.

"My wizard!" Kendra screamed out.

Ficus's eyes lost understanding and rolled up into his head. His knees buckled, and he collapsed to the floor.

"Secure the door and come with us," Jasira ordered the physician,

Stepping over the body, she gripped Kendra's arm and vanished.

"Jasira, we are friends"—she forced a smile—"and I have missed you so."

Take us to the altar!

Her demand sent a chill through Kendra's veins.

* * *

In the background of Truth's efforts, Murn continued to feed the warriors, as Mote attended to the injured.

Riker reported back to the cottage. "Their snipers remain active above the entry."

"An insulting decoy." Maze shook his head. "Our presence encourages the charade."

"And the warkins?"

"Extinguishing flames and digging ditches."

"Their numbers are concerning," said Riker.

"Jasira will slash their ranks. It is happening as we speak."

* * *

"Bring me the book of potions."

"I don't know where—ahh!" Kendra flinched with pain. The tip of the dagger broke through her skin.

"Would you like to join Sten, and slither as a snake?"

"Jasira . . . no—"

"Do as I say or I will send this blade through." *Understood?*

"Yes."

"Bring it to me now!"

Kendra stepped gingerly across the room, the dagger magically fused to her spine. She opened the closet and went inside, reappearing with a leather-covered book.

"This has everything."

Jasira took the book and closed her eyes, then held it to her chest.

The physician blurted out, "It's caught fire."

The book fell to ashes.

Jasira's eyes sparked open. "Bring me the minerals."

Meticulously, she followed Elgin's recipe, branded in her memory.

Kendra and the physician watched with empty faces. The potion spilled over the basin's lip, into the bucket Jasira was holding.

"Carry this with your life," she instructed the physician.

Jasira took a clump of white hair in each hand and vanished. *Take us to where they rest.*

They made their way down the narrow room, each side lined with double-stacked cots. Kendra ordered each enforcer to take a sip from the cup.

At the end of the aisle, Jasira handed the cup to the physician. "Drink."

He brought the cup to his mouth, hesitated a moment . . . then drank.

"Lie down over there."

Jasira dipped a final cup and handed it to Kendra.

She looked down at the yellow-tinted liquid and asked with reservation, "Tell me . . . this potion—"

"Drink." The dagger pressed more firmly until she swallowed. *Now, take me to my daughter.*

Kendra managed the stairs, leading to the top. Arnela was kept there, in a room behind the aviary.

Jasira reached around and reclaimed the dagger and then gently kissed her forehead. "Return to my father, before that kiss is forgotten."

"My wizard . . . your father?" she mumbled.

RESOLUTION

The silver warkin asked, "Zuku, the time has come?"

"Yes"—Maze nodded—"remove the grates."

The messenger reported back with urgency. "Guardian, they will not wake!"

"What are you saying?"

"They breathe, but only this."

Kip was under great pressure and determined to fight. Though not at full strength, he was confident in his plan. They would charge through the tunnel and regroup at the western gate, form a battle line, and motivate Truth's retreat, pinning them against the fortress wall to accept their fate.

Jasira passed through the aviary. Surprisingly, the falcons did not stir. She could *feel* Arnela's presence on the other side of the door.

Kendra sat down next to Ficus, her memories fading away. "Wake up, my wizard . . . wake up, before I lose myself." His eyelids twitched—then opened.

"Kendra," he whispered.

"I am . . . I am Kendra."

"What is wrong?" His words becoming clear and forceful. "What is happening?

Her eyes began to cloud.

"You can't leave me!"

He got to his feet with little effort and hustled to the lift, jumping down to the courtyard before it stopped. "Where is the Guardian?"

"Over there—"

He walked briskly to the far end, where Kip was surrounded by enforcers. They opened a pathway to let him through, their heads respectfully bowed.

"We are ready, my wizard," the Guardian confirmed, "and awaiting your command."

Ficus reviewed the enforcers, dressed in full body armor and staring back at him.

His outward portrayal of confidence belied his inner turmoil.

"The others are in the basement?" he discreetly asked.

"It's unexplainable," said Kip. "Those who were resting will not rise."

Jasira . . .

"Call us to battle, my wizard!"

He steadied himself and shouted, "To battle!"

"Down to the basement!" the Guardian ordered.

Ficus went off in a different direction and up to a sniper's perch.

Jasira gazed down at her sleeping daughter. *I will return for you.*

Riker ignited the tip of the arrow and launched the flaming torch. It gracefully arced with a luminous glow, then exploded on the volcanic rock.

I am ready, answered Jasira.

"She is with us," Maze confirmed.

"I will provide the alert," said Riker.

Jasira focused on the dense arrangement of stars, concentrating on their collective brilliance. Channeling the light source, her chest began to warm—Mystic energy, yearning for release.

From an abandoned mine shaft above Lake Sucrene, they responded to her call. And the warkins formed a circle.

"The beasts know something," said the sniper near the wizard. His words interrupted by the howls.

Ficus braced his hands on top of the wall, his sanity wandering away.

Kip slapped the lead enforcer's shoulder. "GO."

In the near distance, a dark formation appeared in the moonlight.

Maze smiled to himself. *I see them, Jasira.*

"What is this?" said Ficus.

"Bats, my wizard," replied the spellbound sniper. "So many."

The swarm of frenzied creatures descended with purpose and a deafening sound. They fractured into swirling masses, each one funneling into a vent.

Frantic enforcers poured out of the tunnel like ants escaping a flooded sandhill. Truth's warriors rose and released their bolts in seamless precision. Those who survived faced the jaws of a warkin, or a warrior's blade.

In the aftermath, Ficus stood silhouetted against a twinkling sky.

Kip had avoided the slaughter, and carefully approached. "We can escape, my wizard . . . rebuild our forces in Lackland."

"You would choose to escape?"

Before Kip could react, Ficus grabbed him with all his strength.

"My wizard—"

"Escape from this!" He lifted the Guardian and, with a powerful thrust, threw him off the perch. His body cascaded down the jagged rock.

The wizard looked up in disbelief. "Great Maker, why have you forsaken us? This was not to be our destiny."

No . . . our destiny, said Jasira, intruding upon his thoughts.

"Never!" he thundered and raced away.

Jasira lay down next to Arnela and held her tightly. "I am with you now."

They shared a magical warmth, then vanished—and became lighter than air.

Ficus barged in with his blade raised high. "*This* is your destiny!"

Incensed that the room was vacant he wildly slashed at the bed.

Floating unseen, they left the raging wizard and traveled down the staircase.

After pacing the floor, Ficus dropped to his knees, his face buried in his hands.

"Jasira—"

You were too late, Father.

Where are you?

You know.

Ficus stepped through the doorway with uncommon trepidation. Jasira had prepared the altar. Arnela yet asleep, was standing by her side.

He held out his arms. "My daughter—"

"Stay where you are!" she commanded.

He tried to take another step but was unable.

"We can revive Arnela together."

"I will do it myself. *Everything*"—she traced a circle around her chest—"is in here."

Ficus nervously glanced at the altar. "I am connected with you both. We are family."

"No longer! Fury will take us beyond your reach."

"Mystic wizard," he pleaded.

Jasira took hold of Arnela's hands and submerged them.

As Ficus entered darkness, the color of his eyes began to change, from blue to gray . . . to black.

"HAH," Arnela gasped, her crystal-blue eyes wide open.

- FIN -

EPILOGUE

The enforcers who woke up without memories were transported back to Lackland and reintroduced to everyday life.

Jasira set the falcons free, and they flew to the Land of Sym, settling deep inside the Dark Forest, where they thrived.

Mount Golder was returned to the locals, and the castle lavishly restored. An impressive fountain was added to the courtyard. At its center sat a large warkin, *howling* a steady stream of water from its mouth.

The warkins themselves were taken to the Ancient Forest and released. By chance, the pack's first litter included not one but two with silver coats.

The Zone's toxic perimeter was carefully extracted, its interior enhanced with meandering pathways and seasonal gardens.

Centurions Lord Hemeth and Lady Rachel abdicated their throne to Nev and Cray, spending the remainder of their days watching glorious sunsets on Montro.

Maze eventually became the leader of Truth.

The Mystic altar was disassembled, and stored in the basement of Star Jasmine.

* * *

Kendra was taken under the care of her sister, Murn.

"This is a nice cottage," said the gray-eyed woman. "Have you lived here long?"

The Kingdom

At Zuku Cove, the king said, "I saved this one especially for you."

"*That* rock . . . is so special?" Jasira made light of Lent's revelation.

"It is," he assured her. "She who sits there will be the next queen of Rivera."

"If that is the rock's purpose, let me sit on this one here." She softly chuckled. "But I have taken notice of that special rock."

"And it's not going anywhere," he said with a smile. "In the meantime, stay with me at Star Jasmine."

"We will . . . until the child is born."

"Stay as long as you like."

FROM THE AUTHOR

Inspiration: a limitless motivator.

A dear friend was off at basic training (Lackland), and I promised to write. After the fourth letter or so, I decided to try something new. I would create a story to share. Fantasy of course, as it was a favorite of hers, and also mine. So . . . that's how it all began.

Throughout the amazing process, there was no mistaking the guidance I received. And looking up at the *Great Deep Sky*, I expressed my gratitude—countless times.

Blessings!
KmCarey

Made in the USA
Monee, IL
09 August 2024

5908abb0-81d4-47ac-935c-ad8df81554acR01